Legon
Restoration

Other titles by Nicholas Taylor:

The Legon Series
Legon Awakening
Legon Ascension
Legon Restoration

The Contractor Series
Pactum

Legon Restoration

Book Three In The Legon Series

by Nicholas Taylor

Legon Restoration
Book Three in the Legon Series

Somnium Press, LLC
PO Box 621458
Littleton, CO 80162

ISBN-10: 1938387066
ISBN-13: 978-1-938387-06-7

www.NicholasTaylor.co

Acknowledgements

I would like to thank all of my family and friends who have supported me and my publishing endeavors. Writing the Legon books has been a true joy and dream for me. Most of all, I would like to thank all of you reading this book. Thank you for taking the time to read my work and thank you so much for the emails and messages. Your emails have been a motivation for me and have made this whole process wonderful. Thank you so much for your support, and I hope you enjoy Legon Restoration.

① Salmont	④ Salez	⑦ Golden City	⑩ Rosae
② Salkay	⑤ Manton	⑧ Mors	⑪ Noris
③ Bailaya	⑥ Seeon	⑨ Coreum	⑫ Bonta

Impa Empire

Cona Empire

Cona Republic

Pawdin Empire

Contents

Prologue
Introductions

"Appearance is just that; what we see, not what is. Still, that is how we are placed in society. If one can master the way others see them, they can then master society and therefore the world they live in."
-Rivulets of Time

Neelya placed her bag on her new bed in the Palace. She was to be Queen Hoelaria's new assistant. This was a great honor and credit to her. To be selected by one so esteemed was no small feat. She stood and looked at the room which was much finer than that of her last home. The workmanship was a little spotty but she didn't judge that; after all, this was an ape-built structure, the first she'd lived in. She walked to a window overlooking the Capitol. Blue skies fell on green hills. Only a few clouds were visible. She opened the window. The sharp and offensive scents of the city assaulted her and she shut it again, deciding that she preferred the sweet smell of her room.

She picked up a notepad as she made her way out of her room, finding a Human in the hall waiting for her.

"Take me to the Queen," she ordered, not looking at the creature.

"Yes, my lady," he said.

She walked behind the ape not paying attention to him, but rather studying every inch of her new home.

The servant lead her to what she presumed were the Queen's quarters. The servant opened one of two large redwood doors letting her in. Neelya marveled at the large apartment's elegance. The room's exquisite lines and symmetry spoke of a master Iumenta craftsman. Neelya walked in the entry room, admiring the fine decor. She noticed that the servant did not enter. The room stood in stark contrast from that of the rest of the

Palace. Her eyes glided over smooth ceramic walls.

"Neelya," a cool voice called from another room.

She followed the voice to a small dining room.

"Un Prose," Neelya said, bowing to the Queen.

"You may rise. When in private; for you it is not necessary to bow upon seeing me," the Queen stated matter-of-factly.

"Thank you."

"Please join me," Hoelaria said.

Neelya was confused -- she'd always heard that the Queen was ill-tempered; but she didn't seem so now. Neelya sat opposite the Queen examining her surreptitiously. Hoelaria eyed Neelya, looking her up and down like a piece of art.

"I take a great deal of time selecting an assistant Neelya, you should know that. With that knowledge comes knowing that you are highly desirable, but it also means that you must meet those expectations," Hoelaria said, no menace or threat coloring her tone; just fact.

Neelya fought the urge to swallow, "Yes Un Prose, I will not let you down."

An Iumenta came in the room with two silver trays; he sat one before the Queen and the other in front of Neelya. He left the room without uttering a word.

Neelya eyed the servant as he left.

"Humans do not enter my quarters," the Queen said, "please eat. You will be dining with me often."

She did as asked, spearing a cooked carrot. For a long time, the Queen said nothing. She periodically looked up at Neelya, nodded to herself, and resumed eating. Neelya didn't speak.

"You seem nervous, Neelya," the Queen casually observed.

"Forgive me, I do not mean to seem scared or weak, Un Prose."

Hoelaria looked at her again, a slight gleam in her eye. "Neelya, I know the reputation that I have; it's one I've worked hard to earn. When you leave my service you will help to spread that reputation. I am ruthless and I am ill-tempered; but you are my assistant, which is a close relationship in our society. You are as obligated to serve me as much as I am obligated to mentor you. In public, I expect you to do as you are told. In private, however, I expect you to speak your mind -- respectfully of course -- and if you feel so inclined, to question me. This is how you learn, this is how our society has flourished for millennia, and this is what raises us above the ape standing in the hall."

Neelya understood.

"I like the food," Neelya said, surprising herself.

The Queen's lips twitched almost in a smile, "Yes, the apes can cook well."

Neelya looked down at her plate, "Humans are capable of this?"

"Yes..."

An Iumenta entered the room, stopping whatever the Queen was about to say. He bowed to the Queen, "You said to enter when I received news, Un Prose."

"What is it?" the Queen asked coolness back in her tone.

Neelya's ears perked up, *what was going on?*

"Un Prose, Noris has fallen."

Chapter One
Ascended

"At times life appears to be more random than it is planned, but I wonder. Is it that life is random or just that we are so blind as to miss the master's plan."
- Conversations in the Garden

Her lungs filled with heavy sea air. Bright white mist strained her eyes as they tried to focus, she lifted herself from the ground, turning to see a bloody figure at her feet. She was looking at herself. *"That's odd,"* Sasha thought. She looked around, trying to see through dense mist. Sasha thought she was alone, but she wasn't sure as the fog was so thick. Absently she wiggled her toes.

She looked down, feeling grass, "I'm naked," she said with a shock. "How come I'm naked?" she asked again and then, "What is this place, what am I doing here?" Memories washed over her. She had gotten hurt when they were ambushed; was she dead? No she decided, she could feel the ground and it didn't feel dead to her, but what did dead feel like? And why was she looking at herself? She remembered Legon pulling her into his mind, was that were she was? Was she just a part of his mind now? A sound from behind her caused her to spin. She was next to a wall ... a wall of diamonds. Looking down, Sasha saw a paw and massive gold claws, her head tilted up to look into the most beautiful blue eyes she'd ever seen. Looking into them, she felt waves of love emanating from the Dragon.

"Hello," was all she could think to say, then feeling rude she added, "my name is Sasha."

The White Dragon chuckled, the sound of it like a deep soothing roll of thunder, "I know who you are, Sasha, but that was very polite of you," he said in her mind. His voice was rich, resonating in her chest and soul.

"Am I dead?" she asked.

The Dragon shook his head, "No my daughter, you are not. While badly injured, your brother Ascended right on top of you, with your minds fully connected."

She thought about that, "So then why am I here?" She felt no fear and wondered why that was.

"It is because you have nothing to fear from me, and you being here is my will. When you wake, you will no longer be Human. What your brother did was so powerful your body could not withstand it; Humans are not meant to experience the magic you did. That aside, I have brought you here for a reason. You are here now to receive two gifts from me," the White Dragon said.

"Gifts?" Sasha clarified.

"Yes, the first is my anger. You are a uniquely kind person, Sasha, truly one of my greatest creations. With your kindness you have been a compass and a guide, something you will always be. You deplore violence in all its forms, but now you and your brother must purify this land. You must restore things to their proper place."

"I'm going to be mad?" she asked, confused. How was anger a gift?

"Anger can be harmful if it is the wrong kind, but my anger is pure; it will be a shield and a motivation for you. With it you will pour out my indignation upon those who have trodden on the innocent, molested and maimed my children. My anger is the refiner's fire.

"You cannot now comprehend, but soon will," he said lowering his head to hers, touching the tip of his nose to her forehead. With his touch came energy and emotion, shaking her; her whole being feeling as if it would explode. She saw the pain and suffering of a thousand years and more, she felt the sorrow of the land, felt the hopelessness. It was like what Legon would do with people; but what she saw now was not the pain of one small event or even a lifetime's worth, but thousands of lifetimes. The power in the White Dragon kept her mind safe, but she felt the pain nonetheless. Deep inside her a flame began to grow. It spread throughout her, making its way to her heart where it bloomed. Anger the likes of which Sasha had never experienced took over, and with it a drive, a need to stop the wicked. She looked up into his blue eyes. She now understood. Her whole frame trembled with the force of her rage; but with it love, an overwhelming love, even for those that caused her anger.

The Dragon spoke, "You will not live like this, but when you see the suffering of my children, when that pain in others stirs you up to anger or when you are facing battle; this will be the anger that you feel. This anger is tempered with love and that is why I send it with you into the world. My final gift to you is the power to use my anger."

Once again Sasha felt ready to burst, but this time not with anger. It was something different, something raw and familiar; it was magic.

Iselin lost more altitude, being driven toward the sea below. One of the two Dragons that had attacked her sent a jet of emerald flames, scorching her right side. Her healing wards were all but gone and she winced in pain. She turned to look at a blue Dragon as its tail lashed out; she screamed as her front left leg broke. Blood drained from her unchecked as the last of her magic was spent.

Time slowed. She could no longer feel Legon or Sasha, *they must be dead,* she thought. She knew she would be soon as well. One of her attackers, a green Dragon, seemed to sneer at her as its body glowed with a spell that ran up its length, turning into a ball of energy that hurtled its way towards her. Her mind didn't even register the flickers of ruby and lavender that surrounded her. Her vision went amethyst. Confused, she looked around.

From above she heard a deafening roar. She looked up to the cloud-covered cliffs, and from the mist a figure dropped. Still her mind was not working at full speed; Iselin could hardly understand what she was seeing. Her mind registered the massive form of a lavender Dragon diving down at them. Two minds reconnected with hers, both a tangle of rage. A figure detached from the back of her husband, a beautiful Elf with long brown hair waving behind her. Seeing what Dragons could see, Iselin took in the girl cocooned in a nimbus of ruby energy. The energy around the girl condensed into an orb that shot from her hand, streaking by Iselin. She felt something touch down on her back and immediately sending spells at the blue Dragon. Iselin felt her heart race with energy from Sasha, dulling pain and steadying her in the sky. From Sasha's mind, she felt rivers of power, but she couldn't focus on that at the moment; she needed to stay alive. There was a crack of magic on ward and time resumed normal speed. Iselin turned, seeing the blue Dragon tumble in space, its wards glowing hot. It corrected itself as three more ruby spells hit it. In the next moment, she looked to the green Dragon, a jet of emerald flames spewing up at Legon. He opened his maw and a torrent of violet fire erupted from him, pushing back the green fire with little effort.

The two Dragons hit, sending them down further. There was a wet snap and the sound of something getting the wind knocked out of it. Iselin thought the green Dragon must have broken a bone when Legon hit it.

Sasha's mind boiled with anger and spoke to her. "Ise you need to focus. We have to hold this thing until my brother is done killing the other one. You keep yourself in the air, I will deal with the filth," her mind said with an edge Iselin had never heard from Sasha.

Legon looked down at Sasha's unconscious form. He could see from the ever-growing cloud of ruby energy emanating from her body that she was very alive. Her heartbeat was increasing and her chest rose and fell fast. *What is it, Sash?* his mind sent; but her mind was closed to him, a strange alien feeling. Her body didn't look the same as it had before; she was an Elf now. Her eyelids fluttered and slowly opened.

Legon's heart stopped for a moment. Sasha's once blue eyes were no longer blue. Her corneas didn't sparkle with flecks of red as if she were Ascended; but rather were ruby mirrors, the natural blue color completely gone. Before Legon could think further, she smiled up at him and reached up, pulling herself to his nose and kissing it.

Legon heard what sounded like rocks grinding as he chuckled at her. Her mind connected with him and aside from a feeling of immense joy he felt power in her; it was like when Iselin was in her Ascended form … but Sasha was no Dragon. "It looks like I'm going to be stuck with you a bit longer," he said.

She smiled again. "Yes," she laughed.

Their moment was interrupted by the sound of a Dragon's scream. Both tensed, remembering; *ISELIN!* Sasha's mind went from joy to fear to anger, an anger the likes of which Legon had never felt. She was on her feet. Legon looked over to Emma and Mage. Emma crawling, dragging her broken leg; Mage out cold. With a shrug of his magic Emma and Mage glowed purple as their injuries healed instantly. Legon sent a mental message to his, Iselin's and Mage's familiars telling them to protect Mage and Emma.

Emma looked amazed but Legon didn't have time, Sasha leapt on his back without effort. Legon ran at the cliff spreading his wings. He'd been told that Dragons knew how to fly by instinct and he hoped that was true.

His wings drove down and he jumped into the air. He felt a temporary sense of joy as he lifted into space. With two powerful strokes of his wings he was clearing the cliff. The cloud was dense but he could hear his wife being killed below him. Both he and Sasha placed wards around Iselin, but almost at once Legon felt the wards being tested.

"That was like getting hit by a toddler," Sasha said, amazed as felt what little energy Legon had needed to repel the attack.

Legon dove, snapping his wings to his sides. The clouds parted and both he and Sasha filled with rage as they saw Iselin's extensive injuries. Iselin was barely keeping herself in the sky; blood poured from her and her leg was clearly broken. Legon roared, causing Iselin and her attackers to look up.

"I'll hold the blue one!" Sasha thought to him, leaping from his back and sending a ball of magic at the blue Iumenta. Legon bore down on the green one as it breathed emerald fire at him. He responded with flames of his own, feeling the other Dragon's magic buckle. He slammed into the green Dragon, sending them plummeting to the ocean. It bit at him but compared to Legon, he hardly noticed it. Without effort, Legon clamped his jaws at the base of the Iumenta's neck, tasting his mouth fill with a wonderful, sweet, tangy blood. The Dragon roared and Legon reached with his front paw to grab the Dragon's wing at the base. With all his might, he ripped with his paw and pulled with his jaws. The Dragon howled in pain and Legon heard a slurping pop as the wing came loose from its joint and flesh ripped away from bone. The wing tore away, taking strips of back muscle with it. Legon kicked the green Dragon, sending its body -- now missing a wing -- to knock against the sheer cliff, thudding against the jagged rocks and into the surf below. He tossed the wing he was holding and started to ascend to Iselin and Sasha.

Legon strained to climb to where Iselin was dodging attacks from the blue Dragon. Sasha was doing her best to defend with magic but could only spare so much energy to keep the exhausted Iselin in the air. Legon pushed harder, gaining altitude with more and more ease. The blue Dragon looked at him; fear on its face. Legon didn't bother with charging it, but rather let energy run down him and out in a blast of magic. The Dragon's head burst from the spell; sending bone, flesh, and teeth in every direction.

Legon came alongside his wife; seeing her hurt tore at him. He closed his eyes and sent healing spells her way. She yelped in surprise and he opened his eyes, seeing that there was no longer a scratch on her. She looked at him in amazement; never before had she seemed small to him, but she did now.

"Are you all right?" he asked, still concerned.

Her thoughts were warm, "Yes, I am now." She paused, looking at him, "Look at you ... I've never seen a class eight before." She was silent for a moment. "Did you see him?" she asked.

Legon knew she was referring to the White Dragon. "Yes, and you were right: it was truly sacred, he spoke to me..."

She stopped him. "You don't have to share that."

"I want to; you have the right to know."

Legon played her his memories of when he spoke with the White Dragon; how he'd confirmed that Legon was indeed the Everser Vald. She was silent for so long that he became concerned. "Are you still with me?" he asked.

She shook her head. "Yes. So it's true you really are the Everser Vald, I mean I always believed you were, but knowing..."

They turned out to sea and Legon heard the thumping of wings in the distance. He looked to see formations of Ascended heading towards them. As they drew close he started to hear roars and bugles of celebration as Opes and Sydin drew in next to them.

Sydin looked him up and down. "We need to confirm it, but you're an eight. How does it feel?" he asked.

"How does what feel?" Legon hedged.

"Being Ascended," Sydin said.

Legon took a moment to think about it. How did it feel? "Amazing, I've seen and felt through Ise's eyes and controlled the bodies of birds, but never like this. The wind in my wings, the feeling of power ..." he looked over at Sydin and without warning headed towards him. Sydin dodged him with ease.

"Whoa, sorry about that," Legon said.

Sydin and Opes laughed, as did the growing group of Ascended around them. "Flying is natural," Opes said, "flying with confidence and skill, on the other hand, is not. We are going to a Carrier. I am sorry Un Prosa we just can't risk you being in Noris."

Legon didn't understand his apprehension. "Is there something I should know?" Iselin's thoughts of *you have to land* gave him a clue. Carrier landings where supposed to be hard to master with the ship moving and all, but Legon thought he would be fine. Iselin did it all the time and he was connected to her.

"I wouldn't hold your breath, love," she said and then corrected, "actually, maybe holding your breath is a good idea ..."

"Please, I'm not going to fall in the water. Come on guys, I'll be fine. How hard can it be?" Legon asked, confidently.

Sasha piped up. "I don't know, I mean look at how small that thing is," she said, thinking of the Carrier in the distance.

From far out it did look small, but he knew it was massive and built to hold a class eight; he'd be fine ... he thought. The ship came closer and Legon didn't think it was looking all that much bigger.

"Not so cocky now, huh?" Iselin thought.

"Aren't you supposed to be supportive?"

"I'm your wife. In what way does that obligate me to be supportive? My job is to tell you when you screw up."

"Fair," he said.

Sydin broke in, "Now Legon, when you come up to the ship you need to slow down; it's going to come at you fast. You need to almost stop midair and then touch down with your back legs, got it?"

The ship was coming up a little fast, "Yeah, yeah I'm fine. Don't worry; easy."

He could see Elves in the Dragon hold he'd be landing in; they were looking at him with pride and excitement.

"Legon, you want to slow down now..." Opes said.

"Right, right ... slow down ..."

The Elves on the ship didn't look so excited anymore and … a*re they running?* The ship was closing in fast. How was he supposed to slow down? He thought he heard screams from the ship ... it was right in front of him now. He reared up, opening his wings wide, slowing rapidly. He was going to make it right in the opening. He wobbled in the air. A swell came, the ship moved up with it, and WHAM!

Most of Legon hit the hull of the ship with a dull thud. His upper body hit the floor of the hold, and Elves were screaming and running around. Legon dug his claws in the floor trying to keep from... SPLASH! The water felt good, but his pride? Not so good. He could hear the thoughts of every Ascended in the area laughing or trying not to laugh. Most found it inappropriate to laugh at the Head of a House but he had just flown into the side of a ship. Everyone's nerves had been on edge with the battle, nerves that were now releasing; *at least you helped with morale.* The water around him glowed with black and red magic from Sydin and Opes as they hoisted him up to the Dragon hold. Legon clambered inside. He was so thankful that scales didn't show blushing.

Legon stood in the hold trying to retain what little dignity he had left. A quick spell dried him and the area.

Iselin was in her Elf form walking over to him, as were Sydin and Opes. Sasha followed Iselin. Up to this point no one had noticed her, but people were starting to. The Elves grew silent as she passed them. Opes and Sydin turned to look at her.

"Sasha?" Sydin asked, dumbstruck.

Sasha wasn't covered in scales that hid a blush, and seeing everyone look at her she turned red with embarrassment. "Yes, it's me..." she said timidly, a tone in her voice Legon knew all too well. His heart sank; it was the same tone she used to the people in Salmont when she knew they were talking about her.

Opes approached her with a crystal that would test for magic. She took it without looking him in the eyes, and it lit up immediately.

He spoke to the hushed room. "Class six in a fully Ascended form, Elemental. Only someone in their Ascended form can score this high, but you look like an Elf now," he said flatly.

Legon could feel her emotions, her fear. "I'm a freak?" she asked, almost like she was going to cry.

Opes raised his brows and the Elves in the room looked amazed. Sydin spoke, "Not a freak, a miracle."

She looked up at him, "How is that, how can you think that?"

Legon spoke so the whole room could hear him, "Because the White Dragon doesn't make freaks. Think about what he told you; does he think you're a freak?"

Her head lifted and she smiled a bit, "He loves me."

"And so do we," one of the Elves in the hold said. Sasha looked around the room as if seeing the Elves for the first time, and smiled.

Legon noticed Opes next to him. "Legon?" he said, holding out the crystal. Legon bent his neck and touched the stone. It lit bright green. Opes exclaimed in a loud voice, "Class eight, Biologic!" The sound on the ship was deafening, the Dragons in the air roared and word passed from vessel to vessel. Magic flew in the air, bursting like fireworks. For the first time in two thousand years the Pawdin Empire had a class eight Ascended.

In the Capital city of Seeon, Edis sat with his wife Laura waiting to hear any news they could about their children. They had listened to the broadcast about the battle and then were told by one of the house caretakers that Sasha and Legon were missing. Now they sat waiting for information, a worried-looking Rachel with them.

A bronze-haired Elf came running up to where they sat on their terrace. "Un Prose, Sasha is a class six Elemental and the Everser Vald is a class eight Biologic!" the Elf crowed.

They were what and what? Edis asked what she was talking about and if his kids had been found.

The Elf apologized. "Yes please forgive me; they made it to a Carrier. Your son Ascended and that is why we lost contact with them. Your daughter was close by and is now, from what we've been told, an Elf and is a class six, but she is still in an Elf form."

Edis was happy but confused, "Elf form?"

"Yes, you see Dragons are most powerful only when in their Ascended form; but your daughter isn't a Dragon, she is just like any other Elf woman but she has the full power of a class six in Ascended form!"

Edis was still confused. "Is she all right?"

The Elf looked a little exasperated, "More than; she is an immortal now and one of the most powerful ones in history at that!"

It took a moment for what Edis heard to sink in, and then he looked at his wife. "Our kids won't grow old and die," he said. It was just then he heard the excitement in the city. "What is that? Are people yelling?"

The Elf laughed, "Yes the whole of the empire is being told!"

Edis looked out in the streets, seeing people running out of their homes hugging each other and waving house Evindass banners in the air.

Chapter Two
Fallen

"It isn't until we see the effect on the living that we truly understand the loss of the dead."
-Excerpts from The Diary of the Adopted Sister

"Ankle, Tony, John, Seth -- take teams up the gate towers and clear them. We will have supplies and civilians coming in soon and I don't want any problems. The rest of you on me; we need to check the walls' defenses to make sure we aren't going to get any surprises. Who knows what the Iumenta left behind," Barnin said to his men. They rose and started on their way. Noris had fallen but that didn't mean it was taken. Barnin looked to the north and noticed blue and green magic by the cliffs.

He called Heath over to him. "I thought we were told the north cliffs were clear?"

Heath's eyes went out of focus, "We haven't gotten word otherwise; but that magic is over the water, it has to be Ascended fighting."

"Great," Barnin grunted.

Dragons weren't his problem, what was his problem was losing six men in the fight for the town. Six wasn't a lot of losses for taking a major city, but he also lost Josher on the flight in and wouldn't be getting replacements for some time to come.

Around him was a city in disarray. Most of the buildings near the town entrance were on fire, along with much of the town's defenses. When Barnin and his men dropped in, the Elf Dragons started taking out structures that would slow the troops hitting the beach. This, he had to admit, saved a lot of resistance lives but made for a madhouse for the time being. The four teams he'd sent were busy making sure the two towers on either side of the gate weren't booby-trapped.

"Sir, do you really think there will be traps in there?" a man asked.

"The Iumenta aren't dumb; they must have figured there was a strong chance of losing Noris. I don't see them leaving it in pristine condition for us." Barnin said.

As if to enforce his point there was a loud boom in the distance. They looked to see fire and smoke rise over the town. Barnin looked back at the man, "Step lightly."

Barnin started down a road that ran the length of the city wall. There wasn't a lot of damage to the wall, but all of the buildings around it were rubble. Barnin could see men and women covered in black ash and grime trying to dig around the wreckage of buildings. He spoke to a man in his group, "Do we know anything about this city? What part of town are we in?"

The man looked at a map and told him that they were in a light commercial and residential district. *So ... a bunch of homes and shops,* he thought. For being the type of area it was, there was a surprisingly small amount of people; most of the bodies they were passing were men in armor, charred by Dragon fire.

The area they were in cleared into what looked like a small park, but where children once played there was a Trebuchet, or what was left of one. Behind it were ordinances that the enemy never got a chance to use, and a smattering of bodies.

"Check it out! I'd wager not everyone here was killed. Check the buildings, see what you can find, stay in groups. Heath, make sure there is nothing here that can be used," he ordered.

A few men stayed to help Heath as he made sure that weapons were collected and that the ceramic balls filled with flammable oil were either piled up for teams to collect or destroyed.

Barnin felt heat as some of the balls were lit on fire; he turned to look at them. Heath and the two others with him were taking the downed men's weapons and placing them near the fire. *Good thinking Heath, no one will be able to take those while they're hot,* he thought. He knew there were other teams with carts collecting every weapon they could find; not that the resistance was running low, but rather to keep locals from being able to arm themselves and push out the resistance.

Barnin walked up to an elderly man who was poking around in rubble.

"Did you see anyone leave this area that looked like military?" he asked.

The man looked him over, "No I was in the shelter along with the bulk of the town when your lot attacked. The shelter is up the street a ways, out of the range of siege weapons."

Barnin pulled out his copy of a map of Noris and looked around. "I don't know where anything is, can you help me out at all?"

The man frowned, "You burn our city, kill our people and you want help? Why should I help you?" he asked, angrily.

Why should he help Barnin? That was an easy question, "We have ships with healers, food and supplies that need to land. They can't come in and help anyone out until we clear the area. Now, based on what I'm seeing around me, you could use some food and shelter tonight. If you help me out, I'll make sure you're one of the first to get assistance, you and the people living around you."

The man looked angry, but then looked around at the groups of people picking through rubble, "How can you do that?"

"I know people, but it's first come, first served with aid; whatever gets cleared first gets help first, you got me?"

The man's head bobbed, "Yeah I got you. Come on, I'll show you around. Can you help me real quick? I'm trying to find something for my wife," the man asked.

"Yeah, that's fine," Barnin said, walking over in the ruins of what he presumed was a house. "What are we looking for?"

"A jewelry box, it's been in the family for years. We don't want to lose it."

Barnin huffed; he didn't really have time for this. Some of his men followed him over, "Keep looking around, once I find this box we'll help you out," Barnin said to them.

The men left and Barnin began moving beams around, looking for the box. "So how long have you lived here?" Barnin asked, trying to make conversation but not really paying attention.

The answer came from close by; too close. "Not long," the old man's voice rang cold. Barnin spun just in time to avoid getting hit in the head by a hammer. He stumbled, falling back; the man yelled and came at him. The man's head snapped to the side with a crack and he fell to the ground.

The sky darkened as Umbra glided down and landed in the street. "This isn't going to be like when refugees come in, Barnin. These people think you're the enemy; they will try to kill you," she was agitated.

His heart slowed a bit and he stood, "Guess I forgot; we are the bad guys to these people."

She eyed him. When she spoke again her tone was softer, "They have been influenced for years by the Iumenta. It will take our Ascended time to break that cycle of thought."

He nodded, "What can I do for you?"

She told him about Legon and then Sasha; his mouth hung open by the time she was done. "We need to go find Arkin and Stacy. No one has been able to contact either; it's likely they were killed before Legon and Sasha were attacked. We think that maybe Stacy's contact they were going to see was compromised. Legon wanted you to go because you knew Arkin."

Arkin hurt? Barnin didn't buy it; wouldn't buy it. He yelled to Heath, "Heath, get everyone up here on the double. We are going on a trip." Then back to Umbra, "How do we get there?"

"The two other Ascended you came in on will take you, as will I. Legon and Sasha were attacked by Ascended so we don't know what's in the area," she informed him.

Umbra scanned the area with her mind and senses. She couldn't detect anything amiss, but that didn't mean there wasn't anything wrong. The load of Humans on her back was lighter than before; she didn't know most of them very well, just Barnin and Heath. She felt bad for the death of Josher. It wasn't her fault, but she still felt guilty. Had she not been engaged in a fight with that other Ascended, he would have lived -- she could have saved him. That was neither here nor there, she told herself. What was done, was just that; done.

Over the beach of Noris she soared, rising above the open water as she went. Her group was joined by a brown Dragon from House Evindass, who was to find and extract Emma and Mage.

The clifftops were still socked in with dense clouds and she resigned herself to having to stick close to the ground. The cliffs passed below her and she flew over a charred patch of trees with two figures and three familiars.

"Shouldn't we go down and make sure they're all right?" Barnin asked worried.

"Legon healed them both and that brown is going to pick them up. Our mission is to find Arkin, Stacy, and if possible their contact, to find out what went wrong," she explained. She could understand his desire to go and help Emma; after all, they had been childhood friends.

They passed over a monastery at the top of the cliffs and she landed, dropping off Barnin and his men. "Look around, I will stay connected to you if you need anything."

She took off again and started circling around the cliff tops. The other two Dragons were doing the same but weren't finding much. Other than a few townspeople running from Noris, everything looked clear. But then she smelled something. It was blood and a lot of it. Umbra turned, following the scent. She was still having a hard time with the fog, so she was close to the ground when she saw it. On the ground was a group of Humans, bodies littered everywhere. She landed, instructing Barnin where to find her. Scattered around were several men in black. They seemed to be grouped around a badly injured brunette girl who fit the description of Stacy. Her chest was barely moving. Umbra looked further and found the form of another person on the ground. He was blonde with long hair; not as torn up as Stacy, but obviously dead. Arkin's body did not look peaceful; his face was a mask of sorrow. *That's an odd look,* Umbra thought.

Umbra could hear Barnin and his men running to where she was. She turned her attention to the girl on the ground, sending energy into her body, keeping her alive.

"What did you find?" Barnin yelled when he was in earshot.

"Arkin is dead. Stacy is in bad shape, I need to take care of her," Umbra said focusing on Stacy.

Barnin stopped mid-run. "Arkin is what?" he said, his voice holding none of its usual bravado. He didn't wait for her to answer but ran to the form of Arkin on the ground. He swore and threw his helmet.

"I'm so sorry. I know that he was a mentor to you," Umbra attempted to sound consoling.

Barnin stood breathing heavily, taking a few moments to gather himself. "Thank you Umbra, I know that you should call this in, but would it be all right if you just -- I don't know -- made it so I could tell Legon myself?"

She agreed and opened her mind to Barnin and the Carrier where Legon was.

Legon was back in his Elvin form. Transforming back wasn't as difficult as he had thought it would be. Iselin was with Sasha in her quarters doing some tests on Sasha's powers. There was a buzz in his head telling him there was a report for him. He broadened the connection, surprised to feel Barnin's presence.

"What is it?" Legon asked worried at the turmoil of Barnin's emotions.

"It's Arkin," Barnin was angry and sad. "He's dead, we found his body. Stacy is here too. She's alive but just barely."

Legon's blood turned to ice and a pit formed in his stomach. He'd known this was a possible outcome -- the only way Arkin wouldn't have warned Legon of an attack was if he had been dead. But the concept railed inside Legon. Arkin couldn't be dead. "You're sure?" Legon asked shakily.

Barnin sounded broken, defeated, all of his unshakable confidence gone. "Yes. He's gone. Looks like they put up one hell of a fight though; there are Dark Warriors all around ...what do you want me to do?"

Legon spoke without thinking, "Have Umbra bring him to the Carrier; have Stacy brought too."

"And what do you want me to do?" Barnin asked again.

Legon's anger flared, not at Barnin but at what had happened. Barnin was not just asking Legon as a friend for direction but also as a leader, as the Head of a Great House. Legon tried not to let anger color his decisions; he needed to be rational, needed to be a leader, needed to be the Head of a Great House.

"This was a trap meant to kill me, Sasha, and I suppose my wife as well. If Stacy is hurt and Arkin dead, then whoever did this to them is still alive; it would take more than a handful of men to defeat those two. You and your men are to search the area. We have several Ascended around there that will assist in search efforts. If there is a group around, they can't be far."

"What do you want me to do when I find them?" Barnin asked.

"Capture them alive if you can. I want answers."

Barnin swore, "You're going to let them live? How could ..."

Legon cut him off firmly. "Yes; until I have answers, I will let them live. This was an assassination attempt and one that very nearly worked. We need answers. I am not interested in the brute force that carry out attacks; I am more interested in those who plan them; the ones who are truly responsible for Arkin's death. Don't you worry, my friend, once we have the information that we need there will be justice. But not before."

"No, no you're right, I'm sorry. I was hotheaded," Barnin sounded more under control. Then softer, "I've seen where these Dark Warriors come from; they are more like animals if you ask me, just following orders. We'll look around and see what we can find, but I'm not going to lie to you. We've heard how these guys are in a fight, we may not be able to take them down alive."

Legon could feel Barnin's mind, feel the storm inside. He wasn't just upset about Arkin; he was thinking of Josher and the others he had lost that day. Legon spoke, "It's been a bad day and we've lost a lot of good people. I don't want you to take any more losses; if you find anyone, don't take any needless risks to bring them in. Notify an Ascended if you locate anything; they will be able to handle a group of infantry no matter the size. And don't worry; once we find out what we need, we can take care of the survivors. After all, we can't have them escaping and telling their command what we know, can we?"

Legon broke the connection with Barnin. His anger faded, replaced by a huge sense of loss. It was like losing Kovos all over again. He righted himself. Iselin's mind was tense, feeling his emotions. He walked into the room where she and Sasha were.

How did he break the news to them? Legon decided to just spit it out, "Arkin was killed in the attack ... Stacy is badly hurt ... she is being brought here. Barnin is looking for the attackers. Emma and Mage should also be heading back now as well."

Iselin's blue-green eyes seemed to melt, Sasha's red ones softened. She attempted to speak first, "Ho ... tha ... no," was all that came out.

Legon walked over to Iselin and took her hand. She squeezed his back, speaking in a hush, "We grew up together. He was older than I am. I looked up to him." She looked into Legon's eyes, "How?"

"They were attacked, but we will have to wait until Stacy is recovered to find out the particulars."

Sasha was looking down at the floor, her emotions a tangle.

"Sash I'm sorry I-I know what he meant to you ..." Legon started.

"I know you do, he was something to all of us. At least he was with Stacy at the end. They seemed to be very much in love, he would have wanted her to live ... it looks like we have another to care for," she finished.

That they did too; Stacy was on an ever-growing list of those close to them they had lost people they loved. In that moment Legon stopped feeling. He was out of emotional energy for the day. He wanted to mourn Arkin – would mourn him – but he couldn't right now.

"I am going to go send word to our parents … and I suppose his aunt and uncle in Coreum," Legon said.

"I'll contact Ivy," Iselin said. "I know her from when I was younger; it should come from someone they know. I think Arkin was like a son to them in a way. It's hard to tell since he was always gone ... I'm sorry, I'm rambling," she was shaking her head as she walked out of the room and toward the communications center of the Carrier.

Legon looked at Sasha who hadn't moved. She stood still, looking at the floor; he took a few steps to stand in front of her. Before he could speak, Sasha's arms wrapped tightly around him and she sobbed into his neck, "Why, why, why?"

"I know," he said reaching into her mind, feeling for pain.

"NO!" She said angrily, then instantly soft, "Not this, we share this, we hold it together."

"I'm sorry; you're right."

She coughed, "Don't be sorry; you're doing what you always do, protecting me, protecting everybody." She looked into his eyes with a fire he hadn't seen before, "You don't have to hold this mantle alone, not anymore; it's ours together."

I know Sash, I know Legon thought to himself.

Sasha made her way to the deck of the Carrier. Legon would take care of informing their family. For now she wanted to distract herself by taking care of Stacy. The salty sea breeze blew her hair in every direction as she stepped on deck. She figured with her new eyes, she probably looked like some monster from children's stories. Her senses were that of any Elf now, but unlike other Elves she saw as an Ascended did – bands of energy weaving in the air as Elves moved around; even the ship was emitting energy. It was beautiful in a way, the ribbons of color, but also disorienting.

Emma was back and running toward her. Sasha temporarily was distracted from her worries as she gazed at Emma; watching electrical impulses run down her legs and arms as she moved. How was she going to get used to that? Emma bounded into her arms. Upon seeing Sasha's changed appearance, she leaned back.

"Ooh, I like the eyes," she commented.

This caught Sasha off guard, "Really? I don't look like a monster?"

Emma stepped back and looked her up and down, "No; in fact I think it works for you, I mean you're an Elf now, right? And you look even better than you did before -- somehow the eyes add to it." Then she added, "Maybe sneak up on me in the dark some time and see how I react then." Emma smiled and then looked more closely, "But there is more, isn't there?"

All lightheartedness left. "Arkin is dead," Sasha said, looking down. "Stacy is hurt. She is being brought here."

Emma huffed out, "I'm sorry Sasha ... you knew him better than I did. Are you going to be all right?"

Sasha saw Umbra coming in to land on the deck of the ship. "Yes I will, but now we need to work," Sasha said, glad for the need to focus on something other than Arkin.

They made their way to Umbra. A black mist rose from her back and the still form of Stacy lowered to Sasha and Emma's level. Stacy looked bad; she was stabbed several times, and was covered in cuts and other injuries. Sasha examined her and with her mind summoned the Ship's Head of Medicine. Another still figure was almost on the deck now. Sasha turned to see Arkin's body floating.

Umbra spoke in her mind. "Un Prose, where would you like him to be laid?" she asked, empathy in her tone.

Sasha walked over to Arkin, tears forming in her eyes. Forgetting about Stacy for a moment, she reached out and took the carpenter in her arms. With her new body, his weight was like that of a child. She couldn't help but think of when he carried her as a child after one of her episodes.

She looked to Umbra. "Thank you, I will take him from here. Emma, will you please tend to Stacy? I will be with you shortly."

Sasha made her way below deck. The Elves in the hall parted for her as she passed; they bowed their heads in respect. It wasn't that they knew Arkin; in fact it was unlikely that more than a handful on the ship knew who he was. They saw Sasha's face and bowed in respect to a man who the Head of House cared for so much; she carried him in her arms. *He is worth the respect,* she thought.

She came to the door of her apartment, Sasha's handmaid opened the door and she walked into her bedroom, laying Arkin on the bed. "His body never touches the ground again," she said with a kind tone and left the room.

One of Sasha's guards, Cynta, approached her in her Elvin form. "Are you all right, Un Prose?" she asked, her brown eyes warm.

"I am, thank you Cynta," Sasha said walking off, not wanting to talk to anyone.

She noticed Cynta keeping up with her. "Is there something else?" Sasha asked.

Cynta was short but she seemed to stretch herself, making herself as tall as she could. "I am not leaving you, Un Prose," she said, the green flecks in her eyes sparkling.

"But I'm on the Carrier, I'm perfectly safe here," Sasha was a little put out.

Cynta looked down, her short black hair falling like a curtain around her face. "Please Un Prose, had I been with you today, you would not have been injured," she said.

Sasha softened. "Or Ascended," she said "I wouldn't have Ascended either."

"Still Un Prose, that Un Prosa Legon needed to use such magic to protect himself and you is a shame the house guard must rightfully carry."

"But you were ordered to ..." and then Sasha remembered, *you were ordered to not guard Legon's birth parents and they were killed.* Sasha understood. She'd always assumed that while in the Palace, the house guard following her and Legon was more of a comfort to the general public, but now she re-thought that assumption. "Cynta, you can stay with me, but please don't be so formal."

Cynta smiled, falling in step next to her as Sasha began walking again.

Emma followed the small precession of Elves taking Stacy to the sick bay. Emma wasn't too sure if Stacy was going to make it. Emma knew that the Elves were good at what they did, but Stacy was injured badly; her cream skin looked like chalk.

The Head Healer, Neenon, placed Stacy on an exam table. Shortly after, Sasha walked into the sick bay with Cynta.

"How is she?" Sasha asked Neenon.

"We checked her vitals on deck. Umbra stopped most of her bleeding, but we also checked her to make sure she didn't have any internal bleeding," Neenon said.

"Did she?" Sasha asked, looking at the girl.

"It appears that her own wards prevented the vast majority of that. Un Prose, do you feel ill?" Neenon asked.

Sasha shook her head, frustrated. "Yes, yes I'm fine. I just see as Ascended do now and to be honest, going from dull Human senses to that of an Elf in Dragon form is a bit overwhelming and confusing. My apologies. Please don't let me keep you from Stacy."

Emma was curious. She'd seen through the eyes of Elves before and it was a bit much, but she had never seen through the eyes of an Ascended. Sasha stepped back next to Emma who leaned in, "What's it like?"

Sasha paused and then opened her mind to Emma. She could see everything in the same detail as the other Elves and hear everything in the room, even heartbeats. Almost tasting the air, she felt heat from people's bodies, but there was so much more. She could see bands of energy undulating around people and objects. She could see impulses running along their bodies. Emma pulled back, "Whoa."

"Yes, I know. Iselin told me that with time I will stop seeing most of that stuff and just see like an Elf. She said that it's common for Dragons to be overwhelmed at first, but as time passes you have to focus on seeing things like energy."

"Really?" Emma asked.

"No. She's so used to me not being able to read her face, but now that I see like an Elf, I think she was lying to keep me from going out of my mind. Sweet of her, really."

Neenon interrupted their conversation, "Un Prose, we have looked her over and she will be fine. She needs rest, but I would like to keep her here for a few days just to make sure."

"Thank you Neenon, please let me know if you need anything and it will be taken care of."

They made their way out of the sick bay and Sasha said she was going to go take a nap. Emma continued walking until she found Legon; he was leaving the ship's communication room, his face slack.

"Hello Em, how do you feel?" he asked.

"I'm fine, you fixed my leg. How are you?"

"I'm not entirely sure; so much happened today that I'm not feeling much of anything." As he spoke, Emma couldn't help but marvel at the purple flecks in his eyes, more than she had ever seen on anyone, other than..."What is Sasha now?"

"She is a class six but in an Elf form, it's never been seen before, that's why her eyes are that solid metallic red. The flecks indicate power, which is why I have so many, I'm a class eight." He seemed to read her shock, "I'm sorry, you weren't there when I was tested. I'm an eight and Sasha a six. How crazy is that?"

Crazy. She didn't say it; instead, "That's amazing, have you told your family?"

"Yes, and I told them about Arkin; Keither and Sara are being told now. I dare say this will not be a good night for anyone."

Chapter Three
Laid to Rest

"Life ripples out like the water of a pond, how far the ripples go and what they touch we truly never know."
-Diary of the Perfectos Compatioa

Umbra stood in the front row next to Barnin as Josher's coffin was lowered into its grave. Only Barnin's unit and a few others were present. She looked around the collection of dirty men still in their armor. They didn't look sad, just tired. In that moment, Umbra felt for them. This was just a small blip in her life as far as time went. She had walked the land for thousands of years, and unless killed, would continue to do so for thousands more. The men around her were not that way -- most were in their twenties, a few even younger. They hadn't lived life, they hadn't loved and been loved, hadn't lived their dreams. Yet many of them wouldn't leave this war alive. And those who did would lose years of their short lives and worse, this war would be what defined them. Umbra's eyes burned; the boy in the grave was evidence enough of that. He was young, trying to help, he had no wife or children and in a way that made it a sadder because his was a life un-lived.

The gathered group started to move away from the grave, leaving Barnin, Ankle, and Heath behind. Barnin turned, looking at her. She felt self-conscious; did they hold her responsible for his death? She wouldn't blame them.

"I'm sorry, I will leave you alone," she said turning.

"Why?" Heath asked.

She was confused. "Don't you blame me for his death?" she asked.

Ankle answered "You didn't know him long but you were as much a friend as any. You have every right to be here, and we don't blame you. How could we? This is war. This is how it is."

"You have saved our lives several times. That we made it to the town at all was a credit to you. No, we aren't mad at you," Barnin said. And then more somberly, "How do you live with this for centuries?"

"What do you mean?" Umbra asked

Ankle answered, "We always have the hope that someday when we pass, we will see our friends and family again; we can live with things like this war because life is short. You can't. If you lose someone it's for thousands of years. How do you live with that?"

She smiled weakly. "And here I was thinking of how awful all this was for you, only having a few decades for life. To answer: time dulls pain. With our connections to those close to us the pain dulls, and sometimes we almost forget … but it never goes away."

Barnin looked away from the grave and spoke to Umbra. "I think this is bad for everyone. Are you coming to Arkin's funeral?" he asked.

"No, I was not planning on it. I didn't know him …" Umbra replied.

"You should come. I could use the company," Barnin said.

Barnin walked toward Noris, Umbra next to him. Heath and Ankle were just a bit behind. Heath wasn't going to Arkin's funeral, saying he had had enough death for the day. Barnin looked Umbra up and down, her black hair bouncing with each graceful step she took. She looked out of place in a crushed black velvet dress, a spark of beauty in a sea of dirt and grime.

Her green eyes bore into him. "What are you thinking about?" she asked.

He sighed, "You. Here we are all armor and grit and you … well," he made a motion that went from her head to her feet, "you're in that."

To his surprise she laughed, "In what, a dress? They are just more comfortable. Besides when I fight it's in my Ascended form; I have no need of armor and swords. I hope your Samantha doesn't find out you've been ogling other women," she said wryly.

Now it was his turn to laugh. "I'm not ogling you; I just think you look out of place is all," he sighed again. "Thanks for cheering me up."

"You take the deaths of your men to heart, don't you?" she asked.

Barnin searched for how to answer her. "I do. You understand. There's a bond between people when they fight together -- it's like we are brothers, you know?" he said. She nodded and he went on, "I see the families of those who are killed a lot of the time -- in Manton we can go find a widow or a father or mother; we find people to come to events like this, it gives them closure. But out here, who is going to come to Josher's grave? Who is going to leave flowers, what closure will his mother and father have? Will they have any at all? Do you know what it's like telling a family their loved ones won't be coming back?"

He watched Umbra as a myriad of emotions crossed her face. "I was ten; this was before the war of course, a war that wouldn't happen for decades. We were in the front garden making poppies grow, my sister and I, when a man came to our house asking after my mother and father ..." her face reddened. "He told us that our brother had been killed. You see, before the war there were minor conflicts with the Iumenta. … anyway, he was gone, so I know what it is like to have a house call, if you will. Later, my sister and I fought in the war; she was almost one hundred years older than I, her husband fought as well. They didn't make it. I was the one who told his family and mine of their deaths. So to answer your question: yes, I do know the feeling you are talking about."

He didn't always remember Umbra's age. While he thought that he had seen a lot in his time, it was nothing to the woman next to him. How many times had she delivered news of people being lost? What would it have been like living in Elf cities after the War of Generations? There wasn't an Elf alive at the time who hadn't lost several friends and family members.

They were to the harbor now. A small ship waited to ferry Barnin, Keither, Sara and Umbra to the Carrier where Arkin's service was to be held.

Keither stood holding Sara's hand as the ferry pulled alongside one of house Evindass' massive Dragon Carriers. A door on its side opened, a gangplank sliding out for them to walk on. The ship sent was that of sap and sea, it reminded him of his time in Seeon. They walked down a narrow hallway lined with crystal bulbs lighting their way.

Even after the time he'd spent living in them, Elf structures still felt odd to Keither. The ship that had brought him and Sara to Noris was Human; he felt the waves fully and heard the ship creak and waves lap against its hull. But now aboard an Elvin Carrier, there were none of those things. The halls were like that of a Dragon Dome, smooth and refined; there was no sound from the outside world and he barely felt the sea on the large ship. It was even more so when they entered the ship, as spells made it so one didn't feel the effects of motion sickness. In effect, the slight rocking of the ship seemed to be nullified; it was like being on land.

The passage they were in spilled into a large cargo hold that was empty at the moment. Sara walked ahead, down the center aisle of rows of padded chairs all facing a podium and altar. Atop the altar sat a coffin that looked to be made of aspen; its cream wood shone with a glossy clear coat broken only by gold embroidery. Keither sat on one of the soft wooden chairs and resisted the urge to peek in the open casket.

Barnin sat next to Keither, who'd finally been able to shower, and now wore clothes given to him on the ferry. The Ascended Umbra sat on the other side of Barnin. The room filled slowly with Elves and some of the Human command. Keither knew that most in the room did not know Arkin directly, but had respect for the work he did.

Emma walked in and sat next to Sara. "Hello Sara, Keither -- I am so sorry for your loss," she said.

"Thank you Em, is Stacy doing better?" Sara asked.

Emma nodded, "Still weak and out of it most of the time. She can't come today, but should be well enough to attend the ceremony in Coreum."

Keither had forgotten about that. The event today was a public one. Arkin had performed great services for the Elves with Legon and Sasha; this was their time to honor him. But Arkin's known living family was in Coreum; the Elves would keep Arkin's remains and give them to his family once Coreum was taken.

Emma contented herself with looking forward at the altar. She didn't have a relationship with Arkin. She didn't dislike him, but she wasn't close to him like the others were. For her, today was sad, but not as impactful as it was for others. Arkin was closest to Legon, Sasha and Iselin; as such it was they who put the event together. They had grown Arkin's coffin, made the clothes he wore, and with painstaking care used magic to remove any signs of his violent end.

Emma had been surprised by the Cona Republic. House Paldin had offered to grow caskets for all of their dead and ship them to Manton to be returned to family members; but they insisted on burying their dead in Noris, most likely in the hopes that at the war's end, Noris would have a monument made. Emma wondered if it was the right thing to do, or if it was the Humans' way of staying independent, if even only in how they handled their loss.

Legon, Sasha and Iselin entered the room. All three dressed in black; the only other color they wore was the white robes of the Head of House. Sasha and Iselin sat in chairs next to the podium. Legon walked to the podium. Emma thought he looked tired, the tiredness of a man who had put in too many hours, and that of a man who knew his work was at the beginning and not near an end.

"Thank you all for coming today," Legon started. "Today we honor Arkin. He was my teacher, mentor and friend. He protected my sister and taught me what I needed to protect that which I love.

"He lived a life of service; he sacrificed everything for what he believed in. I wonder if I could do the same. Arkin was a humble man and would not boast of himself." Legon smirked a bit, "But I am not Arkin; therefore, I can boast about him to my heart's content. As can my wife Iselin and my sister Sasha; and that is what we intend to do today. We are not going to mourn this great loss, but rather celebrate his life. I would ask all of you who have been touched by Arkin to come and share your stories with us."

Emma had wondered why Sasha had insisted on the most comfortable of chairs aboard the ship, but now she understood. Legon started with his stories of Arkin, and then Sasha spoke, her tale bringing the room to tears. Iselin's was that of a young man who inspired her. Sydin, Opes, and even many Emma didn't know spoke. Barnin talked of Arkin helping him escape the empire and teaching him what he needed to fight back against injustice. Keither and Sara spoke as well. It was many hours before people stopped sharing; Emma was stunned at what an influence Arkin had been on those in the room. Now as she observed the gathered people, among whom were some of the most powerful people in Airmelia, she questioned how many in living memory were as influential as Arkin was.

Legon ended the day with a simple "thank you." There was no call to arms, no request for volunteers to avenge Arkin's death; just a thank you. As people left, they filed past the open casket. Emma took her turn, looking down at Salmont's old carpenter. *He looks at peace* she thought, his hands folded around a letter Stacy had written in the sick bay. Emma worried for the girl Stacy, she loved Arkin and he had loved her. Emma decided that she would befriend the girl; after all, they had both lost their loves to the Iumenta.

As she left, Emma followed Sasha to the sick bay to visit Stacy. The room and its many tables were bathed in honeyed tones, giving it a peaceful and relaxing feel. Emma always noted the distinct lack of odor in Elvin medical facilities.

Stacy was sitting up in one of the corner beds. Emma could see that she was feeling better; all of her cuts and broken bones had been healed. Now, she was just recovering her strength.

Legon and Iselin were behind Emma with Opes and Sydin in tow. The later spoke to Stacy once everyone was around her bed.

"Stacy, my name is Sydin, I am the Head of House Evindass' military. I know that you have been through a lot in the last few days, but we need to ask you some questions about when you were attacked."

Stacy looked weak but nodded. "Wh-what would you like to know?"

"Everything," Legon said with gentle simplicity.

Stacy composed herself. "Well, as you know we were meeting a contact of mine. On our way we ran into some trouble ... there were seven or eight of them I think, but I can't be sure." She sucked in ragged breaths and Emma felt her heart break for the girl. Stacy went on, "We fought of course, Arkin tried to defend me ... but ... but," her face fell into her hands and she sobbed. "They killed and then I was on my own. I don't remember a lot. It hurt. I had wards protecting vital organs, so it took them a long time before I fell. I thought I was going to die. It hurt so much I wanted to die ... and Arkin ...," she choked, "I'm sorry."

Legon put a hand on her shoulder and squeezed. "Don't be sorry. You were very brave. You don't have to tell us any more right now. Thank you for being there for Arkin," Legon said.

Stacy looked up at him with fire in her eyes. "They killed him and I'm going to kill them. Please, please, please, let me help. I know what Arkin was doing. He trusted me with so much. I could help; I helped him set the whole thing up," she said almost fanatically.

Emma could empathize, hadn't she clung to what Kovos had been doing prior to his death? Her service to Evindass was evidence enough of that. Yes, Stacy was looking for the same, looking to keep Arkin alive in her own way by finishing his work. Emma would talk to Legon and Sasha on Stacy's behalf, she decided.

Opes broke in with his breathy voice, "Thank you Stacy, for the offer. We have a lot to talk about regarding the work being done in the Cona Empire, but I promise you that you will be a big part of it. Now please rest."

Legon walked out of the sick bay, leaving Emma behind to keep Stacy company. The bay door closed with a soft thump. "We need to figure out what we are going to do. Arkin's network is too important for us to let it die with him. Also, we have a meeting later today with the other Houses to decide a course of action for this war. Opes, can you please gather all of the information available about Arkin's network; we need to find either a new way of running it or a new Head. Sydin, we need reports on our end of the war for the meeting as well."

Sydin and Opes went on their way to complete their respective tasks. That left him with Sasha and his wife. "Love," he said to Iselin, "we need to find out what the Human forces are doing. Keither has given us some details about what he is doing, but we need to find out what all of their plans are. Do you think maybe you could grease the wheels a bit?"

"Are you asking me to flirt with Enrich?" she asked coyly.

He smiled, "I would never ask you to flirt my love, but charm ..."

She laughed, "I will do my best."

"Thank you," he said and then to his sister, "Sash, I know today has been long but we need to do more."

She nodded, "What do you want me to do?"

"The Iumenta had crystals and other magical objects placed in Noris. Aside from being useful for you and your people to study; they are wreaking havoc. Buildings are exploding; things are bursting into fire or freezing. While I don't think we will be able to do much for Noris, it is likely we will find traps in each city we take. I want you to figure out everything you can about these objects and spells, and while you're at it, see if you can learn anything more about Iumenta crystals. From what I have been told, some of the city's defenses were crystal-based, those crystals mostly shattered in the fight but..."

She picked up the thread of his thoughts. "We might be able to figure out how they were constructed, right? Am I allowed to go ashore?" she asked.

He was a little surprised; Sasha didn't really ask for permission to do anything. "Of course, you are a class six, after all. But ... take your full guard and only go to places that have been cleared," he said.

She smiled, "Of course." She turned and left, leaving Legon the task of confirming the meeting with all of the other Great Houses.

Chapter Four
Road Maps

"Tales of the past outline great battles and strategies; we hear of death defying acts of heroes and heroines of the conflict, but of the packman in supply routes we hear nothing. I suspect that is because he is busy working."
-*The Exiled Captain (Author Unknown)*

Keither fought back a yawn. *It's only mid-afternoon,* he thought. Reading his mind, Sara added, "And you have only slept a few hours every night for the last two weeks." She patted his shoulder.

They were sitting at a table strewn with papers in one of the harbor warehouses of Noris. Arkin's funeral, sad as it was; had made for a nice break for Keither to rest. Now he was back to work. Noris posed problems that while not unforeseen, still proved to be irksome. It was his job to manage supplies and take care of the general population of Noris' daily needs, such as food, clean water, shelter, etc. While Noris was a hub and had warehouses and keeps full of supplies, most of those where either burning to the ground, booby-trapped and therefore about to be burning to the ground, or had yet to be cleared by security, who would likely set off booby traps and cause said buildings to burn to the ground.

Sara squeezed his shoulders. "Talk it through with me, you can figure this out," she said encouragingly.

She was right; he needed to just talk everything out. "Here is the situation: our military is fine for the most part; we brought in plenty of supplies for them. The issue is the townspeople of Noris; our people have to finish taking a lot of the town's strongholds. In most cases those strongholds were set on fire as enemy units lost control of them. That's not all the warehouses – some were left unguarded when we took the town. But some of those houses have tainted goods, grain with poison in it and so on. This means that Venefica have to check the contents of each warehouse before supplies can be distributed."

"What of the supplies that we brought with us?" Sara asked.

"Yes those, well most ships with food were for military use; after all if we can't keep our people fed, they won't be able to fight. Also, those supplies are packed for the purpose of easy travel as we push up the Kay-loose, so I can't use any of them. We do have a small fleet of relief ships waiting to dock -- once they offload, things here will get better; BUT we don't know when that will happen or in what order ships will dock and unload." Keither closed his eyes, "It's a nightmare. We did everything we could to minimize civilian casualties and injuries. We knew there was a chance that the empire would destroy food and medical stores but hoped that it wouldn't. I mean, Noris and its inhabitants are still citizens of the Cona Empire; why would they kill their own?"

Legon took his place with Sydin around a large table with representatives of each of the Great Houses and Enrich from the Cona Republic. As Legon was the only Head of House in attendance, he presided over the meeting and started it.

He stood and addressed the room. "Thank you all for coming. There is a lot that we need to cover today, so I am going to get right to it. So far our campaign into the Cona Empire has met with relative success. That said, we will have setbacks sooner or later. Why don't we all give updates on our various duties," his mind flicked out to the ship and a large map of Noris hovered over the table. Legon sat back down as Sydin rose.

"Noris has, for the most part, fallen. There are still pockets of resistance, but that is to be expected. Human and Elf forces will be spending the next few weeks and maybe even months removing these threats. While the town and its limits seem to be under our control, the towns to the east and north are not. Our troops have not moved on these areas with any degree of seriousness yet. As for Ascended, we have had sporadic attacks on all sides of the town; thus far neither side has taken any casualties in those fights. We think that the Iumenta are looking more to contain them than anything else. Enrich, would you mind updating us on your progress?" Sydin sat down.

Enrich stood, not seeming the least bit bothered to be in a room full of Elves. "We consider the invasion of Noris to be a success; we took fewer casualties than estimated and have held our ground. The only issue that we have encountered -- other than those expected -- is resistance in some parts of town. When Cona soldiers left the area, they burned and set traps in most of the buildings with medical and food supplies. We could handle this had they not also destroyed most of their harbor. As it is, we cannot get supplies into the city with any degree of speed. Also, when leaving, the Iumenta set many houses and shelters on fire; this has left us with a large amount of homeless and wounded people. We have made ships with medical supplies a priority for landing and offloading, but I would be lying if I said that wasn't going to put a hold on advancing up the Kayloose. It's a double-edged sword. If we can push our forces up the river, we will be able to offload more ships, but if we don't offload supplies now ..."

"There will be high losses of civilians," Hydra, a bronze-haired Elf from House Floren said. Her green eyes were thoughtful for a moment, "I will send teams to help rebuild the harbor so you can bring in more ships and also task three destroyers to securing more of the Kayloose." Legon had a great deal of respect for Hydra; she was the admiral of House Floren's fleet and therefore the Head in Command of all naval activities in the war.

"Thank you," Enrich said.

Legon had a thought. "Hydra?" he asked.

"Yes Un Prosa," Hydra said.

"I know that it would be impractical to use the small boats that landing parties came in on, but would it be possible to lash them together and create some sort of floating bridge that could extend out into the harbor?"

Hydra's eyebrows rose. "What a novel idea, Un Prosa. With the movement of the water, I don't think just tying the boats together would be stable, nor could they take the weight; but if we took one boat and put it upside down on another and then sealed them so water could not leak in, we would have a set of floats to make the base of our bridge, or I should say, pier." She thought more, "It's not ideal but it should help until we get the rest of the harbor up and running. I will have people start right away." Her eyes unfocussed for a moment and then she was back with them. "Our report is a positive one to say the least; while the Human fleet looked impressive it posed little threat to our own. As we suspected, most of the Impa fleet have moved in along coastal cities to keep their waters clear. We have a team of strategists that have been trying to figure out why the Impa let Noris' water fall with so little Iumenta back up. The reason we suspect is that they knew that Noris was going to fall, or at least at sea, it would. We believe that their goal is not to try to beat our navy -- they know they can't -- however, they can stop landing parties. We think they will focus on trying to keep coastlines clear enough to move supplies and repel landing parties."

Legon listened as she outlined her plans for how she was going to deal with the Impa Navy. After she was done, other Houses gave updates on all of their activities, most either being on schedule with their plans or further ahead than expected. Legon was shocked to hear that the Precipice was being attacked. Tuneal of House Paldin had chosen not to meeting Cona forces at the sentinels but instead to force them to fight in the narrow canyons leading into the valley where the Dome was. The representative from House Coreen reported that the land invasion from Pawdin lands had met little resistance in the open plains area in the southern part of the empire. His report detailed that in many cases, small villages and co-ops welcomed Elvin forces with open arms.

"That goes to show that Arkin's work was effective; however, I do not think all of the war will go this easy," Sydin said.

"No. I do not either," the representative from House Coreen said. "We suspect that the further north we go, the more resistance we will face. In addition, even after a town is cleared, we expect that in the northern areas we will have more insurgency from those loyal to the Cona Empire. Un Prosa Legon, may I ask what reports we have from House Evindass' spy network?"

"Yes I have been receiving reports. Thankfully Arkin made plans in the event that he was killed." There was a collective sigh of relief from the room at Legon's pronouncement. "We are still getting information from each city in his network. From what we can tell, most of the Cona lands don't even know there is a war on; only high ranking officials seem to know anything. In the southern areas there is more awareness, but the closer to the Capital a city is, the less they know. Some of our cells have attempted to start rumors of the war but have had efforts blocked by Iumenta Ascended influencing people heavily," Legon said.

"This makes you happy, Un Prosa?" Hydra asked.

"Yes it does; as you are all aware, when someone's mind is influenced too strongly they become aware of it. From all accounts, the Iumenta have had to divert their more skilled Ascended to handle the threat we posed. As a result, many novice Ascended are influencing people, and in some cases people are starting to become aware."

This seemed to please most of the Elves in the room and Legon went on. "However, while Arkin's network is giving us information, it still needs a new Head. For that, I am planning on assigning Stacy, Arkin's right hand in Salez and also his lover."

"How much do you trust her?" Hydra asked.

"Arkin had one hundred percent trust in her; they were connected mentally almost the entire time he was in Salez. She has the incentive, obviously; though that does concern me. I don't want her to make mistakes as she looks for revenge, but that aside, I think she is our best option. She knows more about Arkin's operation and plans than anyone; she is even responsible for many of the things his network did."

None of the house representatives pushed the subject, Legon knew that their questions were more driven out of curiosity than anything else.

A raven-haired Elf representing House Neephom spoke to Sydin. "Sydin, what are your plans with the Venefica?" Then, turning and gesturing proudly to Legon, "And the newest class eight Ascended in the Pawdin Empire, as well as Un Prose Sasha."

Sydin beamed, "We are going to secure the air space over the land and use Ascended to take out as many targets as possible. As for Legon and Sasha, Opes will be taking them back to Seeon for training; we hope to have Legon and Sasha ready in a few months at best."

Legon smiled warmly. Five years ago, he would have been insulted by being forced back to Seeon to train, but not anymore; he saw it as an opportunity and planned on working as hard has he could to be ready to fight.

It was evening by the time Sara left Keither's side. She was off to help with some of the medical supplies. The air was cool when she left the warehouse that was Keither's headquarters, the sun almost set. She made her way to the docks, passing ravaged buildings as she went. She heard a bell toll in the harbor indicating that residents needed to make their way home. Martial Law was in effect in Noris, a curfew of nightfall restricted all but resistance forces.

The docks came into view and she focused on her task for the evening. As she approached a ship she heard the sound of rumbling thunder in the distance. She looked at the horizon, seeing color flashing in the sky. *Ascended,* she said to herself. As she looked back at the harbor she watched three Elvin destroyers make their way up the slow waters of the Kayloose. Bolts from the decks launched into the hillside on the opposite bank of the river, bursting into fire. She looked upriver, the horizon glowing orange.

"They are trying to take some more land east of here, I think to clear more of the docks," the rough voice of a guard said over her shoulder. "Don't worry, Noris is still secure." There was a boom in the distance and fire bloomed in the air above Noris. The guard seemed to reconsider his previous statement. "Well, it's mostly secure ..."

She laughed, "Thank you, I am here to help with the medical supply offloading."

"See that ship down there?" he said, pointing west, "That's the one you want."

"Thank you," she said, and turned toward the ship.

Sara stepped onto the rough deck. It was an older merchant ship that had been loaned out for the war. Her crew members were either too old to fight or too young to be allowed to fight.

A middle-aged man with several days' worth of stubble walked up to her. "Good evenin', the name's Captain Rich. How may I be of service?" he said kindly.

"My name is Sara. I am here to help offload the medical supplies."

He cocked a half smile, "You're gonna unload cargo?"

She smirked, "I am here to direct and tell the dock crews where to send cargo." She smiled.

Captain Rich chuckled and showed her below deck. "There isn't much here for ya, we only got lots of odds and ends."

Sara looked the cargo over. She would have liked to have seen more in the way of supplies, but anything was better than nothing. "Thank you. When can you have it on the docks?"

The Captain rubbed his chin, "Seein' how there is medicine and the likes, and there ain't much of 'em, I would say I can get them off for ya in less than an hour; if'n I can get clearance from the Port Master."

"Begin unloading; I will tend to the Port Master," Sara said not unkindly, but with authority.

Sara found the port master and her heart fell a bit. The man's name was

James and Sara was not fond of him at all.

"What do you want?" James asked rudely.

"I need you to clear a ship for unloading so I can get medical supplies to the healing centers."

James was at a desk leaning back in his chair. "I just went on lunch."

This was one of the many reasons she disliked James. "Well, can you just sign off on the ship? We really need those supplies," she said.

James sneered at her, "Why don't I finish my lunch and when I get to it, I get to it. Besides, what do I care if some local town folk kick the bucket; we should have wiped them out to begin with."

"James," she said, trying not to sound mad, "we are here to help ..."

He cut her off, "Sorry, I forget you're not real bright, I'M ON LUNCH! Do you understand me?"

Sara's face burned, she felt the power in her flex. *It would feel so good to zap you,* she thought.

Sara and her team needed those supplies and decided to go over James' head. Her mind flicked out to a nearby Elvin ship. "Forgive me, but I need to speak with someone on the Evindass Carrier Kovos, can you patch me through?" She felt the ship connect her with the Carrier. "Hello, may I speak with Un Prosa Legon, Sasha or Iselin? This is Sara." She hated to do this. She knew they were all busy, but she needed those supplies.

Iselin's mind joined hers, "Sara, I am in Noris, what do you need?"

Sara explained the situation to Iselin.

"I was already at the docks, ready to head back to the Carrier. I will be by in a moment," she said.

James seemed to be doing his best to ignore Sara, but still kept shooting her murderous glances. Finally he seemed to notice that she no longer looked upset. "What has you so happy?"

Sara just smiled.

Soon Iselin came strolling in the building and James' mouth dropped open. Sara wasn't sure what it was, if it was Iselin in her lavender dress or if it was the white robe she wore; clearly stating that not only was she in Noris on official state business, but that she was Head of a Great House.

"Good evening Un Prose," Sara said bowing.

Iselin smiled slightly. "I am here tending to matters with the Cona military." Her gaze focused on James and became flinty, "James, I understand that a ship with medical supplies needs clearance. Is there a reason this is not done?"

James puffed up, "I am on my lunch break and I am the port master on duty; so it's my call, not yours ... whoever you are."

Sara winced inside.

Iselin smiled sweetly, the pink flecks in her eyes glittering. "I am Iselin, Head of the Great House Evindass, and while I am here you are not the end-all of decision making." She turned to Sara, "You have clearance to unload the ship."

Sara was happy to see the color drain from James' face and she could almost hear his heart stop when Iselin spoke next. "James, you would do well to be respectful to Heads of House. I will be seeing Enrich shortly, and will be sure to share my concern with him," she closed by gracefully walking out of the office with Sara hot on her heels.

"Thank you, Ise. I'm sorry," Sara said once they were out of earshot.

"It's fine; you needed those supplies. But you need to remember Legon, Sasha and I may not always be in range to help."

"I know, and I'm sorry. I just don't know how to deal with that guy."

"I'm not chastising you; I'm just saying that if we aren't here, you need to learn how to get what you need. May I recommend learning more of the Jezeer?"

Sara was confused, "How do you mean?"

Iselin rolled her eyes but seemed amused, "Sara, the Jezeer is far more than learning to use your body; it teaches you how to read people, how to change your tone and body language to influence people. Learn those tools and you will not need to ever go over anyone's head to take action."

Sara understood. "I guess that it's not all that different from when I was in Salez; I learned to read people there too, and how to get people to do things."

"Yes, in a way; but this time instead of selling yourself you are selling them on an idea, or in some cases trusting you and your opinion. This is how state craft works," Iselin explained. They were near an Elvin ship and Iselin changed the topic. "I have to go, we are heading back to Seeon for Legon and Sasha to train, but if you do need anything or just want to chat, please contact us," she said, giving Sara a hug.

"I will, and you guys take care and thank you again. Also, I think I'm going to look more into this Art of the Jezeer," Sara said.

Iselin stepped onto the ferry that would take her back to the Carrier and then bring Enrich back to Noris. She'd spent most of the afternoon working with the higher-ups in the Human military trying to establish a working relationship between the Cona forces and Pawdin. It was tiresome work. The Humans were all jockeying for position and making plans for advancement, and there was no sense of unity. This was foreign to most Elves; in complex situations they talked things over and often mentally linked, without a desire to be above anyone else. Meetings were generally short and productive; the only thing impeding progress was pleasantries. That had not been her afternoon. Iselin knew that she was good at working with the Human government. She knew Humanity well and had spent lots of time around them, and if she was being honest, she knew that most of the government was male and found her attractive. She didn't flirt with them, but they seemed to be just that much more pliable. Sadly, in her meetings that day, there were several Human women. She had looked them over using her training in the Jezeer. Most were intimidated by her, and as a result they were being stubborn just to prove themselves. Another woman, who had little in the way of mental protection, thought that because Iselin was blonde and attractive she was brainless. There were older men in the room who likely thought the same of her; however, with their time in the Cona military, they had learned to respect Elves and most importantly respect Elvin Houses. Even if they saw Iselin as a twit, they would not think so little of the minds behind her, and knowing how Elves worked, the older generals listened to her input with respect.

She pinched the bridge of her nose and tried to shove the day from her mind. By the time she arrived back to the ship, her head was throbbing. She felt for Legon. Finding him in an office teaching Sasha to grow plants, Iselin smiled to herself, remembering when she had given Legon the same lessons. Legon was next to Sasha, grinning as she made grass grow in a pot.

They both looked up when she came in the room. Legon's mind was warm and welcoming, her own little piece of heaven. Sasha beamed up at her, "Look Ise, I can grow grass!"

Iselin laughed. "I can see that! It's very impressive. Was it difficult?"

Sasha shook her head. "I think being connected to so many Elves for the last few years helped; I've been in all of your heads when you've done it and it's just doing it for myself now. It's really fun," she said. Then reading how Iselin was feeling, she added in a more subdued manner, "How are you doing? Are you all right?"

Iselin sat next to her husband, leaning against him on the soft couch; he put his arm around her. She closed her eyes as she answered, "Humans can be such a pain. No offense, Sash."

Sasha giggled. "I can't really take offense anymore, can I? But I know what you mean, I was one for twenty-five years," she said.

Iselin opened her eyes. "Sorry, I'm so used to you as Human, Sasha. Why did you have to mess that up?"

"It's your fault! I want to meet all of my nieces and nephews and YOU Elves don't start having kids for a hundred years or so."

Iselin shook with Legon's chuckle. "Wow, so that's why we are going to be stuck with you for the rest of time?"

"Mmmm hmmm, yes, that's right. So you better get used to it," Sasha smiled and turned back to her pot of grass.

Iselin thought about making a comment but drifted off to sleep instead.

Chapter Five
Replacements

"Life is like a wild horse, we have a choice, we can hold tight and see where it takes us, or we can fall off and hope to not break a leg."
-Excerpts from the Diary of the Adopted Sister

Legon woke from a dreamless sleep. In the weeks following his Ascension neither he, Sasha, nor Iselin had dreamt of the White Dragon. Legon wondered if it meant that the dreams were over. He breathed in, his nostrils filling with the sweet scent of Iselin's hair. Reflexively the arm he had around her torso tightened, bringing her sleeping form closer to him. Her soft skin was hot against his, a feeling that would have been uncomfortable had it not been for the mattress cooling itself.

He kissed her shoulder and her mind awakened, connecting with his. She rolled under his arm so she was on her back. He ran his hand up and down the silk skin of her belly and side; she turned her head, eyes still closed towards him. He kissed her softly, thinking about how perfect most every morning had been since their marriage.

She smiled and spoke softly, "Yes, mornings are wonderful. You are relaxed from a night's sleep and still not with it enough to think of the day ahead." She rolled again, making Legon move off his side and onto his back. Draping her arm around Legon, resting her head on his chest, with a kiss she said, "Just a bit longer." As he ran his fingers up and down her back he felt her mind disconnect with sleep. Again, the bed's temperature and even the firmness altered; it was almost imperceptible when this happened. Legon knew that the bed he would sleep in that evening on the Lux would be so well crafted that he wouldn't feel any of the changes either. The headboard would produce the faint scent of lavender and the air would have more oxygen, helping them to sleep soundly. The beds were a far cry from that of his home in Salmont. There the mattress he'd slept on was filled with a lumpy tangle of rope. Now his body no longer contoured itself to the bed, but rather the bed to him, as did every bed in the Pawdin Empire.

It was in times like these that Legon wondered if it was right for the immortals to not share their technology with Humanity. He knew that Humans could not grow plants at will and that it was that ability that made the way the Elves lived so much more comfortable. It was a war in his mind, but he knew the answer. Humanity advanced on its own for thousands of years; it was slow, but still growth. That growth stopped after the War of Generations, after Humans moved into the old Iumenta and Elf cities. Early settlers had adapted mostly Iumenta tools and technology, as that of the Elves was organic and faded. But as a result, Humanity seemed to lose its ability to come up with new things on its own as far as technological improvements went. This pattern continued as the Elves began to work with Humans again; each time the Elves would drastically alter something for Humanity, it was like touching the wings of a butterfly, and they didn't work from that time forth. The fear was a valid one. If the immortals continued to heavily influence Human ingenuity, Humanity would become dependent on them. Conversely, the Human lands were always riddled with war and contention, but was it not the responsibility of the immortals to step in to stop injustice? Legon wasn't sure, it was a question that he thought would be an easy one, but after years of being an Elf, he was still undecided. The Great Houses did their best to walk the line between mentor and enabler, but it was a fine line that always seemed to change.

Iselin was waking again, she tried to move away from him and he held her tight. She giggled, "I need to go to the bathroom. Is that acceptable with you?"

Legon stopped thinking about the world and smiled. "You do?" he said poking a spot on her side.

She jumped, her face turned up to his, eyes wide. "You better not!"

He tickled her again. "Better not what?"

She laughed. "No, that's not funny, I really have to go!"

He felt in her mind; she wasn't lying. He grinned wickedly at her.

Sasha made her way on deck, heading toward the side where the Lux was. Emma was next to her and looked happy to be heading back home to Seeon. Sasha felt the same; she didn't care for violence and she was looking forward to getting away from it for a time and also to hone her new abilities.

Emma gave her a sidelong glance, "Are you looking forward to seeing Edling?"

She was excited about that too, and couldn't help but smile. "Maybe," she said and added, "Legon and I are planning on spending most of our time in the Golden City; Edling's family has a house there."

Emma laughed. "Whose family doesn't have a house or apartment in every major city in the Pawdin Empire?" she said.

Sasha didn't comment. Legon and Iselin were making their way on deck, Iselin keeping her distance from her smirking husband.

"Did my brother do something rude?" Sasha asked Iselin.

"Yes, he did," she said, giving Legon a stern look that cracked into an unwilling smile.

Sasha really didn't want to know what had happened. She'd been in constant mental contact with Legon since he was dressed and as far as she was concerned, anything that happened between them prior to the 'ready for their day' phase was not only none of her concern, but did not actually exist. It was like the world right before dawn when she was asleep; it just wasn't real.

Sasha made her way to her cabin on the Lux. Emma would join her as soon as she'd put her own belongings away, which gave Sasha time alone. The Lux was already pulling away from the Kovos. She leaned against the wall and looked out the back windows of the ship. She heard her door thump shut and turned to Emma who was looking more and more relaxed. Sasha wondered if she should keep Emma from coming with her in the future, but decided that it wasn't really her call to make.

Tom sat in the costume shop in Salez, trying to wrap his mind around the consequences of the news he'd just received. *Arkin is dead and once she is back on her feet, Stacy is in charge,* he told himself again and again. Arkin was the mastermind of all things bringing down the Cona Empire from the inside, it was Arkin who made the plans and executed them, Arkin who had the vision. Tom didn't know what to think about Stacy being in charge; she was good at what she did and was Arkin's right hand after all, but the leader? Tom wasn't sure. Seth came in the back room of the shop.

"What's going on?" Seth asked ashe and Brian entered together.

Tom felt a moment of pause; this was the team now until Stacy came back. "Arkin is dead ... Stacy is pretty torn up ... I don't know too much about how it all went down, but Stacy is going to be in charge ..." he just let it hang in the silence.

Seth and Brian both stood stock-still.

It was Brian who spoke first. "Fine. So Stacy is in command, what are our orders?" he asked.

"Do we have a problem? Are we compromised?" Seth asked taking up the thread.

Tom understood, the bond with Arkin's unit was tight, but there was always an understanding that people could be killed. There was always the understanding that if someone did die, the others were to keep functioning.

"We don't have anything new as of yet, I am to take care of things until Stacy is back. The message I got also said that once Stacy is back, she will be busy just like Arkin. He used her to run Salez, now it will be me running that part of this cell. Seth, I don't think we've been made, but there is always that chance. From what I know Arkin and Stacy stepped into a trap, this trap looks to be an assassination attempt on the Heads of House Evindass, who are both now Ascended." Tom held up his hand, stopping any questions, "Now, I don't know how this all played out, Stacy's contact was either followed or was a bad one, I really don't know and I don't think we will know anytime soon.

"Seth, poke around and see what you can find out, see if it looks like we have been found out. I don't think you will find anything, but it's worth a look. Brian, we may have to leave Salez or change fronts, see what you can do for setting up some supplies if we have to leave."

The two men didn't wait around and went to their respective tasks. Tom sat alone again in the back of the shop, wondering how something like this could have happened. Years of being on the fringe of society and dealing with some of the most unpleasant and untrustworthy people in the country had given Tom good instincts, and his gut told him that there was something was off about Arkin's death, but he couldn't place what it was.

Barnin had mixed feelings about how he thought his day was going to go. On the one hand he was happy that his unit's mounts had arrived from Manton. On the other hand, they had come with his unit's replacements. Some of the men who were joining them would be seasoned vets and he wasn't unhappy to be getting them; it was all of the new kids that would be the problem. He didn't think about Josher, he didn't think back to when the kid joined his unit. Sadly, Barnin had lost enough men over the years that he'd learned to deal with it.

Ankle was at the docks already, along with most of his men, waiting to get their horses. Along with the disgruntled-looking animals came a group of men who were really just kids.

"I thought we were getting some seasoned guys too," Barnin said to no one in particular.

"Change of plans, I read the orders sheet. I guess they decided to put all the vets in new units, so we get the newbies. Should be fun," Ankle said.

Barnin cursed. "We are supposed to head up to help take Bonta. How are we supposed to get these kids ready?"

A tall lanky kid – man -- whatever, walked up to Barnin obviously terrified. "Sir, reporting for duty," he said, his voice cracking with nerves.

"DID YOUR VOICE JUST CRACK?" Barnin roared. "For the love of ... have any of you even started puberty yet?" he asked the group. Some of the new guys looked at each other uncomfortably and Barnin went on, "Ya know, start growing hair in places and thinking about girls?"

"Um, Sir, this may not be productive," Ankle said. "Maybe you could see if we have orders at H.Q?" he tried.

Barnin thought Ankle might be on to something, so he walked off as some of his men started taunting the new guys, taking Barnin's lead. *Great,* he thought *I bet I get a lecture for hazing.*

Barnin was calmed down by the time he talked to his men. If he was being honest with himself, he wasn't all that worried about the new guys. Long gone were the days when his unit was alone behind enemy lines.

"Feeling better, Sir?" Ankle asked.

"Yes, I am," Barnin said.

"Good to hear Sir, hang in there," Ankle said.

Barnin gave him a look. "Are we gonna hug now?" he asked sarcastically. Without waiting for a reply he addressed the room full of men. "We are going to be heading out to help take the city of Bonta, like Noris it's not huge, but also like Noris it's not going to be an easy take." Barnin walked up to a map on the wall of the area, and motioned along the Kay-loose river past Noris to Bonta.

"Bonta is just one more step up the Kayloose. The end goal is Salez, but before we can get there we have to cover a lot of ground. We aren't going to have the Pawdin Navy to win this one for us. They will be doing what they can from the river, but most of Bonta is out of range for ships and landing parties won't work, so that means a good old fashioned knock-down-some-stone-walls siege.

"We need to gather supplies and be ready to move out by morning. You will want to find any extra pairs of clothes you can. House Floren says they are expecting rain. We won't have proper shelter for some time unless Bonta falls easily. Any questions?"

One of the new guys, the one Barnin had accosted that day raised his hand, "Sir, are there going to be any Pawdin Ascended helping out?"

His balls may not have dropped yet, but there's hope, Barnin thought. "That will be one of the things that will decide this battle. If the Iumenta can't hold the air space above the town, then we are in for an easier victory. But don't let that make you think we don't have our work cut out for us. The Elves are going to be focusing on Iumenta forces which are heavy in this area. Even if the Elves take the air above Bonta, they will not be able to clear out threats like they did for us in Noris. Any other questions?"

Another man asked how well the city was supplied and if routes were being cut off. "They are well supplied; being a port town they have considerable stores of goods." That was the end of the questions.

Barnin was packed and ready to go, all of his men were; everyone had been living out of their packs since landing at Noris. As for the new guys … well Barnin figured they never got a chance to unpack from landing that day.

Barnin made his way to where Sara and Keither were staying. It was one of the houses near the docks that had been commandeered. It was large and belonged to a naval officer. He knocked on the heavy wooden door and a portly man answered.

"I'm looking for Keither and Sara?" Barnin said.

The man nodded, opening the door, "Down the hall and to the left."

Barnin walked down a hall with maroon carpet and wondered what Keither had done to earn such nice accommodations. He turned, almost walking into Sara.

"Sorry about that. How are ya, Sara? Nice place by the way," Barnin said steadying her.

"Oh thank you, it's not all ours -- we share it with a few other people. This house is dedicated to relief staff. Well, those of us organizing the staff," her eyes shifted around. "I think they put us all on top of each other in this place so we wouldn't stop working," she confided.

Barnin laughed. "Yeah, if you two are working with the Cona Republic now, you're going to be kept in just enough discomfort to make you work for a better tomorrow." Sara chuckled. "You guys too busy to talk?" he asked.

She smiled. "Oh no, no, please come in. We are just over here," she said, leading him to a doorway.

They walked into a medium-sized room with enough space for a bed and desk. Keither was at the desk hunched over some papers. "Evening Barnin, one moment," he said, not looking up.

"You think to him that I was coming?" Barnin accused Sara.

She scowled and shook her head. "You really need to get over that, honestly it's not that weird."

Keither turned to look at him. "She's got a point, I mean it's not like you haven't been around mental networking for -- umm, I don't know -- four or five years now?"

Barnin wasn't going to have this conversation, instead he made sure his mind was protected and changed the subject. "We are leaving to go to Bonta tomorrow morning, are you lot doing anything for that battle?" he asked.

Sara looked down, and Barnin didn't need to network with her to know what she was thinking. A few years ago he would have told her not to worry, that he would be fine and so would those she knew in his unit ... but that was a few years ago and Barnin knew that he couldn't make those promises, not anymore.

Keither answered. "No, we are dealing with things here. I suspect that we will spend most of our time in Noris unless they decide to move us closer to the front to handle coordination there."

"That's good, Noris is a good town and the further into the war we get, the safer Noris will be," Barnin said, feeling comforted that at least some of his friends might not be in harm's way.

Iselin leaned over the back rail of the Lux and looked out at the empty horizon. The sun was just a sliver, casting the sky in deep oranges and blues. Her eyes swept the black water, looking east to where the moon rose higher in the heavens. Noris and the coast were long out of sight even for her powerful eyes. So much in the world had changed in just a few short weeks. Emma came up next to her.

"Hi Em, how are you?" Iselin asked.

"No Ise, how are you? I've been that person staring out at the waves before. What's on your mind?"

Iselin breathed out heavily. "I don't know; it's a lot to take in. I mean, life feels so out of control on the one hand, but on the other, I know that my parents were my age when the War of Generations started. Also, my husband is a class eight. I've always believed him to be the Everser Vald, but part of me ... most of me ... wished I was wrong, you know? I'm sorry, that sounds selfish," Iselin confessed.

Emma nodded sagely. "You think it's selfish to want a peaceful life for you and your husband? You want to not have to deal with the burdens that come with him being the Everser Vald?"

"See, selfish, right? I'm honored really ..."

"Look Ise, I know you, you are like a sister to me. You're not being selfish; in fact, if you weren't worried about all these things I would think you were mad." She laughed, "I mean, really, Iselin, who in their right mind wants to be the wife of the person who is supposed to rid the land of the Iumenta? It's like when I was a little girl and thought that having twelve kids would be fun and easy."

Iselin smiled, "You mean it wouldn't be fun and easy?"

Emma grinned, "Well, I used to watch some of the kids in town when their parents were out to harvest and it was fun, but easy? Look, all you can do is your best today and that's it."

Oddly, this made Iselin feel better. She breathed out another sigh imagining all of her stress leaving. "Thank you Emma, you are like a sister to me, too," she said, smiling.

Chapter Six
Bonta

"How can we see the good while living the horrors around us? Is it really possible that the suffering of today will mean peace for tomorrow? And is that peace worth the cost? These are the questions every leader must ask themselves. Yet these are also the questions that only time will answer, leaving us only with the faith of today."
-Conversations in the Garden

Umbra glided on a thermal, silent and unseen. The only light in the cloudy night was that from Bonta. It lay to her right like a lake of gold, a thousand little points of candle, fire and torchlight; as the night wore on, those lights dimmed in the city. Outside the city to the west, the fields also glowed with many camp and watchfires of the Cona Republic forces there to take Bonta. She banked away from the city as color flashed in the sky. Since the invasion, both the Iumenta and Elves were fighting smarter, like they did in the War of Generations; if an Ascended was getting too hurt they would retreat and rest. This meant that even though the battle for Bonta had been raging on both land and air for over a week, there were no Ascended fatalities on either side. At some point, the turmoil inside the Cona Empire would brim into rioting and panic; on that day the war would turn fully in the favor of the resistance. Umbra knew this, every Elf did, and so did the Iumenta, she suspected. They weren't stupid and she figured it was for that reason that both sides were fighting smarter. For the Elves, it was wasteful to lose lives now when progress would be slow, and for the Iumenta it was unwise to diminish their numbers before things became difficult. Tonight her mission was twofold. She pushed her mind far out, using magic to gently influence all of those in the area. It was something all Ascended were doing, they were trying to undo years of influence by the Iumenta Ascended and also to increase the morale of resistance forces.

She soared over the landscape, looking for anything that could help out Elf and Human efforts. Her eye caught the glint of something in the distance. She narrowed her focus on where she saw the glint and found a convoy of carts and men. They appeared to be bringing supplies to Bonta. Her mind reached out to the Human command, asking if they had anyone in this area. They did not. *Good. Something to do,* she thought.

Umbra hugged the hilly landscape and made her way to the convoy. She glided almost right above them without notice. A nudge from her mind was all it took to see that there was no magic protecting her prey. She came around, coming at the group from behind. Still she made no sound. Tree tops were all but tickling her belly as she passed. When she was all but on top of the line of carts, she breathed out a long steady stream of fire as she flew up its length. The trail lit with the glow of flames as screams of pain and terror rang out.

She circled back around. There were ten carts, all burning. She noticed bodies on the ground, a few on fire and running. A burst of magic killed her suffering victims. She passed over the scene again, being able to see perfectly in the firelight. From what she could tell, there were no survivors. Umbra flapped her wings a few times, returning to her previous altitude and original course.

Sasha did her best not to grin. She admired the rose in front of her as it grew. She'd all but mastered making plants grow. It was easy for her, much to Legon's frustration; it had taken him months to make it as far as she was.

"Ha! Look at that! How long did that take you, Legon? A month?" Sasha taunted.

Legon smiled good-naturedly, "Now concentrate and see if you can turn the blossoms from red to white."

From red to white, she could do this. Sasha focused on the plant in front of her. The feeling for making plants grow wasn't like using magic, it felt as though she was extending herself and her mind's eye to the plant. It would grow to her will if she understood what she was doing. The ruby petals of the flower seemed to wilt, folding in on themselves. She corrected what she was telling the plant to do and the flower popped back up to life, the petals a bright vibrant...

"GREEN?" she exclaimed falling back into her seat.

"You know, I think it did take me a month to master growing ... but after I had that part down, altering plants came pretty natural to me. I don't know, maybe it's my minor that made it so simple for me and not for you," Legon poked.

Sasha had that coming, but she wasn't going to lose with grace; instead she stuck out her tongue and leaned back over the plant. She knew Legon was right; he was a biologic and she an elemental. Elementals always had a harder time altering plants, but that was on large scale projects, not making a flower turn a different color.

She tried again and this time the rose just died. "Oh no, I killed it," she said, feeling awful. It may have only been a flower, but she was the one who grew it to death.

Legon placed his hand next to the plant. "It's not dead yet," he said, and she watched as the rose bounced back to life, its petals now back to a deep red.

Barnin mounted his horse and tried not to cake the stirrups in mud. The rain was finally letting up and Barnin couldn't be happier. While in one aspect, poor weather meant that Iumenta Dragons were more likely to stay grounded, it also meant that the Elf Dragons wouldn't fly either. Putting all of the responsibility of breaking Bonta to ground units, that with heavy rain made incendiary siege weapons ineffective. As a result, little in the way of progress was being made on the city of Bonta. Barnin was hopeful that with the weather getting better, progress could be made. He was tired of living in constant wet and mud.

Barnin and his men rode out from camp, clods of mud flinging from horses' hooves. The sun was rising over the hills and Barnin relished its warm rays. The mounted units were on what they called 'fishing patrols'; it was their job to find enemy units in the surrounding area and likewise make it harder for the Cona Empire to support Bonta.

As they ascended hills and trails, the sun rose higher in the pale blue sky. The air grew muggy as the saturated ground lent up its moisture to the sun. Barnin stretched in his saddle, enjoying the feel of being dry.

"Feels good doesn't it, boys?" he asked his men.

They all agreed.

The patrol had been uneventful but good for Barnin and his men and he thought he would tell them so. "I'm glad we got called out on this; it's go-"

"CONTACT!" Heath shouted.

Barnin and his men moved off the trail, drawing weapons and looking around, seeing nothing. Above the hill in front of them, a pink Iumenta Dragon crested the horizon. Barnin fought the urge to panic, ordering his men to spread out. He knew there was no way to fight a Dragon; all they could do was attempt to minimize casualties. Ahead was another Iumenta, this one brown. Barnin could see their shiny armor strain to sparkle as the Dragons themselves leached light from the sky, only their black claws and teeth gleaming. Instantly he began to sweat and his heart raced.

"Help is on the way," Heath said softly.

There was a roar from behind them and Barnin turned to see an Elvin Dragon approaching, its green scales bright and vibrant. The three creatures engaged each other, coming in low to the ground. Barnin turned to the south, seeing that more Elvin Dragons were on their way, but likely wouldn't make it in time to help their brave comrade.

The green Dragon was being forced closer to the ground, taking heavy damage. Its blood spattered the hillside. Barnin was about to give the order to run when a thought came to him: *that Elf saved us. It could have waited for back-up and won this fight easily, but we'd have died...*

The pink Iumenta was just overhead. "HEATH! Distract it!" And to the rest of his men, "Arrows, fire everything you've got!" They wouldn't be able to hurt the Dragon; but take its head out of the fight -- give the other Elves time to arrive -- that they could do.

Heath sent a bolt of yellow at the Dragon. The spell flashed before its eyes, making it turn to look at Barnin and his men. In that split second, the green Dragon lashed out with its tail and hit the pink Iumenta's wing. There was a crack as bone broke and the beast fell the short distance to the ground.

As the pink Iumenta dropped, Barnin could see magic run the length of the Dragon's wing, and it looked at them furiously. "CHARGE!" Barnin yelled holding his sword aloft.

It was a credit to his men that not a single one hesitated, all spurring their horses toward the angry Dragon. Barnin saw a flick of green just before the pink Iumenta sent a spell at him and his men. There was a crack like thunder and a flash of pink and green, but Barnin rode on. His men split as they reached the Dragon. It launched forward, snapping at them.

Barnin saw Ankle swing his sword, hitting the Dragon's nose and doing no damage whatsoever. *You aren't supposed to win,* he told himself. Another of his men ducked, avoiding the Dragon's tail.

Barnin saw two more flicks of color around him. He saw the two incoming Elf Dragons sending spells at the Iumenta. There was more thunder and the pink Iumenta refocused on the Elves, taking flight and joining its companion in the sky. They stayed close together, holding off the Elves' spells. The green Dragon backed away from the Iumenta. The Iumenta turned and retreated. The green Elf waited for the other two Dragons to join it and then they flew after the Iumenta.

Barnin looked to his men. He enjoyed the looks on their faces, some looked ready to fight; others starting to realize what they had just done. The new guy Barnin had snapped at the other day was also the one who avoided the pink's tail. The man looked up in the sky, angrily, "You'd better fly away!" and that did it; everyone broke down. Barnin was laughing so hard, he had to keep from falling out of the saddle.

Later Barnin was surprised that he didn't get a reprimand from command about what had happened; they seemed to be in shock about the situation.

"And why did you do this?" one of his commanding officers asked.

Barnin wasn't ready to tell the whole truth. "If the green Dragon lost, then we would have been taken out anyway. It was a narrow shot but a shot nonetheless." He paused, making up his mind to be honest, "And whoever that was that saved us would have died; that Elf was going to lay down their life for a bunch of people they didn't know. I couldn't in good conscience run."

His commander seemed to think about that for a while. "Most would have run; it would have been the safe decision to make. However, staying like you did ended up working. It saved lives and I daresay earned some respect with the Elves. Good job son, I wish I had ten more like you."

Barnin looked down, "Sir, respectfully, you have twenty-nine more like me; not one of my men hesitated. Each and every one of them did their job."

The commander nodded, smiling, "That's good to hear. Thank you, I stand corrected."

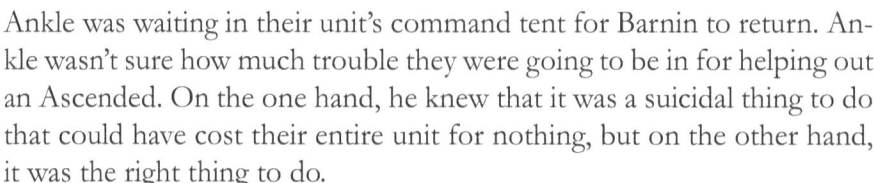

Ankle was waiting in their unit's command tent for Barnin to return. Ankle wasn't sure how much trouble they were going to be in for helping out an Ascended. On the one hand, he knew that it was a suicidal thing to do that could have cost their entire unit for nothing, but on the other hand, it was the right thing to do.

Heath was sitting at the one table in the tent on one of four chairs. The table and chairs weren't really theirs, they'd found them on the side of a road during patrol and thought they would add to the overall feel of the muddy burlap tent. Ankle pulled out a chair and sat.

Barnin walked into the tent, taking Ankle and Heath by surprise. "That went better than I thought it would," he said.

"Are we going to be punished?" Heath asked.

"No, they were happy with us. I think if we had taken losses, it would have been different; but we didn't, so we are the good guys," Barnin explained.

Ankle was about to speak when an Elf walked into the tent. Seeing Elves was not uncommon, so Ankle didn't think anything of it, until he noticed that the man's brown eyes had green flecks in them.

Ankle got up as Barnin turned to the Elf. It also took Barnin a moment to register who the Elf was. "Oh, you must be the Dragon that saved us. Thank you," he said.

The Elf's face was emotionless, "I could say the same for you, and thank you."

Barnin nodded, "Well, you're welcome. May I ask if your lot killed those Iumenta?"

The Elf glanced around the tent, taking in all of its muddy glory. "No, we did not. It is rare for Ascended to be killed, though I most certainly would have been if not for your unit. May I ask who the magic user was? Forgive me; I didn't get much of a look at any of your faces."

Heath stood up from the table and looked uncomfortable. "It was me," he said.

"What class are you?" the Elf asked.

"Class? I-I'm a class one, Sir."

Ankle knew that Heath was always overly critical of his own skills, almost seeming ashamed to call himself a Venefica.

"Why did you choose the spell you did? It was only burst of light, if I am not mistaken."

Heath looked more uncomfortable, "I was only trying to distract, is all, Sir. I couldn't hurt an Ascended if my life depended on it, but I figured a blast of light could at least make it hard for it to see or take its attention away. Sorry for making a poor choice, Sir."

The Elf looked confused. "Poor choice? I think you misunderstand me. I was not criticizing your choice; most would have tried to hurt the Iumenta, which would have not even gotten its attention. Instead, you chose to do something that would accomplish your goal; a choice I might add, that saved me, and also gave my companions time to help us all. Good work."

Heath looked like he was going to faint. "Thank you, Sir."

The Elf turned his gaze to Barnin, "You ordered this?"

"Yes I did."

"Why?" the Elf asked.

"You saved our lives and more, we are on the same side, and it's our job to protect each other, no matter the cost."

"Many would call you reckless or stupid," the Elf pointed out.

Barnin smiled, "I know, but the same could be said for you taking on two Iumenta Dragons to help some Humans."

For the first time, Ankle saw the Elf smile, his thin lips turning up at the edges. "We are fools both; but I think better men as a result, don't you think?"

Barnin laughed. "Yes on both counts. Ankle here actually made contact with his sword on the Dragon's nose," Barnin said gesturing to Ankle.

"And?" the Elf asked Ankle.

"Didn't get a good swipe at her, but she was scared, I'll tell you that much. Next time Sir, next time!"

"Her?" the Elf asked confused.

"Wasn't that a girl Dragon?" Ankle asked. "She was pink."

To Ankle's surprise, the Elf laughed loudly. "No my brave friend, she was a he; the color of our magic has no effect on our gender," he said laughing again.

Ankle laughed too,. "Whoops, I always just figured since Ise is pink ..."

The Elf calmed. "Do you mean Un Prose Iselin of House Evindass?"

"Yeah, I mean Un Prose Iselin," he wondered if he had spoken disrespectfully.

A light seemed to turn on in the Elf's eyes, "You are that Human unit Un Prosa Legon speaks so highly of. I should have guessed. Well, today I am truly honored." The Elf looked at them all differently. "You must be Barnin, and based on your rank, you must be Ankle," then to Heath, "and you're Heath."

"You have heard of us?" Heath asked.

"Why yes; you are the Human unit Un Prosa Legon so readily trusts and it was you who found Mors, if I am not mistaken."

"You know about that?" Barnin asked.

"Mors? Yes, it was your mission that compelled the Great Houses into action. All Elves have been told of Mors. Though most of us do not know mission specifics, I rank high enough to have been told. You must remember your mission was secret mostly from Humanity, it would have been bad for the Iumenta to have known you were coming."

Ankle felt a bit of ice in his gut thinking about Mors, and "Rachel," he said softly.

The tent went silent.

Ankle looked at the Elf. "Do you know how the girl we found is doing?"

He shook his head. "We know almost nothing of her. I know your names for the simple reason that you were on that mission and many others for Evindass, and therefore you could be a possible target for the Iumenta. Other than that, I don't know much. I have family in the golden city; they told me there was a Human girl living there who no one seems to know." The Elf looked solemn for a moment, "I don't know everything you boys had to see there, but I'm sorry you had to see any of it."

The Elf, spent a little while longer with them, but Ankle wasn't paying much attention to the conversation. All he could think about was Rachel in that cage where they found her. As night drew on, he stood outside his tent, watching the horizon light up with the glow of fire as Bonta burned.

Ashley was running as fast as she could back to her house. Behind her were burning buildings that were too close to the city walls of Bonta. Wooden balls filled with burning oil hurtled over the wall, exploding when they contacted buildings and streets. Ashley told herself she wasn't going to turn around and look at the devastation. It had been a mistake to go looking for her sister and brother-in-law; their house was in cinders.

The smoke turned the setting sun red. A flash of color and a clap like thunder caused her to jerk her head skywards. Above her, Dragons were fighting. The sky turned calico and in some places rained blood from the battle above. Ashley refocused on what was in front of her as her legs pumped, taking her away from the wall. She saw plumes of fire to her right; she looked to see some of the Elf Dragons dropping the same type of balls that were being lobbed over the city wall. *That's the government district,* she thought.

As she rounded a corner she all but ran into an Iumenta, his yellow eyes only flashing to hers for an instant before he went back about his business. She saw what looked like an odd ballista being manned by several Iumenta. They were not loading bolts into it but rather packages. *It's like a slingshot* she thought. The Iumenta launched the package into the air. She watched as it exploded near an Elf Dragon with a loud boom. A moment later she heard what sounded like rocks hitting nearby buildings and she looked down to see a metal spike fall to earth. *That's what the Iumenta are shooting,* she thought. She heard other booms and looked to the sky, seeing more of the little packages in the air all around the city.

The Dragon the Iumenta had shot at turned its attention to them, and Ashley ran again; not wanting to be around when the Dragon attacked. As she ran, the nearby buildings were lit with emerald, the same color as the Dragon she'd seen. The light came with a small wave of heat. Ashley didn't turn around; having no desire to see whatever was left behind her.

Sara rubbed her eyes. She was exhausted. Though she was in Noris, the city of Bonta was no more than an hour away, and had fallen late the night before. She needed to be ready to receive the injured by dawn. Her day was spent with wounded people, mostly civilians. She walked out of the warehouse and turned from the healing facility to the medical supply warehouse.

One of her staff was with her. "Tammy, what all do we need again?" Sara said, looking at a much-too-small cache of supplies.

Tammy fished a piece of paper out of one of the pockets of her bloody apron and read off a list of supplies. They had maybe half of what they needed; Sara looked over at Tammy, her red hair escaping from under its bun.

Tammy looked at Sara. "What? Does my hair look bad?" She said with a wink, "Well, you're not one to talk; I think birds are nesting in yours."

Sara laughed. With the hurt and dying all around, it was an inappropriate time, but there wasn't anything she could do to stop it. She got serious, "We need to find supplies ... I will-"

"I'll try to find more. I can't use magic like you can, and maybe you can save some people while I look. At any rate, you're in charge and you need to be here. I'll go fishing," Tammy said, picking up an armful of supplies. Sara did the same and walked back into the healing center.

She was greeted by the smell of blood and infection. Most people were not seriously injured; the seriously injured were still in Bonta, unable to be moved. But Sara was still dealing with the wounded from Noris as well. The Iumenta had burned healing centers as they left, leaving the town with nowhere to go. But unlike Bonta, Noris hadn't been under siege, which meant that most people were able to seek help before infection set in. For the people of Bonta, this had not been the case. The town wasn't under siege for long but infection set in quickly. Sara knew there would be teams working around the clock removing limbs, trying to save people.

For her part, her magic was drained, along with her physical energy. All she could do was mix herbs for fever and infection and tell her medics who they should try to save and who to just make comfortable.

A frantic mother holding a child grabbed her attention. Sara rushed over to them and saw that both were burned. She helped them over to an empty bed where the mother laid the child down. Almost the entire right side of his body was charred, his breath relatively nonexistent.

"Help us," the woman begged.

Sara's mouth opened and closed without sound. There was no helping them; the boy was too far gone, and Sara could see it. "I'm sorry, I'm so sorry, there's nothing I can do."

The woman's face fell, tears in her eyes. "My husband is dead ... my son is dead ..." her eyes lifted to Sara's, "Why did you do this to us?" her broken voice asked.

Sara was at a loss for anything to say. How could she tell a grieving mother that the war that killed her whole family was necessary? There were no words of comfort that she could offer.

Hours after the boy died, his mother collapsed with infection from her own injuries, and still Sara had no supplies. She stood outside, knowing that the woman wouldn't make it through the night, knowing that so many wouldn't. Sara didn't question why the war was happening; oddly, she felt more confident than ever about the need for the Iumenta to be pushed out of the land, but she wasn't happy about her current situation.

Tammy had returned with a few supplies she'd gotten from the Elves, but had also been reprimanded by Command for going to the Elves for help; the Cona stance was that they could take care of their own.

Sara was furious with her superiors for not letting the Elves help. But then she had a thought: *those orders aren't mine; I am still under the command of Legon.* She was on loan, more or less with the Cona Republic; her title was that of a liaison. She remembered Iselin's advice on taking care of things herself.

"Come, Tammy," she said.

Tammy followed Sara. "What are we doing?"

"Do you still have a list?"

"Yes; why?"

Sara didn't respond but continued on to where the Elvin command was. She walked into the building without fear, grabbing Tammy's hand and bringing her in too. "Sara, we are going to get in trouble ..." Tammy protested.

Sara was not stopped by anyone as she walked up a set of stairs to a door labeled 'Sydin' and knocked twice. Sydin opened the door smiling at her, and then his smile faded. "Come in Sara, I dare say you need something."

She entered with Tammy, who was turning a special shade of green and white. Sara held out her hand to Tammy who gave her the list of supplies. "Sydin, we don't have enough medical supplies, and people are dying."

Sydin looked serious. "Yes, I am aware the Human leadership has been pigheaded about us helping out."

"I too am am aware of that, but we need help."

"Do you want to go against your command?" he asked her.

Sara beamed, "Well you see, I'm not really under their command now, am I?"

Sydin caught on. "That you aren't; you are really under our command, but you are in charge of that healing facility."

"... which is under the control of the Humans. But," Sara said "there is no rule that a Human healing facility can't use Elvin medicine ... just that the Cona staff isn't allowed to ask you for it."

Tammy seemed to be catching on as Sydin spoke. "But that doesn't hinder you, does it, dear?" he held out his hand. "Let's have a look," he said, taking the list from Sara and reading it over.

"There is an Elvin healing center to the north of town I think you know about; I will have them give you everything you need, mostly herbs you need for infection. I will have them give you some other medicines I think you became acquainted with when you lived in Seeon. The center has two Biologic Ascended, along with a team of other Biologics. I will have a few of them, including both Ascended come down to your center and see if they can help with your backlog. Does that work?"

Sara felt like a weight had been taken off her chest. "Sydin, I would hug you if I weren't covered in blood."

Chapter Seven
Cremo Terra

"Hate is the natural byproduct of life, with it we know love and we find motiva-
tion."
-Articles of the Mahann

Cinto moved through the rafters of the building with ease, Kora behind him. He sniffed the air, trying to catch the scent of a Twig.
He knew they would be coming; now that Bonta had fallen, he knew he
and Kora didn't have long. They continued moving, stopping when they
heard Dragon wings hiss in the sky above the building. Cinto felt for the
crystal at his belt; he couldn't use magic but he knew what it felt like to
have a crystal drain energy from him. There was no pull on him from the
crystal.

"They do not know we are here," Kora said softly.

"That they do not, they may not even know any of our kind are left in
the city," Cinto said hopeful.

Kora peeked out of a gap in the roof, his silver hair and gray skin hardly showing in the light. "They must know; not everyone came back from
Noris, did they?"

Indeed they hadn't. It was a moot point; Cinto and Kora had a mission
they were to complete. They continued on, high in the building that held
government records. They were above the room they needed to be in.
There was a heartbeat inside and soft breathing. Too soft for a Human,
Kora signed to Cinto, Elf. Like a spider, Cinto turned himself upside
down, crawling along the building's outer wall, getting purchase on un-
even stones. The room they needed to be in had a ceiling they couldn't get
through, but an adjoining closet did not. It was into that closet that Cinto
now went. He looked through the keyhole, seeing a room of shelves
stacked with papers. With her back to Cinto was a Twig, she pushed back

her brown hair behind a tapered ear. She was reading something from one of the shelves, not paying attention to her surroundings. As silently as was possible, Cinto drew a knife from his belt, placing his hand on the doorknob.

He opened the door which to his great pleasure made no sound. He tiptoed his way up to the Elf. He was about to grab her when she spun in shock. Vivid green eyes flashed and she opened her mouth to call for help. Cinto slashed at her with the knife. She backed away, but not in time, and the knife cut into her throat. She spluttered, unable to cry out, she turned to run. Cinto grabbed one of her hands and pulled her back to him. Kora was in the room now, rushing up to Cinto.

"If she dies too fast, her mate will know," Kora hissed, stopping Cinto from breaking her neck.

Cinto stopped what he was doing. It was true. His blade was coated with a drug that would make it difficult for the Elf to talk with her mind, but if she died, her husband would too, and in so doing give away Cinto and Kora.

"Fine," Cinto said. He broke the Elf's arms which was far more effective than cuffs could ever be. She only gurgled a scream. Kora stabbed her in the liver. The wound would take a little while to kill her and the pain would make it impossible for her to move around or focus enough to work past the drug in her system. Cinto tossed the Elf to the corner of the room to let her die. They went to work finding and destroying documents.

Umbra flew over Bonta, pushing soothing emotions to the people. Light rain and fog made the already smoke-filled air catch in her lungs and make her want to cough; she resisted and searched for anything amiss with mind, eyes, ears, and magic. She wasn't finding anything with any of those senses. The city was full of people, limiting her seeking spells to those using large amounts of magic. Even those using just a little were everywhere with Elf and Human Venefica using their powers.

She glided by the city's government sector and in a heartbeat she felt the mind of Sydin.

"Are you finding anything?" he asked.

"No Sir, nothing. I am sure that Cona and Impa units are still in Bonta; they just haven't made a scene yet like they did in Noris."

"I agree; keep your eyes peeled for anything out of the norm and let me know if you find anything."

"Yes Sir," Umbra said.

Kora looked over at the dying Twig on the floor, her chest rising and falling in ragged, painful breaths. He and Cinto were done with what they needed to do and could go now.

"Should we put it out of its misery?" Cinto asked

Kora looked down at the Twig, sneering, "Where is your Everser Vald to save you now? Worthless Twig, do you really think you can win this war?"

Her mouth moved, trying to form words; Kora stomped down on one of her broken arms, making her moan. "Nothing to say?" He placed his foot on her bleeding abdomen; she coughed up blood this time, still unable to speak around the cut in her throat. "Does that help?"

Her other hand was groping pathetically at her side; Kora saw her trying to pull something out from behind her. He smiled, thinking she was going for her faloon, and then his blood went cold. She freed a tiny crystal from her back. It lit up blue.

"Tracker!" Kora barked

Umbra jerked in the sky, her mind abuzz with the signal of a tracker. If it had been activated, then the Elf holding it was in trouble. She spun in the sky, heading back towards the government sector, pumping her wings as hard as she could. Her lungs filled with air and she roared, terrifying people below. She yelled out with her mind, "TRACKER!"

Barnin heard a Dragon roar and looked around him. A ball of black magic streaked across the sky, stopping above a government building and pulsing brightly. Barnin jumped on his horse, calling to his men, "MOUNT UP! COME ON, COME ON, COME ON!" He rode through the streets toward the building, his unit was close. People dove out of the way, a few even getting clipped. "MAKE A HOLE!" he yelled.

Ahead of Barnin and his men were five figures moving so quickly they were blurs at the entrance to a building. He knew they had to be Elves and Iumenta with that speed, and he hoped that there were more Elves than Iumenta. As they drew in, he saw more clearly that it was two Iumenta fighting three; no two Elves. He pushed his mount harder as another Elf fell.

"Come on!" he growled.

The Iumenta looked at Barnin and his men as the last Elf died. As he drew his sword, Barnin let out a war cry that ripped the inside of his throat. Yellow shot at the Iumenta as Heath tried to take them out before they could use their fenrra. The spell missed and one of the Iumenta grabbed a stone on the ground, hurling it at Heath. Instead of contacting with one of Heath's wards, the stone struck his horse's leg, sending the animal tumbling with Heath still on its back.

"HEATH!" Barnin shouted, but he couldn't think of Heath anymore, they were in battle with Iumenta.

The world moved in slow motion as Barnin targeted an Iumenta. Its raven hair was the most defining thing about it; Barnin's eyes could make out each strand as they flowed in the air like waves. The Iumenta turned to the gray stone wall behind it, taking several steps up it, and then pushed off from the wall high above Barnin, pointing one of its razor fenrra at him. Barnin's vision was blocked by his shield as he raised it instinctively to protect himself.

There was a sound of screeching metal and time resumed its normal speed. Barnin yelled as the fenrra pierced his shoulder, going through the metal shield like a butterknife through butter. His gaze met cold yellow eyes as the Iumenta's other fenrra was driven into Barnin's back. There was the pressure of something on him and then nothing at all.

He felt his lungs fill with blood and he coughed it up in a great mouthful. He slumped in his saddle, not even registering the screams of his men as they were killed. His vision swam as he tried to breathe, the world tilted and he felt himself fall, hitting the ground.

Cinto finished killing the last of the Twigs when he noticed a group of Human cavalry moving in on them. The lead Ape seemed over-confident in its shiny armor; it yelled at the top of its lungs, as if that would do anything. The other Apes were following suit. Kora dodged a yellow spell and hurled a stone at the Venefica Ape's horse, sending it cartwheeling with its rider.

Cinto turned to the wall, taking fluid steps up it, he leaped into the air at the lead ape. It raised its shield, likely thinking it would stop a fenrra, but of course it didn't. Cinto stabbed the Ape's shoulder with the fenrra in his left hand. This allowed him to come around behind the Ape and stab him through the back with his other fenrra. He jumped to the next horseman, not waiting to see if he'd killed the commanding animal. It was of no consequence to him; it couldn't fight anymore.

Blood spattered Cinto's face as he decapitated the next one and then again as he killed another. Kora caught his attention, "Ascended!" Cinto listened, hearing its approach.

He swore and they ran into an alleyway. They jumped from one wall to another as they went, freeing them from dodging the people and junk that littered the ground. They couldn't see the Ascended yet, but they could hear it roar. They moved quickly, faster than any horse could in the narrow alleys, sometimes jumping from windowsill to windowsill, but never being far away from populated areas. If they moved fast and stayed close to people, the Elf Dragon wouldn't be able to lock onto them with magic, or at least it couldn't with ease, and not without hurting civilians.

They zigged and zagged between buildings, always trying to keep out of view of the Dragon. They were heading to a park. In it was a tunnel that would lead out of the city; but more importantly, the Ascended wouldn't be able to find them. They were going to have to jump from one of the city's roofs to make it.

Cinto saw the red roof and flung himself into the air, Kora behind him. There was a thud of wings but Cinto landed on the roof unscathed. He jumped again for the park just in view. As the wind buffeted him, he noticed something in his peripheral vision. It was a Twig archer.

Pain erupted in his calf as he touched down, an arrow sticking out of it. He drew one fenrra but felt another stabbing pain that made him cry out as his kidney was punctured. He spun as his injured leg gave way. He watched as another Twig fired and an arrow buried itself in between Cinto's collar bones.

———————⌠⌡———————

Umbra passed over the building where the tracker had been activated, seeing both Elf and Human bodies as she passed. She could see the Iumenta trying to flee. They kept to the alleys, making it hard for her to stay on them. She tried to use magic but was unable to lock on to them and just them; if she used magic, she ran a chance of hurting innocent people. She would have to wait until she could get a direct line of sight to use magic or until she could use her claws or teeth.

She could see up ahead a park they seemed to be heading for. She told her command, and kept following the Iumenta. It wasn't hard to tell where they had been, Humans screamed as they saw two Iumenta running along above them. She caught glimpses of them jumping back and forth from wall to wall to keep going. She had to admit they were doing a good job of using the buildings for cover.

Umbra took a chance and assuming they were going for the park; tried to head them off. She came in close to a building, folding her left wing in, almost brushing its stone side. As she rounded the building, a figure launched into the air and headed for a red-roofed building. She opened her mouth as she saw a second silver-haired Iumenta jump. Its yellow eyes flashed to her in fear as she clamped her mouth shut. The Iumenta's ribcage cracking and snapping almost didn't even register with her, so powerful were her jaws. Salty blood filled her mouth and ran down her chin as the Iumenta's lower half hung out of the left side of her mouth, his head hanging out of the right.

She snapped down twice more as she came in to land by the park, seeing the other Iumenta dead. She tossed the limp and slightly masticated body next to its companion. She touched down next to some grass and rubbed her face on it to wipe the blood from her chin.

Several Elves were already there. "Do we know anything yet?" she asked.

"No; the Elf who activated the tracker is dead, along with three other Elves and about six Human soldiers. Several more Humans are badly injured," a woman said.

Umbra took flight again, saying over her shoulder, "I'll see if I can help."

She made her way back to the government building. When she arrived, she stopped the spell that was shining brightly above the building. She floated down, seeing familiar faces. As soon as she realized she knew this unit, she felt concern. She found Ankle, "Where are Barnin, Heath, and the others?"

Ankle looked shaken and covered in blood, though it didn't look to be his own. "Heath is mostly all right; a horse landed on him, but his wards kept him from serious injury. Barnin is hurt bad … Some Elf is trying to keep him alive; can you help?"

Umbra searched the area, finding an Elf healer tending to a downed Barnin. He was awake, but having a hard time breathing. "Is he going to live?" Umbra asked.

The healer, a man Umbra knew, looked up at her. "Can you help me stop the bleeding so I can heal his cuts? His lung was punctured, but nothing else vital."

Barnin's body glowed black as Umbra sent spells to stop his bleeding. He hacked up more blood, and Umbra thought he looked scared. It was the first time she'd seen the emotion on his face. His wound glowed peach as the healer stood up.

"Better?" the healer asked.

Barnin coughed up a bit more blood, but not as much as he had been, "I feel like I can breathe a bit now, thank you. Please help my men."

The healer left to tend to the other hurt men without a word. "What happened?" Umbra asked.

Barnin looked up at her, his face pale from loss of blood. "I forgot what it's like when Elves and Iumenta attack Humans, ya know? And these guys ..." Barnin shook his head, "they were good, I really thought the two of them were going to kill us all," he said.

Umbra was thankful they hadn't.

Chapter Eight
Aftermath

"The victory of today is always followed by the battle of tomorrow."
-The Exiled Captain (Author Unknown)

Keither surveyed the field that he was to turn into a refugee camp. He was happy with it; there was a small mountain-fed stream that would keep the people in clean water. The field had access to main roads and there was enough room to accommodate many people. In the weeks preceding the fall of Bonta, the Pawdin Empire had managed to get both cities' docks fully functioning, so no longer were Keither and Sara forced to work without supplies. Now the task had turned to one that Keither thrived on, which was how best to use those supplies.

Sara came up, leaning on his right side. "It has potential," she said. "I'm a little surprised we were given such a nice plot of land to use," she continued.

"Well, it's not in a good spot for the military, and I'm sure we will be getting far more people than we are planning on, but I'll take it. Do you have your team organized?" he asked, looking down at her.

She told him she did.

Keither spoke to Sara's staff, figuring out everything they were going to need, and then he met with his assistants. His people were a collection of carpenters, engineers and smiths; it would be these people who would bring everything together. They were joined by one Elf who would, with the help of ten others of his kind, take care of growing things that might be necessary.

Keither had worked with everyone in the command tent, which was going to make life a lot simpler for him, he thought. He addressed the room at large, pointing to a drawing of the field. "This is not going to be like it was in the Cornis Mountains. In the peaks it got cold; it doesn't here. We are in a temperate area, so we don't need to worry about building cold weather structures, like we did in the peaks. Also, unlike the Cornis Mountains, this camp is for displaced peoples, so they won't be here for long. Many of them, once we clear out their home lands, will go back to where they came from to rebuild ... hopefully."

"The issues that we are going to have are that first; this camp is not permanent. Therefore, no fixed structures if we can avoid them. We will have to make do with tents and other temporary buildings. Second, there will be a lot of wounded coming in, so we need to work around the needs of the healers when laying this camp out. Third, we are going to get a lot of rain in this location, which means we need to consider using stone roads in the camp. I don't want to have to deal with being in a swamp or pit of mud either, so we need to look at drainage options."

Keither went on to outline what needed done. Trenches needed to be dug that the Elves would then lay pipes in; these pipes would let water in so they could drain the field of excess moisture, and yet other pipes would move water from the stream to wells in camp. The Elves would grow structures to handle waste, which could then in turn be used to grow food and other day-to-day supplies.

The day grew warm as the normally overcast sky opened to blue and the sun. The sun's rays felt wonderful on Keither's shoulders as he walked the field, making sure that everything was running as it should. Prisoners of war from Bonta and Noris were helping to dig trenches for the Elves to lay pipe in. Others were in the nearby woods and fields collecting large rocks to form the roads of the refugee camp. He saved going to the Elves for last; they didn't need any supervision, but Keither loved to watch them grow plants.

He watched as an Elf pulled a small wooden box from a pack. She opened it to reveal a seed the size of an apple, and looked at Keither. "I know you have lived with us for a while, but where you lived were cities that were already built; have you ever seen a master seed before?"

"No, what are they?" he asked walking up to the woman.

"We can alter a plant to will, but there is no reason to create from scratch all the time. This seed comes from an altered structure. When I make it grow, it will already have most of what this building will need; all I have to do is make corrections to give the building function and tell the seed how to grow. Do you understand?"

"I think so. What is that seed supposed to be?"

"Merely a basic structure, but in it there are functions ranging from lighting, heating, things of that nature. This seed will be the building that cleans this camp's water supply. You may watch if you like," she said.

"How long does it take?" Keither asked. "I am sorry; I want to watch but I am always running behind."

The woman smiled warmly in reply. She placed the master seed in a small hole in the ground, not bothering to cover it with dirt. She placed both of her slender hands on either side of the hole and Keither watched as green shoots shot up from the seed. At first it was slow but became faster as the plant grew. Once there was a substantial stalk, the Elf rose, holding a branch. An odd-looking tree took shape, bulging in some places, branches reaching down to the ground, digging in and creating tree trunks. The tree creaked as more branches went into the ground and others reached skyward; after a half hour the growth seemed to stop and the Elf looked at him.

"There is still much more to be done, but it will be underground with the roots," she said in a sweet voice.

Keither stared at the small one-story building before him in amazement.

"That is amazing. Does everything grow that quickly?" he asked.

"No; master seeds help, though we only use them when working on simple projects. You must remember that plants naturally filter and clean water, so building a sanitization unit does not require near the work most buildings do."

"How long will it live on its own?" he asked, still mesmerized by the building.

"Without an Elf to support it, maybe ten years; with an Elf near to maintain it, this tree will never die," she looked at him more closely, "Are you all right?"

Keither looked down, laughing once without humor, "Just remembering something is all." He wasn't going to say anything, but changed his mind. "When Legon and I were traveling south, the first town we saw was Salkay. I remember seeing its sanitizer and thinking to myself, the Iumenta must be great. I thought the others in my group were crazy to see the Iumenta as bad. Arkin said that Humans fought Elves putting in sanitization units like the one you've made here. It all just seems so different to me now."

She paused, "Your race did fight us; I think that growing plants seemed ... unnatural to them, but the Iumenta sanitizer is ceramic and stone, something that Humans can build on their own. Perhaps if we had not thought of our own technology to be the solution for your race and taught them that of the Iumenta, they would have embraced it sooner."

A question came to him. "Did it ever bother you? You know, dealing with us?"

She laughed. "Frequently." Then she stopped. "Forgive me, I do not mean to be rude. You are a different race; you think differently than we do, you see the world differently. It is not your unwillingness to listen that frustrates, but our inability to figure out why."

They didn't speak any more after that and Keither contented himself with inspecting the work of his teams, all the time asking himself, *why is it we don't listen?*

As Barnin looked over the roster of yet more replacements, he absent-mindedly rubbed where his wounds had been. The healer healed them all the way -- he knew that -- but it didn't seem right to him. After that Iumenta had worked him over, Barnin fought to stay awake, knowing that if he let himself lose consciousness, he would cease to exist. Then he was healed, his only suffering from shaken nerves and the loss of blood. He shook the thought from his mind and went back to what he was doing.

Ankle walked into the command tent, "Morning Sir, do we have a plan for the day?"

They were still in Bonta; the front was slowly moving north and Barnin figured that at some point, the front would be where his unit was going. The only reason they weren't there now was due to Barnin being torn up by an Iumenta, and that was fine with him.

"We are going to do knock-and-talks today on the east side of town," Barnin explained.

"Is there any reason we are doing it and not regular infantry?" Ankle asked.

After an army took over a town or city, regular infantry performed knock-and-talks. Units would knock on every door in the town, collect information like names, jobs, family, etc. While one unit performed the knock-and-talks, other units would search buildings for contraband. Barnin hated doing it; people did not like having an invading force in their homes looking in their belongings, but it was a necessary evil.

"Yes actually, the area we are going to has been hit before, but command thinks there are insurgents there. I'll explain more with the men," he said.

Ankle didn't push the subject anymore and waited for their troop's standard meeting time. Barnin looked his men over. In some ways it would be good to get to the front line. He hated dealing with security; most of his men had black eyes or split lips from when townfolk resisted or when they found groups of insurgents.

"We are going on knock-and-talks today," he said. None of the men said anything but he could see their faces droop. "We are looking for specific people this time; we will not need to question people with the normal questions," he pointed to a map of the section of town they were going to. "As you can see, we are going to a mixed part of town; there are going to be houses and a few businesses. We are looking for a group of three men we think tried to burn a supply depot the other night." Barnin pointed to a man with a hand raised.

"What did they burn, sir?" the man asked.

"We think they were going for medical supplies that were due to go to the front; at least the map they dropped showed medical supplies as the target. That being said, you know the amount of materials moving around here; the supplies had moved out that day and instead they burned ..." Barnin looked at his paperwork, "they burned a crate of clothing, looks like; socks and undershirts."

There was a chuckle from the group and the same man spoke sarcastically, "Sir, how are we supposed to win this war with smelly socks?"

Barnin smirked, "You're missing the point son, what if we get killed with dirty underwear? Think of the shame." Everyone laughed. "But on a serious note, we got lucky; if these guys have gotten past security before, they could do it again. Our job is to find them, arrest them, and bring them in. That's it," Barnin dismissed his men so they could get ready for the day's work.

Ankle walked with two other men up a street of tightly packed homes. They had been working the area for some time and had found neither hide nor hair of their targets. Ankle knew that didn't mean much; the problem with people like the ones they were looking for was that they were normal. No one in the area would think anything of them. He made his way to a two-story house with graying wood and knocked on the front door.

A woman answered, looking up at him. "Yes?" she asked.

"We are looking for some people who have been burning medical supplies." he said, thinking *there is no need for her to know that they only got some socks*.

Her brow furrowed and he went on, "Have you seen anyone acting oddly lately or has anyone new come to town?"

She held her chin in her hand for a moment thinking, "You know what, now that you say something, I have seen all of those things."

"Can you tell me more, please?" Ankle asked.

She nodded. "Yes, not too long ago a bunch of rebels started attacking the town. Since then they have moved in and acted quite oddly; you see they spend their time harassing people as if they have the right to be here when really ... you don't," she said with venom.

Ankle rolled his eyes. "Right, right ... we are going to search your house now," he walked in, moving the woman out of the way.

She shouted at the top of her lungs, "COMPANY!"

Ankle heard a thud from the floor above him and another at the bottom of a staircase. Running from the second floor, three men spilled out into the first floor of the house. All three matched descriptions of the men Ankle and his unit were looking for.

"STOP!" Ankle yelled as all three made for the back door.

Ankle tore after them, turning to yell to his companions to go around to the back of the house and call for backup. Glass exploded by Ankle's head as the still-screaming woman threw something at him; he ignored her and ran after the men. He passed through the kitchen and to a back door as it closed. He rammed the door with his shoulder, almost falling out into an alleyway behind the house. Ankle ran into the back of another house and turned, following the men. They were running along the alley, and as the last one passed by the edge of the house, he was tackled by one of Ankle's companions, sending the beefy man to the ground punching and kicking. Ankle couldn't jump over the two men on the ground, the beefy one wasn't getting an upper hand on Ankle's man, but he wasn't going down either. Ankle drew his sword and smacked the suspect on top of the head with the flat. He dropped.

Ankle made his way around them and kept running after the retreating forms of the two other men. He watched as both were hit by others in Ankle's unit.

Heath entered the house where the three insurgents were found. The woman, whose name was Ashley, was still in the home, her hands bound, and to Heath's surprise she was also gagged. "Can I talk to her?" he asked a man standing next to her. The man nodded and Heath noticed a bruise forming on his chin, "Did she?" The man nodded again.

Heath untied the gag and understood at once why it was in place. She started to yell at him, her voice growing higher with each word, and she spat at him too. Heath leaned in to her, looking right into her blazing eyes and holding up his hand, "Flamma," he said, as yellow flames burst into life in his palm. Ashley went dead silent. "Better," Heath said.

He closed his hand, stopping the spell. "I need to look around your house and ask some questions, will you be cooperative?"

Ashley looked scared now and spoke with fear, "Y-yes I will, I won't make trouble."

Heath looked at some papers. "Our list says no one lives with you here. Can you tell me who those men were?"

She eyed him, apprehensive with just the hint of defiance. "My brother and his friends," she finally said.

"Thank you, and what does your brother do for a living?"

"He doesn't have a living anymore," she said a little angry.

Heath smiled, "But before that ..."

"He worked in a storage yard," she looked down.

That made sense. "That was how he and his buddies got in then, wasn't it?"

She looked up. "They are brave t-"

Heath cut her off, "Were trying to burn medical supplies designated to helping refugees of the war; not those for military units."

Her eyes widened. "I don't believe you," she said, sounding unsure.

"I promise you that; I have no reason to lie to you. Did you know that's what those supplies were for?" he asked, trying to nudge her mind slightly.

She looked up at him, trying to read his face, "They told me it was weapons. I didn't know it was for hurt people." She looked down.

"We found their map. They knew exactly what they were hitting. Thankfully the shipment had been moved and instead they only took out some clothing items."

Ashley breathed out a sigh. She chewed her bottom lip for a moment. "What is going to happen to them?" she asked.

"We will question them and then decide from there, they will likely be prisoners for a short time at least." Heath watched as Ashley's eyes teared up. "Look, I'm sure your brother isn't a bad guy. I'm sure he was told to do this. It may not have been his choice; we find that a lot."

She looked up, "What do you mean?"

"Most of the people we've caught -- like your brother – we've found had no intention of actually doing anything bad; most are angry with us for being here and a few will fight back. But what we see most times is that the people who do things like burning supplies are forced into it. Has your brother seemed odd in the last few weeks or months?"

She looked confused. "Last few weeks or months? You lot attacked us by surprise," she said.

Heath shook his head. "That's not true. It has taken months of preparation for this invasion. In addition, we had to sail here before we could attack, not to mention that the Elves and Iumenta announce their intentions when they are going to start a war. I am sorry to tell you this, but Hoelaria received a declaration of war several weeks before we landed. That's why there have been so many Dragons around here for so long. You must have noticed."

Heath watched as her eyes darkened. "We were told that there were training exercises in the area ..." she looked up from the floor, "if the government knew that you were coming, why didn't they tell us?"

Heath was unsure of what to say to her. He needed information, and she was starting to warm up to him. If he was being honest, he felt for her. He wondered what it would be like thinking that everything was peachy in the world and then to have an invading force at your doorstep. That in and of itself would shake someone, but to find out that the people in charge of keeping you safe knew an attack was coming and didn't tell you ... "I'm sorry, your town has been preparing for a long time now; for years I suspect. The tension between our nations has been getting stronger and stronger for some time now. That being said, does it really surprise you that you were not told of an impending invasion?"

Before she could answer, Heath heard Ankle speak from behind him. "You get anything yet, Heath?" he asked. Heath looked at Ashley, she was staring up at Ankle from behind a curtain of bronze hair, not looking as hostile as she did before.

"No, she doesn't know anything," Heath said.

"Right, cut her loose then. We have other things to do."

Ankle continued on with his day, walking down a street of small businesses. After the morning's success, they'd be assigned to working a new part of town. He left his men searching a wig shop to talk to the store owner next door.

Ankle pushed open the door of the butcher shop to the sound of tinkling bells. "Hello."

There was no answer. Ankle looked the shop over, gazing behind the waist-high counter to a peg board lined with knives and cleavers.

He walked behind the counter, looking around. *Maybe the owner is in a cold cellar,* he thought. He looked under the counter and walked further back in the shop. It didn't look like the butcher was working on anything at the moment, so Ankle figured he was gone.

"Oh well, I guess we can cross this off the li-"

Ankle huffed as he was hit from behind, his sword being pulled from its sheath. Ankle turned, knocking over his assailant and falling with him to the ground. There was a clang as his sword hit the stone floor. Ankle rolled on top of his attacker and raised a fist. Below him was a man with a bushy beard and wild eyes. He grunted, bringing his head up, smacking it into Ankle's.

Ankle felt his nose break and fell back. He stumbled to his feet, blood pouring from his face. He reached for his sword, *where is it?*

He looked at the man in his white apron. It was covered in blood -- *at least you found the butcher* -- and in his hand was Ankle's sword. The butcher swung it at him, Ankle jumped back; *I'm not going to get killed with my own weapon.* He backed into the wall and a knife fell to the floor. The butcher paused as Ankle turned, looking at the assorted knives and cleavers. Ankle looked back at the butcher, the butchrs momentary pause over, he bellowed rushing forward.

Ankle turned, grabbing a three-foot splitting cleaver and blocked the blow. The butcher backed off. Ankle swung the cleaver a few times and quickly got used used to the feel of it. He could tell by the way the butcher was holding his sword that the man had little to no training with one; Ankle, however, had extensive training with both sword and ax.

"Look sir, you can't win this fight. Put down the sword, there's no reason for you to die today," Ankle said.

The man thought for only a moment before rushing forward, the sword high above his head. Ankle dodged to the side, swinging the cleaver. There was a whoosh of air from the man as the cleaver made contact with his side. Blood sprayed the ground and Ankle felt the blade jerk to a stop midway through the man's body. Ankle tugged; with a slurp, the cleaver came free. The man stumbled forward, slipping in his own blood, and dropped to the floor. Ankle slumped to the floor himself, breathing heavily as blood pooled around the butcher.

"FLAMMA!" Sasha yelled as she landed on the deck of the ship. Steam hissed in the air as a column of ice evaporated from her flames.

"With the fenrra," Legon growled. "INIS!" he roared, sending a lavender bolt of lightning at her.

Remembering the point of the lesson, Sasha raised her fenrra to deflect the bolt. She crouched to the deck and launched herself into the air. "Communis infirmus," she said as shards of light shot from the palm of her hand. Legon deflected a few of the shards before realizing that it was a harmless spell. Sasha, still in mid-air, took advantage of Legon's moment of distraction to send a powerful freezing spell at him. The deck of the ship was engulfed by steam as she landed on it. "HA! You aren't allowed to do that in this lesson," she said, enjoying her victory, knowing that her freezing spell was too strong for him to hold back.

Legon's voice was a soft whisper behind her. "The steam was just a screen. I didn't need to deflect a spell that was easily dodged," he said as she felt the cool edge of Tento, Legon's fenna, rest on the back of her neck.

A breeze cleared the deck as Sasha huffed. "No fair," she said.

The blade left her neck as she turned to her brother. "How is that not fair?" he asked, smirking.

"You used magic to screen the deck of the ship; that's cheating," she accused.

Legon sheathed Tento and put his arm around her shoulder. "Sash, the lesson was for YOU to learn how to block with a fenna, and for YOU to learn how to better fight with magic. There was no rule about using spells on your surroundings," Legon pointed out.

She sighed, "I am going to be a horrid fighter, I'm avoiding combat if at all possible." Then pointed out, "I don't even have the nerve to fight unless I'm connected to you."

It was Iselin who had first made the connection about how Legon affected Sasha. When Sasha was only weakly connected or not connected at all to Legon, she was just as timid as she was when she was a little girl. It was only when connected to her brother that she was able to even make an attempt at aggression, and even then it was a poor attempt.

Legon responded to her inner monologue, "Sash, that's a good thing."

"Normally yes; but we are at war, Legon. What if I need to fight and you are not close enough for me to connect to?" She gestured around the deck, "It's one thing here when we are in training and I'm connected to you. I can fight with you but only because I know that neither one of us could ever get hurt because of our wards."

Legon took his time answering. "Fair, but when you were with the White Dragon, he gave you his anger didn't he?"

"Yes; when I see injustice, I will feel it."

Legon squeezed her shoulder. "Then you will be fine, when you are with me you can train connected to me and if you find yourself in a combat situation I assure you that you will have the White Dragon's anger." Then he added brightly, "Now let's go see what's for lunch."

Chapter Nine
Flight of the Dragons

"Growth is almost always painful; it's the world's way of reminding us that there is a price for everything. For us, we need to figure out that price and then pay it."
-Confessions of Love, The First Wife

Legon closed his eyes, breathing in deeply the sweet scent of Seeon. They would soon be docking. He was surprised by how much he'd missed the city. They hadn't been gone for very long, but he suspected that his feelings had more to do with the fact that when he'd left the Capital, he wasn't sure if he would be returning.

Sasha joined him by the rail. He could feel her apprehension.

"What's wrong?" he asked.

"Do you think he will see me as a monster?" she asked.

Legon could see in her mind that she was thinking about Edling, the Elf who had told her he loved her. She was concerned about what he would think of her new appearance – her red eyes and her new power. Legon held back a sigh, knowing that while Sasha's concerns seemed silly to him, to her they were far from that. He thought humor might be the best course of action.

He turned to her placing his hand on her shoulders, looking her square in the eyes. "Sash, Edling is a smart, talented man. I promise you he figured out women were monsters long ago," he said with mock sorrow.

Sasha's face softened and she fought back a smile. "I hate you," she said looking back over the rail of the ship.

Iselin approached them and said coolly in Legon's mind, "Don't think I didn't hear that."

Legon turned to her. "Hello my dearest love, you look radiant," he crooned.

Iselin thought for a moment. "Better," she said, walking up to him and wrapping her arms around his waist, "But you did say that all women are monsters ... and I am a woman."

"Who has threatened to eat me on a regular basis since we met," Legon argued.

She smiled, "True ..."

Legon kissed her. "I think you are just upset that now it is me who can eat you," he said, kissing her again.

"Love, you can eat me anytime you want," she said suggestively.

"Eww," Sasha said, making a disgusted face. "That's my cue to leave. Honestly you two, how many years does the newlywed syndrome take to wear off in Elves?" she left without waiting for an answer.

Sasha left Legon and Iselin alone. The ship was pulling into dock now and she was excited to see her family. If she was being honest, she was both excited and nervous to see Edling. Emma stood with her on the deck, lightly bouncing on the balls of her feet.

"You're on edge today," Emma noted.

"A little. You seem a bit keyed up yourself," Sasha pointed out.

Emma stopped bouncing. "Just restless; we've been on one ship or another since we left Seeon to go to Noris. I'm ready for immobile ground and something to do."

Sasha smiled. "You didn't bring enough to read, I take it?" she asked.

Emma snorted. "I was sure you'd leave me here when the fleet left so I didn't bring much in the way of reading, but also ..." she paused, looking thoughtful, "also Seeon is my home now. I never thought I would truly see it that way, but I love the city. It feels like where I belong. I'm happy here. If I'm being completely honest, I'm happier in Seeon than I have been anywhere else."

"Even more than Salmont?" Sasha asked, thinking of Kovos.

Emma thought for a bit. "Salmont was a different life. I miss Kovos, you know that better than most. But I don't dwell on it anymore, and it doesn't hurt the way it did before." She breathed out, "When I left Salmont, I felt something inside me die and I will never get it back. I won't love again; not the way I did with Kovos. But he would have wanted me to be happy and so I am. Does that make any sense?" she asked.

"Yes, it does," Sasha said.

The ship was stopped and they were getting ready to disembark. As Sasha made her way down the ramp of the ship onto the dock, she could see her parents waiting for them. They knew about everything that had happened during the battle and Sasha wondered what they would think of having two immortal children. Her mother came to her first, hugging her and then pulling back, looking Sasha up and down, and finally looking into her eyes. Sasha could see herself reflected in the bright blue of her mother's eyes. No longer were Sasha's the same vibrant blue, but now red that shone like mirrors. Her mother was confused; she looked as though she recognized her daughter, but didn't at the same time.

"Will they go back to blue?" Her mother asked.

Sasha shook her head, "No."

Her mother's face saddened. "You have always been like a mirror for me; if it weren't for our ages, we'd have looked like twins."

"You're upset," Sasha said, feeling a sting deep inside her.

"Not in the way you think. I am happy for you. No longer will you have episodes, or so I've been told. No, it's the bittersweet feeling every mother has when she realizes that her daughter is no longer her little girl," her mother smiled patting her cheek.

Sasha smiled, understanding what her mother was feeling. She looked to her father who looked down on her, disapproving.

She felt herself shrink like when she had done something wrong as a child. "I thought I made it clear you were not to get hurt," he said.

"I- I didn't get hurt," she spluttered.

Her father put his hands on his hips. "Really? The way I hear it, you just about died on top of that hill."

"Oh that ..."

She looked down, trying to think of something to say. And then she felt his hand on her chin, pulling her head up to look into his eyes. "I know I can't stop you from doing anything, but no more mortal injuries, young lady. You are still my daughter, no matter what your title is and I'm not going to lose you again."

"Sorry Daddy," she said, just like when she was little.

And just like when she was little, once her father had scolded her, his face softened and he pulled her into a tight hug. "I am so happy for you now; and don't think that you being a class eight, or whatever means I don't get to worry about you and can't get yell at you."

She laughed, "I'm a class six, and I will always be your little girl."

She felt the mental presence of another and turned to see Edling a little way off. She slowly walked up to him. He ran his fingers along her cheekbone and brushed back her hair, taking in every detail of her face. His mind felt wondrous to her. He held her shoulders, the look on his face disbelieving. "You really don't have episodes anymore?" he asked breathless.

"Not once since I've changed; it's been almost two months now," she explained.

"And you're immortal," he verified.

She nodded. His hands moved down her arms to her waist and then he wrapped them around her, bringing her in close. She could feel the heat from his body, hear his heart race, and even see his skin flush. She opened the connection of their minds, timid at first, but then feeling what he felt. He was happy and relieved.

"So you don't think I'm a freak," she needed confirmation.

Edling pressed his forehead to hers, "Always thinking so little of yourself. You are not a freak, and you never have been."

Unexpectedly, he kissed her. Sasha felt her whole body get warm and tingly. She knew others were watching them, her family included; but she didn't care. When they broke away, she pulled him close to her and whispered in his ear, "You know you're going to be stuck with me for the rest of eternity, don't you?"

She felt him chuckle. "I already was."

Legon made his way along the rooftop garden of the Palace hand-in-hand with Iselin. They walked until they met up with Tenick, Legon's uncle, Opes and an Elf Legon did not know. He was not as tall as most Elves, with short brown hair that matched his eyes and to Legon's astonishment, he saw brown flecks sparkle in his eyes.

Tenick spoke. "Legon, it's good to have you home," he said, shaking Legon's hand. "Anna sends her regards," Tenick said, speaking for his wife.

"It's good to see you, and where is Anna?" Legon asked.

"We are staying in the Palace, but since she is not Ascended, she declined coming this afternoon," Tenick said warmly.

Now that he was an Ascended, Legon was to begin training. It was for this reason they were meeting on top of the Palace roof. The brown-haired

Elf introduced himself, "Un Prosa My name is Gratook, and I am the Head of Biologic training at the Venefica School in Seeon's Central Academy. I believe you have met the Dean of the school, but we have never had the honor."

Legon shook Gratook's hand. "It is a pleasure to meet you."

Opes spoke. "Legon, as you know, today we are going to start your training as an Ascended. We are going to gauge what your natural abilities are -- each of us will be working with you on one thing or another. Iselin is one of the best flyers I know, so she will be working with you in the air. Gratook will be working with you with your minor. I will be assisting you in up-close, physical combat. Tenick will be here to help you on a general level," he explained.

"Is this common?" Legon asked.

Gratook answered in a smooth voice, "Yes. You see Iselin, Opes, and I will be focused solely on our perspective topics. For example, if you are learning to fight with Opes, Iselin will try to only notice your flying during a fight and comment on that. In this way you are able to get intensive training. Tenick will be the one who ties everything together for you as he will not focus on any one part of your skillset. Both we and the Iumenta do this when first training new Ascended. Once you have mastered your minor, you will be taught by Ascended with other minors along with me. So, shall we go to the training arena?"

Legon watched as Tenick, Opes, and Gratook ascended, and hovered above the Palace. Iselin spoke in his mind, "You've haven't ascended since your first time; the important thing to remember is that ascending and flying are mostly instinct. Don't think about it," she said.

He remained in her mind as she transformed into a pink Dragon and took off. *You can do this,* he told himself. He closed his eyes, focusing on the power within him, letting the urge to change take over, heat rushing down his limbs, and he felt himself grow. He opened his eyes and saw the world only in the way an Ascended could. Legon looked down the length of his body, flexing his wings, loving the way they felt.

"Very good Legon," Opes said in his mind. "Now take off."

Take off? The last time he'd flown it had felt easy and natural, but now the prospect of taking off seemed a bit daunting.

"The last time you flew you didn't think; you were acting to save me and as a result you just used your natural feelings. You need to do that now." Iselin said supportively.

Legon extended his wings, coming in close to the ground he jumped in the air, driving his wings down. He lifted higher but it didn't feel right. He moved forward slightly, but it felt awkward. "Whoa!" he said, lurching unsteadily in the air.

Iselin spoke, "Stop thinking about flying and fly."

"Fine, I'll do that. Thanks," he remarked tartly.

"Empty your head Legon. That shouldn't be hard for you, there's rarely anything in it anyway," she said acidly.

"What? How is that supposed to help? And what do you mean there is never anything in it? You always tell me to stop talking so much in my head and ..."

"You're flying," she interrupted him smugly, "just don't think about it."

And he was. Legon was flying -- not with any level of grace -- but he was moving around without issue. He could only go forward and turn a little bit; hovering was out of the question, but he was still flying.

"Basic maneuvers like hovering and going backwards will come easily to you. After a few days, basic flight will be second nature for you; it's just a matter of trusting yourself," Iselin said.

Legon wondered why none of the others were saying anything when he remembered that it was Iselin's job to teach him to fly. They all flew away from Seeon over the forest. Legon loved the way the air felt and the freedom that the sky allowed.

"It feels wonderful, doesn't it?" Tenick asked.

As they flew, Legon noticed a large circular clearing in the trees that looked several miles across.

"That is one of the training arenas," Opes said, "there are many; each one has specific duties. This one will suffice for what we are going to do today."

As they came over it, Legon could see high walls with tall poles extending a few hundred feet in the air. The poles were about one hundred yards apart from each other, spaced out along the length of the arena. "What are those for?" Legon asked.

It was Gratook that answered. "Prior to training, we will each fly around the arena. In each of those poles are crystals with power in them. They can hold simple spells, so we will each place a 'stop all' ward in each crystal. Once we begin, some of the crystals will levitate up even higher in the air, and this will insure that all of our spells stay inside the arena," Gratook explained.

Legon followed the others around the arena activating crystals, and as he flew, he noted the diversity of the ground below him. Some areas had rocks like little crags. Others were open field and still others were water. They landed in the center of the arena which was just grass.

Iselin spoke. "Now, I will be working with you first, and we just need a guage to see what your levels of expertise are. You can't fail here," she explained.

They took off, this time Legon noticing that it was easier than before. Legon was to place several wards on himself; one was so that if he got too close to anything, he and others would be shielded. This was done because of his size; if he ran into Iselin or the others they could get hurt, or so he was told.

His job was to follow Iselin as her maneuvers went from simple to complicated. At first Legon was having fun. It was easy; they flew around the outside of the arena, and then she would climb and dip in the air. As time went on, the climbs became steep and the dips became dives. It was on one of these dives that Legon learned the real reason for the ward he'd placed on himself. He was diving down behind Iselin, elated with the rush he was feeling, and while she was still high above the ground, she rose out of the dive. Legon attempted to do the same ... he tried again and panicked. All he could see was the ground rushing up to meet him. He turned himself in the air and drove his wings down; he slowed drastically and then ... WHAM! He hit the hard dirt of the arena, and his surroundings glowed magenta from his ward.

Iselin looked down as she heard her husband hit the ground with a dull thud. The wards he was using would prevent him from getting hurt so she wasn't very worried about him. He was doing well so far, for a beginner. "Now take off and let's try again," she said.

"How come I fell? What did I do wrong?" he asked.

She could tell that he was bothered by not being perfect on his first day. "You did fine; I am smaller and more agile, plus I have years of experience on you," she said, trying to be supportive. She could feel it wasn't working. "Look, when I first started flying I was horrible, it was like I wasn't even a Dragon. I felt embarrassed every time I flew so I worked at it," she said. It was true; she could remember being one of the worst flyers around. But now after years of work, Iselin was known for her abilities.

She came back around as Legon took off again, following her in the sky. She turned slowly, weaving around in lazy circles. From what she could see he was having a hard time with his turns; it wasn't power that was his problem. She banked tighter and tighter. With each turn she could hear Legon behind her losing control. Tenick was sharing his sight with Iselin so she could see as Legon wobbled in the air. She tried slowing down and he steadied a bit. Then she sped up going faster and faster. Legon kept up with her, though he couldn't accelerate at her rate. This time when she turned, Legon cartwheeled in the air, crashing to the ground.

Legon found himself on the ground again … and again ... and again. It was making him crazy. Finally, Iselin called an end to the flying part of his test. Then he went on to working with Gratook. He'd thought the magic part of his test would be the hardest, but Gratook said that Legon was advanced for how new to magic he was.

The last of his tests for the day would be with Opes. The test was on close-in combat and this was what Legon was looking forward to the most. He knew that Opes was going to dominate the fight; he had literally thousands of years on Legon, but this was at least something that Legon normally excelled at. Oddly enough he was looking forward to getting worked over; Opes would give Legon a goal to achieve, a spot to shoot for on the horizon.

The two Dragons circled slowly as they faced off in the air. In this test, neither would be using magic. Legon watched the smaller Dragon as he flew, biding his time, letting Opes make the first attack.

"Not going to use your size and strength to end the fight right away, Un Prosa?" Opes asked condescendingly.

Legon didn't fall for the bait. "Not until I can control how I fly, or how to best attack as a Dragon."

"Very good, that is wise," Opes said.

Legon figured Opes was trying to lull him into letting his guard down, so Legon relaxed a bit, trying to look unprepared. He'd read Opes correctly. Opes twisted in the air and rushed Legon, but Legon was ready. Right before Opes hit him, Legon folded his wings, dropping. His wings snapped back open unsteadily but he lunged at Opes as he flew past.

The red Dragon twisted in the air to face Legon, lashing out with his tail. Legon caught the blow with his front paw, feeling it sting and burn with the impact. The two Dragons came together. Legon used his size to try to dominate Opes with sheer force. Legon found flying to be simpler now that he wasn't focused on it. Wards they had placed on each other made their claws feel like feathers as they slashed at each other. They bit and clawed for what felt like forever to Legon, and finally it was Tenick's voice that rang out over the network.

"I think that will do," he said, sounding amused.

Legon panted, pleased to see that Opes also looked worn out.

"That was incredible Un Prosa, you have almost no skill with fighting but you are extremely good at reading your opponent and fighting within the skill set that you have," Opes said and went on, "So often when someone is a good fighter in their Elf form, it is due to spending years on the technical aspects of fighting; but you, you have learned to read what others are doing and you're willing to take risks within reason."

"Thank you Opes, that means a lot coming from someone as skilled as you. Had this been a real fight, you would have defeated me," Legon said.

"But not without a great deal of effort. If you can learn technique, I dare say you will be one of the greatest fighters in our history," Opes said proudly.

Legon was happy to be done for the day. As they flew back to Seeon the sun was setting, turning the sky orange and making the bay glitter.

"It's wonderful isn't it?" Iselin asked.

"Yes. I love being in the air, even if I still have a lot to learn. I've been in your head when you're flying. I've seen the world from your perspective more times than I can count, but even after all of those times, this feeling I have right now of flying is so much better."

"I really never tire of it. I'm glad we can fly side by side now," she said warmly.

They landed in the Palace gardens and Legon transformed back into an Elf, as did Iselin. Opes and Gratook flew to their respective homes and Tenick flew off to run an errand before dinner, leaving Legon and Iselin alone. They walked back in to the Palace hand in hand.

Chapter Ten
Day to Day

"I saw a group of children playing today and I asked myself: Do I spend too much time worrying of the things of tomorrow and not enough time enjoying today? Instead of answering the question, I contented myself with a walk in the garden and spent the afternoon reading my favorite book."
-Diary of the Perfectos Compatioa

B arnin walked back to his tent wondering what he was going to do. He'd just gotten a promotion. Now he had command over three units, making him responsible for ninety men; a responsibility he'd managed to skillfully avoid for years now.

Ankle was next to him. "Sir, this is a good thing," he said for the tenth time.

Barnin huffed. "What am I supposed to do with this many people? Honestly, it's been hard enough to keep one unit alive," he complained.

He wasn't feeling sorry for himself by any stretch; he had done a good job with his current – well, past – command. His concern was that he didn't have a clue how to take care of more than one unit, and with the war raging he wasn't likely to get any guidance from his superiors. "Aren't you nervous about taking command of an entire unit?" Barnin asked Ankle.

Ankle shook his head "Nah I've been running it for years, I just let you think you were in charge. Besides, you're still going to be with our unit, aren't you? Well, at least most of the time."

Barnin was still expected to fight, but now he would take time with each of the three units he was over. "Some time sure, but to be honest, I'm going to have to work with the other two units a lot more. One is a patchwork of other units that took heavy casualties and the other one is new guys right out of training."

Ankle winced, "Oh, now I know why you're not happy. At least the unit with the vets can fight."

"But they don't know each other, there is no unity, half of these guys have just been transferred out of healing centers. I'm sure they'll get it together, but it will take a bit of time and I'll have to spend most of my time with the other unit that came from Manton," Barnin explained.

"So, what? Simple missions for the new kids and moderate missions for the vet unit, and ..."

"Advanced for yours," Barnin said.

Ankle's jaw tightened a bit as Barnin went on, "You know I hate putting the brunt of the dangerous work on your shoulders, and maybe in a week or two the other veteran unit will be able to handle more."

Ankle relaxed. "No worries Sir, I'd do the same thing as you and truth be told we've had it easy for a while, but now I'm nervous."

Barnin laughed. "Why is that?"

Ankle smiled, "Because I have to lead on my own without you as a babysitter."

"Oh really? I thought you'd been in charge for years; are you telling me that's not true?" Barnin jabbed.

Ankle smirked, "I don't recall making such a comment, Captain … you must be mistaken."

Sasha peeled back thick plant skin that covered the crystal she'd just grown. It was like peeling a banana, but instead of a sweet fruit, in her hand rested a slightly opaque, square crystal. She held it to her eye, gazing inside. She could see flaws and it wasn't supposed to be clouded. Her mind reached out to the crystal and she started to fill it with a small amount of energy. It glowed red, flickering a bit. She kept putting in energy. There was almost enough to heal a small cut when it cracked, losing what energy it had.

She placed the broken pieces back on the table and sighed. "What did I do wrong?" she asked Edling.

"The plant isn't forming the crystal's structure properly," Edling said touching the plant, reading its makeup.

"Why can I make crystals with magic that can hold power just fine, but not grow them?" she asked, exasperated.

"We use magic when growing the crystals but that's not the point of this lesson. You need to create a basic functioning crystal with just plant life before you augment the crystal's creation with magic. You are doing well for how long you have been able to control plants."

"I know, I know, but it bothers me that I can do a better job working with the enemy's technology than my own." Sasha said.

"I'm not bothered," Edling said. Then reading her face added, "Because you're not the enemy. We have seen many breakthroughs in the last few years because of your thinking," he said sincerely. "Now come on, we are done with crystals for the day. I want to work with you more on growing plants into structures," he said taking her hand.

Sasha went without a fight. She walked with him outside the Palace, her guard coming with them as they walked through Seeon until they came to one of the magic academies.

"What are we doing at the Biologic Academy?" she asked.

"They have a training ground for Venefica who are learning how to build large or complex structures," Edling explained.

Edling lead her through a set of tall heavy doors opening to the inside of the academy. They made their way to the front desk, Edling telling the attendant that he had an appointment. Sasha noticed some of the Elves looking at her, some looking twice.

Sasha turned to Cynta. "What are they looking at? People see me all the time."

"Yes, but not in the academy and not since you've Ascended," she said.

Sasha felt self conscious but tried to ignore the onlookers. Edling came back to her side, leading her further in the building. They entered a courtyard that was approximately one hundred yards on all sides.

"This is one of three training grounds," Edling said, taking her hand. They walked to the center of the yard.

Sasha looked around, grateful to see there were no windows looking in on them. Edling pulled a master seed from his pocket. "We aren't doing anything big today, just a small building," he said, handing her a master seed.

Sasha knelt down, using magic to dig a small hole. She placed the seed in it.

"What do you want me to grow?" she asked nervously.

Edling smiled. "Anything you like; I want you to focus on the functionality already built into the seed. Learn how it makes climate control and water management work. When you grow it, feel how weight is displaced along the structure and how to weaken and strengthen places."

Sasha reached out to the seed with her mind and power. She was amazed at the complexity that she found. Edling was right; the seed had the ability to grow far more than a simple tree that looked like a building. She found everything Edling had said and more. There were functions to grow windows and lighting, she found colors of every shade. Sasha found herself getting excited.

She told the plant to start growing a thin shoot rising up. She stood, holding a branch from the shoot. The plant kept growing, Sasha directing it, doing as Edling said, feeling where weight was misbalanced. She sent branches into the ground correcting the balance and thickened support beams. When she was done, she looked at her handiwork and frowned, "I forgot to add a door."

Sara contented herself with cleaning. The healing centers in Noris and Bonta were starting to clear out. It had been a lot of work but Sara finally felt like things were getting better. She knew that at any time she and Keither would be moving closer to the front, but she wasn't going to think about that.

When she was done cleaning she decided to look at inventory reports. She looked over reports for centers in both Bonta and Noris. Her eyebrows knit as she read them. Bonta was running low on things like bandages and other basic items. The cause was increased insurgency in the city. Sara knew that both Elf and Human forces were working to contain insurgents but it was slow going. Most insurgents were targeting things that were easiest to hit, like Sara's medical supplies, but there were also many that were willing to kill those in the resistance. She shook her head as she put down the report, telling herself, *this is what war is.*

Sara looked up to see a family of three enter the center. The father was holding what Sara presumed was his son in his arms. She walked over to them, the mother eyeing her child nervously.

"May I help you?" Sara asked.

"We need a healer," the woman said.

"You're in luck; what can I do?"

The woman eyed her. "Perhaps there is someone a bit older, with some more experience? I don't mean to be rude, but my son broke his arm and ..."

"I am the Head of this center and more than capable of fixing a broken bone. Please come this way," Sara said firmly, but not unkindly.

She didn't get upset at people anymore when they implied or said that she was too young. People were sick and scared, so Sara allowed them some room to be a little rude. She led the family over to a bed and asked the father to set the child down. The small boy was cradling his right arm, his face scrunched in pain and determination not to cry. Sara reached out gently, placing her hand on the boy's arm. She closed her eyes, feeling with magic, inspecting the bone. It wasn't broken all the way; just a minor fracture.

"Excuse me," the mother was frustrated, "but my son is hurt and shouldn't you be doing something like making a splint instead of feeling the injury?"

Sara didn't pay any attention to her, she felt the magic grow within herself; the energy shot down her arm to the palm of her hand as she whispered a spell. The family gasped as there was a slight silver glow from Sara's palm. The little boy's face softened and he rubbed his arm.

"It was just a minor fracture, nothing serious. It's completely healed now; there is no need for a splint," Sara said turning to the boy's parents.

"You're a Venefica?" the man asked.

Obviously, Sara thought. "Yes, we try to always have one at each center at all times. Is there anything else I can do for you?" she asked.

"Thank you for taking care of my son, but we don't have the money to pay for a Venefica..." the mother said.

Sara smiled shaking her head. "There is no charge; this is only a temporary center to help townspeople after the invasion. The Pawdin Empire and Cona Republic are paying for everything. Even if that were not the case, I used magic and not very much at that; I wouldn't have charged you. I can't remember how many times I hurt myself as a kid," she said, then addressing the boy, "Fall?" she asked.

He scowled, "From a tree," and then brightened, "but I made it real high up!"

Sara laughed, "I'm sure you did."

"Thank you so much for your help and I'm sorry if I was rude," the mother said.

Sara told her not to worry and after a few moments the family was on their way.

Barnin rode out ahead of the rest of the unit he was working with. He had decided that giving all three of the units names would be annoying, so he would call them by number. Today he was with unit three; it was comprised of all men who had just gotten out of training back in Manton. Based on Barnin's experience with new guys in combat, he was pretty sure he would be killed in the next week or two.

To the North of Bonta were steep, rolling hills. While the terrain made it hard to build towns and cities, there was also an occasional farm. The good thing about the hills, though, was that they made a perfect place to hide people and supplies which one could use to fight back against an invading force. That was why Barnin and all three of his units were in the area. They were looking for anything that could hurt their side. Thus far they'd found nothing, which suited Barnin just fine.

The other two units had separated from Barnin's current group so they could search a larger area. Barnin crested a hill and saw the charred remains of a caravan below. He held up his hands, stopping his mount. The others in the group where not as fast to stop and there was some chattering about people running into other people.

"QUIET!" he barked back to them. "Three teams, two check the perimeter and the other on me to the caravan."

A kid next to him snorted, "Not taking any chances with this burnt wood, Sir?" Some of the men snickered.

Part of Barnin wanted to just hit the moron next to him but he decided to make this a teaching opportunity. "Burnt wood, huh?"

"Yeah, it's black and there's smoke" he sounded like he thought Barnin was an idiot.

"What does the smoke tell you?" he asked.

The man frowned, "I don't know, that the fire has only been out a little while. Does it matter? The Elf Dragons hit caravans like this all the time."

Barnin nodded, "And tell me, when was the last time you saw a Dragon in the area today?" The man said nothing. "And since we are the only unit dispatched to clear this part of the land around Bonta, what does that tell you?"

There was an uncomfortable hush with the men now, as the one who'd spoken said, "That means that whoever did this was an enemy."

Barnin smiled sarcastically, "Very good, I'm glad you figured that out. What we are going to find down there is either our own people dead or refugees fleeing the area are now dead. If we are lucky, the ones who did this are still in the area. If we are unlucky, that burnt caravan is a trap." He spoke louder to everyone, "This isn't some training exercise; you have to start thinking faster and you cannot look at everything like it's harmless. If you see something that seems off, then treat it like a possible threat. Now move out," he ordered.

He started down the hill toward the blackened wagons. As he got closer, he saw charred bodies. The smell was horrid, but sadly something Barnin was starting to get used to. The men in this new unit were not, however; and he heard one vomit from high up on his horse. This shouldn't make Barnin happy, but it did. When soldiers died right out of training, it was for one of several reasons; one of those was that they were cocky and had no sense of reality. Now the new unit had a sense of just how real war was.

It looked as if there had been four wagons in the group, all burned. From the lack of debris, Barnin figured they were stripped of valuables prior to being set on fire. There were bodies scattered about.

He looked out to the two groups searching the surroundings. He asked each if they had found bodies. Both had. The team to the west had found significantly more; it was a collection of men, women, and children, something that bothered the new guys.

"Listen up, look at these bodies, look how they lie, look at their tracks. This will tell you in what direction they were heading, and in turn tell you how they were attacked." He pointed to the east. "People were running west, meaning they were running from something over to the east. You can see that most of the people were killed with arrows, and they were shot in the back."

Barnin started moving slowly east, away from the wreckage, looking for clues to the number of those in the attack and where they might be heading now. He found the remains of a camp, the grass flattened in the form of bodies in about five places. He showed his men how they could read a camp to learn more about the enemy, explained to them that all of the skills they learned -- if they had hunted growing up -- could apply now.

"What do we know?" he asked.

One man answered, "We know that there are only a small number of them, which will make them harder to find. We know that they are archers and if they managed to kill that many people, they are good ones, and we know by the tracks that they went northeast."

Barnin grinned at the one who'd spoken. "Hunter?" he asked.

"Four sisters; it was all my father and I could do to stay sane, Sir," he explained.

Barnin laughed, "I'm sure it was and he is correct, so now it is our turn to go hunting."

Legon banked to his left, keeping on Iselin's tail. He was using their mental connection to help him learn how to keep himself more stable in the air. When he'd first met her, he didn't give any thought to how difficult flying was; now he was thinking about it.

"Stop overanalyzing everything; flying is about feeling the air in your wings, about letting yourself go," Iselin said sagely.

"That's fine for you, love, but every time I let myself stop thiking of it, I go straight to the ground," Legon said

She ignored him, instead choosing to show him her point by gracefully gliding through the sky, turning and rolling like a dancer suspended in space. He tried to follow her movements, but had a hard time, though to his credit he didn't crash once.

It was late in the day when they turned back for home. The air cooled as the sun set and it felt wonderful.

"You really are learning quickly," Iselin said.

"Thanks, I have a good set of teachers," Legon said warmly. And then, his tone cooler, "and I don't have a choice, time isn't on our side."

She didn't say anything. He could feel that she wanted to disagree with him, tell him that there was no rush, but then she'd be lying. Legon knew that he didn't need to be ready in the next week or month; he had several months to get ready for going back to the war. But he wanted to be there with his people fighting, doing everything he could to rid the land of the Iumenta, but despite that, he also knew that if he wasn't ready he would be more of a hindrance than anything else. It was that plain and simple truth that kept him working himself to the bone every day. Sasha was doing likewise. Now that she was able to grow plants to will, she was learning everything she could on growing crystals so that she could assist her team. She was also learning how to use the fenna and already working on Binnon. Years of being a class two magic user had taught her many lessons, now all she had to do was learn how to master her new power.

"How long do you think it will take her to master Binnon?" Legon asked.

Iselin thought for a moment. "Not as long as most; she's been using magic for years now and has been pushing herself during that time. Sasha has a lot of power; she just needs to learn how to control it and how to sustain it."

Legon sensed how proud Iselin was of Sasha. "She reminds you of yourself, doesn't she?" he asked.

Iselin was embarrassed. "Yes and no; her drive is much like mine, and I think of her as a sister."

"You know she sees you as a mentor. Every tip or suggestion you give she takes to heart."

"I know, and it's sweet of her. Whenever she trains with me, it's fun to watch how hard she tries. In truth it makes me want to work harder myself; both of you have done that. Others see the work you two are putting in and that news makes it to the front lines, let me assure you. Don't think those fighting the war feel you have abandoned them," Iselin said

Seeon was rushing below them now and Legon focused on landing properly. The Palace was right ahead of them and he slowed, letting his back feet touch down. Before his front paws made it to the ground he shifted back into Elf form. Iselin did the same next to him. They walked along the rooftop gardens hand in hand on their way down to dinner.

Chapter Eleven
The Plains

"Realizing the place I held in the world and the place of my love put a troubled world at ease for me. From that point on I have been able to see things how they really are and in them find joy."
-Confessions of Love, The First Wife

Through dint of much effort over the months since she'd Ascended, Sasha finally had a familiar. The ruby-flamed cat looked up at her, its mind connected with Sasha's.

"So," Legon said, "what are you going to name it?"

Sasha scratched behind the cat's ears. "Princess," she said, and then turned when she heard more than one stifled chuckle.

"Princess, huh?" Legon said, but instead of responding to him, Sasha narrowed her gaze on Edling, whose thoughts she could read all too well.

"What's wrong with Princess?" she asked acidly.

Before Edling could defend himself Iselin spoke. "I like it," she said approvingly.

Legon rolled his eyes, "Love, no offense, but you named yours Cat. You really aren't an authority on naming things..."

Iselin gave her husband a stern look, "I'm naming all of our children."

Legon laughed, "Great, what are you going to call them? Child One, Child Two, and so on?"

Iselin smiled sweetly, "I will eat you..."

Legon laughed harder. "I'm bigger than you now, HA! You didn't plan on that one, did you?" he said, blocking Iselin when she tried to punch his arm. The two went tottering off, bickering playfully.

"Do you think we'll be like that?" Edling asked, eyeing their retreating forms.

Sasha stood up, holding Princess. She liked how Edling had assumed that they would be married some day.

"What, you don't think that way?" he asked smirking at her in challenge.

Mental networking meant that there was no such thing as a bluff, so instead she just leaned in and kissed him. He kissed her back, putting an arm around her, "You are good at changing subjects, you know that?" Then looking down at Princess, "And what form do you take when you're released for battle?" he asked the cat, petting it.

"A Puma I think, that was my goal. But she won't be strong enough for that for a bit, maybe a day or two. It was amazing how much energy she took to make."

Edling scooped Princess up in his hands, looking at the glowing crystal in her center. "And with you making her from a hybrid of Elvin and Iumenta crystal technology, it will be hard to determine her true power," he pointed out.

This was true, once Sasha had mastered growing crystals with the Elvin techniques she was able to focus more on combining what they knew about the Elf and Iumenta styles. She'd also managed to get her hands on several Iumenta crystals from Bonta, which had proven useful. "It's amazing, now that we have found some common ground, the advancements we are making are incredible, I thought it would take us ten years to get where we are today."

"But do you think we will be able to apply anything we have learned into the war?" Edling asked.

Sasha nodded, "Yes in fact, I do. As you know, there is a small Iumenta Dragon Dome that lies between us and the Capital city Bailaya. Its size suggests that it was built for the same reason we built the Precipice Dome; it's a public relations piece."

"Yes I know; most people think that it will fall if we hit it hard enough."

"It would yes, BUT, what we have learned can be of use. I think now that we understand the makeup of Iumenta crystals, we will be able to use that to try to weaken the Dome's defenses," she explained.

Sasha didn't care to talk about the war anymore; it was all that was being talked about these days. And if it wasn't being talked about, it was seen. Sasha hated going out into public seeing men and women fall dead to the ground as their spouse was killed in battle far, far away. The whole thing made her sick. The thing that bothered her most was the looks in the eyes of those who were old enough to remember the War of Generations;

there was always fear in their eyes and a deep sorrow that would never go away. It was this, she realized, that was the curse of immortality; the things that wounded one for a lifetime stayed with immortals for millennia.

She started walking with Edling, wondering what it would be like if he were to die. The thought made her gut hurt. "I am not going anywhere and neither are you," he said softly.

Princess leapt out of Edling's arms and into Sasha's, rubbing her head under Sasha's chin. In essence, the familiar's consciousness was inside of the Venefica who created them, making them extremely adept at knowing what their masters were thinking and feeling. It linked both ways and Sasha could feel the little animal's concern for her. She held the cat closer and tried to push her mind away from the war.

Barnin was thankful that his unit was being transferred out to the plains. He was looking forward to the change in scenery, and being in the plains liberating co-ops and villages meant that he didn't have to deal with sieges on large cities. Both of his new units had come together nicely. The unit of veterans came together well and Barnin had a high opinion of most of the men. The rookie unit was still coming along, but had been making progress.

They headed southeast away from Bonta and the Kayloose River. Ahead of them lay the vast plains of Airmelia, to the north were rolling hills and forests, things nearly nonexistent in the plains. Barnin knew that there were small forests, but from what he'd seen on maps they hardly deserved the name. The plains were riddled with lakes and streams that fed the Empire's farmlands.

The road they were on was wide enough for two horses so Ankle was riding next to Barnin. "Do you think we will see the main army?" Ankle asked, referring to the Pawdin forces that were moving north from the Elf lands.

Barnin answered "I don't think so; when I received our transfer orders, command said that Coreum had fallen to the Elves. From what I was able to gather, the Iumenta and Elves are doing most of the fighting with both sides ignoring Human units."

Ankle nodded. "So what we can expect -- pockets of Human resistance but not a major force?"

"That's what I was told. Reports also indicate that the plains have started to rebel; they are in a state of civil war in some of the large cities. I don't think we are going to see a lot of Cona soldiers in the co-ops and villages we are liberating," Barnin explained.

"So some of the villages we come to could be friendly and others hostile?"

"I think so. At any rate, we will need to keep sharp. It's possible that some of these towns don't know which side to trust and I dare say that in some of the more secluded co-ops, the people may not even know about the war yet," Barnin said.

The land before them was flat with the horizon stretching on forever. It was an odd sort of feeling for Barnin and his men; all had grown up in mountains, and the wide open plains made everyone feel exposed and vulnerable. Ahead of them, a small town came into view. A stockade wall surrounded the town. As they approached, Barnin told his men to be ready for a fight, but not to draw their weapons.

A man in each unit was responsible for carrying the flag for the Cona Republic. Barnin checked to make sure those flags were in full view as they came in close to the town. The town didn't have a gate and Barnin could see groups of people at the entrance looking at them. They were armed, eyeing Barnin and his men, presumably trying to figure out which side Barnin's unit was fighting for.

When they were close enough to make out people's faces, Barnin saw them shouting at each other and oddly enough, waving at him and his men. His units slowed down. The townspeople came streaming out from behind the wall, all cheering and waving colored banners. Barnin slowed his horse to a walk as he entered the town. The mass of people parted before them. A young woman with brown hair and brightly colored clothes bounced up to him, extending her hand, looking like she wanted to talk to him. Barnin leaned in his saddle to try to hear her and to his surprise, she kissed him full on the mouth. Red-faced, he straightened up and turned to his men who were experiencing some of the same, others were being handed kids who climbed up on the men's shoulders and waved to the people.

He saw Ankle who smiled, yelling at him, "I guess we should classify this town as hostile?" He laughed.

Legon lowered himself into a pool that would only hold four or five people. Its water was hot and steaming as always, from walls in the side, jets of water and bubbles relaxed sore muscles. It wasn't late but still dark out. Legon leaned his head back, looking into the heavens. Above him the sky was filled with the tiny points of light that were the stars. He breathed out, seeking constellations, wondering who else was looking upon the same scene as he was.

"Would you care to join us, Edling? Iselin is changing and will be out shortly," Legon said, hearing footfalls. Legon turned to look at him.

Edling smiled. "How'd you know it was me?" He asked.

"You passed my guard when you came in, and you step louder than my wife."

Edling nodded. Just then Iselin came into view. She greeted Edling and dropped her robe as she approached the pool. Skintight fabric wrapped around her waist and chest, leaving most of her smooth skin exposed, Legon smiled, remembering the first time he'd seen a bathing suit. She got in the pool with him, groaning as she sat down. "I am sore everywhere. I'm making you train with Opes tomorrow. Really Edling, you are welcome to join us. Legon has a spare suit if you need ..." she said.

"No thank you, I was just hoping that maybe I could speak with you for a moment," Edling said to Legon, sounding uncomfortable.

"Go right ahead," Legon said.

Edling took a moment before speaking. "I am aware that this is a custom where you come from, but I'm not too sure how to go about it. But ... I want to marry your sister," he blurted.

Legon laughed, "Well Edling, I appreciate you asking my permission, but you're supposed to ask her father, not her brother."

Edling frowned and muttered something to the effect of, "Knew I was wrong."

Legon spoke again, serious this time, "Edling, you promise to take care of her the way I have?"

Edling paused for a moment. "Better than," he said with conviction.

Legon felt himself relax in a way he never thought possible, knowing that Sasha would be taken care of. "Then let me welcome you into the family," he said his voice surprisingly heavy. Edling thanked him, leaving Legon and Iselin alone.

Iselin came up close to Legon and put her arms around him. "I don't understand your feelings. You are happy for her and you like Edling, but somehow you feel sad. Why?" she asked.

He thought of how to explain. "It's an odd sort of thing. I have wanted this day for my sister for almost as long as I can remember ... but in a way I feel like I'm losing her. She no longer needs me for her episodes or to grow things for her, or even ... even to protect her from people in town. That's been my life and hers for as long as I can remember. We are so connected emotionally and mentally; in many ways I am just as connected with her as I am with you. We have always been like that, even from before we could talk in each other's heads."

Iselin thought for a while and chose her words carefully. "When you and I first met, I was so jealous of Sasha. Not in any perverse way, but because she was so connected with you. I remember when I Ascended for the first time and I saw and spoke with the White Dragon. From that point on, my confidence never wavered, but for the first time since then, I was unsure. I always worried what would become of you when Sasha grew old and passed away. After you Ascended and so did she, knowing what was said to the both of you -- your purpose in this world -- it honestly frightened me.

"You two are to do so much together and I worried for your safety and hers, but another part of me wondered about where I fit in to all of this. She is your compass; the White Dragon made that clear. She, your sister; not your wife ..." she looked down.

"Love, you know-" Legon started.

"I am not sad. I didn't understand, but since then I have tried to just have faith that everything is the way it ought to be. And it was just now that I realized that you two are one person. The reason why I feared her death was that I knew she was your morality; she was your conscience and compassion. I thought that was because of how you grew up, your connection; but I see now you were never meant to be without her or her without you. You are like twins in so many ways, not sharing some of the same organs but instead sharing part of your cores. Do you understand what I'm saying?"

It was Legon's turn to look down; when Iselin had said they were like twins he thought otherwise, thought about them having different parents and her being older than he. But that aside, she was right; they had always been in-sync with each other, separate but the same ... like twins. A warm feeling fell over him at the rightness of what his wife was saying, and all of his worry of losing Sasha left. He'd never lose her; he couldn't. "Do you think that's why she was on the hill?"

Iselin's eyebrows knit together, "Excuse me?"

He looked into her confused eyes, "On the hill when we Ascended, do you think that's why she was there? You're right; at our cores we live off each other, I get my empathy from her and she my strength. Neither one of us could live if the other passed away. Do you think that's why she was there? Was it fate that she Ascended when she did?"

Iselin shook her head. "I don't know. All I know is that you are both destined for greatness and that I love you both." Then she smiled, "But if I'm being honest, I love you a lot more."

They both laughed, breaking the tension. Legon pulled her in close, feeling unnaturally calm as he continued gazing at the stars.

Chapter Twelve
Atrocity

"In all of the creation there are none save us that are more cruel to our own kind, none more capable of hate and destruction. What is it that makes us this way? How long will we be suffered to exist before justice mercifully blots us from time?"
-An Island of Sorrow

Sasha moved to her left, keeping on the balls of her feet and eyeing Legon with caution, trying to predict his next move. He held his fenna Tento like he was going to lash out at her with it, but she thought it more likely that he was bluffing and would attack with magic instead. She was right; Legon shot a spell at her that she deflected with her own fenna. She smiled, thinking that for once she was going to win.

"INIS!" she yelled, sending a ruby bolt of lightning at Legon.

He held up Tento, trying to deflect the spell pushing him back several feet. She could see him panting; she could almost taste her victory. If she defeated him today, then she would be able to start working with Elves in their Ascended forms. Once in an Ascended form, magic users were significantly stronger than when in Elf form. This was not the case for Sasha; she was Ascended and able to use her full abilities as an Elf, but she had yet to prove herself. In fact, to her dismay, she wasn't performing at near the same level of power she knew she was capable of. She pushed the thought from her mind.

Legon smiled a hard smile at her. "Don't get cocky, you haven't beaten me yet."

Then he held Tento high in the air and said in a powerful voice, "Binnon Toriso-vetis!" Tento pulsed lavender, but Sasha did not see any attack, Legon drove Tento into the ground all the way down to the hilt. There was a rumble and the earth trembled, *what is this?*

Too late she found out. All of the plants around her shot out, vines as thick as grapefruits launched at her. Even now as an Elf she had a hard time moving fast enough to avoid them. She swung her fenna, feeling genuine fear for the first time when sparring with her brother. Power ran down Sasha's arm and into her fenna as she used cutting spells to defend herself. She tried to jump in the air but was cut off. She looked at Legon, still with his blade in the ground. In her moment of hesitation, she felt a vine thick as a python wrap around her wrist pulling her sword. There was more vines around her waist. She freed her fenna as another wound around her neck. Still more encircled her whole body. She couldn't see anymore, with her breath cut short she forced out, "Ignotis ... aurium."

There was heat and then her leafy prison glowed crimson. The vines burned away and she caught a fleeting glimpse of Legon before the vines around her neck shone with a lavender light that signaled the end of the skirmish. Had she been in a real fight with Legon, the vines would have broken her neck. She relaxed as the vines released her. Legon pulled Ten-to from the ground and came up to her, breathing heavily.

"Better," he panted. "I had to go full power that time."

She sheathed her sword. "But it's not good enough! Even at full power you should be nothing for me. What was that attack you used?"

Legon looked confused for a moment. "Oh that's right; you haven't ever seen Toriso-vetis before have you? Binnon is the highest release of magic as you know; at Binnon all of your other spells are stronger but you can channel that power into one spell. The attack I used on you was my most powerful one. Like anything else, we all have certain spells that we are better at. Take for example Mage. He is an Elemental, so when he uses Binnon he uses elemental attacks. He prefers fire. Does that make sense?" he asked her.

"I think so ... I just don't seem to have anything offensive that sticks out to me," she lamented.

Legon scoffed, "What was that spell you used at the end?"

"Umm, let me think. I was scared so I just said something that came to mind -- I think it was Ignotis-aurium," she said.

Legon shook his head, impressed. "You infused the air with fire! It was strong. Had you used it before I attacked, you would have won," he said.

Now it was her turn to scoff. "Please; all it did was cut away vines..."

Legon became serious, "Sasha, you countered my most powerful attack when I was at full strength, and you did it with a spell you used for the first time..."

She thought for a moment. That *was* the first time she'd used that spell and it *had* broken Legon's Binnon attack. She nodded, noting the new-found information. "Thank you. I will try harder," she said.

Emma looked down on the practice arena as Legon and Sasha spoke. Next to her was Rachel, the girl Barnin and his men had found in Mors. Over the months since Rachel had been in the Elves' care, she'd grown back all of her hair and gained a healthy amount of weight. Still, there was always a look in her eyes that said that even though her body was healed, her heart was far from it. It was those same hazel eyes that were wide after watching Legon and Sasha go at it.

"Do you need to leave?" Emma asked.

Rachel looked over at Emma; her face the same age as Emma's but again, it was her eyes that looked like those of some of the Elves. There was a sorrow in them that spoke of a millennia of sadness. But unlike the Elves, there wasn't the light of hope and the signs of a millennia's worth of joy.

"Forgive me," Rachel said, always polite. "It's just ... just that I don't see Un Prosa Legon and Un Prose Sasha like this often. He is so powerful." She looked to the arena again, "Why does Un Prose Sasha look sad?" Rachel asked.

Emma had given up telling Rachel she could call Legon and Sasha by their first names. "She is disappointed that she still cannot beat him in this form," Emma said.

Rachel thought for a moment, "But isn't Un Prosa Legon extremely powerful? He is a Dragon, is he not?"

Emma took her time; she understood magic a great deal, but never found herself in the situation to explain it. "When Legon is in the form of a Dragon -- what you would call Ascended -- then he is powerful, yes; he is a class eight. But in his Elf form he is not as powerful; he is stronger than a class five by a long shot but not anywhere near full strength. Sasha, however, is a class six just as she is, how you see her now is her Ascended form, her only form, as an Elf. She has all of the power of a class six Dragon focused in her small body; that makes her very strong. So strong in fact, that from my understanding it would likely take a powerful class six or a class seven to overpower her."

Rachel's eyebrow rose, "Then why did she lose?"

Emma smiled tightly, "That is the question, isn't it? It seems that she has not been able to fully use her power. In his current form, Legon should be no challenge for her, but for some reason Sasha has been unable to use her full abilities."

Rachel seemed satisfied but thought of another question. "Why didn't Un Prosa Legon use that attack when you were all on the hill when he Ascended?"

"Binnon takes almost all of a Venefica's energy, Legon had been fighting all day long and I doubt he had the strength left to use Binnon. That aside, Binnon is not practical in conventional battle, had he used that attack he would not have been able to defend himself from any other attacker. It would mean giving yourself only one chance to defeat all of your enemies," she explained.

Legon and Sasha were leaving the practice area and coming toward Emma and Rachel.

"Em, Rachel, it's good to see you. Would you two like to join us for lunch?" Legon offered warmly.

Rachel bowed deeply. "Yes, thank you, Un Prosa," she said, "and may I say it was a privilege watching the two of you fight."

Emma noticed just the hint of tension cross Sasha's face. "Thank you Rachel, that is sweet of you."

"Thank you, Rachel. Let's eat -- I'm hungry," Legon said.

Sasha rolled her eyes, "When aren't you hungry?"

Keither cracked his neck and stretched, feeling the baking sun warm him. He was ready for a break and made his way down to a bakery that he liked. when he saw someone there he knew.

"Aren't you a little old to be eating something that fattening?" he asked.

The man in front of him turned around, eyeing him. "You should respect your elders," Sydin said with a smirk. "How are you?"

"I am doing well and so is Sara. You?" he asked.

"Doing well."

Keither got a pastry of his own and joined Sydin at a table. They sat silently enjoying their food for a little while before Keither brought up the only conversation he seemed to have anymore. "How is the war effort?"

Sydin sighed, "It could be going better, but we are winning and I suppose that's what counts in the end."

"Is it?" Keither asked.

"I guess that will depend on what we count as a victory won't it?" Sydin said "I think we will rid the land of the Iumenta, but as for our losses ... well, we will recover."

"What's it like?" Keither asked.

"What's what like?" Sydin asked.

"Living forever, with this," Keither said gesturing around him.

Sydin smiled without humor, "You try to remember the good things I guess, but in some ways I wonder who has it worse. The immortal who will have centuries of happy memories in exchange for centuries of heartache, or the mortal who only gets a few short decades to make memories at all."

They talked about how the war was going for the Elves, and how Keither was doing at his job; all in all it was good to see Sydin. Keither didn't get a chance to talk to many people from his past anymore, with Legon being in the Capital and Barnin being deployed to the plains. All Keither had to talk to these days was Sara.

"You know if it wasn't for the mental networking, I don't even know how my marriage would function," Keither said.

"How is your marriage?" Sydin asked.

"It's good, but we don't see much of each other; it's more like we just live together we are so busy. But, we talk all day in our minds, and in that way it makes it all right that I don't get the time with her that I used to."

"Have you thought of starting a family?" Sydin asked.

Keither laughed, "That would mean having energy at the end of the day to make a family." Then he got serious, "We want to, but ... with the war it's not easy."

"It never is, and I suppose that for now it's good to wait. But Keither, don't lose your youth and life to this cause. You aren't an Elf; you do not have thousands of years for memories with your wife."

Too soon both Keither and Sydin had to leave. Later that day, Keither went back to where he and Sara were staying. He thought back on his conversation with Sydin. When he got in Sara was reading some paperwork. Keither walked over to her and kissed her passionately.

She smiled, surprised. "Where did that come from?"

"I don't want us to lose our youth. Come on, we are going out," he pulled the papers from her hand.

"Bu-but I have work that I need ..."

"To do tomorrow. We are going to dinner and then I am going to try not to step on your toes as we dance," he said, pulling her along.

She laughed. "Dinner and dancing? But I look horrible," she tried to protest.

"You look radiant and I'm not losing a moment more of the night," he said, pulling her outside.

Barnin observed the village before him. Up to this point they hadn't met with any real resistance as they cleared the plains of the Empire. This latest village had already been taken once as the Elves moved through the land, but as soon as the Elves left the area a small factions of those supportive of the Queen had resumed control of the village.

"Sir, this is a hostage situation if anything; how could those inside possibly repel us?" Heath asked and added, "They don't even have any magic users, we can get in without issue, I'm sure."

Barnin thought for a moment and decided that Heath was right. "The Elf liaison I connected with said when they came through there was a catapult left. They were moving quickly through the area trying to out-flank the Iumenta, so they didn't get a chance to destroy it. We will have to watch for that, but otherwise Heath is right; there can't be more than a couple hundred people behind those walls and most will be hostages." Then to his commanders, "We are going to hit them head-on. Heath will take care of the village gate. Once inside, kill anyone who is hostile, but be careful not to hurt the villagers. Most of these people are probably scared and harmless."

The wall before them was a tall stockade fence made for keeping robbers and animals out of a city; not a military unit. Barnin fully anticipated having the village under control by lunch. He and his men rode up to the village gate, holding their shields up and hearing the occasional clang of an arrow bounding off the metal surface. As they approached the gate, Heath barked something in Glosso and a flash of yellow smacked into the door. There was a crack and a groan as the door shifted but then nothing happened.

"They must be holding it closed, Sir, but the bar is broken!" Heath said.

Once at the door, Barnin pulled on Poison's rein and the horse reared, its front hooves connecting with the door. But nothing happened; it didn't budge. Barnin and his men pushed as much as they could to no avail. The door seemed to be stuck.

"Heath, a little help?" Barnin said, exasperated.

The people holding the town were on top of the wall throwing rocks -- and whatever else they could get their hands on -- down at Barnin and his men. Barnin ordered his men to move back out of range as he thought of what to do.

"They may have carts or something of that nature on the other side of the door, but you'd think we could move those without that much difficulty."

Ankle spoke. "Maybe we can find another way inside, Sir," he offered.

Barnin agreed. Ankle took a group and rode around the village, looking for weak spots in the wall. Barnin wasn't happy; he had promised himself that he was going to have the town taken by lunchtime, which was fast approaching. Ankle and his men didn't find much in the way of a weakness in the wall.

"Heath, can you break through the wall?" he asked.

Heath eyed the wall, "It's just wood, but the timbers they used when they built this thing are thick. After attacking the gate, I don't have the strength right now; maybe sometime tonight. I will just be able to weaken the wall, maybe cut some of the support beams."

"Will it be enough for us to tear down the wall?" Barnin asked.

"Yes I think so; if we can get some ropes on the top of it, once I break the supports, the horses should be able to pull down a section."

Barnin told everyone to set camp. He was confident in Heath's abilities, but wasn't going to underestimate those holding the town again. The day wore on hot and dry, and Barnin couldn't wait for the sun to go down. As the sun set, lines of smoke made their way up from the village and Barnin wondered if the smoke was from cookfires or from those holding the village. As the last of the sun's rays faded, he got his answer. Arrows with flaming tips ascended into the sky, landing just shy of Barnin's camp.

"Everyone up!" he ordered.

He remembered that there was still a catapult inside and he wondered if they could expect anything from that. His thought was answered as a form engulfed in fire cartwheeled in the air. It landed with a thud not far away from him. *What is that?* he wondered. Whatever *it* was twitched on the ground and Barnin craned his neck, making out the shape on the ground. "HEATH!" He whirled, "Heath you need to be ready now! They are using the villagers for ammunition!"

Another form came through the air and this time Barnin heard a scream along with it. *They're still alive!* He shouted orders to his archers, "Those people are alive; shoot them in the air!" he ordered.

"Do what, Sir?" a man asked.

"We can't save their lives, but we can end their suffering! The rest of you on me. We are getting past that wall!"

Every few moments another person came hurtling over the wall. Barnin, with Ankle and Heath at his side, rode to the wall but away from the gate. His men threw ropes over the top of the wall with hooks on them, catching at the top of the wooden structure. Heath sent magic at the wall and Barnin heard wood break. "PULL!" he shouted, and his men coaxed their mounts away from the wall.

The wood groaned and popped as the tall slats parted with the rest of the wall. Arrows came hissing out. "PULL! PULL!" he yelled and finally the section of wall came down.

Behind the wall was an assortment of men in normal clothes; they held swords, staves and wooden shields. Barnin's breath caught in his chest. When he'd seen villagers used for the catapult, he'd assumed that real soldiers were on the inside of the village, or worse -- the Dark Warriors. But that's not what met them. It was normal people, normal people who had used their neighbors as ammo. He rode forward, the people inside the walls running, only a very few staying to fight. His men found almost no resistance once inside the walls; the untrained people were killed with almost no effort whatsoever.

They made their way along the wall, headed back to the gates and Barnin saw what had been blocking their way. Piled in a haphazard heap in front of the gate were the bodies of men, women and children, a pool of bloody mud forming at the base. Barnin saw one of the new guys stop and stare. He looked sick.

Ankle rode into the village, killing as he went. The sight of people flying over the wall was disgusting, but he had seen much worse. As he made his way, he got to the gate and saw the pile of bodies blocking the way, and that's when he stopped. Memories of Mors came rushing back to him and he felt his body grow cold even though the night was hot. Gooseflesh covered him as he remembered. Mors was worse, that was for sure, but

Ankle hadn't expected anything like this. There were no Iumenta here, there was no breeding camp, and the heap of people in front of him now was new and fresh. Their eyes were clear as they stared up at him, and blood still oozed from some of the corpses. He looked into the eyes of a little kid, no older than nine or ten. Blood was coming from his mouth, covering his neck and upper body. He hadn't been killed by some army; he'd been killed by someone in the town, by another normal Human.

Pain shot in his shoulder and he turned to see Heath. "Hey, hey, get it together ..." Heath trailed off reading Ankle's face, "Are you all right?"

"How did this happen?" Ankle asked, not really expecting an answer.

Heath shook his head, "I don't know, but right now we can't think about that. There are still people alive here and others who are hurt pretty bad. We need to work."

Ankle didn't really feel time slip by as they cleared the village. Some of those responsible for the atrocities in the village had tried to sneak back in amongst the regular villagers; but they were soon found out. They took maybe ten prisoners, who they put to work clearing the bodies from the gate and burning them. Ankle sat at a little table outside a shop staring off into space, ignoring flakes of ash from the burning pyre of bodies. He wasn't seeing the dirt road in front of him or the people moving about, he was seeing Mors and Rachel.

"Snap out of it," Barnin said, his voice harsh and demanding.

Ankle turned to look at him. "How ..."

Barnin's hard expression softened. "Apparently after the Elves came through, a group of villagers took the town over and killed anyone who had been friendly to the Elves, or tied them up so they could be used later. There were some other things that they did, too ..." he paused and shivered, going on, "but needless to say it was a group of sick people." Barnin shook his head and breathed out, "The women were in on it too, some of them up and killed their own sisters and brothers in the sickest ways, I just don't get how people could go so wrong ..."

"I wish I could tell you," Ankle said hollowly.

Heath was at a loss for what to do for Ankle. A week after they had re-captured the village, Ankle still wasn't responsive, Heath looked at Barnin seriously, "I'm worried about him."

Barnin frowned, "Yeah, me too, but I don't see what we can do about it."

"You could transfer him back to Manton," Heath offered.

Barnin scoffed. "He'll be all right, he'll come back to us. It will just take him awhile. I can't transfer him back to Manton; I don't even have the power to do that. I just wish ... sometimes ... that I hadn't taken him to Mors," Barnin admitted.

"Sometimes I wish you hadn't taken me either, but someone had to go and it may as well have been us," Heath said.

"Yeah, but you and I didn't get affected by that place like he did. I mean, I have nightmares about it, heck I see those people killing each other in my sleep every night. But Ankle ... something in him broke when we were up there."

"Do you think maybe it was that Rachel girl? Seeing her like she was, in that cage, do you think that's what broke him?" Heath asked.

Barnin's brow furrowed, "Nah, she saved him, he was broke before her. I think having her to protect was the best thing in the world for him. It gave him some freedom from guilt."

Heath was confused. "What should he feel guilty about?"

Barnin eyed him. "Come on, you don't feel just a little guilty sometimes? We left those people there. And I know we couldn't have done anything ... but sometimes," he paused, "Sometimes when I dream, I see the girls in those cages, the dead ones and living, and in my dreams they look at me ... they don't talk, but it's written plainly on their faces. They're saying, 'Why didn't you save me?' ..." Barnin's eyes watered and his voice grew thick, "and I can't say anything, so I turn away from them and behind me there are thousands of them; millions, the same dead faces all saying nothing." Barnin looked at him, "You don't feel guilty sometimes?"

Heath swallowed hard. "Yeah, I feel that way most of the time; I just try not to think about it. But you're right; fact is Ankle did something we didn't. We could have each taken someone with us ... but they're dead now." He closed his eyes, "I hope now that they are dead they aren't suffering anymore."

Why hadn't Heath taken someone? He could have; they all could have. Two more wouldn't have had to suffer if only he wasn't a coward. But what if they had all taken someone, what if the weight would have slowed them down, gotten them captured? It was a sin he'd just have to live with; he thought of the White Dragon. *Forgive me.*

Chapter Thirteen
Jump

"The purpose in our life often times doesn't matter just so long as we have a purpose."
-Conversations in the Garden

Firelight lit the horizon to the west as Umbra flew. Several of the coastal cities had already fallen to the formidable Pawdin Navy. But as the fires in the distance attested, some cities still held on. Below her were the Laetuc Mountains, which split the Empire in two. Her mission was not to engage the enemy, strictly speaking. Hers was a game of cat and mouse. She glided in the silent night air looking for targets, not just land targets like bridges and caravans, but more importantly, she hunted Ascended. Stealth was her primary tool. She spent her evenings looking for other Dragons and when she found them, she followed them and relayed their location to Elvin Ascended who would then attack the Iumenta.

It was hard for her to not engage the Iumenta; all she could do was watch as her kin did that work for her. But she understood why she needed to stay out of fights; she couldn't be seen. She wasn't the only one in the skies with this mission; there was an Iumenta equivalent to her in the air, a whole squad of them. Some she even knew from before the War of Generations. She'd been playing this game for over two thousand years, and the sad part was that in a way, those Iumenta were friends to her. Well, as good of friends as Elves and Iumenta could be. They had a working respect for each other.

The Iumenta stealth units were also her greatest threat. They were also experts in hiding themselves and in hunting down other Dragons. On occasion she would catch a glimpse of one but could never follow them. She knew this went both ways; on more than one occasion she'd lost an Iumenta following her. Sometimes Umbra would act as bait. She'd let herself be found and when the Iumenta came to attack, she'd be joined by other Elves. It was dangerous work, but Umbra fed off it.

The night was clear, no clouds to hide in, and the moon was almost full, lighting the landscape below her. She hugged the mountain tops, doing her best not to be seen but on nights like this, she could only be so stealthy.

She decided to move closer to the coast, as the lights from the cities would help keep those on the ground from seeing her. As she moved closer to the coast, the air became thick with smoke. She flew high above the city, staying well out of the way of any Ascended fighting below her, seeing the flashes of light from magic to the north. Ships burned in the water as did much of the harbor. Streaks of fire licked the sky as Pawdin ships fired on the city's defenses. Umbra wondered how much longer the city would be able to hold off the onslaught. So long as the Iumenta controlled most of the city's airspace, the town would hold.

Sasha leaned back into her fiancé, Edling, wanting to take a break. She closed her eyes, tempted to call it quits for the day.

"Why don't we go for a walk by the bay my love, it would relax you," Edling whispered sending her thoughts of the bay. "We could even talk about the wedding," he said, and kissed her neck.

Why was she fighting this? "Fine," she relented. "I'll test this last set of crystals and I'm all yours." She eyed him, "By the way, that wasn't fair," she accused.

Edling smiled, stepping away from her with a chuckle. Before her were two crystals: one that was grown in the fashion of the Elves, the other a hybrid of Elvin and known Iumenta techniques. She placed them inside a device that would test how much power each could hold, how quickly the crystals could be filled and drained of power, and their overall performance under pressure.

Sasha started the test, watching a display that showed results as they came in. In every test prior to this, her hybrid crystals had shattered or under-performed the traditional Elvin crystals. She and Edling waited for a moment for the test to run. As she waited, she thought of plans for her own wedding … well, the plans she had control over. Just as Sasha had planned Iselin's wedding, Iselin was planning Sasha's wedding. She was nervous; Sasha had gone a little overboard with Legon and Ise's wedding. Since then, she'd been asked to plan no less than twenty other weddings for heirs of Houses both Great and Minor. But in all those other weddings, she'd never expended the resources that she had with Legon's. Now it was Iselin's turn to get revenge on Sasha. Iselin and Legon had wanted a small wedding, not unlike Sasha; but Sasha had made sure the affair was anything but small.

Edling tensed beside her, reading her thoughts. "What I don't understand is why I'm getting punished too," he said. "You planned that wedding; not me ..."

She smiled up at him. "Sorry," she said warmly.

The testing device beeped and Sasha turned, "Well, I didn't hear anything shatter, that's a good sign."

She opened the device, removing the crystals and reading the display. "Edling," she breathed.

"What is it?" he asked, concerned.

She pointed to the display and he gawked, "It's a fluke. Run the test again," he said. "There's no way it out-performed our current technology by thirty percent, nothing has advanced that far for a thousand years!"

Sasha ran the test two more times with the same results. All thoughts of the bay left both of them as they worked to re-create the test crystal. Sasha called in all her staff and they worked through the night.

Morning found Legon sitting with his wife on their terrace, watching the sun rise. In the back of his mind he could feel Sasha frantic about something, but he really didn't care. He sipped his Poti and held Iselin's hand.

"Her wedding is soon; do I need to do anything?" he asked her.

Iselin sighed and smiled wickedly, "Yes actually, I have commissioned a new hall that will be the size of one of the old Human cathedrals. It will be a good thing for the people; they need the excitement. I need you to grow the super structure for it this week; all of our largest buildings were grown by class eights, so it shouldn't take you too long in your Ascended form, maybe three or four days. From there, artisans will do the detail work."

Legon nodded. "I can get to it in two days. I've almost mastered jumping. Do you think I have the skill for that kind of building?" he asked.

She laughed. "No. Sorry love, Gratook will join you. Really, you'll just be lending him your strength; though since he is your teacher, I am sure he will use it as an educational experience too. Also your uncle Tenick will be there as well; he is a master builder. As for jumping, I think you'll get it figured out today. I am going to work with you on it," she smiled.

Before he could say anything Sasha came bursting out of the Palace onto the terrace looking slightly psychotic, hair strewn in every direction like she'd been in a windstorm, red eyes shining. Legon wanted to make a comment but decided better of it. "Are you … all right?" he asked.

"All right? How can you ask that? Haven't you been paying attention to my thoughts?" she demanded.

"Umm no … was I supposed too? I was asleep for about eight hours, you know," he said.

She shook her head. "Of course, of course," then she looked at both him and Iselin. "We've done it!" she announced excitedly.

Iselin smiled. "That's fantastic dear. Done what?"

Edling joined them, grining. "Sasha had a major breakthrough last night," he said.

Legon sat up as did Iselin, both getting serious. "What is it?"

Edling handed Legon and Iselin a sheet of paper. Legon read it over, "How is this possible?"

Sasha was bouncing on the balls of her feet. "I can tell you -- I want to tell you -- but Edling made me promise to make sure that you really want to know all of the mechanics behind it …"

Edling placed his hand on her arm, stopping her. "Sorry," she breathed. "I had a lot of Socolata last night." Then she went on, still in a rush, "In short, these new crystals are stable in the extreme and can hold and transfer massive amounts of power without losing too much in the process. They are super efficient. They are tricky to make, however, and we still have tests to run on them, but I think they will be ready for field tests within the next month," she said.

Legon thought for a moment, *they may not be in full production for the war.* He sensed more of Sasha's thoughts. "There's more?" he asked.

She nodded. "In testing when we found the breaking point of the old hybrids, the fail point was in their Iumenta making. It's something small, but we think there may be a way to affect the Iumenta parts. But it's just a theory at this point," she said.

Legon felt a chill run down his spine and Sasha frowned, "What is it?"

"Are you saying there may be a way to attack crystals directly or weaken them?"

"Yes," she said looking shocked at his concern.

"This needs to be your top priority. If we can attack a crystal in a Dragon Dome, we will have a significantly easier time taking the Capital. But also, if we can do it; so can the Iumenta. We need to find our own technology's weaknesses and find a way to secure them," he said more firmly than he meant to.

Sasha's face paled as did Edling's. "You're right," she said. "Should I take time from mastering Binnon?" she asked.

Legon frowned. "No, you need to master that. Edling, this will have to fall on your shoulders," Legon said.

Edling's face hardened. "Yes Un Prosa, I will not let you down."

After Sasha and Edling left, Legon sat talking to Iselin.

"It's not likely the Iumenta have found a weakness in our technology," Iselin said with a surprisingly high amount of confidence.

"But we don't know that for sure," Legon pointed out.

"They have never done anything ..." she started.

"We thought we knew the Iumenta had stopped their breeding programs, but I'd say Mors proved we don't know as much as we think," he said firmly, and then reading the worry on her face added more softly, "Love, I agree they more than likely don't know about any weaknesses our technology may have, but it's our job to find and fix those weaknesses regardless." He squeezed her hand, "Let's get ready for the day; I want to get jumping down."

Iselin watched Legon's retreating figure. This was one of her favorite qualities of his. Legon was able to simplify anything to its most basic component. She knew that Sasha's news would have caused weeks of speculation in the other Great Houses and still likely would, but not for Evindass. There were going to be a lot of questions that needed answering about whether or not the Iumenta could hurt the Elves in a new way. For Legon it was simple; it didn't matter what the Iumenta knew or didn't know. There was a problem and he ordered it solved. She also liked that even right after hearing the news he had, he was not dwelling on it. She could feel his mind; it was fixed on what he needed to do that day with the task he had at hand.

She sat outside for a bit before getting ready for her day. She was going to be spending most of the day in her Ascended form, which shortened her morning prep time significantly. *If you always stayed Ascended you'd never have to worry about your hair,* she thought. Iselin met with her assistant, giving her a few things to do for the day, and then she made her way outside. Legon was already Ascended and flying out over the bay. She transformed and took flight.

Iselin slid through the air, coming alongside Legon. "So, are you ready?" she asked him.

They flew west out over the ocean and away from main shipping lanes. Once they were on their own, Iselin began to instruct him. "Now love, so far you are doing great. Remember the two key things needed to jump are knowledge of your destination and using your power to get you there." She'd been working with him for a while on jumping, which so far had proven to be the hardest thing for Legon to learn. She broke the lesson into two different sessions. The first was fixing a spot in space to jump to; this he had mastered. She would connect with him fully and he would fix a spot for her to jump to. The next lesson was on the actual jumping itself. This too he could do, though not as well. Iselin would join his mind and give him a fixed point to jump to. Legon made the jump most of the time but wasn't proficient yet. The problem that Iselin was having was trying to get Legon to both plot a jump and execute it.

Legon tried a jump. Iselin was in his head monitoring him. He locked on to a spot in front of him, his magic moving in him and about to propel him forward. He started his countdown by folding his wings in. A purple dot glowed in front of him. He sent power down his body and he started the jump. There was a flash of lavender but Legon didn't move.

"Ahh, what now?" Legon said aggravated.

"I don't know; maybe it's because you are so big, jumping could be difficult for you. There aren't any class eights around to ask."

"Do you really think so?" Legon asked.

She thought about it. "Yes I do actually, I mean Sasha picked it up no problem ..." she stopped.

He was incredulous, "Sasha? She can jump? I didn't even know she was learning!" He was flabbergasted, "How come I didn't know about this?" he demanded.

"I'm sorry," she said. "I didn't teach her; my father did, and she didn't want you to know because she thought you would get upset if you found out she mastered it in a day-"

"IN A DAY?!" he was stupefied. "I have been trying to learn this for almost a month, how did she do it in a day? And how were you able to hide this from me?"

She winced, "Well, you see it all happened rather fast, and you were in meetings that day and not connected with me, so really it wasn't all that hard ..." Her voice trailed off. She looked over at him. He wasn't mad at her or anyone, he was happy for Sasha, but Iselin could tell that he was thinking hard.

Finally he spoke, "No, this is good to know, nobody masters jumping in a day. I think you're right about the size thing, it has got to be what is holding me back."

Legon decided that he wasn't going home until he mastered jumping. Oddly, knowing that Sasha had mastered it in a day motivated him. Not that he thought he was better at magic than she was; he knew he wasn't. Sasha was extremely talented with magic. The only thing she didn't excel at was combat; he knew that had little to do with her abilities, but rather was tied to her attitude. He decided the latter was likely true for him as well. Legon had mastered many things with magic and in many ways was far ahead of most users. This was because he worked hard and never stopped trying. Iselin had been like that as well, she excelled more due to her attitude than because of raw talent.

"I just need better resolve," Legon told Iselin.

He tried again, and again, and again. He was getting tired and the sun was starting to set, but still Legon didn't stop trying; he was going to jump. He fixed his gaze on the horizon, locking it into his mind *5,* he felt magic build in his body *4,* he double-checked his location *3,* his wings snapped to his side *2,* a dot of light appeared in front of him *1,* and the dot expanded revealing his destination as power ran over his body *jump.* Legon was surrounded by purple and for a moment, the world didn't exist. Then his wings opened, supporting him on the air. He looked back to where Iselin was in the distance. He'd finally jumped.

Evening found Edis walking down the streets of Seeon with his wife Laura. He loved the city with its growing buildings and near constant activity. In the months following the start of the war, he found that the normally vibrant streets had lost some of their life. And on occasion when he was out walking, he would see an Elf keel over dead, as far away that person's spouse died in combat. For the people living in the Pawdin Empire, the war was always at home, no matter where the front line was.

He and his wife had gone to a play and dinner for the evening. His life had changed in the years since he and Laura left Salmont. Now he spoke Glosso, the Elves' language, and he could speak with his mind. Just by virtue of being mentally connected with others, he had learned more in the last few years then he thought possible, and he got to see his children often. Sasha was due to be married shortly, which made both him and Laura happy and despite the gloom of war, life seemed good to Edis, but somehow it didn't feel like he was living his own life.

"We don't do what we used to," Laura said reading his thoughts. "We had a routine before; we had a purpose in our days. That purpose was to get by and to work but it was a purpose nonetheless," she pointed out.

"So … we have no purpose now?" he asked.

She thought for a moment. "In some ways, yes; I suppose that's true. I can still work as a healer, but I use crystals for most things now. No longer do I have to worry if a fever is going to break or if a treatment I used is going to have an effect. As for you, you worked with your hands all day, and while I can keep myself busy as a healer and learning more about medicine, you do not have that; there are no butchers in Seeon."

This was true; Elves grew plants however they wanted, even making fruit that was seemly no different than meat. "So you're saying I need to find something to do?"

She shrugged, "Perhaps. If you think about it, we don't have to do anything. We live in the Palace and we cannot go back to a Human city, nor would we want to. Maybe you need a hobby that can take your time, isn't there anything you've always wished you could do?"

Edis thought and smiled. "When I was a boy, we lived near the sea. My father and I would go out sailing sometimes; his friend had a small sailboat that we would all take. We would try to fish a bit, but mostly I just liked being out on the water and diving in the reef," he said.

Laura smiled up at him. "You've never told me that before; why not?"

"I don't know, I didn't think about it. When I moved to Salmont, there wasn't an ocean nearby and I always assumed that's where I would spend the rest of my life, you know? There was no need to think about it, and after so many years, I guess I haven't thought about it much here either."

Their conversation was cut short by a thud behind them. They were almost back to the Palace so Edis wasn't surprised to see Legon and Iselin in their Dragon forms landing behind them.

"You look happy," Edis said to his son.

"I can jump!" he said and added, "It's beautiful this evening. Iselin and I are going to go for a flight. Would you like to join us?" he asked.

"But dear, haven't you been flying all day?" Laura asked.

Iselin answered. "That was training; this is just for enjoyment. Don't worry Laura, flying for us is like walking for you, we aren't too tired," she said warmly.

Edis knew that flying wasn't Laura's favorite thing to do, but he put his hand on the small of her back and gently pushed her toward Iselin. Laura glowed pink and rose up in the air to rest sidesaddle on Iselin's shoulders. "You just need to loosen up a bit," Iselin said to Laura. And then she took off.

"Do you need help, old man?" Legon asked.

Edis scoffed, "Do I need help?" Then he looked up at Legon's towering form, "Yes, I could use a hand," he said.

Edis felt himself rise in the air and then settle on Legon's shoulders. He, unlike Laura, enjoyed flying immensely. It was a thrill for him each time he was on a Dragon. Once they were in the air, Edis connected his mind with Legon's. "I have a question for you," he said.

"What is it?"

"I'm thinking about taking up sailing, can you think of who I need to talk to?" Edis asked.

"That's wonderful, and yes, I have a few people who can help you. Do you need a boat? We have plenty," Legon said and then added, "If you like, I could grow one for you."

Edis beamed, "Thank you Son, that would be nice of you, but are you sure?" Edis was touched. Legon didn't have much in the way of time, and there was something about your child making you something that made a man feel good. He relaxed on Legon's shoulders and began looking forward to his new hobby.

Chapter Fourteen
A Dream Come to Life

"Life is a sea of memories, dotted with islands of choice events."
-Excerpts from The Diary of the Adopted Sister

Tom, from Arkin's old unit in Salez, looked across the table at a stone-faced Stacy. Things in Salez and around the rest of the Empire had been on a steady decline over the last few months. Tom glanced over to Seth and Brian, trying to see what their reaction to Stacy's news would be.

"Well? Does anyone have anything to say?" Stacy was irritated. "We have had four contacts killed this week; doesn't anyone have something to say?"

Tom cleared his throat, "I'd say we have a mole." He tried not to sound dramatic or on edge.

Stacy blinked, "A mole?"

"Stacy," Tom said, "think about it. We have people getting killed left, right and center. Information we have collected has been leaked and even law enforcement seems to be getting wise to us. We have a mole."

Seth answered, "How do you know we aren't just being followed? I mean, we knew that at some point in time the Iumenta would create an organization like ours, right? So maybe that's what this is."

"Thank you Seth, followed is more likely," Stacy said. "Tom please; a mole, honestly?" she scoffed.

Tom shrugged, "That's what I would do."

Brian raised his eye brow, "What is what you would do?"

"If I found a clandestine organization running operations in my city, I would follow them, find key people and then try to plant someone in that organization. Kind of like ... oh yes, what we did in Salez with the local government."

"But we didn't come up with that plan, an Elf Lord did and my ..." Stacy stopped talking for a moment and then went on, her voice thick, "and Arkin."

Tom's face fell, "Stacy I'm sorry, I didn't mean to ..."

She waved him off, "Don't apologize, I should be able to keep myself under control and after all you're just doing your job. Look, I don't want you guys to think about moles or people following you; just do your jobs and let me handle this. Good?"

Seth and Brian agreed and Tom did only grudgingly. There was something that was off to him about the whole situation that they were in. *Why now?* He thought. *Why were they being targeted now?*

Sasha looked herself over in the mirror. Her dark hair was piled atop her head with jewels and fine silver and gold bands wound throughout. A delicate lace collar rose to just below her chin, connecting with a flowing white gown. She felt as though she'd run out of breath and couldn't quite catch it again. It was her wedding day; a day she had both dreamt of and yet hadn't believed would happen in her whole lifetime. She, like most little girls, had fantasized about this day, imagined a day fit for a princess, though no one expected that to happen. But here stood the girl who would never be with anyone; here she stood on her wedding day. She was the heir to a Great House; today she was a princess.

"You look breathtaking," Iselin said from behind her and then asked, "Does it feel real?"

Sasha turned to her, "Real?"

"Yes, on my wedding day it didn't feel real to me, more like a daydream that I hadn't snapped out of yet. Here I was marrying a man I could have never in my wildest fantasies conjured up, and the ceremony, the one you put together, was like nothing I could have ever hoped for," she said reminiscing.

Sasha turned back to the mirror, smiling. "Yes, actually I was just thinking about that. I keep thinking that I am going to wake up in my bed back in Salmont. I never thought today would happen. Edling is perfect for me in every way and I am perfect for him. If it weren't for the turmoil in the world at present, I would say that the life I have now was too good to be true and I must be in a dream. But I am not going to think of anything negative today," she promised herself.

Her mother entered the room. As Sasha turned to look at her, Laura's eyes filled with tears. "Oh dear, you couldn't look more perfect," she gushed.

"Are you going to cry all day?" Sasha asked warmly.

Her mother sniffed. "Of course I am, it's a mother's job to spend her child's wedding day in tears. Today is a great day for your father and I; our last child is getting married. And, if we are very lucky, you will not follow in your brother's footsteps and Edis and I might actually get some grandchildren," she glanced over at a red-faced Iselin.

Before Iselin could be chastised more, she was saved by Emma and Sara walking in. Sara and Keither had jumped in the previous morning and Sasha was elated to see her again. Sadly, Barnin was unable to attend the wedding. Legon had to do some work to get Sara and Keither to come and still they couldn't stay long.

Legon stood next to Edling by the altar. They were in a large hall that Iselin had had specially built for the day's events. It was massive, with an arched ceiling towering overhead. The ribbed beams of the ceiling were separated by Circular windows below, and long stained glass windows extended to the floor. Chandeliers hung from the arched tops of the beams, bathing the room in warm light. The altar was on an elevated platform below which were row upon row of chairs with guests in them. Behind Legon and the altar was a wall wrought in gold and silver. The wood Iselin had ordered grown was pure white from floor to ceiling, and along the walls ivy grew with flowers of pink and red blossoms. Legon couldn't have imaged a more elegant setting.

Legon looked to his left; Edling looked as if he'd stopped breathing. "Are you going to be all right?" Legon asked softly.

Edling glanced over at him, "I don't know, there are a lot of people here and I'm nervous on top of that."

Legon chuckled. "I remember that; just be thankful you don't have to walk down the aisle, and as soon as she's here you won't be thinking about anything else, trust me," he assured him.

Sasha stood at the entrance of the hall as everyone rose to face her. Oddly, no fear of the crowd gripped her. In her years of service, she'd addressed the masses many times, and she found that she wasn't actually scared of the ceremony or of being married. She was filled with the giddy apprehension that comes when you know that your life is about to change permanently. She felt her father next to her tremble slightly. Standing at the altar was Edling, and that's all that mattered to her. She started down the aisle, doing her best to pace herself. The room seemed to extend with each step; it felt like an eternity before she reached the two small steps onto the platform and stood before her husband to be. Her father deftly gave Edling her hand. Edling's palm wasn't clammy or cold, his hands were warm like his eyes and face. His mind was a blur of emotion and neither one paid any attention to the world around them.

Edis looked down the aisle. When Legon got married, all he had to do was stand up by the altar and shake hands with people; but not this time. This time it was his little girl getting married, and if that was not enough pressure, he had the privilege of walking her down the aisle and giving her away. It was an honor to him, a moment he'd hoped for since her birth. But now standing at the edge of the crushed red velvet carpet that would take them to the altar, Edis was nervous. Sasha and Legon spoke in public; Edis and his wife didn't, and even now Sasha was the center of attention, but he stood just to the right of her. It was a sea of faces. He felt himself tremble just a bit.

Sasha was the one who started walking, not he. He was supposed to be leading her down the aisle, not the other way around. He tried to compose himself. He passed by Elf Lords and Ladies, all smiling warmly at him and Sasha. The hall itself inspired reverence and spoke to the regal nature of his daughter's people. Her station never left his mind and even today, her wedding day, it rang clear. Behind Legon in his white robes of the Head of House was a wall of gold and silver; on it hung banners of House Evindass. His Sasha, his sweet little girl, was far from being the toddler he'd once played with and bounced on his knee.

He passed Sasha's hand to Edling's and sat next to his wife. Had some-one told him what Sasha would become on the day of her birth, Edis would have laughed. But now he looked at his daughter, at his own blood, and tried to see the amazing woman she'd become. He saw her kindness and beauty; saw her drive to make the world a better place. In so many ways she didn't seem like she could be his child. Sasha was brilliant and special in so many ways that he couldn't fathom. He was blessed to have been allowed to raise her. He closed his eyes and tried not to weep as he said a silent prayer of thanks to the White Dragon.

Emma watched as Sasha twirled around the dance floor with Sydin. Emma was happy to see him again, and while he seemed slightly more haggard than normal, the strain of the war didn't seem to get to him. Emma had found this to be true with all of the Elves she had met from the front. Unlike their Human counterparts, the Elves' centuries of life experience appeared to keep them mentally and emotionally balanced. The war was more of a bad dream to them than a reality, just a terrible spot in time.

Other than Legon, Sasha and Iselin, Emma only had one Elf friend who she counted close and that was Opes, who was making his way over to her. He held out his hand and asked her to dance. She accepted and joined those already on the floor in a waltz.

She could see pain in his blue eyes and commented on it. "Weddings," she said like an accusation.

He nodded his agreement. "I can see that you too have bittersweet feelings today," he said, referring to the fact that both he and she had lost their loves.

It wasn't healthy that Emma still dwelled on the death of Kovos; it wasn't something that he would have wanted. But for her she did want it, she worried that if she ever let herself let go of him, she wouldn't be able to remember him. For her, keeping Kovos' memory close and painful was better than letting it drift. For Opes, his wife was killed in the War of Generations and for him, like any Elf, there was no letting go, too con-nected were their minds by the time that she was killed.

"Weddings remind me of something that I will never have," Emma said. "They remind me of what was stolen."

Opes never tried to tell her to move on with her life; he understood her perfectly, which in a way made him Emma's closest friend and vice versa.

"Yes, today for me it is not memories of an opportunity missed. No, I can still see my wedding day as clear as if it were only yesterday. Ours was not as lavish as the Head of a Great House, but it was a beautiful venue. Ever since I lost my wife, I have performed many marriage ceremonies, did you know that?"

"I didn't know that; why?" she asked, wondering why someone would do that to themselves.

"Well for one, even though part of me feels sad at these events, they are a happy day and I remember how happy I was and look forward to that for the couple getting married. But I perform the ceremony because it reminds me of my own." His eyes got a far off look in them as Emma listened, "Every time I do one, it's like feeling my own again. That was the happiest moment in my life and it was my wife's too, so happy was it that not even her death can taint the memory. Do you have any memories like that?"

Emma smiled "In fact I do. It wasn't the happiest day of my life but it's oddly memorable. I was trying to hint for Kovos to ask me to marry him but men don't seem to do well with hints," she chuckled, "anyway, I took him to look for linens and things of that nature, I thought maybe if we did something domestic together he'd get the hint ... he didn't, of course. It wasn't until after I came to Seeon that Sasha told me that Kovos hadn't gotten a single one of my hints. I can still remember the look on his face when I asked him to pick out a color for a tablecloth," she giggled.

"I don't think I understand," Opes said.

"Forgive me; you see Kovos wasn't what you would call refined. I had laid in front of him swatches in varying colors of white. The look on his face was like I had just given him an unsolvable puzzle. It was the funniest expression I'd seen him make, I tried to explain to him that there was more than one color of white," she laughed again. "He looked at me like I was insane; to Kovos there was only one white, no off-white or bone, just white." She sighed, "It's a silly, inconsequential memory, but for some reason it's the most pure one that I have."

When she was done dancing with Opes, she walked over to a table where Rachel sat looking wide-eyed at all of the guests. Emma had taken the girl under her wing; she'd tried to help her integrate into society, which had been a success for the most part. But Rachel wasn't comfortable with large groups of people or when there was a lot of activity.

"Rachel," Emma said. "How are you doing?"

"It's like a dream, isn't it? You wouldn't know the world is in turmoil."

"Is that a bad thing?" Emma asked.

Rachel cocked her head to the side, considering Emma "No, it's good. I feel like today in this room, the war doesn't exist, it's like when I was a girl living by the sea and the fog burned off to reveal the bay. That's how it feels in here, like the fog is gone and in its wake is a beautiful world."

Emma thought about what Rachel said. She was always amazed at how insightful the girl was.

Sasha's wedding was coming to a close. It had been perfect. Her feet were sore from dancing and her face ached from smiling; these were the marks of joy, in her opinion. Before her was Sydin in his Ascended form, his black scales shining in the fading light. He would be flying Sasha and Edling to the town of Rosae for their honeymoon. Rosae was small; the Family House there was nothing like the Palace that she lived in now. She and Edling were looking forward to the slower pace of the town and its quaint atmosphere.

Edling lifted her onto Sydin's back and he took off. The people below cheered and waved to them and Sasha found herself leaning back into Edling's warmth, closing her eyes.

Thank you she thought to Edling. He responded by squeezing her harder.

Sasha was vaguely aware of Sydin's mind. He was connecting with a jump crystal in preparation for the jump to Rosae, and so blissful was she that she didn't even feel the jump. Her lungs filled with the thick sent of Rosae. The town was named aptly, when her eyes opened she was greeted by the sun setting over a valley of vineyards and a town lined with streets of roses of every different kind.

Sydin glided over the town center, none of the buildings being more than two stories tall, as he made his way to the edge of town. Sasha stepped off onto the soft lawn at the Family House. She and Edling said their goodbyes to Sydin and he took off to jump back to Seeon.

Sasha and Edling walked hand in hand toward the cottage that was the Family House. Its walls were draped in roses like the rest of the town and they happily entered the small living room.

"Two bedrooms," she said, looking at Edling, "that's it. That is all this entire house has -- just two small bedrooms! No servants, no guests, no nothing, and it's wonderful!" she gushed, truly relaxing.

"Perhaps someday we can live here," Edling said.

"That would be nice; we could jump to Seeon or the Golden City for my research and then come home here in the quiet."

"It's too bad most Elves wait a century before having their first child. If Legon and Iselin produced an heir now ..."

Sasha wrapped her arms around his waist, "Well, I think they might. You see my family is mortal, and I think Legon wants at least one of his kids to know their adopted grandparents." She ran her fingers through Edling's dark hair, "And with each niece or nephew I get to play with, it moves me one step further from being Head of House. Not that it will matter anyway, I suppose."

Edling cocked an eyebrow and Sasha answered his unasked question. "The White Dragon told me that when Legon or I died the other would too, so we will never inherit House Evindass, but as time goes on, I will have less responsibility."

Edling kissed her. "I forget you aren't used to how things normally are. You and your brother have been busy with a war since you arrived. Once the war is over, much of life will slow down, the fifteen hour days and weeks that never seem to end will go away. It is not uncommon for Heads of House to take several months off for holiday, indeed this is the norm for our entire race."

"That sounds most welcome. Now enough talking about what will happen years from now and more kissing and enjoying our wedding night," she said, pulling Edling in close.

Legon and Iselin walked with Sydin toward the war room in the Palace. Sydin was giving them a report of how House Evindass was faring in the war effort. The three of them entered the war room where the rest of the Heads of each of the Great Elvin Houses were already sitting. Legon greeted each of them in turn.

"Thank you all for coming not only to this meeting, but my sister's wedding. It meant a great deal to her," Legon said.

Each person in the room networked their mind with everyone else, giving Legon as well as every other Head of House a complete view of the war and the Pawdin Empire's overall standing. Legon trusted each Head of House completely as did they him; as such, the members of the

Pawdin government thought as one mind and while in these meetings an overriding consciousness tapped each person's memory and abilities.

The war was going relatively well; they were taking fewer casualties than expected and taking ground. Their efforts over the years to thin out the Iumenta Dragon population had paid off. As a result, the Elves were increasingly using Ascended to take out ground and sea units. The Naval battle was all but won, the Cona and Impa fleets were futilely trying to keep their northern shores safe, but almost all of the waters in the western seaboard were under Pawdin control. The fleet was working closely with ground units to bombard and take coastal cities.

The fight on the ground was slowly progressing up the coast and Kayloose River, and thus far there had been no major setbacks. Everyone knew that the war would get harder the closer to Impa lands and the Capital they got; it was for this reason that Legon wanted to be in the fight. He knew that he was only one Ascended, but he was a class eight which meant something to the people. Legon being in battle would increase morale across all the Elvin and Human forces.

Chapter Fifteen
Ignotis-Aurium

"Once I was asked to view the latest work of a young artist. It was a painting that took a whole wall. He asked me to stand close and look. I looked at it from up close seeing only dots of color. Then I stepped back to see that from a distance the dots made a picture. The piece was speaking to the fact that if we change our perspective of an object we can, in a way, change the object. It wasn't a new style of painting but I found the experience enjoyable none the less."
- Conversations in the Garden

Keither landed hard on his backside.

"Haven't you practiced since we left Manton?" Barnin asked, referring to Keither's long-standing inability to fight with a sword.

"If you must know; no I haven't. I've been a bit busy, if you haven't heard," he said icily.

They were in Ripensis, a city on the banks of the Kayloose River. Ripensis itself wasn't as large as Salez, but it was interconnected with many smaller towns and villages, giving its metropolitan area a sprawling nature. Keither had been in Seeon when the city was taken, so he hadn't seen any of the fighting himself, but he knew that both the Elves and Cona forces had taken heavy casualties.

Barnin and his unit were in Ripensis to re-fit and take on a few replacements.

Barnin continued their conversation. "Yeah, we've all been busy. How was the wedding?" he asked.

Keither sheathed his sword, effectively ending their practice, and earning a disapproving look from Barnin. "It was amazing, to be honest with you, but I don't know. Seeon just didn't feel the way that it used too."

Barnin sat heavily on a chair. "How do you mean?"

Keither tried to think of how to describe Seeon's change to him. "It's like the people are always living in a state of fear."

Barnin laughed, "What, like they think they are going to get attacked? Come on Keither, the Elves aren't cowards."

"No, no, not like that. It's hard to describe, it's like people are always waiting to drop dead, which in a way, I suppose they are." Barnin gave him a look. "You haven't been there since the war started, but I was talking to Emma and she was telling me that she hates walking the streets now. The Elves die when their spouse dies, so when someone gets killed at the front ..."

"You mean their wife or husband just drops dead in the street?" Barnin asked amazed.

Keither nodded. "If your spouse is in the war, you not only worry about losing them but also yourself."

"That is eerie, did you see that when you were there?" Barnin asked.

"Yes, once. Sara and I were having breakfast at a cafe and some guy was walking down the street. He dropped something he was holding; it was glass and it shattered as he made this horrible pained sound and keeled over," Keither explained.

"What happened then?"

"Nothing really, everyone around him got real quiet and scared looking, and then some Elves picked up his body and took it off somewhere. Things went back to how they had been before the man died. Seeon is a tense place to be right now."

Barnin shivered on the inside. He'd always assumed that the Elves had the war pretty easy -- well not the units that were on the front -- but the people back home in cities like Seeon. Now he was starting to reassess his views. *How horrible would it be to go through your day knowing that at any moment you or someone you know could drop dead?*

He thought again and asked Keither, "Would that happen with you and Sara? If one of you, you know, kicked it, would the other one go too?"

Keither shook his head. "Sadly, no. She and I are mentally linked just like the Elves but a connection strong enough to kill takes decades. No, right now if one of us dies, the other one will merrily spend the rest of their life looking forward to death. It's so bad for the living person, in fact, that in the Pawdin Empire, people generally do not join the military until the connection with their spouse is strong enough to kill."

Barnin was shocked, "They do what? Why would you want the other person to die?"

Keither gave a dark chuckle, "You and Samantha don't share a mental connection so I can see why you're confused. Do you remember Opes? He is one of Legon's guards." Barnin indicated that he remember him. "Well, Opes' wife was killed in the War of Generations; they had only been married for a decade or so. You see back then, everyone fought and she died. When she passed, so did part of Opes. Think of how much you love Sam, and how much it would hurt to lose her."

"I can't even imagine that kind of pain," he said honestly.

"The pain you will feel when she dies is nothing to what Opes felt and with a connection like that, not even time heals the wound; you just learn to live with the pain. It's for that reason that I hope, as does Sara, that if one of us is killed, then the other is only moments away," Keither said.

Barnin tried to clear his head. "That's one more reason not to use that freaky mental linking trash." He said, thankful yet again that he didn't go for any of that type of nonsense. "A man's thoughts are his own, and that's that. Now break's over, get your sword," he said, changing the subject.

Sara spent the bulk of her afternoon organizing supplies. This was the task that felt like it took most of her time, but she was thankful for it. The war was wearing on Sara; it seemed to her as though she couldn't get the blood of the wounded off her hands and clothes. The sound of grown men crying for their mothers was a constant echo in her ears, not even sleep brought relief. The only bit of rest she'd had lately was Sasha's wedding, though even in Seeon the war was at their doorstep.

The army wasn't pushing ahead right now; it was all but stopped, giving time for troops to secure the countryside and to build up supply routes before they pushed for Salez. Salez. Sara wondered how she would feel being back in the city. She had no doubt that she would go there, Salez would be a major hub; taking the city was a must. From there, all that stood in the way of them and the Capital were some towns and a Dragon Dome. The latter would not be easy to take. She thought again of Salez, she wondered if any of her old co-slaves were still there, and if so, how were they doing? She found it unlikely that any of them had survived since she'd last been with them. Most had probably long since died from diseases they had caught from horrid clients.

She pushed those thoughts from her mind and went back to what she was doing. By the time she was done working for the day, the sun was setting. The sky was deepest orange from the smoke of fires. Ripensis, while taken, was still putting up a fight. The city with its flowing metro area had many strongholds that were not going quietly into the night. Fires burned, licking the skyline with bright orange and yellow. Smoke rose like columns over much of the north end of town. Flashes of magic could be seen on the ground and from Dragons above the city. Not for the first time, Sara asked herself if she would ever see Airmelia whole and complete in her lifetime.

"You are morose today," Keither said from behind her.

She turned to him. "Yes, I suppose I am. I think it was going back to Seeon that did it to me. Before when I was feeling worn out from the war, I could think of Seeon and its flowered streets, calm and serene. But now I know that there is no place in the land that is calm or serene.

"I was listening to your conversation with Barnin, the things he has seen in the battlefield." She looked at her husband seriously, "Keither we cannot allow our children to grow up in this world. We cannot allow another generation to be laden with the burdens of war and oppression."

"I know, but that's what this is all about isn't it? This war, it's about making sure that there is a brighter tomorrow."

"But how?" she said, her voice cracking. "Barnin told you what he's seen, what Humans have done to other Humans. And the Iumenta, how many times have the Elves tried to defend us and the Iumenta just come back like some deathly fever? What happens when they cannot defend Humanity? What then?" she asked, not expecting an answer.

Keither looked down; Sara could sense his thoughts tumbling on themselves before he spoke. "I have gotten to know the Elves rather well over the years and also Legon. The Iumenta have proven that they will always be a threat. I do not think the Pawdin Empire is planning on letting that threat stand any longer."

"What do you mean?" Sara asked.

"Think about it, has the Pawdin Empire faced any real adversary in the Cona lands? Has the Impa Empire unleashed the full force of its power yet? Think love, you watched Legon train in Seeon, saw how hard he worked, his determination to get ready for the front. No, the fight hasn't begun yet, not for the immortals. No, the real war will start at Salez close to the Impa border, after months of wearing ourselves down, that is when the Impa Empire will truly start to fight. And after the Cona lands have been retaken, I would be very much surprised if the Pawdin Empire didn't continue to push in to Impa land. Sara you know Legon, growing up when he got in a fight, did his opponents get back up?"

A chill ran down her spine, she did know Legon; his restraint came from Sasha, without her he was an unstoppable force. After thousands of years of hostility from the Iumenta would Sasha stay her brother's hand? A voice almost like a whisper in her head said *no she wouldn't*. Memories of when Sara and Sasha had spoken of the war after Sasha's Ascension assaulted her mind. Sasha was never angry; never felt the need to strike out, but she did now. When Sara thought about it, she knew that both Legon and Sasha's anger was kindled against the Impa Empire. No, Sasha would not stay Legon's hand. With her at his side there would be no mercy nor rest for the wicked, not for those who had hurt so many for so long, and there would be no prisoners or slowness to action. Once the Heads of House Evindass returned to the Cona Empire, they would pour justice out on the land like a dam bursting.

Sara didn't say anything. Instead she held Keither's hand, looking out at Ripensis' skyline, praying as she had so often for the Everser Vald to come and cleanse Airmelia.

Sasha finished lacing her boots and placed her fenna Indigntio on her belt. She looked at herself in the mirror admiring Indigntio, its cream sheath matched its white handle. Her fingers ran along the handle and the gold filigree running up it. She would have never admitted it, but she always wanted a fenna. She thought they were beautiful; she always liked to look at Legon's fenna Tento. She suspected the reason she found them so appealing was her connection with Legon and his fascination with anything that was a blade, but nonetheless, over the years she had grown attached.

Her eyes moved to her reflection and she could help but notice just how different she looked. Gone today was her normal flowing dress; instead she wore dark leather pants and doublet. Her normally long hair was up in a tight bun and her red eyes shone. Today she had to admit that she looked like a warrior, almost frightening. She didn't like it. Sasha was not a warrior, was not violent; just the thought of herself in a fight made her sick to her stomach. She opened her connection with Legon more than it already was and the sick feeling in her vanished.

Edling walked up to her and rubbed her shoulders. "When it comes time for you to really fight, you will have the White Dragon's anger, remember?"

Of course she had told Edling about when she met with the White Dragon, how could she not? He needed to know. "I know and for that reason I shouldn't be worried, but it's odd. When I Ascended and Legon and I fought those Dragons ... it felt like it was me fighting but not really, almost like being in a dream. I felt no aversion in the least bit to killing and in truth I felt no guilt about it either."

"Why would you feel guilty?" Edling asked.

"Do you remember when I told you about how Legon and all of us were making our way to the resistance?" He nodded. "When Kovos was killed, we were in a clearing and all of us were fighting. I was in a full Mahann state and obviously thinking with only pure logic. At the time, I felt no emotion, no feeling of apprehension to hurting people. I was shooting my bow, and I didn't kill anyone, I just injured them. Anyway, at the time I didn't feel bad about what I was doing, but after -- when I had a chance to think about what had happened -- I would feel bad about hurting people, even if they were enemies. It didn't bother me a lot and whenever I'm connected with Legon it doesn't bother me ... but when I fought with the White Dragon's anger I felt no remorse afterwards, none, not a bit."

Edling frowned in thought, "Why do you think that is?"

"It's a perfect anger, I know that sounds odd to say, that anger can be perfect, but his is. It is perfectly just and therefore there is no need for remorse of any kind. Does that make sense?" she asked.

"Yes, being privy to your thoughts as I am it makes perfect sense to me, but what I don't understand is why you are worried now. If his anger is perfect and you will feel that anger only when it is appropriate, shouldn't you be comforted?"

She smiled and gave an uncomfortable laugh. "It's not using it that worries me, it's being worthy of the honor to use it that does. It's a lot of pressure, you know?"

Edling's expression changed; there was a light in his eyes. "That's it!" he said.

"That's what?"

He spoke in a rush, "You have not been able to use your full power yet, have you?" She indicated that she hadn't. "Oh, why didn't we see this before? You are putting too much pressure on yourself, don't you see? How could you use your full power if you think the only time you can is when the White Dragon is giving you his anger?"

"I'm not sure I follow ..." she said.

"We have been trying to get you to go full power when fighting; but you aren't a fighter, you have always been hesitant to fight, even with magic. If you are going to see that you are capable of going full power, it can't be with combat, or at least not at first."

Edling pulled her out of their apartment and past a confused Iselin. "Wait, aren't we supposed to train?" Iselin called after them.

Sasha could only manage a helpless look, she had no idea what Edling had in mind and he was keeping his thoughts closed off to her.

"Welcome to married life!" Iselin yelled.

Edling pulled Sasha into a giant storeroom in the Palace's basement. In front of her was a musty old sheet of burlap over something that looked to be thirty feet high. Edling pulled the fabric to reveal a crystal.

"Edling, that ... that is huge ... is it a Dome Crystal?" she asked.

"What gave it away?" he asked.

"Its size and shape; Dome Crystals are tall and rectangular, but other than that I don't know much about them, just that they are really powerful. Are you going to open up your mind now?"

"That I'm not. Look, this thing has been dead for years; most people don't even know that there is a crystal in the Palace basement. I want you to power it up, not a lot of power just enough to activate it with a small charge. Any class five can do it, but I think it could be a good object for you to practice on," he said in a rush.

"Are you ...," she began, still incredibly confused, "whatever you say ..."

She reached out with her mind and found the crystal. Every crystal had a minimum threshold of power that it needed in it before it could do anything. This crystal was empty. She pushed with her power and to her surprise she felt resistance. She pushed harder and still the crystal didn't seem to respond. Finally frustrated, she pushed as hard as she could, Sasha was a master of crystals and wasn't going to let this one get the best of her. As she pushed, something in her mind clicked. The magical power she was holding on to exploded in her, suddenly she found herself full of energy. The crystal in front of her flashed red and started to accept energy.

Sasha backed away, releasing her power, though she could feel it just under the surface in her mind. She turned to Edling who was bouncing on the balls of his feet and looked to a slack-jawed Iselin in the doorway.

"You found your power," Iselin said.

"I wha?" Sasha said.

Edling explained, "I'm sorry but I lied to you, only Ascended have the strength to activate a crystal of this size, you did it!"

"Wait, what? You lied to me?" she tried to sound annoyed but he looked so happy she couldn't quite put the menace in her voice that she wanted.

"How did you do that, Edling?" Iselin asked.

"I realized that Sasha couldn't use her full abilities because her head and distaste for fighting were getting in the way. But with a crystal … she doesn't see them as a threat, and I told her that a class five could activate it, so …" Edling explained.

"So you tricked me," Sasha said, and then felt inside herself. Now that she had done it on her own once without the White Dragon's anger she knew she would never have a problem again. "You're forgiven" she said to her husband. Then she turned to Iselin, "Come on, let's train!"

Iselin followed Sasha out of the storage room. She was having a bit of a hard time keeping up with her; Sasha was excited about being able to use her full abilities.

"Where do you want to train today?" Iselin asked.

"The training arena by the bay," she said.

Iselin was surprised by Sasha's choice. The inside of the bay arena was entirely water. It was designed to help Ascended learn to use the element of water in combat and then also to train them how to fight under water. Iselin continued to follow Sasha without commenting on her choice of venue. *If she wants to get soaked, what business is it of mine?*

Before them was the training arena. It was unique in that it was built into the bay; there were no high walls for the space, just towers around the perimeter holding crystals that rose from the water. They both reached out with their minds and activated stop all wards in the arena's crystals. Iselin transformed into her Ascended form and looked down at the tiny Sasha.

Sasha looked up at her, radiant. "Ise, don't hold back, I'm not going to. I'm going full power from the word go and I expect the same from you." Iselin saw a flick of ruby as Sasha protected her with a stop all. Iselin did the same and took off.

She didn't want to go full power against Sasha, the fight would be over before it even started and she didn't want to snub the girl's enthusiasm. But she couldn't really hide anything from Sasha either, so she was at a loss of what to do.

Legon's voice interrupted in her head, "Love, if she really can use her full abilities now, you are going to need to do everything you can to not lose, and she's an Elemental, in an arena of water."

What Legon was saying clicked and Iselin turned to see Sasha about fifty feet away from her. She was glowing red and flying through the air. The flying part didn't bother or confuse Iselin; all magic users could use spells to fly, though most couldn't sustain the spell for long. No, Sasha should be able to fly with ease as a class six. The thing that had Iselin worried was that Sasha's fenna was also glowing which meant the spell she was using to fly wasn't taking up much of her energy ... *She can use her full abilities!*

Sasha slashed at the water and Iselin rolled in the air just in time to avoid being hit by a chunk of ice the size of a horse. *And she's an elemental!* Iselin thought.

"I told you so," Legon's voice sounded smugly in her head.

"Quiet, I've never seen her be so aggressive!"

"Oh about that ... I'm giving her a little help on that front, do you mind?" Legon said.

He was helping Sasha so she could be more aggressive. Iselin thought about being mad but changed her mind. This was the only way Sasha could learn to fight; she needed her brother to give her the strength and confidence in mock combat. In real battle, she'd have the White Dragon's help. Iselin could live with that.

Iselin stopped in the air as Sasha sailed past her. Sasha turned just in time to raise her fenna up to meet Iselin's tail. There was a flash of crimson from one of Sasha's wards and a crack like thunder, and Sasha was sent rocketing through the sky by Iselin's blow. She righted herself and sent more ice at Iselin. *That was a weak attack; Legon is lending her the will to fight, but none of his skills. I'm going to have to push her to get her to try something new*, she thought.

Iselin sent five bolts of magic at Sasha. Being the small target she was Sasha dodged them all with ease, but in the time it took her to do so Iselin managed to get close to her again. Iselin snapped at her with her teeth sending Sasha retreating, trying to block with her blade. Iselin swiped with her claws and tail, completely catching Sasha off guard. Sasha was doing her best on defense but had yet to attack again.

"This is your weakness Sasha; in combat, your size gives you an advantage with long range but makes it impossible for you to attack directly in close quarters," Iselin explained.

"I can't get an attack off, what should I do?" Sasha asked.

Iselin took another swipe with her left paw while she thought, "Anything that will separate us, find a way to give yourself some room."

Sasha deftly blocked a few more hits and then to Iselin's surprise, Sasha came at her swinging her fenna. Iselin moved to block but Sasha didn't connect, instead she used Iselin's movement to move past her and then behind. Iselin spun in the air trying to face Sasha, but she couldn't. The small girl was too fast. Iselin heard and felt her wards being tested as Sasha attacked her from behind. Iselin faked a roll and caught Sasha off guard; again she hit her with her tail. This time Sasha didn't tumble through the air but just went sailing back.

Iselin gritted her teeth and charged Sasha, who responded by flying away from her, shooting freezing spells in the water, making columns of ice erupt from the surface. Iselin had to bob and weave to avoid the ice and then finally started using magic to clear a path. *You may be a class six, but your power isn't limitless,* she thought, knowing that soon Sasha would start to lose strength.

Iselin blasted ice from in front of her, revealing Sasha. Sahsa was launched in the air as she created a wall of ice. Iselin, ready to melt the ice, realized that they were at the edge of the arena. She pulled up, looking skyward at the tiny girl above her.

"FLAMMA!" Sasha yelled, sending a torrent of scarlet flames at Iselin.

Iselin opened her maw and breathed a bright pink jet of fire. The two magical flames met in the air and Iselin pushed against Sasha; Iselin was not going to be out-muscled by a hundred-and-twenty-pound girl. All of a sudden, Iselin felt no resistance as Sasha's spell stopped. To Iselin's right, out of the corner of her eye, she saw Sasha swinging her fenna close by. "Ignotis-aurium!" Sasha said.

Too late, Iselin couldn't avoid Sasha's most powerful attack. The spell hit the base of her neck and Iselin felt her own protective wards shatter. Her vision flashed crimson as Sasha's block all ward saved Iselin from what would have been certain death in a real fight.

The fight now over, Iselin hovered in the air looking at a gawking Sasha. "I … I defeated you." Sasha said. "I don't even feel that tired!" she added.

Iselin scowled. "We all keep forgetting you are a class six in an Elf's body; you have less area to guard and to move … it should be no surprise that you have more endurance than the rest of us, your body isn't taxing your power like a regular Ascended," Iselin said, shaking her head.

Iselin could tell the moment Legon weakened his connection with Sasha, her bravado faded and she looked concerned. "I'm sorry Ise, are you going to be all right? It was really mean of me to try to get you to run into the side of the arena like that, and thank you for helping me so much."

Iselin laughed, "Only you would apologize for exceeding your teacher's expectations. Come on little coward, that's enough for today; let's go home."

Sasha floated over to rest on Iselin's shoulders and they flew back to the Palace.

Chapter Sixteen
Tooth and Claw

"There's a thrill to battle, testing one's self against an unknown adversary that can bring some to joy; while to others it brings near crippling fear."
-The Exiled Captain (Author Unknown)

L egon glided in the air with Iselin and Opes on either side of him. On his back were Sasha and Emma. The day had come for them to leave Seeon and return to the war. They flew towards a Carrier named the Actuaries, she was new and this was her maiden voyage.

As he made his approach, Sasha's mind spoke to his, "What is so funny?" she asked.

"Do you remember the first time I tried to land on a Carrier?"

She laughed, "Yes I do, that was amusing."

This time as Legon came in close to the ship, he slowed and easily landed in the opening in the Carrier's hull. Each Dragon's hangar opened to the sea, allowing them to fly directly in or directly out. He heard the soft thuds of Iselin's and Opes' wings as they too landed in their own respective hangars. Once inside, Sasha jumped from his back and Legon used magic to lower Emma to the hangar floor.

"Are you going to stay in that form the entire time?" Emma asked him.

"Yes, Ascending takes energy; in this form I'm more able to handle any emergencies that come up," Legon explained.

"Un Prosa," somone in front said. "Welcome aboard. We are within a few weeks of reaching the rest of the fleet, please let me know if there is anything that you need while aboard," the Elf Captain said.

"Thank you, Captain. What do you think of her?" Legon asked, indicating the ship. He saw Sasha perk up a bit. The Actuaries was fitted with Sasha's new crystal technology and Legon knew she was bursting to find out what the Captain thought.

The Captain looked over at Sasha, his green eyes twinkling, and Legon thought he saw the hint of a smile. "Thus far Sir, she has been a dream come true, she is fast and about as nimble as a Carrier can be and as far as her magical capabilities go, she is everything that I could have ever asked for in a ship. I will withhold the rest of my judgment until she is tested in battle, but I dare say that House Insa has much to be jealous of," he said.

Legon saw Sasha beam at the praise. Legon suspected that the Captain was right; House Insa controlled the largest, most advanced and powerful Navy of all the Great Houses, and it was they that commanded the Pawdin Naval action in the current war. If the Actuaries was half of what Sasha and the ship's team of designers promised, House Insa would be jealous indeed.

After the Captain left, Emma frowned. "I didn't think there was any rivalry amongst the Houses," she said.

"There isn't," Iselin answered. "When we say jealous, we mean that the way you would be if a friend made a better cake then you did; you're not really upset, but rather looking forward to getting the recipe."

Legon stopped paying attention to Iselin's and Emma's conversation and looked out the enterance of the hangar to the wide open space of the ocean before him. The ship moved up and down with the waves and he found it relaxing. He closed his eyes, just listening to the sound of the water and the low buzz of conversation behind him. He closed his mind to all but Iselin's emotions. His mind was clear except for the sounds and smells of the ship and sea.

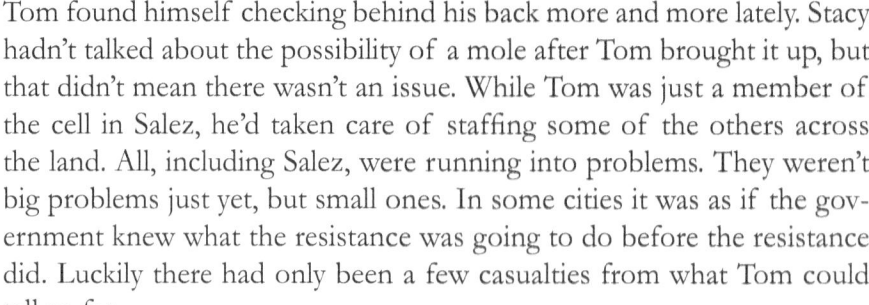

Tom found himself checking behind his back more and more lately. Stacy hadn't talked about the possibility of a mole after Tom brought it up, but that didn't mean there wasn't an issue. While Tom was just a member of the cell in Salez, he'd taken care of staffing some of the others across the land. All, including Salez, were running into problems. They weren't big problems just yet, but small ones. In some cities it was as if the government knew what the resistance was going to do before the resistance did. Luckily there had only been a few casualties from what Tom could tell so far.

As far as Salez went, Tom was finding that he had the hardest time with propaganda campaigns. He could feel the Iumenta Ascended working the people's emotions over. He'd found that his group's continued tactic of creating chaos by murdering key people wasn't affecting people as much as it should.

Tom looked up to the sky, feeling his mind being pushed on by the Iumenta above. He dropped his mental defenses, feeling waves of calm wash over him. There was no reason to be worried, there was no war … he brought his defenses back up. Again he was wracked with worry. A few people on the street paused as the Dragon flew overhead, some even looked around. *They're starting to feel the influence.*

He caught a glimpse of something out of the corner of his eye. *Same one as earlier* he thought. His tail was obviously not overly skilled. Tom kept on walking. He wasn't doing anything right now; when he needed to work, he'd lose the tail easy enough.

He made his way back to the shop. Inside Brian and Seth sat behind the counter, staring off into space.

"What's going on with you two?" Tom asked.

Seth shook himself, "Bleedin' Ascended, isn't it?"

"Aren't you blocking them?" Tom asked, wondering why Seth would allow himself to be influenced.

Brian snorted, "Tom, you can't be telling me you don't see what's going on out there, can you?"

He just raised a brow.

Seth spoke, "I was out last night, you know, up on the roofs doing some recon. Anyway, an Ascended came overhead. It didn't seem to care much about me, but on the street I saw the people's steps pick up a bit. So, I let down my defenses some. Sure enough, I felt pretty dang happy and safe. A few people looked around, wondering what gave and that's when I saw them."

"Who?" Tom asked.

Seth winked, "A couple Iumenta, they were watching the people."

"So?"

Brian spoke, "Come on Tom, think about it. What would they be able to see?"

Tom was about to say he didn't know and then it hit him. People who were noticing the touch of an Ascended would look around in confusion, people who didn't know would pick up their pace and look happier. But those who were blocking the Ascended …

"They are looking for people trained to block Venefica …" Tom was stunned.

"That's what we think. That's why we have been leaving our mental defenses down; it helps us to blend in better. You may want to do the same," Brian said and looked at the door as a customer walked in.

Laura closed the book she was reading. On the couch opposite her was Rachel; they were both enjoying the Palace library. Rachel looked up at her and a small smile touched her face.

"You like it here, don't you?" Laura asked, referring to the library.

Rachel put down the book she was reading. "Yes I do; it's not just the quiet of the place, but everything about it." She motioned to the bookcases that towered above them, "This room is quiet not for lack of company but because nothing in the room speaks with sound," she said.

"I'm not following," Laura said.

"The books -- even when I am the only person in here, I don't feel alone; I have the books for company. I know it's an odd sort of thing to say, but that's how I see this place. Anyway, when I'm in here I don't really feel threatened or sad; I can pick a volume off one of the shelves and be taken to a different place, a different life. There is no war or death or suffering."

"What do you like to read?" Laura asked, intrigued by the girl's point of view.

Rachel gave a small chuckle; something Laura had never heard her do. "It's embarrassing really, but children's stories. Compared to my life, there is no real conflict in these stories and everything is always happy and lighthearted, simple ... at the end of the story everything fits together into one small life lesson. Wouldn't it be nice if the real world were like that?" she asked.

Laura sighed. "Yes, yes it would be nice if that was the way the real world was. So, does it really make you feel better reading them?" Laura asked.

"Yes, you should try it," she said offering a small book.

"Oh, I'm not that stressed ..."

Rachel smiled again. "I see Un Prose Sasha gets her inability to lie from you. Your children are going off to war; right now they are likely on a Carrier that is going off to battle. You live in a city where people randomly die in the street and you are a Human in an Elf world, how can you not be stressed?" Rachel asked honestly.

Laura frowned. "You are a lot more observant and clever than I gave you credit for. Yes, I am stressed," she explained.

"I know that people try not to show how they feel around me. I understand and am touched. No one wants me to get upset. But I'm much better now, after months of being here I feel much more ... sane," she finally said. "Your son and daughter have done that for me, more so Legon than anyone, but everyone has shown me compassion and that has helped me come back from that dark place I was in when I was rescued. But please Laura, don't feel you have to hide around me, I may not be completely better yet – maybe I never will be -- but I assure you ... I know fear and worry; those were my companions for years, you can always talk to me."

Laura wasn't sure what to say to that, so she held out her hand and took the book Rachel proffered. As Rachel had said, it was lighthearted and Laura was surprised to find that as she let herself fall into the pages of the book, her worries did seem to vanish for a short time. The book was a collection of short stories and she read three before closing it. She looked for Rachel but the girl was gone, so enveloped had Laura been she didn't even notice that she was alone in the library. The light from the window at the end of the row where she sat was soft orange. The sun was setting and when she looked across the harbor, she saw the hill opposite the Palace crowned with the fire and golden rays of the sun. She breathed out and for the first time since the war had started, Seeon seemed to her as beautiful and magical as it had when she'd first arrived.

Tom had taken Seth and Brian's advice, letting down his mental guard enough to have his emotions influenced. He didn't like the thought of the Iumenta controlling him in any way, but it was better than being found out.

He stepped into an alleyway, keeping from being seen. He was tired of being followed and wanted to know who his tail was working for. Tom became the tail and as he suspected, the man he was following wasn't overly skilled. The man was trying to keep from being followed but not doing a good job of it. Still, Tom stepped lightly, not letting himself get lulled into overconfidence. The last thing he needed was to walk into a trap.

He followed the man to a small shop. The man walked in and Tom watched from a secluded spot outside. The man walked up to a woman and tapped her shoulder. She turned and Tom almost gasped in surprise.

The man was talking to Stacy, and she was speaking warmly to him. Tom wished he could use magic to hear what was being said, but Stacy was too far away and there were too many people around making noise.

They only spoke for a moment before the man left, but Tom felt his blood run cold. Was Stacy the mole? She couldn't have been. Arkin trusted her with his life, and she had almost died when Arkin was killed.

Another thought popped in his head. What if Tom's tail had figured out who Stacy was? What if she was in danger? Tom thought that more likely. He dashed across the street and into the shop. He walked up to Stacy, who jumped in surprise.

"Tom wh-" she started to say.

He shushed her, "Do you know that man?"

"Man?"

"The one who was just talking to you," he insisted.

Her face lit up, "Oh, no not really, he was just asking me if I'd like to go to dinner sometime. I told him no. Why? And why are you here?"

"This isn't a good place," he said pulling her from the shop.

Once on their own he explained to her that he was being followed and then he explained how he was now doing the following.

Stacy looked severe, "So this man works for the Iumenta, you think?"

"I would think so."

She nodded, "Right. We need to handle this discreetly and soon."

"How?" Tom asked.

Stacy smiled coolly, "Tomorrow allow yourself to be followed again. Go down by the markets."

"Then what?"

She smiled, but this time with her usual warmth, "Shop for dinner, just stay in the market."

The next day Tom did as he was asked and went to the market. Sure enough, there was his tail. Tom decided to play his role and started to look for things he needed. Soon he had several items and was wondering what Stacy was going to do. Tom walked by a group of draft horses harnessed to a cart with wine barrels. Tom talked to the peddler, trying a few of the drinks. Wine wasn't really his thing, but he was running out of things to do. As he moved along, he noticed his tail walk by the horses. One of the wine barrels toppled, startling the animals. They launched forward. Tom's tail tried to move out of the way but was knocked over by the horses. Tom spun with the rest of the people and watched in detached horror as the man was trampled by the horses and the cart pulled over him. When Tom turned again, Stacy was next to him. She looked at his day's purchases, "What's for dinner?"

A light rain pattered against the hull of the Actuaries. Legon gazed out the opening of his hangar at the gray sky. As a Dragon, his eyes were keener than as an Elf, and as such he could see the coastline in a haze of rain and smoke. They had made it back to the Cona lands. Little pricks of light were on the horizon as fires burned. Legon watched as the rain extinguished the fires, making them disappear in plumes of steam.

Emma came and sat down on Legon's leg. "Is it supposed to rain all day?" she asked.

"No, it should clear up in a few hours," Legon said.

"Are you going to fly any missions today?"

Legon sighed. "Yes we are; nothing too major tonight, just a standard patrol. What will you and my sister be doing?"

Emma looked a little confused. "I'm not sure exactly, I'm on a very need to know basis. All I know is that whatever we are doing involves water."

Legon laughed, "Live in fear, Emma."

"I do, so why isn't Edling here?" she asked.

"He would be a liability. In general, only one person in a couple will go to a war zone."

Before they could talk more, a group of Elves came in the room. "Un Prosa," one of them said, "we have been sent to help you with your armor."

Legon looked back down at Emma. "Sorry Em, got to go, unless you want to help me with my armor?"

She smirked. "Lifting giant pieces of metal, how fun! No thank you. I think I'll go hide from Sasha," she said as she walked away.

Legon really didn't mind wearing the armor all that much, it was designed to not limit his movement and didn't feel all that heavy on him. Still, he didn't walk around much in it as the plates on the bottoms of his feet made him sound like he was wearing tap shoes for giants. In the hangar next to him, Iselin was also putting on her armor. They were both excited; they'd trained together for years but never really fought alongside each other.

Legon made his way to the lip of the hangar's opening. The rain had stopped a while ago, giving the air a clear smell that Legon knew would disappear once they were over the coast.

He leaped from the hangar, opening his wings and driving them down; within a few flaps he was gaining altitude. Iselin, Opes, and a member of his guard were behind him. His mind was joined by the others and Sydin.

"Sydin, how are you? It's been too long," Legon said.

"Yes it has Un Prosa, how was your trip out here?"

"Peachy."

The group formed up in a standard V formation. Legon had learned that there was a lot that went into the Dragon formations. Because of the varying size of Ascended, based on what class they were, formations were set. The one they were in now was the most basic. As a class eight, Legon was in the lead. This was because he was the most powerful member of the group, but also the one with the least amount of speed and maneuverability. On either side of him were Sydin and Opes, both class seven, and bringing out the outside of the formation were Iselin and Legon's guard, an Elf named Pondos, both class six. If they got into a fight, Legon would directly charge the enemy, Sydin and Opes would take his wings and Pondos and Iselin would try to outflank their opponents. With the Iumenta being outnumbered in the sky, the Pawdin Empire had found formations like this one were giving them a significant edge.

They headed toward the coastline. Below them the sea rushed by as did Elvin and Human ships. As they passed over the beach, Legon could see the bodies of soldiers strewn along it. His nostrils filled with smoke as they flew over the city wall. Most of the city had been taken, with just the northeast holding on. Legon and his unit were just flying over the city on the way to their patrol route when to the north they saw three flashes of light.

"Three Iumenta Ascended to the north!" Sydin said.

Legon's formation turned and sped up. "Looks like three sevens," Legon pointed out.

As he said this, three more Iumenta jumped in, two of them class sixes and a class seven. Legon and his unit were now outnumbered but not about to back down.

Sydin took charge, "Iselin, Pondos, keep them off our backs, we will have to hold them until reinforcements come. Opes, you and I need to force them into Legon's line of fire. Legon, you focus on one opponent at a time, I want you to try to get in close, save your magic."

The Iumenta formed up in front of them, three sevens lined up with the sixes on the outside and just back a bit, the last seven was right behind the center Iumenta. Legon knew the technique they were going to use. The Iumenta were going to try to force Legon to fight more than one opponent, the first Dragon would try to expose Legon's back.

The two formations closed in on each other. Iselin and Pondos separated out from the formation, giving the appearance that they were going to try to outflank them. Legon bore down on the Ascended in front of him, its blue scales pulling light from the sky. It showed no sign of fear of the upcoming fight. Legon found himself looking forward to the conflict, his body vibrated with the desire to kill the thing in front of him.

Mere feet away from the blue Dragon, Legon folded his wing, rolling in the air as he passed the blue, he saw it trying to double back on him. Iselin and Pondos twisted in, converging on the blue Dragon as Legon collided with the red Iumenta that had been in the back of the formation. Its eyes were wide with shock as Legon plowed into it, driving out its breath.

The red tried to back away from Legon, sending a spell at him that cracked against one of Legon's wards. Legon pushed harder into the red Dragon, trying to gain purchase on it, he blocked a blow from the red's tail blade and grabbed on with his front paws. He pulled on its tail, un-balancing it in the air, Legon swung with his own tail. It hit the other Dragon's hind end, cutting down to the bone. The red twisted its tail away from Legon, but not before Legon got two more hits off with his tail.

Legon breathed pure fire with no magic in it. The other Dragons' wards blocked the flames with ease, but also impeded the Dragon's view. Legon closed in on the Dragon, finally able to lock in with him. They bit and clawed at each other and tried to bite the other's neck. Being locked together, they were losing altitude fast. Legon remembered that the key to his unit's formation was to stay in a tightly packed group. He broke away from the red and back-pedaled in close to the other Elves.

They were in a close pod with the Iumenta surrounding them, the red Dragon circling, giving itself time to heal.

"Legon, you can start using magic," Sydin said.

A green Iumenta seven was in front of Legon. *Inis,* a bolt of lavender lightning shot from Legon's front paw, colliding with a wall of green. There was a crack of thunder from the Iumenta's wards as Legon pushed with his lightning. The green Dragon sent an arch of emerald that smacked ineffectually against Legon's wards.

All of the Dragons were fighting with magic now, the sky strobed. Legon felt Iselin still fighting the blue Iumenta Dragon, she wasn't losing yet, but before long she would. In the first stages of the fight Iselin and Pondos had taken some hits, trying to ward off one class seven and two sixes.

"We need to even out the playing field," Legon said.

He felt the power in him well up into a ball that ran down his body, *Nu-close,* the ball streaked across the sky hitting the green Dragon. There was a blinding flash of light and a deafening boom as the spell hit. Legon felt a wave of heat from the explosion and saw the green Dragon tumbling back in the air, rivulets of blood spinning off its body from the many tears and burns now covering it. Its left wing in shreds, unable to steady its descent to the buildings below, Legon watched as it crashed into what he assumed to be a warehouse. He turned his attention back to the fight at hand, clearing his mind from the sudden loss of energy the spell had taken.

"Which one will have the most strength?" Legon asked.

Pondos responded, "The blue."

"Its mine, then," he said. Opes and Sydin engaged their own targets, while Iselin and Pondos went for the two class sixes. Legon twisted in the sky, making for the blue Dragon. It tried to evade him by flying down and away. Legon gave chase. Every time the blue Dragon would try and make a tight turn, Legon would send a spell in front of it, keeping it from out-maneuvering him. *He must be waiting for that green one to recover* he thought.

The blue came in close to the ground over the Iumenta-controlled part of town. As Legon followed, anti-dragon flack filled the air; he tried to dodge as best he could but took some minor hits. *Fine, if you won't fight in the air, we can fight on the ground.* Legon sprinted forward and sent another exploding spell, this one not as powerful, but right in front of the blue. Legon's plan worked and the blue Dragon was taken off guard by the explosion in front of it. Legon took the opportunity to make the air under the blue Dragon thin, making it drop a few feet and clipping a tree. The Dragon tumbled to the ground and Legon followed. He was going to land in a park controlled by the Iumenta; he had to end the fight with the blue Dragon quickly.

The blue Dragon tumbled on the ground but before it could recover Legon landed, driving his claws into the dirt *Toriso-vetis!* The trees next to the blue Dragon came to life, growing branches as thick as a horse, entangling the Iumenta. Legon became aware of Iumenta approaching behind him. There was a glow behind his horn as his familiar, Bill, detached as a ball of light that turned into a lion to defend Legon's back. The blue Dragon roared in pain and frustration as it tried to fight against the trees, their branches becoming sharp and piercing the blue Dragon, running it through. It gave a gurgled scream and bloody stakes jutted out from its chest and neck between its armor. Legon altered the spell, making the trees behind him swipe out at twenty or so Iumenta and sending them flying. Bill returned to Legon as he took off and headed back for Sydin and the others, leaving the dead blue Dragon behind.

Iselin and her unit were heading right for the group of other Dragons. She and Pondos moved out, away from the formation just a little bit to give the Iumenta the impression that she and Pondos were going to try to flank the other formation.

It was obvious what the Iumenta planned to do. The War of Generations taught both Elf and Iumenta not to mess around with class eight Dragons, Legon would be the main target. The Iumenta knew that if they didn't defeat or distract Legon, they would be in trouble.

She could feel her husband's thoughts; he was looking forward to a fight. Normally Iselin would say that he felt that way because he was a new Dragon, but the reality of it was, that was just her husband.

The two formations were on each other. She saw Legon dodge the lead Iumenta Ascended, a blue one that twisted in the sky. She and Pondos flew in on either side of the blue Dragon. Pondos slashed with his front paw and Iselin lashed out with her tail. Pondos made contact but she didn't. The blue Dragon turned on Pondos who was in closer.

The ancient and skilled Dragon fended off the blue Iumenta with grace and ease. Pondos was only a class six, but seasoned and had been in the house guard for Evindass for nearly six thousand years.

"I have this one Un Prose, focus on the other sixes," Pondos said.

Iselin turned in the sky to try to keep the two class six Ascended at bay. One was a sickly orange and the other canary yellow. Iselin needed to not focus on one Dragon, her job and Pondos' job was to keep the yellow, orange and blue Dragon away from Opes, Sydin and Legon so the latter could use his superior size and power in one-on-one combat. Iselin's hind leg exploded with pain as the orange Dragon smacked her with the spiked blades on its tail. She tried to ward off a few attacks and make a few of her own, but for the most part Iselin was just getting torn up. Pondos pushed the blue back and was able to help her a bit.

Iselin became aware of her husband severely hurting the red Iumenta and rejoining the group. She squared off with the blue Dragon as Sydin gave the group the go ahead to start using magic as a primary attack. Iselin's minor was Energent, meaning she was more naturally at ease with energy type spells -- jumping and things of that nature. Energent's are the most versatile of magic users, but at that moment, Iselin would have rather been an Elemental. Her ability to more readily control magical power was ineffective against a stronger adversary like the blue class seven she fought now. That didn't stop her from sending every spell she could at the thing. It, in turn, was bombarding her with spells.

Iselin was feeling rather happy with her performance with the blue Dragon when the sky lit up and there was a boom. Air buffeted past her and with it, a blast of heat. Legon had attacked the green Iumenta with a powerful spell, causing his adversary to cartwheel in the air. The blast disoriented the fight, both sides backing away from the other. Only Legon was unfazed as he asked which of the Iumenta was the strongest. Pondos said that it was the blue Dragon. Without argument, Iselin turned in the sky and attacked the orange class six.

They locked in the sky and Iselin felt her sides burn as claws raked down them, cutting into her. The wounds healed instantly and she tore into her opponent. They fell toward the ground and separated, breathing orange and pink fire at each other. Again they came together; this time Iselin received a scratch across her face that nearly pierced her eye. Iselin swiped at the orange Dragon's neck; it pulled back in time to only receive shallow wounds. They continued to fight back and forth, each taking and then losing the advantage. Her mind was aware of Legon using his most powerful attack and then leaving the ground. The orange Dragon instantly disengaged her, backing away in the sky, sending torrents of magical fire at her. Iselin let the Dragon go. All of the Iumenta were leaving the area; the green one was still unable to fight and now with the loss of the blue Dragon the Iumenta were not only outnumbered but outclassed.

Legon rejoined the formation. "Are we going to follow them?" he asked.

"No," Sydin responded, "we aren't, we are going to return to the Carrier. We are too tired for a full patrol."

Iselin could feel Legon's emotions, he wasn't happy. "What is it, love?" she asked, narrowing the mental network so they could talk privately.

"I wasn't much good today. I only killed one of them," he said sullen.

Iselin tried not to laugh. "Oh my, you forget that Dragons do not often die in battle; normally once they are badly hurt, they retreat. That is a victory, love. And today you severely wounded one Dragon to the point where it couldn't fight any longer; also hurt another one pretty bad as well. You did kill the blue Dragon, along with a mess of Iumenta ground units. So ... try not to beat yourself up too much, you know?" she said.

He laughed a bit. "I guess when you put it that way, I wasn't a complete idiot today," he said.

She decided not to comment on him saying "complete idiot."

Chapter Seventeen
Hurry Up and Wait

"Speed is of the utmost importance to an armed force, without it they cannot make it to a destination in enough time to wait an annoying amount of time for new orders."

-The Exiled Captain (Author Unknown)

Barnin and his units rode through the remains of a burnt and destroyed forest. For several days they'd been following the Pawdin Army, making sure that towns and villages were secure as the main army pressed on. He didn't enjoy playing clean-up and trying to suppress insurgency before it started wasn't easy or safe, but it was a lot better than being in conventional combat. When the war first started, his unit of new guys would have been disappointed at the prospect of months of not seeing what they would call "real combat", but after what they'd seen and dealt with thus far with the "not real combat," he figured none of them were looking forward to the real thing.

Thick smoke crossed the road and Barnin put a cloth over his mouth and nose. He was assaulted by the acrid scent of burning flesh. As they rounded a corner, the source of the smoke came into view. Before them were piles of burning bodies -- both Human and Iumenta -- heaped together. Barnin knew that there were no Human resistant forces fighting alongside the Elves, so no one he knew was in the piles, but he still found them hard to look at.

"Why don't they bury the dead?" said the commander of Barnin's youngest unit.

His name was Timothy and for the most part Barnin liked him. "I know that the spread of disease plays a factor," Barnin said, "but also the Iumenta cremate their dead, so I think in a way it's the Elves trying to be respectful."

They were past the piles and cresting a hill. Barnin couldn't remember the name of the town they were going to. Whatever its name was, the town looked bad. Smoke rose from several spots including a large stone building that Barnin assumed was the town keep. They made their way to the main gate which was ripped from its hinges; thus far all they spotted were Humans walking around the town's burnt surroundings. Inside the wall they found a lot more activity and to Barnin's relief, a group of Elves standing next to a cache of supplies.

Next to the supplies were the Elves' tents, they looked like giant leaves that had been folded into a Dome; he knew that any Elf could grow one of these tents in a matter of minutes. An auburn-haired Elf woman approached Barnin and his men.

"Good afternoon Commander, my name is Lele," she said in a calm, regal voice.

Barnin dismounted and addressed the woman, "Hello, my name is Barnin; who do I need to talk to about finding out what I need to do here, and where I should tell my men to sleep?"

Lele's eyes went out of focus for a moment. "You may talk to any one of the Elves here; we are from The Great House Viridi. We will be leaving to join our forces within the hour. If your men care to, they may use our tents, or they may take rest in the town's tavern," she said, still formal.

House Viridi, Barnin had heard of it of course, but didn't know anyone from it. He thought it was one of the Houses from the deep southwest; its people had almost no Human contact.

"Thank you; where are your forces headed off to?" Barnin asked, hoping he could maybe get some news of the front.

Lele looked confused for a moment. "Salez of course, to meet up with the rest of the Pawdin and Human Army," she was matter-of-fact.

"Oh, so the push for Salez is on then, I suppose we will be getting orders to head up that way soon."

Lele looked severe, "Yes, I dare say you will."

The look on her face bothered him. "Do you think it will be a hard city to take?" he asked. Barnin assumed that Salez wouldn't be easy, but it was so rare the Elves showed concern about a battle.

"Salez has long been a jump-capable city ..." her eyes went out of focus for a moment, "Forgive me, I have matters to attend to. We have provided food and some basic supplies. We have notified command that they will need to send more food here and a team to re-grow the fields. It was very nice making your acquaintance and I hope all goes well for you," she said and then walked away.

As all of the Elves left, Timothy leaned down from his mount to talk to Barnin. "What's a jump-capable city?" he asked, "And why is that a bad thing?"

Barnin shrugged. "I couldn't tell you about either," then he raised his voice, "Here's what's happening. House Viridi has been so kind as to leave us tents to stay in, also there is food for the people here. This spot is our Headquarters. Timothy, take your men out on the wall, I want a perimeter up. Ankle I want an assessment of the town. The rest of you set up camp here and fan out in the town in groups of three, looking for people who need help. NOW MOVE!" he ordered.

Using the Elves' old camp as a base of communications, Barnin used Heath to keep tabs on the groups of men as they worked on their various tasks. Barnin placed his pack and a few things in one of the Elf tents. When evening came, he slid in his sleeping roll, grateful for the sweet scent of the tent. He closed the flap and sighed. Thin though the tent's skin may be, there was silence inside of it for the most part. He fell asleep with the image of his wife safe back home in Manton.

Heath found Ankle laying on a tarp, staring up into the night sky. "Can I join you?" Heath asked.

"Go ahead."

"You look like you're thinkin' pretty hard there buddy, what about?" Heath asked.

Ankle laughed a bit, something Heath hadn't heard him do in a long time. "I'm thinking about pasta and what it tastes like."

"Pasta?"

"Like at my parents' restaurant back home. I'm trying to remember what it tastes like; it used to keep me grounded." He breathed out, "Before Mors I could always think of my father's cooking and it was like being at home again."

"What changed after Mors?" Heath asked.

"Rachel." Ankle looked at Heath, "After meeting her, whenever I think of home, I think about how she'll never have that. While I was eating and loving life, people like her were suffering in that awful place, you know?"

Heath felt cold. "Yes, I know what you mean, but ... but it's not your fault, you know? That those things happened to her and others."

"I know, but that doesn't change anything." Ankle changed the subject, "So what are you going to do when this is all over?"

"The war, you mean? I don't know, I haven't thought about it all that much, to be honest with you. I don't want to have dreams that probably won't happen. You?"

"I think you need something to look forward to. But I think I am going to go work for my father in his restaurant, I know how to cook almost everything in there," Ankle said.

Heath was shocked, "You know how to cook? How come I've never seen that?"

Ankle shrugged, "I haven't cooked in a while. When I was a kid, my dad used to make me help him in the kitchen and then once I joined the army, I stopped cooking. It bugged me that he made me help him when I was a kid, but now I think he knew something that I didn't."

"And what was that?"

"It makes me happy -- trivial as it may sound -- but those are some of the best memories I have," Ankle said.

"So cook me something," Heath said.

"What?"

"Cook me something … I helped look through the food the Elves left and they left a bunch of spices and other junk that no one around here is going to be using anytime soon, so make me something."

"No, I'm not going to cook for you, I'm not your wife," Ankle said, trying to close the subject.

Heath punched his arm. "Sure you are, now cook for me, woman! I'll make a fuss and then Barnin will make you cook for everyone."

Ankle mumbled something about killing Heath in his sleep but got up and walked over to the supply mound. He grabbed an armfull of supplies and walked over to one of the adjoining buildings where there was a kitchen. An hour later Heath sat down at a table and Ankle put a plate of pasta in front of him; it had some cream sauce and chicken covering it. Heath took a bite, chewed and swallowed.

"So?" Ankle asked.

"Five years!" Heath said.

"What?"

"I've been serving with you for five years, and this whole time I could have been eating this?! I don't know if I should be mad at you or just thankful that I can finally look forward to a decent dinner."

Ankle laughed hard, Heath could see months' worth of tension being drained from him. "I think your father was right, you are happiest doing this." It was true; not only did Ankle look better now, but when he was cooking the food, Heath watched years of stress leave the man. In truth, this was the happiest he'd ever seen his friend.

"I think you're right, maybe I should start doing this more," Ankle said.

"I think that would be a good idea. Now, can I have seconds?"

Almost a week after securing the town, Barnin and his men rode out of the forest enjoying the look of the wide open plains around Salez. When the order to go to Salez came, Barnin wasn't surprised. The city wouldn't be easy to take and the Elves and resistance would need every man available.

They were approaching from the southeast. Barnin could see the sprawling city with its white walls in the distance, but what he wasn't expecting was the lack of smoke or flashing magic on the horizon. That wasn't to say he couldn't see both Elf and Iumenta Dragons in the air; there were plenty of those, but they didn't look to be fighting much. As they got closer to the city, Barnin could see structures outside of the city walls. The closer he got, the more the buildings came into focus.

"Are those Elf buildings?" Heath asked.

"I think they are," Barnin replied.

As they drew in on fields of green-domed tents of the Elves, Barnin was shocked to see all that they had built.

"It's like a small city," Ankle said as they came into camp.

Another Human came up to them and pointed them to where they needed to go. They passed what looked like a hospital being grown and Barnin saw someone he knew.

Keither turned at the sound of his name being called. He smiled to see Barnin, Ankle, and Heath approaching him.

"How are you?" Keither shouted at them.

"We are doing good," Barnin said. When he got to Keither, he dismounted and shook Keither's hand. "How are you doing?" he asked.

"Busy, but that is pretty normal for us," Keither answered.

Barnin pointed around, "Hey what's with all the stuff the Elves built, and how long have they been here?"

"They came here about a week ago but construction really only started two days ago. Salez is a jump city so the Elves are counting on heavy resistance."

"What is a jump city?" Barnin asked.

"Do you know about jump crystals?"

"Yeah I've jumped before," Barnin answered and read the confusion on Keither's face. "Sorry, it's secret and I can't share, but what about it? Does Salez have a crystal?"

Keither nodded, "Two actually, most large cities have them, one is for incoming Ascended and another for outgoing. You have been out in the plains, so it's no surprise you haven't seen anything like this yet."

"So what is that going to mean for trying to take the city?" Barnin asked.

Keither tried not to huff or talk to Barnin like he was an idiot. "Well, the Iumenta will be able to bring more Ascended in whenever they like, and on those Ascended can be replacement units or supplies."

He saw something click in Barnin's head. "So we can't just wait for the city to run out of supplies, got it. Well, isn't this going to be just peachy." He looked around. "But still, what's with all of this?" he gestured to all of the buildings. "I mean, why not just stay in tents, and did they really build all of this in a few days?"

"Barnin, it could take months for Salez to fall; both the Elves and the Iumenta are digging in for a long fight, and honestly, we are too."

Keither was happy to see Barnin, but he was busy and he could see that Barnin had a lot of questions. "There is an Ascended I've seen you talking to, Umbra is her name right?"

Barnin's head bobbed, "Yeah, do you know her?"

Keither had an idea. "Yes, we met in Seeon"

He reached out with his mind, trying to find her. "Umbra?"

"Hello Keither," she answered sleepily, "How can I help you?"

"Barnin and his men just got here; do you want to show them around? Or are you too tired?"

———— ✌ ————

Umbra's mind flicked out to her hangar to check the time before responding to Keither. "No, I've overslept as is, but I need to stay in my Ascended form. Can you give Barnin, Ankle, and Heath directions to my hangar?"

Keither said that he could and Umbra got up, stretching her neck, legs and her favorite of all, her tail. She thought about having something to eat but decided she wasn't hungry just yet. One of Umbra's favorite parts of being in her Dragon form was that she did not have to get ready in the morning. She didn't have to pick out something to wear or do her hair or brush her teeth, no; she just woke up and started her day.

Her mind reached out to her hangar door and it slid open, spilling midday light inside, making her eyes water.

"It's past noon and you're just waking up?" a sarcastic voice accused.

How did they already make it here? She thought and then said, "I swear Barnin, I will eat you some day." She looked down at Barnin, Heath, and Ankle, "And for your information, I work through the night so noon is just fine, thank you very much."

Heath looked over to Ankle, "Right, and here this whole time we thought that the Elves were so dedicated and hardworking."

Ankle laughed and waved at her, "Come on guys don't be like that; we haven't seen Umbra in a really long time. Is that any way to say hi?"

"Thank you," Umbra said.

"You're welcome," Ankle said, adding, "She's just a big lizard and we all know how lazy lizards are; it's in her nature."

She lowered her head level with the three of them, trying to look upset, but Heath just looked in her eye and made a kissy face, "You eyeing me, sugar?"

Umbra lost her composure and started to laugh. "I have missed you guys," she said and added, "So do you want a tour of the camp?"

"Do you mind?" Barnin said seriously. "Joking aside, if you need sleep ..."

She looked more closely at him, seeing obvious signs of wear on him and the others. Her heart fell, seeing it in their eyes, they'd seen a lot in their short lives. "No I'm fine, really. When do you have to report in?" she asked.

Heath answered, tapping the side of his head, "We're checked in. We don't have anything until tomorrow."

"Good," she said, and reached her mind out to command. After a moment she spoke again, "We have clearance."

"For what?" Ankle asked.

"For me to give you a flying tour of the area. I told my command that you are mounted units and it could help if you knew the lay of the land," she said with a wink.

Barnin, Heath, and Ankle climbed onto Umbra's back. Barnin felt himself stick to her as she trotted along a wide path that connected the many hangars.

"Why aren't you just taking off?" Heath asked her.

"There is too much air traffic in this area, and with Salez being just northeast from here, we have to mind all of the Ascended in the sky. We are going to a designated take-off area, from there a ground unit will give me instructions so I don't cause any issues for other incoming and outgoing Dragons." she explained.

"So what happens if the Iumenta attack?" Heath asked.

"If there is an attack, we receive an order to scramble. If that happens, every Dragon that is on the ground will take off from their hangars to meet the threat. Sometimes scramble orders will come, but only for squadrons that are on alert."

"Alert?" Ankle asked. "None of this is making any sense to me," he added.

"Alert means that they are first responders, they sit waiting for a call to scramble. It shouldn't make any sense to you; everything is very catered for air combat and defense," Umbra said.

They were coming to an elevated platform from which Dragons of every color were taking off. Umbra stood in a small line until they were on the platform. A windsock blew alongside the platform, that Umbra said was there to tell her which way the wind was blowing. She leapt into the wind, driving her wings down. Barnin felt the all-too-familiar pull on his gut as he moved upward.

As they got higher, Barnin was able to appreciate the vastness of the base that the Elf and Human forces had built. He could also see lines of Dragons coming in to land in specified areas.

Umbra angled north towards Salez, which was taking up much of the horizon. The city was deceiving in its size; to Barnin it looked so close, but he knew that the Elves' air field was a few miles away from the city. He could see flashes in the sky around the city as Dragons fought.

"I thought we weren't attacking yet?" Barnin asked Umbra.

"You aren't. We, however, have to hold the air space above our units and base, and the Iumenta have to hold the air over Salez. The fighting you are seeing now is more posturing, no one is doing any real damage and neither side is putting effort into it. Don't worry about Salez right now, I want to show you something," she said.

They were getting really close to the city. Barnin wondered if they would get attacked soon, but Umbra didn't seem concerned. She directed their interest to the ground. She was perpendicular to Salez. Below them was the Elvin artillery. Until Umbra said something, Barnin wasn't sure what he was looking at. From the ground grew tall trees whose bases looked like the ends of tuning forks, there were no limbs or leaves on the trees, they stretched straight into the sky. From their tops were vines that touched the ground.

"What are they?" Ankle asked.

"They are our version of Trebuchet," Umbra said, a little smug.

"Can you explain?" Heath asked.

"Of course. You see those tall trunks of the tree are like the throwing arm, an Elf will grow the arm down to the ground where that vine you see will be attached to an ordinance. The arm will be tied to the ground and an Elf will tell the tree to straighten back out. Once the proper resistance in the arm is met, the tie keeping the tree to the ground is cut and then wham, just like a regular Trebuchet, the ordinance is hurled at its target," she explained.

"You grow your siege weapons onsite?" Barnin asked.

"Yes they take about an hour, and then another few for ordinances to be grown. Wait until you see how we take down the city gate," she said cryptically.

They flew away from the front and Umbra, true to her word to her commanding officer, showed Barnin, Heath and Ankle the surrounding country. The sun was setting when they started back for base. As they flew, Umbra showed them one last thing. Two mounded buildings rose from the ground at the back of the base; they were far apart but looked identical.

"These are jump sites. We brought two jump crystals up the Kayloose and placed them in these buildings," Umbra said.

They watched and sure enough, a Dragon flashed into existence above the eastmost building. Umbra explained that Elvin jump crystals were not as strong as Iumenta ones, but that because of the Elves' control of plants, they were able to sustain power longer than their Iumenta counterparts. What it meant was that an Iumenta crystal could bring in a lot of Dragons in a short amount of time, but then it would run out of energy; whereas the Elves' crystals couldn't work as fast but they never ran out of power.

"I thought Dragons had to use energy to jump," Heath said.

"We do most times. Like when I was bringing you back from Mors, I had to provide nearly all of the energy for that jump and even then I had to be in range of the crystal. This is also the case for the crystals in cities; they act more as guides for Ascended. But in combat, you don't want to drain all of your power jumping into a fight, so we can augment our own strength with that of the crystal. When we siege Salez, their jump crystal will be doing nearly all of the work when they bring in Ascended. The two crystals the city has will be powerful and if the Iumenta are wise, with that kind of energy they will be able to bring in a lot of units if they need to, or vice versa; they will be able to evacuate a lot of units."

"Do you think they will do that?" Heath asked.

"Evacuate? Yes, when the city's air space is about to fall they will jump all key people out of the area. Once we control the space over the crystals they will no longer be able to use them; a crystal only guides Ascended into a very small area of space, or conversely will guide an outgoing Dragon out of a small area of space. Once the sky above is controlled, the crystals are all but worthless to the Iumenta. Only in very rare and desperate cases will Iumenta try to come into an area or flee once the crystals have been compromised. Still, our first priority as Ascended is to destroy those crystals," Umbra said and seemed to pause.

"What is it?" Barnin asked.

"I'm trying to find a nice way of saying this. You see the fight on the ground -- while important -- won't decide victory; whoever controls the sky, controls the ground."

Barnin knew what she was saying, "Don't worry about it. We don't take offense to that; we know how battle works. If you didn't control the air, we wouldn't be able to control the ground. It's the same with the

navy, until they control the coastline, there isn't much good in us getting ourselves killed on the beach, you know what I mean?"

Umbra came in low to the ground on her approach, banking slightly left and right to slow herself. Barnin always found landings to be the most relaxing on a Dragon. The sun was going down and the Elvin base lit up with magical lights. Umbra seemed to be following a lit path, culminating in a landing pad that she touched down on.

"Thank you for the tour," Barnin said, once he dismounted.

She winked at him. "Any time ... hey," she said and paused, "the battle is going to start in a few days ... it's going to be long and bad. In your downtime if you ever need someplace to go, you're always more than welcome in my hangar," she told the three of them.

Barnin nodded, taking what she said to heart. Despite the joking tone they had with Umbra, all of them knew how experienced she was in combat. Barnin headed toward his tent, not looking forward to the days, weeks and probably months ahead.

Umbra watched Barnin, Ankle, and Heath leave. As soon as they were out of sight, she made her way back to the take-off pad. She'd spent too much time with them that day and she still had to fly her patrol, but she didn't regret it. Experience had taught her to enjoy downtime in war.

She took off with the sun almost completely set. She was one of three from her squad present at Salez and she connected with her companions.

"What do we have for the night?" she asked.

Tacita, Umbra's second in command answered. "We are staying in a team tonight, cleaning up the countryside if we can. Command wants to control supply routes in and out of Salez," she said, her voice soft and wispy.

"Festina, Tacita form up in a V, I'll take lead," she said.

Her mind was touched by another Dragon. "This is Lamma, with Salez squad eight, we are three class sevens," she said.

The Elvin Ascended assigned to the Salez base were broken up into squadrons, each with a squad leader and four other units. Lamma was stating that she was in charge of squad eight and that the units with her were all class seven.

"I'm Umbra, stealth squad, one seven, two sixes," she said and added, "Any on the ground?"

"Two sixes on the ground, both on alert," Lamma said.

Umbra spoke to her squad, "We have friends in squad eight, they are short two that are on alert." Tacita and Festina said they understood and Umbra addressed Lamma, "Good to know you're there; are you to engage ground targets or only Ascended?"

"We have clearance for ground and air targets but would prefer the latter. What are you sweeping for?" she asked.

"We are on the lookout for ground targets tonight, but if we are lucky we will find some Iumenta stealth units. We know they have some here, we have been playing cat and mouse for almost a week now."

"Understood, we will watch our backs; let us know when we can be of assistance."

"Will do"

"Happy hunting," Lamma said and broke off the connection.

Umbra focused on looking for caravans and convoys as she hugged the ground. Tacita and Festina were on either side of her, allowing them to cover a large area. To the north were the main Impa and Cona Empire forces; they were being fed by large supply lines that had Iumenta Ascended flying patrol. Umbra would avoid those areas and try to concentrate on smaller parties that were out of the way.

There wasn't a lack of activity below her, but it was figuring out what was a target that was hard. The countryside around Salez was clearing out as people left the area, wanting nothing to do with a battle. Refugees clogged roads and bridges, along with any paths they could find out of the area. She glided over camp after camp without being seen or heard. If there were any hostiles in the area, they were blending in well. She was looking at a small camp when she saw it; just a shadow in the sky to her left.

Her head snapped around as she connected with her squad and Lamma's, "Possible contact. I think I saw an Iumenta stealth unit just west of us."

"What do you want us to do?" Lamma asked with a little unease in her voice.

"Go high and watch yourselves, we will try to pin down the Iumenta and give you directions from there." Lamma took her ascended higher and Umbra scanned the horizon. Finding stealth units was most Dragons' least favorite thing to do. It wasn't easy and even with all her years of practice; Umbra only occasionally would find an Iumenta stealth. But Umbra loved the chase as did her entire squad; after all, this was the game they played best.

Tacita spoke. "I have it!" she said relaying her thoughts to Umbra and Festina.

"Do you want us now?" Lamma asked.

"No," Umbra said, "it could get away, let us pin it down first." She addressed Festina, "The Iumenta is northwest of here, go north and see if you can get ahead of it."

Festina sped up, leaving the formation. He was the fastest in Umbra's squad and ideal for interception assignments.

Umbra and Tacita stayed on the Iumenta's tail, closing in on it, from what she could tell, it wasn't aware of them yet. Umbra instructed Lamma where she needed to go and that the Iumenta would come to them. Umbra closed in on the Iumenta, it was a class seven. She and Tacita could take it out, but she wasn't sure that was a good idea. It was a fair bet that the Iumenta wasn't alone in the area. Tacita dropped back, circling around and making sure that Umbra's team wasn't flying into a trap.

"I'm out in front, what do you want me to do?" Festina asked.

"Slow up, cross its field of vision and head east toward Lamma and her squad. I told them to get in close to the ground and take cover. When you pass overhead with the Iumenta, they will take off and engage."

Festina acknowledged his orders and allowed himself to be seen. Festina had to be careful, he couldn't be obvious about being seen, the Iumenta had to think that it got lucky. The Iumenta changed course to follow Festina. Umbra fell back some, making sure the Iumenta wouldn't detect her.

Festina passed over the hill where Lamma and her units were hidden. As the Iumenta flew over, Umbra saw flashes of red, blue and brown as her units shot spells at the Iumenta. There were cracks of thunder as the Iumenta's wards blocked the magic. It turned in the sky to see three Dragons coming at it. Festina turned to cut off the Iumenta's retreat.

"Tacita go up! We need to get above it!" Umbra ordered.

The Iumenta wasn't trying to fight, but rather just making an attempt to get away. Umbra pushed as hard as she could to get high up in the air to cut off the Dragon's retreat. Festina was doing likewise and was shooting up; Umbra took comfort knowing that Festina would be able to easily outstrip the Iumenta.

"Contact!" Tacita yelled across the connection. "South, three Ascended," she said as Umbra turned to see three Iumenta Ascended making their way to Lamma and her group. *Of course, the stealth had support,* she thought.

Umbra and Tacita dove down toward the Iumenta. "They don't seem to know we are here," Umbra told Tacita. "Come in behind and on top of them, there are two sevens and a six. I should be able to take out the six and we can hold the other two until Lamma can assist." Umbra knew that she needed to be fast with the six. If she could break its neck right away, she could focus on other targets. It was rare for Dragons to get in that close undetected, but this was how most of the stealth squad made its kills.

Umbra came up fast on the tails of the Iumenta, who were almost in range of Lamma and her units. Umbra was all but on top of the Iumenta six when it noticed her, but too late. She struck like a snake, biting the base of the Dragon's head. Umbra twisted in the air, snapping the Dragon's neck. It fell to the ground.

A teal Iumenta turned on her. Unlike Umbra, the Iumenta were in full armor and she dodged his tail blade, unable to block it with anything. It lashed out again and Umbra closed the gap between them, taking a swipe at it with her front paw. Her hind leg screamed in pain as the other Dragon clawed her and hit her with its tail. She got in a few shots of her own before she started to use magic to fight.

She didn't have to fight long, as a jet of ruby fire made contact with the Iumenta. Lamma and her team had killed the stealth Iumenta and were coming to assist Umbra and Tacita. Festina was coming in too when Lamma's voice rang out, "Good work, stealth squad we'll take it from here."

Tacita and Umbra didn't need to be told twice. They regrouped with Festina, watching Lamma and her fully armored squad take out the two remaining Iumenta Dragons. When they were done, Umbra and Lamma's teams turned back for base, spent for the night.

"I owe you dinner," Lamma said to Umbra.

"Oh, why is that?"

"I had a squad member get taken out by the Impa stealth squad. I've been wanting payback for months now. I contacted base, we have permission to take our Elf forms for the rest of the night, if you feel so inclined."

Umbra smiled, "I think I do feel inclined."

Chapter Eighteen
The Calm before the Storm

"When I look back at what it was like back then, I think the times of greatest discomfort were just prior to battles. I may not have been a warrior on the field, but never the less my heart flew in the azure sky above and trod on the turf below."
-Diary of the Perfectos Compatioa

Legon did a final check on all of his gear. Sasha entered the hangar with Edling, who'd just jumped in. He turned to look at them. Sasha was clad in the standard Elvin armor with her hair up in a tight bun. The look didn't suit her but Legon chose not to comment on it. They were going to be jumping to Salez and while Legon wasn't happy about it, he knew Sasha would probably see combat.

Reading his thoughts, Sasha commented, "I'm not happy about it either, BUT remember, I will only fight if I feel the White Dragon's anger. Besides, when I'm like that it doesn't really feel like me, you know what I mean?"

"No, I don't," Legon said. "But based on the look on your husband's face he isn't real thrilled about you going off to siege Salez either," he pointed out.

"It's not that," Edling piped up. "I want to come to the front."

Legon gave his brother-in-law a look.

Edling rushed on, "I'm not going to fight. But when Salez falls there will be Iumenta crystals left behind, I could be of some use, we need to learn everything we can," Edling argued.

"He's got a point, Sash," Legon said.

Sasha crossed her arms, "And what if he gets hurt?"

"He'd be far away from the front; really he wouldn't be in any danger unless we got overrun," Legon said.

"That's not the point," Sasha said.

"Umm, you guys do know that I'm in the room and I'm not a kid, right?" Edling said, looking put out.

"Shh," Legon said, "Let Mommy and Daddy talk." Edling scowled and Legon went on, "Sasha, he could be useful and we are going to be at Salez for a long time. Do you really want to go that long without seeing your husband?" Sasha was about to argue when Legon butted in, "Look, if he stays on the Carrier he will have a higher chance of getting hurt. Once we leave, they are heading north, they will be fighting the Impa navy. But if he comes with us ..."

Sasha looked over at Edling and sighed. "Fine, but Legon is taking you. I will ride with Cynta and Emma can go with Opes," she closed the subject by walking away.

Edling mouthed, "I owe you" to Legon.

"I can read both your minds!" Sasha yelled from the hallway and Edling rushed off.

Legon could hear Iselin laugh in the hangar next to him, "She is so funny when she's trying to be upset."

Legon agreed.

When it was time to leave, Edling came in Legon's hangar. He was in his traveling clothes and looked nervous.

"You all right?" Legon asked.

Edling nodded, "Yes, I'm not scared to fly; it's just the whole ..."

"Your first time going to a battlefield?"

Edling said it was and Legon did his best to try to placate Edling's fears. Edling climbed onto Legon's back. Legon looked out of the opening in the hull and the rushing surf below him. He walked up to the edge of the opening and asked the Carrier for clearance to take off. When he was told to take off, he leapt out of the opening, driving his wings down, moving up in the air. He climbed as his guard formed in a star behind him. To his right was Sydin, and to his left Opes with Emma. There were two others with them, Mage and the rest of his guard on the other two Dragons' backs.

Iselin took off as Legon and his formation circled. Iselin had a guard similar to Legon's. They were followed by Cynta with Sasha and her guard. The three formations floated in the sky and prepared to jump. Carriers held jump crystals in them and Legon connected to the ship's crystal, as did the rest of his guard. He started his count down, *four* he connected with the crystal, *three* Legon locked in on his destination, *two* he felt Edling's uneasiness, *one* his wings closed in and he saw lavender light, *jump.*

Legon's wings snapped open and his lungs filled with dry smoky air. Below him was the sprawling base at Salez. The rest of his guard was still in formation and Iselin and Sasha's groups materialized behind them. On Legon's back, Edling shifted.

"I've never seen the plains of Airmelia before," Edling said, "and Salez looks so large ..."

"Salez is big, but not unlike many of our cities, the openness of the plains make the city seem bigger," Legon explained.

Then he was contacted by the base's ground control. He followed their directions, heading to the part of the base that was designated for House Evindass. He turned into the wind on his approach. Tents raced by below as he slowed, heading toward a landing pad.

Elves were starting to come outside, no doubt informed that the Everser Vald had arrived. As Legon came close to the ground he could hear people cheering and chanting.

"Whoa there, big guy, are you all right?" Edling asked. He was connected to Legon's mind and could feel Legon's nerves.

"Don't worry; I'm not concerned about landing ... I just feel uncomfortable with lots of attention," he said.

Edling laughed, "Look at it this way, you're going to have thousands of years to get over it."

"Thanks."

Legon came up on the landing pad and reared up, coming in and touching down. Without the wind rushing by, Legon could hear just how loud the people were, and he had to admit a very small part of him liked the attention.

Sara looked out at her old home. Were any of her old co-workers still alive? Probably not, she thought. It had been years since she'd walked the streets of Salez, since she'd woken in the morning hoping to find out it all was some nightmare. The city looked a little worse for the wear since she'd left. Its once bright white walls were now dingy. *I suppose there isn't any point washing something that's going to be under attack soon, is there?*

Slightly below her were ranks of soldiers preparing to hold the front line. As her gaze swept the faces she was struck by their youth.

"Were we that old when we were thrust into this war?" Keither asked, coming up next to her.

"No," was all she said.

They turned around and made their way back to the medical center where Sara worked. She was not in charge of the facility but rather the Elves were. Still, Sara had a large team she was responsible for, but for the first time her responsibilities didn't involve inventory.

A healer named Jenny bounced up to her. "Ma'am, is there anything you need me to do?" the girl was young, right out of training.

Sara smiled, "Rest; soon you will have plenty to do."

Jenny gave her an odd look but did as she was told and plopped down on a cot to take a nap. *Sleep tight today because soon, sleep will be the last luxury you get.*

A familiar voice called her name and Sara turned, "Hey Ankle, how are you?"

Ankle limped up to her and frowned, "Sorry Sara, but I twisted ... well ... my ankle, can you take a look at it?"

Sara fought not to smile and instead directed him to sit down. "How'd you get hurt?" she asked.

"Playing ball. It was stupid but I need to be in top shape for tomorrow ..." he said and trailed off.

"Oh, so it's tomorrow then," she said, all of her previous amusement leaving her voice. Sara wasn't in the loop on when the army was going to start its assault on Salez. She figured most of the base wasn't in the loop either, but Ankle was an officer, so of course he knew. "Don't worry, I won't say anything," she said, reading the look of worry on his face.

"Thanks, I'm just so used to you and Keither being more informed than I am. I forget you aren't running this center."

She was feeling around his swollen ankle and didn't look up. "It's so nice not to be in charge, let me tell you ... hmmmmm you're not hurt badly; you'd be fine in a few days, but I'll take care of it," she said and muttered a spell. Silver light bathed his leg and Ankle turned his foot around.

"Thanks Sara," he said, standing up.

"So why didn't you tell Heath you were hurt?" she asked.

Ankle smiled. "What, and give him the satisfaction of besting me in a game? No thanks. See you," he said, trotting off.

"Men."

———————— ⟨⟩ ————————

Tom was losing people left, right and center. He couldn't figure out how. But it was a problem he needed to solve. The Pawdin Empire was at the doorstep of Salez and Tom couldn't afford to have problems at the moment. But everything he was doing was turning into a bust. He hadn't been followed since Stacy had killed his last tail, but that wasn't to say that he was comforted. If anything, she scared him now. She'd had a man trampled to death and it didn't seem to affect her.

Stacy aside, Tom had had more than enough with people getting killed. He knew that they had a mole and he was going to find out who it was. There were only four people in their team, four people who Tom himself had recruited. There was also a handful of others from other teams that he knew of in different cities. So he was digging, rechecking everything he knew about everyone. It wasn't an easy task. Like Tom, all of the members of the teams tried to hide their past lives, but still Tom was making headway. He'd managed to clear most everyone that he had brought on.

He'd started with the teams outside of Salez first. He wasn't able to find anything that spoke to anyone being a threat. He was now onto the Salez Team. Tom didn't want to think that anyone in his team was the mole, but prudence dictated that he make sure.

He walked back into the shop, seeing a bit of folded parchment on the counter. He reached down and read it. It was one of his only remaining contacts. The contact, named James, said he'd found something important. Tom needed to meet with him right away. He was about to burn the paper when it hit him. James' note shouldn't have been on the counter, nor should it have been open. That could only mean one thing …

Tom ran from the room. The mole was in Salez. It was one of the people he'd spent every day with for years, but who? Tom didn't have time to think about it, he had to run and run fast. James was in trouble. He knew where James worked and rushed there just as the sun set.

He could see the street he needed to turn down. As he got closer, he noticed people walking away quickly, looking uncomfortable. His own emotions darkened. He wanted to not be here. He wanted to go some place else. The emotions were not his own.

Tom entered the mind of a dog on the corner. He directed the dog to look down the street, which was empty. From a shop, a man came bouncing out, not seeming worried in the least bit. It was James. Tom was about to reach out with his mind to James when the form came from the shadows in front of James. The dog jumped and Tom lost sight of what was going on.

He reached for James' mind and found nothing. Tom pressed himself against a wall, wondering what to do. To his right an Iumenta walked by, coming from the direction of James' work. Tom saw the flash of a crimson coated blade being put in a pocket.

A woman screamed in the street. Tom walked away, not needing to see James to know his fate.

Emma found Sara and Keither at their barracks. They looked tired but happy to see her when she came in.

"Em, how are you?" Keither asked, trying not to sound tired.

"I'm good; is it too late? You two look tired," she said.

Sara waved her off, "Tired is a way of life and the sun has barely set. We can sleep tonight."

Emma looked down without thinking.

"We won't be sleeping tonight, will we?" Keither said. "I thought the attack was tomorrow."

"So they told you, I take it?" Emma said.

Keither sighed, "Yes, I just got back from a meeting, but why aren't we going to sleep tonight?"

"The Ascended will attack tonight. They are the first wave. I think Sydin only told a few of the higher ranking Human command about it," she explained.

A tea kettle started to whistle behind Sara and she took the pot off a small silver fire that went out. "Tea?" Sara offered.

Emma joined them and they talked for a while. It was tense like all conversation had become and Emma longed for a time when the only thing that worried her was if Kovos was going to fall out of her window. But those days were gone. She knew that her life would never be like that again, and in some ways -- though it pained her to lose that innocence -- she preferred her new life.

They heard a thud outside and went to investigate.

Salez shone bright on the horizon, almost peaceful. Emma looked up to the sounds of wings, seeing Ascended upon Ascended pass overhead, armor glinting off the light of campfires. A chill ran down her spine and she noticed Sara take Keither's hand.

In the distance Emma heard a siren sound.

"The Iumenta know what's coming," Keither pointed out.

Yes, Emma thought, she knew that sound. It was not unlike the siren she'd heard on the Carrier, the order to scramble, the warning that an attack was coming.

"What's going on?" Keither asked Sara, and Emma turned to see Sara's eyes had a silver film over them, she was enhancing her vision.

"The Iumenta that were flying cap are falling back, I think to group up. The Pawdin forces are midway between our base and Salez. I can see the Iumenta now but I can't tell who has more Dragons, there are so many on each side."

Then the night sky flashed with magic and Emma didn't need Sara to tell her any more. Magic in every color and shade imaginable streaked across the heavens, exploding and booming. Fire lit up the night and the sound of roars and metal on metal could be heard as the two groups of immortals met.

From the forward edge of the base Emma heard the groans of trees as the Elves fired their Trebuchets and other siege weapons. The missiles burst into flames once airborne, arching across the sky to smash into wards just outside of Salez. She saw similar projectiles come from Salez to break apart on Elvin wards being maintained by Pawdin Ascended on the ground.

Emma looked up again to see that the battle above was raging ever harder. She tore her gaze away from the sky, feeling her head start to hurt from the sound and flashing light.

She looked at Keither, a grim look on his face. He spoke in a near whisper, "And so the battle for Salez has begun."

Chapter Nineteen
Breach

"What is security? Is it knowing that you will be safe at home as you sleep? Or is it something else...is it just an illusion we play on ourselves to think everything is OK?"

-An Island of Sorrow

Legon looked down on the burned field that separated the Pawdin army and Salez. The week following the Elves' attack had seen no progress for either side. He flew above the ever steady stream of fire from ballista, catapults and Trebuchets. The Pawdin line glowed with wards of Ascended who stayed on the ground protecting artillery. He looked at the once-white walls of Salez. Wards now only stopped a portion of projectiles; the Iumenta saved the magical power of their Ascended for battle with almost all of the power from store crystals fueling the city's jump crystals.

Legon re focused on what was ahead. Before him was the air battle that had been going at a constant pace since he and the other Dragons first attacked. At any given time, there were around fifty Ascended in the air fighting, and now he would join the melee for the day.

"Un Prosa, how would you like to proceed?" Opes asked him.

Legon thought for a moment and responded, giving orders to his squad. "Fly ahead of me and try to engage targets. Once you have someone engaged, I will come in and take over," he said.

He'd found that the Iumenta Dragons were giving him a wide birth, making it hard for him to fight. Iumenta would attack him and after a few blows would back off to let another Dragon take a shot. It wasn't that Legon was taking a lot of damage, but that the attacks wore him out and kept him from being able to do any real damage himself. His squad would try to push targets to him, but as soon as he started using magic they would retreat. *Not today,* he told himself.

Opes flew ahead of him, taking on a blue Iumenta. Legon faded back, taking his time approaching the Dragon. He feigned an attack on a red class six, allowing himself to get in close to the blue Dragon. The blue Dragon was right below him when Opes spoke, "NOW!"

Legon dropped in the sky, the blue Dragon not even having time to turn in the air to defend his back. It felt cowardly to Legon to fight this way, but he didn't see himself having a choice. He landed on the blue Dragon, who tried to twist. Its back spikes glanced off of the heavy metal on Legon's feet as he tried to grab onto the blue with his front paws. The Dragon's head turned and bit at him. Legon slapped his tail blade into the blue's hip. In the blue's moment of pain, Legon was able to get purchase on the blue's shoulder and he breathed fire on the Dragon's neck and head. Wards blocked his flames and Legon felt himself descending.

Opes and the rest of Legon's guard were circling around the two Dragons trying to keep the Iumenta from helping their comrade.

"Anytime, Legon!" Opes said.

"I'm getting to it!"

Legon was loath to use up too much magic this early in the day, but he didn't have a choice; the ground was coming up fast. He felt the well of power deep within him, letting it bubble in his gut, and spewed forth a stream of amethyst flames that engulfed the blue Dragon's head. Legon felt the blue's wards blocking him but soon they buckled under the pressure of Legon's magic. Legon let go of the blue Dragon, its head a mass of charred bones. Its body fell toward earth as Legon tried to engage another enemy.

Barnin felt a rain drop hit his cheek. *Wonderful,* he thought. *More rain.* Another drop hit him, followed by others. He turned on his mount to look at Heath who was looking up at the clouds.

"Do you remember what it's like being dry?" Heath asked, as it started raining harder.

"Feels like it's been forever, doesn't it?" Barnin said.

There were rumbles in the distance, along with flashes of light; Barnin had no idea if it was from lightning or Dragons. The rain was starting to come down hard. Barnin couldn't see far ahead of himself and the sound of the downpour made it all but impossible to hear anything.

He came up next to Heath and yelled. "We need a network," he said, hating what he was asking for.

"You sure?" Heath confirmed.

"Ya, I hate the mind talk junk but it's not worth lives."

Barnin felt his mind join with Heath's and then the rest of his men. Several of them shied away from the contact but didn't sever it.

They were in the nearby countryside of Salez, making sure the Impa and Cona Empires couldn't flank the resistance and Elves. He told his men to stay sharp. The Elves were in control of most of the air space outside of Salez, but when the weather took a turn for the worse, the Dragons didn't fly. It was during these times when ground units would try to move in on the area.

Barnin rode, keeping close tabs on all three of his units. He knew at some point they would run into resistance. It was just a question of when and who. Poison, his mount, splashed along, her hooves making slurping sounds in the mud. A nearby creek had burst its banks early in the week, turning the field they were entering into a sort of shallow lake.

Barnin's eyes strained to see across the field and his heart dropped. From the other tree line was a group of figures running at them moving as fast as horses.

"IUMENTA!" he yelled across the network.

His units clumped together drawing swords. Barnin looked at a large group of Iumenta, their fenrra drawn, bearing down on them. When they were twenty feet away, Barnin saw a flick of orange that became a ball of orange magic that flew from the sky, striking the ground in the heart of the Iumenta formation. Barnin was blinded by an explosion and despite the magic protecting him; he felt a blistering wave of heat and steam. His eyes focused again; the field in front of him was shrouded in steam. Before it could clear, there was another flash of light, this time purple and coming from the other direction. The air rent like thunder as he saw more orange and purple streak the sky.

Two Dragons came into view - an orange Elf and a purple Iumenta. They were clad in armor and met above Barnin's men. His face was peppered in blood from one of the Dragons. He looked down, seeing more blood that was not his own. Crimson covered him and his dazed mind remembered the Iumenta. His head snapped to where their formation had been; the steam was clearing and a few were left alive, recovering from the orange Dragon's spell.

"Charge!" he ordered.

No one hesitated. He spurred on Poison. As he reached a staggering Iumenta he removed its head. Time was not something they had a lot of; once the Iumenta's shock wore off ... he heard a scream. His head snapped to his right where a man went down, an Iumenta on his horse getting ready to jump. A ball of yellow struck the Iumenta and it died.

Barnin looked to where the Iumenta had come from to see another group entering the area. Above them the Iumenta Dragon had been joined by a second. Any moment now, the orange Elf Dragon would flee or be defeated.

"Heath, contact command, tell them the perimeter has been breached," then to the rest of his men he said, "fall back!"

He turned Poison and galloped out of the field. He looked back as the orange Dragon fell.

Sara blew into the mouth of a dying patient. The man's lungs filled with air that didn't find purchase. She lifted herself, looking down at the soldier below, and then she wrote a note on a piece of parchment next to the man and placed it in a tube next to his bed. Beyond being rattled by death, she turned to see a familiar face.

"Sasha!" she said.

Sasha's smile reached her ruby eyes. "Hello Sara, I was wondering if you could use a hand?" she asked.

Sara smiled at her friend. "Always. Are you sure you don't mind?"

Sasha laughed, "I offered, didn't I?" Her smile wavered, "I don't like combat ... even with the White Dragon's anger ... it doesn't feel like me. Well, I suppose when I'm angry like that, it isn't me, is it?"

"I wouldn't know I've never seen you when you feel the White Dragon's anger, but I can't see you fighting."

Sara tried to picture Sasha killing in her mind and couldn't quite see it.

Popee, the Elf in charge of the healing center, walked up to Sara and Sasha. Her dark brown eyes looked tired. She bowed to Sasha. "Un Prose, it is an honor," she said lifting herself.

"The honor is mine. Popee, correct?" Sasha said, sounding formal.

"Yes Un Prose, how may I be of assistance?" Popee asked.

"That question should be the other way around; I am here to assist you. I understand that you are shorthanded on Ascended help," Sasha said.

Popee looked taken aback for a moment and then looked around the crowded healing center, running her fingers through her dark brown curly hair. "Yes Un Prose, we are shorthanded, perhaps you could assist with minor injuries?"

Sasha nodded, "It would be my pleasure, where shall I start?"

"Sara will take you around," Popee said.

After Popee left, Sara asked, "Are you sure you are OK with just doing minor injuries?"

Sasha spoke warmly, "Of course, she is shorthanded and I have the power to heal many minor wounds in this center. I dare say it will clear up a lot of beds and resources."

"Allowing her to focus more on people who are worse off," Sara noted.

"Perhaps, or maybe just to give her staff a break. Who is our first patient?"

Sasha spent a few hours in the center. Sara took her from bed to bed where she would fix lacerations and broken bones. As soon as a bed was free, it was taken up again, but Sara could see a difference. The load of work really had been lightened.

Popee came up to them. "Thank you Un Prose, you have done much to help us today."

Sasha was at the entrance and looked back at the people still in bed with a sad expression. "I wish I had more time, Popee ..." she kissed Sara on the cheek "I have to go now, keep safe," and with that, Sasha left.

"Sara, would you mind walking with me?" Popee asked.

"Of course, may I ask why?"

"I need help getting some odds and ends at one of the storage buildings and I thought you could give me a report of your afternoon."

Sara walked with Popee, talking, telling her about who Sasha had healed and how many. Popee seemed happy and relieved about everything that Sasha had done. The rain was coming down hard now, forcing Popee and Sara to hide under eaves. They came to a tent near the north edge of the base. Lightning flashed in the sky and thunder rolled.

She and Popee rummaged through supplies and chatted. They were looking outside at the rain when a crystal rose in the air. It flashed red and the air filled with a droning blare.

Sara clapped her hands to her ears, "Wh-"

Popee looked terrified. "It's the Warning Crystal siren; it's the signal for Dragons to scramble!"

Popee grabbed Sara's arm and pulled. Sara tried to speak, " Warning Crystal? But the weather ..."

Sara heard a boom. She looked toward the edge of camp to see a plume of fire. The Warning Crystal blared on. Popee pulled Sara to the ground and she felt a wave of heat cross over her body.

"WE NEED TO RUN!" Popee said, pulling Sara up.

The tent they were in was on fire. Sara was pulled out into the street. There were explosions all around her and she looked to the sky to see a group of Iumenta Dragons coming in, preceded by torrents of magical flames and spells of every kind. From further inside the base, anti-dragon flack filled the air. Streaks of magic and ballista bolts sailed over her and Popee. Packages burst in the air. A ball of pink came from an Iumenta and struck the building next to her. The explosion sent Sara and Popee flying ten feet to land on the muddy lane. Sara landed hard and turned to Popee.

She's out cold, Sara thought. She wasn't without injury either, her leg hurt as did the side that she landed on. Rivers of fire were raining down everywhere. Sara knelt down, trying to wake Popee. Her eye caught an Iumenta coming in close to the ground, braving the barrage of ballista fire. As it came in, Sara could see figures fall from its back. *Oh no! They are caring ground units!* She spoke a spell, reviving Popee.

"We need to go; there are ground units here!" Sara said.

Popee stood up but too late, the Iumenta were on them. A memory from long ago came to Sara. It was when she'd been fleeing this land and the one and only time she'd used magic to fight. Silver light shot from her, hitting an oncoming Iumenta. Its body glowed with green. *It has protection!* When the first one was on her, Popee pushed Sara out of the way and drew her faloon. The Iumenta blocked the thin blade with ease and Sara sent another spell at it, just a flash of light that distracted it. Popee took the Iumenta's distraction to her advantage, stabbing it in the chest with her faloon.

More Iumenta were there, none of them paying any attention to Sara, but going after Popee instead. Sara grabbed some wood she found on the ground and swung it at a female Iumenta. It sidestepped her attack and lashed out with one of its own. The Iumenta hit Sara with the back of her hand, sending her careening in the air. Sara landed hard on her side and bent forward to wretch and spit blood.

"Popee!" Sara said, reaching out with her hand.

Popee was on the ground, an Iumenta readying to stab her. Sara's vision turned red for a moment as a ruby familiar in the form of a Puma crossed her vision. The Puma attacked the Iumenta that was about to kill Popee as an Elf came into view.

Sara tried to raise herself, falling back down as pain exploded in her leg and side. She clutched her side, forcing out a spell that mended her broken ribs. Popee was lifting her and Sara looked to see the other Elf woman with her back turned to them, fighting the Iumenta. She had a fenna that blazed scarlet with blood. She and her Puma fought viciously, Sara watched as she killed several Iumenta. Then she used magic to take down others that were further away. She cut an oncoming foe in two, splattering the area with gore.

The woman growled a spell, making the rain in the immediate area coalesce into orbs that froze into ice. She sent chunks the size of heads at the Iumenta, driving them back. The woman turned, her face smeared with blood, and Sara's own blood ran cold. The face was a mask of rage and anger so frightening that Sara knew it would haunt her for the rest of her life, but the eyes ...

"Sasha ..." she whispered.

"Popee, get Sara out of here now!" Sasha ordered without a hint of her usual warmth.

Popee lifted Sara and they ran away from the edge of base, the whole time avoiding arrows and magic. The air above her was roiling with both Elf and Iumenta Ascended. Human and Elf soldiers ran past them, heading toward the edge of base.

As soon as Keither heard the Warning Crystals sirens, he tried to fully connect with Sara. He caught flashes of her being attacked but then her mind closed off to him. Never in his life had he run so fast. He sprinted toward the edge of base, passing soldiers on their way to defend the wall. Kovos' sword bounced against the side of his leg and Keither was thankful to have it. He came to the top of a small hill overlooking most of the north side of the base.

He took in the scene before him. Buildings were burning and exploding with magic from Iumenta Dragons, the air was filled with Anti-Dragon flack and arrows. The flashing red siren crystals blared. Elf Dragons passed over his head, joining the battle. Keither looked to the healing center where Sara worked to see it shattered and smoking. *She wasn't there,* he said to himself.

He started to run again -- he had to find Sara -- but the Iumenta were on the ground! He felt waves of heat from buildings and the sky. Dragon blood fell like rain as the fight in the sky escalated. Keither lost his footing when a group of scared people ran by. He fell to his knee. In the moment it took to pick himself up, he saw Sara with Popee. The Elf was carrying her. *Sara is hurt!* Popee saw him and ran to meet him.

"Is she hurt?! Is she going to live?!" Keither asked, looking at his wife, her face pale.

"She'll be fine; she's had a shock and her leg is hurt. Take her away from here," Popee ordered.

"Where are you going?"

Popee didn't respond but turned and dashed back toward the fight. Keither didn't hesitate before leaving the area. Some of the Elves' siege weapons had been turned and were firing on the Iumenta. He could see toward Salez that the rest of the Elf artillery was firing, the air filled with both Elf and Iumenta Ascended.

Sara groaned, "What's going on?"

"The Iumenta are making their counterattack!"

He got Sara inside the small barracks they lived in. Even when he shut the door, his ears rung with the sound of spells on wards and the windows flashed like a freak storm raged outside. He found a few other support staff in the building, hiding out in a small cellar. He and Sara joined them. There was a glow of silver and Sara relaxed in his arms.

"You can put me down, I'm almost healed now," she said.

He did as she asked and he saw her wince. Her eyes met his and she answered his unasked question. "When the attack started I fought back, it took most of the power I had. It will take me a bit longer to completely heal my injuries," she said.

The building shook and everyone in the cellar screamed. Everyone hit the ground, and Keither tried to cover Sara. The building shook more.

Legon gazed out of the opening of his hangar at the rain coming down in sheets. He was grateful for the break from fighting. The rain washed the base of its ever-present stink of smoke and death. Iselin lay next to him, also craning her neck out of the opening.

"Thinking about a nap?" Legon asked her.

She shrugged, making her armor clink. "I'm considering it, but not seriously." A tendril of water formed and flowed to her mouth, "I'm not that tired."

"Yes, it feels nice just to watch the rain."

In the distance, Legon saw a red crystal rise in the air and start to blare.

A voice came into their minds from ground control, "Scramble, scramble, scramble, Iumenta attack imminent at the north gate ..."

Both Legon and Iselin shot up. Dragons in hangars across from them were taking flight and Legon waited for an opening before propelling himself in the sky. Opes and Sydin's minds joined his.

Sydin spoke, "Legon, head over to the north gate and take charge, I am going to take command near the city. It's safe to assume that the north of the base isn't the only thing that is going to be attacked."

Legon's mind opened to all the Dragons in the area. "All squads heading north, this is Legon of Evindass taking command." He waited to hear which squads were going north and connected only with their leaders to relay orders. He could see the north side of the base in a blaze as Iumenta Ascended attacked. Ground command connected with him and he relayed information to the Dragons. "Ground is setting up a defensive line and growing artillery, Anti-Dragon flack is one hundred feet."

"Orders?" a commander named Lamma asked.

"Contain the Iumenta near the gate, target Ascended carrying troops. We need to give the ground units time to evacuate the area and provide support as needed," Legon said.

Below him, streaks of smoke trailed Anti-Dragon flack. Legon rose in the sky, Iselin and Opes in formation. They plunged themselves into the battle, Legon using powerful spells in an attempt to push the Iumenta back. To an extent it worked, but he had been fighting all day and what little energy he had left was dwindling.

Legon, Iselin, and Opes soon were covered in wounds and their healing wards were failing them.

"Legon, we need to pull back," Opes said.

Reluctantly he agreed. This was fighting as a Dragon; you fought until you were badly injured or tired, then you would pull back and recover. It was that reason that made Dragon fatalities more of an exception than the norm.

Ground command connected with him, "Sir, we have a defensive line and have turned artillery on the gate. There are several new batteries that are nearly grown; once complete, they will level anything past the defensive line."

Legon acknowledged and asked for a timeframe before speaking with his commanders. "We have less than a half hour before ground levels the area. Ground units are pulling out of the area but a few can't get out; I need four squads to assist with evacuations," he said.

Sasha's mind connected with his, "Legon, we need to be pulled out; my guard and a few others are pinned down."

Legon could see her position in his mind and said, "Make red smoke and we'll get you."

He was too tired and too focused to pay much attention to Sasha's situation or the seething anger he felt from her mind. He found her smoke and came in with Opes and Iselin. Two other Dragons circled the area so Legon and the others could come in close to the warehouse Sasha and her people were in.

Sasha was on the roof fighting with magic, along with the rest of her guard. She was sending spikes of ice at Iumenta ground units. Behind her lay several figures who looked hurt.

As Legon came in, he breathed fire around the building and Bill detached from him to join Iselin, Opes, and all of the other Veneficas' familiars on the ground. Legon hovered over the building, feeling Elves climb his tail, Sasha making it up to his shoulder.

"We're all on," she said.

Legon turned and drove his wings down, feeling the strain of so much weight on his back. Large burning projectiles from the main artillery whizzed past him, giving him motivation to try harder as he forced himself higher in the sky. Once he was moving forward and up, things got easier. Below, he passed the defensive line.

Sasha felt the anger from the White Dragon fade. In its place was pain and fatigue. She started to tremble just a bit as fear and sadness gripped her. The ground units had grown new artillery that now fired on the north gate. Below them, dozens of burning wooden balls rushed by, their hollow insides filled with a flammable liquid. She turned to look as they hit the north part of the base, bursting on the ground, covering the area with fire and death. She turned her head away and looked at Popee, covered in injuries. An Elf had secured her to one of Legon's spikes. The healer stirred a bit, opening one of her swollen eyes to look at Sasha.

Sasha brushed Popee's hair from her face and spoke to her as warmly as she could, "Shhhh it's all right now, I am going to take care of you."

Popee smiled weakly and muttered, "Sara was right ... perfect," and then she passed out.

Legon landed and Sasha and the others got off his back. Sasha could hear chatter in his head as he coordinated the air and ground attacks up north.

"Sash, can you take care of the wounded?" he asked.

"I'll take charge, don't worry," she said and added, "Be safe."

Legon laughed. "Yeah, I'll go be safe in combat, thanks for taking care of the wounded," he said and started to fly off.

Before she could retort about his comment about being safe in combat, the wind was knocked out of her as a pair of arms wrapped around her.

"You stupid, brave, reckless woman!" Edling's voice sounded behind her. "What if you'd died? Are you hurt?" he asked spinning her around.

"N-no I ..." she started to say something but was cut off when Edling kissed her. He picked her up, spinning around. Sasha wanted to be mad with him for manhandling her, but if she was being honest and the tables were turned, she'd likely do the same thing. He put her down.

"You can't get mad at me dear, you know that," he said reading her mind.

A smile forced its way on her face, "But I can try, can't I?"

He kissed her again, "How's that going for you?"

She gave in to being happy for a moment. "Not well," then she paused, "only you could make me happy in the middle of an attack," she accused, then got back to the matters at hand. "I need your help; we have wounded to take care of."

Edling held her tight. "I know, I will behave now, but a husband is allowed a moment of joy when his wife comes back unharmed," he smirked.

"Well ... has it really been a whole moment?" she matched his smirk. They allowed themselves several more happy seconds before duty called them back to reality.

Chapter Twenty
Aftermath

"Despite my insistence that I am the only one in the world, life seems to go on without my presence."
-Walking Through Time (Author Unknown)

Keither listened to the distant rumble of magic. His arms were loosely wrapped around Sara's sleeping form. The night had been a long one; the air was thick with dust and smoke. He knew that some of the fighting had taken place over their barracks but he wasn't sure how much, or how much was left of the area.

Sara stirred. Bleary-eyed, she held her side and muttered something. Her palm glowed silver and she sighed, "Finally."

"Are all of your injuries healed?" Keither asked.

She sat up. "All the ones that count; are you hurt?" she asked.

He said that he wasn't. Others in their hiding spot were starting to leave the cellar and Keither decided to join them. He helped Sara up and stumbled a bit.

She steadied him, "I thought you said you weren't hurt."

"My leg is asleep," he said stamping it on the ground, trying to get blood flow again.

When they came out of the cellar and left the building they were met with relative calm. Only a few buildings around them had any damage, but when Keither turned to the north, he could see pillars of smoke rising.

"I'm sure we are needed," he said.

Sara frowned, "I can't seem to get in contact with Popee ... you don't think she ..."

———————— ∽ ————————

Sara's mind reached for Popee but found nothing ... *she could be asleep still.* Protocol said that Sara needed to make contact with command for instructions, so that is what she did. The mind she was led to was Sasha.

"You're all right," Sara said.

"Yes I'm fine; were you injured?" Sasha asked.

"Yes, broken ribs and leg but they are healed now; I should be ready to work. Do you know where Popee is? Did she make it?" Sara asked.

"She is unconscious. She got hurt in the attack, but my guard pulled her out. We healed most of her wounds, but she escaped from bed and started working. I dare say she worked too hard and passed out; I gave her a sleeping draught so she can heal. Can you please report to Center Six?" Sasha asked.

"Yes, I will go there right away," Sara said and broke off her connection.

She hurried to the center, feeling guilty. Popee had started working as soon as she could, but Sara ... she'd hid during the night instead of doing her job. She clenched her fists, feeling her nails dig into her palms. *Pathetic,* she thought.

Her feelings of guilt didn't ease when she made it to center six. It was full of people, with a pile of dead outside of it. The healers inside looked ready to drop; all showed signs of working through the night. Sara threw herself into her work, not letting up until she needed to get supplies.

As she came up to a supply tent, she saw Sasha talking with someone. Sasha waved her over and Sara recognized Barnin. He was covered in dried blood and she couldn't tell if it was his or not. Some of his other men were in the area; they looked like they were eating as quickly as they could and gathering supplies.

"Hey Sara, how are your ribs?" Barnin asked.

"Fine; what are you guys doing?" she asked.

Sasha raised an eyebrow and Barnin spoke. "Re-fitting," he said, as if it were obvious.

Before anyone could say anything, they all looked up as a group of Elf Dragons passed overhead in a V formation. In the center was a massive purple Dragon Sara recognized as Legon. His armor looked worn, his scales covered in dirt, smoke, and blood. Even from the sky he looked like he'd been through hell. Next to him were Iselin and Opes. They descended as they flew over.

"They haven't rested since the attack started, and even then they were just taking a small break. They have been fighting since yesterday morning," Sasha said, leveling her gaze on Barnin, "and if reports are correct that Iumenta class eight is in the area." Sasha looked behind her, "I need to go ... something's up; command is meeting. Sara, I hope you feel better." She took Barnin's hand, "Be safe," she said, and walked off.

Sara's head dropped, "How can she even be talking to me with what I've done?"

"What? You mean, hiding all night and not being at the healing center helping out?" Barnin asked frankly.

"You're mad at me, aren't you?" she said "You should be, you were doing your job all night, Legon and Ise and Opes and everyone else was but I ..."

Barnin put his hand on her shoulder, "Had reached your limit. Look Sara, I'll be honest with you, we needed everyone last night, but we needed everyone clearheaded. Sasha told me about everything. You've never seen combat like that before. The center you worked at was destroyed and you were scared and stressed along with having broken ribs and a leg. You could have somewhat healed your injuries, and pushed through the pain and worked, but at what cost? Sasha isn't mad at you because she understands. Don't beat yourself up; just keep doing your best. Got it?"

"Barnin, that was a really kind thing to say ... I-"

"You're worried that I got hit on the head or something right? Because I'm being nice? That's fair, but it's the truth."

"Thank you. Is there anything your people need?" she asked.

Barnin thought for a moment, "Do you think you could tend to a few of my guys? They don't have any major injuries -- well a few do -- but they aren't going back out with us. But it would be nice to go back into combat with everyone at one hundred percent."

"Sure, lead me to them," she said.

Emma sat with Edling, waiting for Legon and Sasha. Legon trotted up in his Dragon form, entering the hangar, dragging his tail, Iselin close behind. A group of Elf blacksmiths were on hand to make any needed repairs to their armor. Once inside, Legon wasted no time shedding his worn and blood spattered armor. As soon as he and Iselin were out of it they took their Elf forms.

Legon stretched his arms above his head and said, "I never thought I'd be so happy to have a meeting."

A haggard-looking Iselin agreed.

Emma raised an eyebrow and Legon answered her unasked question, "I can take an Elf form and get out of that armor."

Sasha came in the hangar and Edling went to join her, taking her hand. Emma liked to watch Edling with Sasha, every time he saw her it was like he was breathing for the first time. Emma thought it was cute and wondered how long his reaction would last.

Emma reached down to her bag, pulling out a stack of papers and spoke to Legon. "Legon," she said, taking a business tone, "would you like me to brief you on the way to the meeting?"

Legon looked at the stack in her hands and seemed to reconsider his earlier statement about being thankful for a meeting. "Yes please, but after it starts I want you to get some rest."

Emma smiled. "I will," she said, following him out of the hangar, filling him in on what the meeting was to be about. Once Legon, Sasha, and Iselin were in the meeting, Emma met back up with Edling.

"So what did you find out?" he asked.

"Well, it could have been worse, from what the reports say. We pushed the Impa back out of the base and they didn't breach any other sections of the wall," she explained.

"But ..."

"But the north end of the base is mostly ashes; House Coreen used artillery to keep the Iumenta from being able to keep any ground. The forest outside the wall is likewise gone. We only lost a few Ascended and most of those deaths occurred at the onset of the attack. From what we can tell, the Iumenta didn't lose any Ascended in the attack, or if they did; we didn't find the bodies. However, the Iumenta took significantly higher infantry casualties than we did, so overall we fared well, I suppose.

"The reports that I read said that this could be the first of many attacks. We can expect all sides of our perimeter to be hit from this point forward unless we keep the Impa on the defense."

Edling nodded and asked, "Do you know the state of Salez?"

"It's good the city will fall, most likely in the next few weeks. Doesn't Sasha tell you this stuff? You are an heir to House Evindass, after all."

"She doesn't like to think or talk about the war. I try to keep her distracted with crystals and helping out with healing centers," he said.

Emma should have known that. "I can see that, well if you ever need info, you know I'm your girl," she said.

"Don't think I'll forget that," Edling said warmly. "Now, we both need to get some rest."

Emma agreed and went to her quarters, falling on the bed without even taking the time to change out of her clothes. She thought it would take her a long time to quiet her mind, but as soon as her head hit the pillow, she fell asleep.

Chapter Twenty-One
Betrayed

"When trust is lost, we lose something essential to our makeup, something that sometimes can never come back."
-Excerpts from The Diary of the Adopted Sister

Tom flinched away from the heat of fire. Salez was falling, there was no doubt about it in his mind, and it would fall soon. Tom still didn't know who the traitor in his group was; everyone checked out from what he was able to tell.

Right now he needed to figure out how to stay alive. He dashed down the stone streets, dodging soldiers as he went. Most of the civilians were out of the area, those left were heading toward shelters.

Tom saw a girl with long brown hair in the distance, running in the wrong direction. It was Stacy. *What's she playing at?* He went after her. She was a good distance ahead of him and Tom was having a hard time keeping up. Stacy ran without fear as she moved. Then the obvious struck him. Brian checked out; Tom had known him for years, and Tom was the one who found Seth. He was just a thief before … Stacy was the mole.

He slowed his pace, needing to confirm what should have been plain as day to him. She was in a commercial area of the city now; most of the people were long gone. She ducked into a shop. Tom went across the street. He climbed up the wall of a small building. Once on top, he looked out toward the main city wall. Magic flashed and crashed in the air. He knelt down, coming to the lip of the roof.

He used magic to magnify his eyes and ears. His head throbbed with the sound of magical fighting and he refined his spell. He heard voices, both speaking in Glosso.

"What do you mean?" Stacy's voice asked.

Tom leaned over, his enhanced vision allowing him to see Stacy in the shop. In front of her was an Iumenta. Tom went ridgid; it was the same one who killed James.

"I told you. You are of no use to us anymore, if you ever were to begin with," the Iumenta said harshly.

Stacy didn't seem to care. "So what is my new assignment?" she asked.

The Iumenta laughed, "You don't have one. You're finished, which I think you already know."

Before Tom could register what was happening, the Iumenta's hand slashed at Stacy in a blur of speed. She fell back, blood pouring from a cut on her head. She hit the ground and felt the wound while looking up, her eyes fearful.

Tom fought the urge to help her; she was the enemy.

Stacy looked scared. "Please, don't kill me!" she cried.

The Iumenta looked at her with disgust and walked forward.

Stacy barked a spell and metal spikes shot up from the wooden floor of the shop. The Iumenta howled in pain. Before it could react, Stacy was up, all of her fear seeming to vanish. She pulled a knife and stabbed the Iumenta in the gut. Tom watched it fall forward, and then Stacy slashed its neck in several places. She backed away, panting a bit. Tom's mouth fell open. Never had he seen someone kill with such precision, not to mention the skill it would take to kill an Iumenta.

"I did know you were going to try that. Why do you think I chose to meet you here?" she said to the dead Iumenta.

Stacy cleaned off the knife and walked out of the shop. Tom ducked back down on the roof.

"You can come out now, Tom," Stacy's voice came from below.

Tom's heart began to race. He was no fighter.

There was a slight sound of boot on stone and Stacy came over the wall and onto the roof. *How had she moved that fast?* She was always a happy, bouncy girl, but that wasn't the Stacy in front of Tom now. He rose.

"So you're the mole," he stated.

"Tom, I told you not to look for the mole, didn't I?" she said without a hint of warmth.

Tom's eyes flicked about, looking for a way to escape. "You did tell me not to look into it; yes," he admitted.

Stacy took a step forward, "Too bad really, now that we're on the same side and all."

Tom stopped, looking around, "Same side? You work for the Iumenta."

Stacy came a step closer, "Really? See, I thought they just tried to kill me."

"So … you're on the Elves' side now?" he asked, not trusting her.

She nodded, "Yes, you see where I come from you learn that survival is most important, and I plan to survive, Tom. So yes, now I am on the Elves' side, and a good ally I'll be."

"So what, then? We just leave here?" Tom asked, though he doubted that was her intention.

Stacy frowned, "Sadly Tom; no. You see, soon the Impa will lose Salez and when they do I can't have you telling House Evindass that I tried to kill Legon and Sasha and did manage to kill Arkin. So Tom, you have to die." Her voice warmed, "But this does work out well. I can now go to Legon and Sasha, having killed the mole that has caused so many issues. Issues that will now stop."

"It won't work." he said "you can't have been working alone all this time, Evindass will find out!"

Stacy laughed "Oh, about that. You see, Arkin did do a good job of training me how to run an organization. Did you know he had measures in place to have everyone in each city killed if needed?"

Tom wasn't sure how to answer that.

"I take it from your silence you didn't know that. He did. It's the best way to seal leaks if a group gets compromised. I took that policy of his to heart. Prior to my meeting with my Iumenta handler today, I sent out kill orders for every cell I was running. The entirety of the organization I created will be dead by nightfall." She paused "after all, I can't have them hindering the work I will be doing for the Elves."

Tom shuddered on the inside. She really had changed sides and was now working for the Elves.

Tom's gut clenched. She was going to get away with everything. He had to act. "FLAMMA!" he shouted, as ruby shot from his hand. Stacy deflected the magic and dodged to her side.

Tom jumped from the roof, letting magic stop him. Stacy was a killer, but she was only a class one. Tom was a class two; he was more powerful than she and older. He could win this.

Stacy laughed from above. Tom hid behind an overturned cart. Stacy landed on the ground.

"Tom, you can't beat me," she said confidently.

Tom felt concealment wards being tested. He jumped from behind the cart, sending more magic at her. She countered, and Tom blocked the spell.

"Why?" he asked as he ran into an alley.

"Why what?"

He used magic to project his voice, trying to throw her off, "Why join the Iumenta in the first place?"

"Tom dear, I didn't join them; I was raised by them," she said it as if it were obvious.

She went on, "Well, while we are playing this game I suppose I can tell you the story. You all were so happy to find Mors. That's not where I'm from. The place where I was born and raised is deep in Impa lands. Even after this war, the Elves will never find it."

Tom blanched. He lost his focus, taken aback by her statement. Stacy came around a corner, and Tom deflected a burst of gold. Pain exploded in his leg. He tried to get up, pulling a knife from his leg. He backed away from Stacy.

"Do you know what it's like training with Master Venefica, Tom?" she asked, moving to stand over him.

Tom pushed against a wall, trying to get away from her. Fear and pain were gripping him.

"N-no," he said.

She smiled faintly. "I didn't think so. See, I was the top of my class. They pulled me aside at the age of six. The Iumenta trained me to be an assassin. I've trained one-on-one with Masters who have been doing magic for thousands of years. Couple that with the hand-to-hand training Arkin gave me …" she paused, "Well, don't be hard on yourself for losing."

There was the rumble of wards. Stacy looked up and then back to Tom, "Sorry Tom, but I have to go now. Don't worry; I'll make it fast. Any last words?"

Tom didn't have anything to say. He'd been such a fool. He simply closed his eyes.

Legon stared ahead as he flew toward Salez. Weeks of fighting were drawing to a close. He knew that this day the air space over Salez would fall, and with it, the rest of the city would follow. Legon figured the Iumenta must have known this would happen too; they weren't fighting with the same vigor that they had over the last month since the siege had begun.

"Surround the city," Sydin ordered.

Detachments of Ascended broke off from the main attacking body to circle around Salez. Legon stayed in a forward group with his guard, Iselin, and Sydin. Formations of Iumenta lay ahead of them; dead center in front of Legon was a pale green Dragon. The Iumenta class eight. None of the Elves knew the Dragon's name; all they could figure out was that he was recently Ascended like Legon. Sydin said one could see how new he was by the lack of control he had in the sky, something indicative of all new Dragons.

"So do you think Green is going to fight me today?" Legon asked Sydin, referring to the class eight.

"I don't think he will have a choice. I can tell he's new but none of our forces have seen much of him so it's safe to assume that you have more actual combat experience," Sydin said comfortingly.

Legon was a little irked, "I'm not worried about fighting him Sydin, but thanks for the pep talk."

Legon thought he heard Sydin mutter something about the pep talk not being for Legon, but he decided not to comment and focused on the fast approaching green. Legon looked into the Dragon's yellow eyes, trying to read them. He could see excitement in them, a desire to prove himself.

"We will have your wing," Sydin said.

"That won't be necessary; he wants single combat. I can see it in his eyes, and I want the same," Legon said.

"Don't be a fool Legon, there is no way he's fighting you alone," Iselin barked, but Legon wasn't paying attention to her. He too was excited, he too wanted to prove himself against this Dragon and he didn't want any help.

Before Iselin was able to argue more, Legon leapt forward at almost the same time Green did. Legon let out a savage roar that was matched by Green. Torrents of emerald and amethyst flames collided and Legon felt Green's power pushing against him. Never had Legon felt the kind of resistance he did now.

The two Dragons smacked into each other, the force of it making their chest plates groan and grind together. The sound was horrific. As Legon suspected, none of the Iumenta paid any attention to him, and he paid no attention to anything other than Green.

Claws cut deeper into Legon than ever before, Green's jaws snapped at Legon's neck and in turn Legon bit down on Green's shoulder, tasting blood and flesh. They separated before they hit the ground. Below them, Humans, Elves, and Iumenta ran to avoid the two massive Dragons. Legon swung his tail. Green caught the blow and returned with one of his own. Legon stopped it as magic ran the course of his wing, making a poison gas that he then used his wings to drive toward Green.

The gas met pale green wards and was countered by blasts of wind so focused they could cut steel. Legon's wards stopped the attack. *So you're an Elemental,* Legon thought. They both rose in the sky trying to gain the upper hand on the other. Legon felt healing wards strain as he was cut by claw and tooth, but for every wound he received, he dealt one of his own.

They were above Salez's main wall now and Green seemed desperate. Magic rebounded off of both Dragons as they fought. Green faded back and Legon -- too eager -- shot forward. Green's tail came swinging up at Legon's exposed head.

Green's tail blade made contact with Legon's jaw, cutting armor and flesh, shattering bone. Legon screamed as the lower left-hand side of his jaw separated from the upper half and flapped in space. The force of it was too great and the other joint in his jaw broke, leaving his bottom half hanging by muscle and scales alone. Pain fogged his vision and he felt healing wards drain as they tried to heal his jaw. In Legon's moment of disorientation, Green lashed out, getting in two more tail hits to Legon's sides before he could block. Ribs cracked with one of the blows and Legon feebly tried to ward off attacks. He felt his jaw snap back together and finish healing, but he'd lost ground in the fight and was losing badly.

There was a sound from Salez and Green separated from Legon and looked back. Legon recovered, but before he could attack, Green turned in the air and flew as fast as he could back toward Salez. Legon looked to see the other Iumenta doing the same. Many were going to the ground and picking up other Iumenta and then using one of the city's jump crystals to leave.

Sydin's voice boomed, "They are jumping out; secure the city's air space!" he ordered.

There were collective roars from other Elf Dragons and Legon joined them.

He fell back to be be in formation with Iselin who eyed him. "You almost died today," she said angrily.

"I know," Legon said, remembering.

"You're happy about it?" she was incredulous.

"Of course; Green is my equal in every way and he beat me. That hasn't happened since Kovos, and I know Green feels the same," Legon said warmly.

"I married an idiot," Iselin spat and broke connection with him.

Keep yourself alive until we meet again, Legon thought, thinking of Green.

Barnin finished tying his gear and looked up at Ankle, who said, "Is there a reason why every time people need to be dropped behind enemy lines now, our unit has to do it? I mean, you can't tell me the Elves want us on this mission."

Barnin laughed without humor, "I'm sure they don't, but I think the Human command wants to prove that our race can be of use too, and we've done this before so ..."

"Oh, goody for us," Ankle said.

Barnin left the tent and went to the field to speak to the rest of his men.

"Listen up," he said, addressing them. "We have several objectives today. We need to help clear battlements looking down on the entrance of the city; if we can secure those it will save a lot of lives when that main gate comes down. Next up, if you see Anti-Dragon flack we are to take it out. The Pawdin Empire has units dedicated to this, but we need to do our part. We also need to watch for artillery and if we can, deal with that too. I'm aware that sounds like a lot to do, and it is. We are here today as backup; we do not have any hard and fast targets, so be ready for things to change fast on the ground."

Barnin looked to the sky, seeing a group of Dragons approach, and burst out laughing. His men looked at him like he'd gone mad, and maybe he had. The massive form of Legon landed in front of him, Opes and Iselin on either side, along with a few others.

"Need a ride?" Legon asked.

Legon's body was covered in thick metal armor; the metal smudged with dirt and speckled with dried blood. With his dark purple scales,

Barnin thought he looked menacing, a defiant force to be reckoned with. This made him smile.

"Where you headed?" Barnin asked.

"Me?" Legon said. "Oh, I'm going to go destroy a city's defenses; you wanna come?" Legon said with a chuckle.

This whole conversation Legon had kept between the two of them. Barnin's men were looking at him, worried about the grin playing on his face; he raised his voice and turned away from Legon. "Team one on me; we mount up on Legon; he's the purple one! Team two Ankle, you're on Ise!" he said, giving orders. The men jumped into action, loading up on the Dragons with Barnin climbing up Legon's side.

Barnin had been on Umbra many times and she was a class seven. He'd even trained on a few sixes so he knew the difference in size between class six and seven Dragons. But the difference in Legon's size shocked him; Legon felt more like a small mountain to him rather than a living, breathing creature. Once atop his shoulders, Barnin stared at the cords of muscle running up Legon's neck. When all ten men were on, Legon took off, rushing up in the air. Barnin could feel that Legon wasn't as fast as a class six or seven, but his command of the air was impressive. As they banked toward the city, Barnin could feel how smooth the flight was and he was reminded of when Umbra told him that the larger the Dragon, the smoother the flight.

Legon's mind came back into his. "Barnin, I have a request to make of you," Legon said.

"What's that?"

"Do you remember Stacy?" he asked. "She has a team here in Salez. She said they were betrayed and she doesn't feel secure right now. I need you and a team to find her and get her to an extraction point. Use Heath to get in contact with her and then again to tell me so I can come get her and her people."

Stacy was in trouble? Barnin hadn't thought about her much in the last few months, but he remembered her. She was the young, cute, bubbly girl Arkin had fallen for; she'd nearly been killed at Noris. *Don't worry old friend, I'll keep her safe,* Barnin thought, thinking of Arkin.

"We'll get her and her people out. Where are we dropping in?" Barnin asked.

"Just past the main wall; you'll be dropping with the rest of the teams. Stacy has her people near that area. You will be getting her and two others; one named Brian and another named Seth."

"Arkin told me about a third person when we were in Salez. Tom was his name?" Barnin said.

Legon was silent for a moment, "Tom was a double and the one who betrayed Stacy and Arkin. Stacy took him out right before I picked you lot up. That's when she asked for extraction."

Barnin's attention was drawn by the sound of Anti-Dragon flack ahead of them. The Iumenta Ascended were pulling back and in their wake were waves of flack in the air. Barnin could make out flashes of wards around the city as the Elves attacked.

Barnin turned back to his men. "New mission! We have critical personnel who need extraction in the city; we are to secure them until the Pawdin Empire can pull them out!" he shouted the descriptions of Stacy and her people. "Hang on tight, things are going to get bumpy until we are on the ground!" he finished.

Barnin turned his attention back to Salez. Its main exterior wall was teeming with activity. Elves were growing vines that wound up the stone wall, making ladders while two Dragons were in front of the main gate. From right under the Dragons, trees as thick as horses shot from the ground, pushing against the gate and making it groan and creak. From inside Salez, all manner of artillery were firing over the wall. Elf Dragons strafed the battlements with Magic and flame, trying to weave through the flack as they laid waste to ground units.

Barnin coughed as they flew through thick smoke and then he sucked himself in to Legon as close as he could. Legon had reached the Anti-Dragon flack and was weaving. Barnin felt the breath pull from his lungs at the concussion of flack exploding around them.

Legon roared and Barnin felt heat from fire as Legon swooped down at the wall, sending a jet of flames at some archers. Barnin's vision flashed lavender with Legon's wards. *I hate this part,* he thought. *At least he's not fighting any other Dragons.*

"We are almost there!" Legon said.

All of Barnin's discomfort left and he turned, "It's go time! Remember, civilians have been evacuated from the area, so kill anything not on our side!" he reminded his men.

"Dare I ask?" Legon said.

"Cona units will dress as civilians," Barnin said, speaking from experience.

"Right," Legon said, and then went into a dive.

Barnin felt his stomach drop to his feet. Legon came to almost a complete stop in the air. They were right above what looked to be a residential district; slate roofs were right below. Arrows shot from a nearby window but were deflected by Legon's wards. Barnin watched a set of vines wind around the building where the arrows came from. The vines became thick and squeezed the building. Its stone walls gave way and the structure collapsed, killing anyone inside. Before Barnin could thank Legon, he and his men glowed purple and were lowered to the ground.

Once his feet touched earth, Barnin led his men to where Stacy was supposed to be.

"It's a ghost town," Heath said, commenting about the lack of people in the area.

"This is far away from main streets and from the gate; I don't think we will see too many other people."

A plume of fire filled the street behind them and Barnin looked skyward to see more balls of fire from Cona artillery.

"Let's get this done fast!" he yelled to his men.

They didn't see another person until they made it to a small costume shop. In the window, Barnin thought he saw a knot of red hair disappear. He entered the shop and shouted, "Stacy! Come on, we don't have time for games!" And then turning his head back a bit, he spoke to a figure behind him, "and we're on the same side, so you don't need to point that knife at my back."

"How did you know I was here?" a male voice said.

Barnin turned to look at Seth, his shaggy red hair disheveled.

"You aren't real good at sneaking up on people, are you?" Barnin commented.

Before Seth said anything, Stacy came from the back room with Brian and said, "No he isn't, and this is all of us."

Barnin looked at her, noticing a cut along her forehead and said, "Are you injured?"

"That bastard Tom got her," Brian growled. "I swear if I had known ..."

"I'm fine," Stacy said and added to Brian, "It's not your fault and he's gone now." Stacy turned back to Barnin, "The traitor who had Arkin killed was named Tom-"

"And you killed him just a little while ago, yes; I know. This isn't the time; this whole area is going to be leveled soon, and we need to get your people to an extraction point," Barnin said, cutting her off.

"We will be meeting a Dragon from Evindass at a park near here," Heath said. "We have two minutes to get there," he added.

Barnin all but pushed Stacy and her team into the streets, which were becoming more and more clogged with smoke and fire. They moved quickly, trying to avoid debris until they found what at one time was probably a nice park. At present, it was no more than a small clearing where a burned and mangled catapult could be found.

Barnin and his men stayed close to the walls around the clearing and Heath called the Dragon that was to get Stacy. There was a thud as a bright yellow Dragon came into view, hovering over the area.

"Wait! We are flying?" Seth said. "You didn't say that!"

"Honestly, you are in high places all the time," Stacy said.

"Yeah but…AHHHHHHH," Seth screamed as he and the others glowed yellow and rose up to meet the Dragon.

Barnin turned to one of his rookies who hated flying and said, "See, at least you didn't scream like a little girl when you flew out here."

"Don't trip on anything today, Sir," the rookie said sarcastically.

Barnin laughed and then they ran as the area around them began to be bombarded with artillery.

Chapter Twenty-Two
Memories

"Guilt is the worst of poisons; it creeps into the veins of our mind and heart, stopping us from healing. Often times it can even prevent us from action. But on the other hand, guilt can motivate us to greater heights as we strive to do better. Indeed, guilt is a double edged sword. The key seems to be feeling guilt only when it is deserved and only in the right amount."
-Diary of the Perfectos Compatioa

Ashes floated to the ground like snowflakes around Sara as she walked the streets of her old home. Up the hill she could hear the sounds of the Salez north fortress in its death throes. Around her were ruins, piles of rubble of a once booming city. She stopped in front of what was once a tavern, the same tavern that Legon and Sasha found her in. *What was its name again?* She strained to remember but couldn't.

Blackened remains of Iumenta and Humans were in heaps on street corners. Some were women and children, but Sara was happy to see that most of the dead were soldiers.

She walked up the street, weaving her way through Elves and Humans as they worked to clear the area of corpses and debris. Supplies moved in a steady stream up the hill toward the fortress. Sara decided to see if her old home was still in one piece. She very much doubted that it would be; there wasn't a building in the area that wasn't damaged, with most being all but destroyed.

I need to stop calling it home, she thought. *It was a prison, nothing more.* She came to the brothel that once was her prison, where she was forced to do things that still crept into her dreams. She wondered if any of the girls she'd known were still alive. Part of her hoped that they weren't, hoped that death had spared them from suffering years ago. People in her old line of work normally only lasted a few years at best, and it had been …

four or five years? The roof was caved in and the street-facing windows shattered.

The door still stood and she pushed it open, feeling herself go cold. Could she handle being in this place? Sara shook herself and walked in the front lobby. Only part of it was burned, the floor wet from recent rain and the lack of a roof. She made her way to the cellar door, feeling more nervous. Down there was where her old cage was, and so many other things. She walked down the narrow steps to a cold, stone floor. Sunlight came in from the missing floor above. Ahead of her was a row of cages. At the end of the row was an open space with chains hanging from the ceiling. A burned whip draped over a hook in the stone. She looked away from it; she could almost feel it on her. It had an enchantment, making wounds heal within moments of being inflicted. The owner would hit Sara with it all over her body; she remembered hanging from the chains, screaming. She wasn't the only one who spent time there, everyone did.

Sara dabbed at her eyes and walked down the row, looking into the first cage. She was met with a sight she didn't expect to see. On the floor were the charred remains of a woman. *He didn't even let them out!* She thought in disgust. As she looked around, every cage was occupied. The owner had left these women to die. Sara wanted to vomit, but didn't. She walked up to the last cage and gasped.

"Penny."

How had she lived all these years? Sara opened the cage door with magic and knelt next to her friend's body. Only part of her was burned, but she lay lifeless on the cold stone. Sara leaned over her, touching Penny's face. She sobbed.

There was a footstep behind her and Sara whirled, ready to defend herself; convinced that the owner had come back to punish her. But it wasn't the owner of the brothel.

"You knew her," Sasha said. It wasn't a question, just an observation.

Sara was at a loss for words. Part of her was scared of Sasha after seeing her fight, after seeing anger etching her face, but that wasn't the face that looked at her now. It was soft and caring, just as it always had been.

"I failed them," Sara said weakly.

Sasha knelt next to Sara and for the first time she could see that Sasha was alone.

"I'm alone; my guard is outside. It's just us," Sasha said, and then more warmly, "Who did you fail, Sara?"

Sara pointed at the bodies, "Penny...all of them, I could have come back to save them I could have..."

"Shhhh, stop Sara, this is not your fault," Sasha said.

"But it is! Don't you see? She's been here for years ... she comforted me when I was ..." Sara's voice broke. "I won't let them pile her with the rest of the bodies," she said determined.

Sara collapsed into Sasha, who wrapped her arms around her, "Of course not. Do you know where she was from?"

Sara looked up, "A small town around here, I don't know."

Sasha stroked Sara's hair "We will figure it out and take her home to her family, all right?"

Sara nodded and Sasha went on, "But we can't take her like this and Legon is almost here."

Sara was confused at why Legon was coming. She wasn't upset that he was coming; if anything, Legon was the only one who truly understood her.

She jumped a bit when the wood around her groaned and there was a snap.

"The building isn't stable," Sasha said aloud.

Legon's voice rung in Sara and Sasha's mind, "Yeah, I figured that out. Sara, what's wrong?" Legon asked, craning his head over the hole in the floor above them. Then almost at once he said, "Penny." Of course he knew who Penny was, Legon knew so many of Sara's memories of her time here.

"We are taking her to her home but her body is in bad shape," Sasha said.

"I need room," Legon said. With a flick of magic, the cage flew apart, allowing him to hang his head next to Penny.

Penny's body glowed lavender. Tentacles of energy ran over the damaged flesh and Sara watched her burns disappear and her skin pink up. When he lifted his head, she looked as though she was asleep. She lifted in the air as flowers grew under her. Legon set her on the bed of flowers.

"She looks so lovely," Sara whispered. "She looks peaceful, but that's how it's supposed to be though, isn't it? She doesn't have to worry about this world any more; she's free."

Sara stayed with Penny, Sasha by her side, until Elves brought a new dress for her to be placed in and Sasha grew a casket, with Penny's favorite colors and flowers decorating it. Sara placed her friend in the coffin, shutting the lid with a faint farewell.

Four of Sasha's guard carried Penny back to the base.

Sara stood next to Sasha, who took her hand. "Are you going to be all right?" Sasha asked.

Sara nodded. "I'm sorry for being scared of you," she said, ashamed.

"Don't be, you should have been scared. When I'm like that, it's not really me fighting."

"But still, I shouldn't have been ... and thank you for Penny. I will cover the costs ..."

"When have we ever asked you to cover any costs?" Sasha asked. "Besides, had we ended this war two thousand years ago when we should have, Penny would have never died."

Before Sara could say anything, Sasha squeezed her hand and walked away.

Iselin glided over the fields that separated Salez from the base. She looked at the blackened landscape and wondered if this is what all of the land had looked like during the War of Generations.

She flew toward the north hill and fortress of Salez. Only a few Iumenta Ascended still held unable to jump out of the area, long ago the fortress jump crystal had run out of power, and soon the building's other defenses would collapse under the constant pressure of attack. Iselin wanted to be there when both fortresses fell. Long had Salez been one of the Iumenta's top strongholds.

"Did Salez even fall in the War of Generations?" Legon asked in her mind.

"No, it didn't. The city was abandoned eventually, but Pawdin forces never took it with force, we had several cities like that as well."

The north hill lit up with magic and Iselin recognized the sound of wards failing.

"It's happening!" she said, speeding up.

Elvin ladders grew over the walls and Iselin watched as Elves and Humans surged into the fortress.

Sydin's voice rang in her head, "Iselin, we need you to help secure the building with the jump crystal in it for Sasha and Edling's people."

Stacy had told Legon where the jump crystal was thought to be and Iselin focused on that section of the fortress. There were no more Iumenta Dragons in the area to defend the air and what little Anti-Dragon flack remained was being abandoned. On the south side of the fortress was a tall square building with no windows. Iselin came in on the building, touching down on the roof. As soon as she did, Iumenta spilled out, attacking her. She took off again. *Well, I'd say there is something in there,* she thought.

She reached out to her guard, "We need to end this before they are able to destroy the crystal."

Members of her guard converged on the buildings, raining down flames and death. Special units from the Pawdin army jumped off Dragons, running into the building to secure it. Iselin stayed in command until one of the ground units came on the roof, telling her they had secured the building.

Her mind reached out to Sasha and Edling who were close by on a Dragon's back. "Sasha, you two are up; the building is secure," she said.

The emerald Dragon, Cynta, landed on the building, and Sasha and Edling dismounted.

Sasha stepped down on the roof of the building and turned to her husband. She didn't need their mental connection to see that he was uncomfortable. The area they were in was far from being free of battle.

"Are you all right?" she asked.

"Not really," he responded honestly. "How can you be?" he asked.

In reply, she broadened her connection with him, allowing him to feel her connection with Legon. "The more connected with my brother I am, the less fear I feel." She felt Legon's mind reach out to Edling and he seemed to calm.

"How does he do that?" Edling wondered as they walked to a door on the roof.

Iselin spoke into their minds. "Legon is inherently a violent person; combat doesn't scare him and that's why you feel better," then in a bit more of a rushed tone, "Hurry please, we need to know if the crystal is still working."

Sasha rushed inside and down a set of stairs littered with bodies. She focused on the Mahann, trying to keep any unpleasant emotions from her mind. They entered a vast room.

Elves were moving around the room and around a giant square crystal that sat above a circular shaft. Edling seemed to forget his fear and jogged up to the crystal, placing his hand on it.

He frowned, "It's functioning but it won't respond to me. That's no surprise; ours will only respond to Elves."

Sasha ran her hand along its smooth side, "That's fine; we aren't interested in the data it holds, just its makeup." She pointed into the shaft, where gold bars ran into water with blackened filth in it. "It looks like they killed the algae."

Legon's mind came into hers, "Algae?"

Edling responded, "Yes, magic comes from life; we use plant life to power everything. While the Iumenta cannot grow plants at will like we can, any Venefica can affect plant life. The Iumenta grow algae to sustain their crystal's power supply. They dip gold into the water the algae is in to conduct the plant's life force to the crystal."

"Ah, that's why their crystals don't charge as fast as ours; algae doesn't produce much power," Legon said.

"Correct," Sasha said. "I suspect they killed the algae just to slow us down."

"Why would we care about that?" Legon asked.

Sasha rolled her eyes. "I don't know, so maybe we couldn't develop a spell that would wipe out the algae powering Dragon Domes … maybe…" she said. Then added, "I would like to send some samples to Seeon and have you look at them; you are a biologic, after all."

She leaned in, looking at the crystal in amazement, "Dear, are you seeing how it's constructed?"

"Yes; it's so perfect, it's almost like it was produced by a Master," Edling said.

She looked at him, "Of course!"

"Of course what?"

"Think about what you just said! Iumenta can't grow crystals like we can. That means there has to be a handful of Master Builders, and I bet they all use the same techniques."

Edling's face lit up, "So their crystals will likely have the same weaknesses!"

Sasha reached out to Emma. "Emma, we are going to need all of the samples we've collected since the war started and we need the rest of the team here. Have them jumped in from the Capital," she said, peering back at the crystal.

Chapter Twenty-Three
Salmont

"I wondered what it would be like going home, returning to the land of my birth. When I arrived however, I found that while home had not changed, I had."
-*Excerpts from The Diary of the Adopted Sister*

Emma relished the cold bite of the morning air. This was one of the things that she missed the most about her homeland. Next to her stood Sasha, and with them were Keither and Sara, along with Legon's and Sasha's guard. Sara's friends' hometown had been destroyed, so now they stood in a small mountain co-op. The season was changing; the aspen were turning gold, and leaves scattered the ground.

Before them was a tree with the whitest bark, Legon's claws dug into the ground around it. Flowers the shade of Penny's favorite colors bloomed, their petals catching the breeze and floating around the tree.

All of the Elves had their heads bowed in prayer. Emma looked to Sara and whispered, "Do you understand the tree?"

Sara looked at her, eyes shining, and shook her head no.

Emma explained, "The tree planted above her will have her name, and when she lived, etched into the tree forever. It will never grow taller and always keep its shape. The flower petals grow quickly so that they can fall and drift in the breeze, but this tree will only bloom on the day of your friend's death. Every Elf who passes this tree will impart some of their strength to it, keeping it alive for millennia. A mark will be on the tree indicating that she was Human."

"Does her being Human matter?" Sara asked, almost sounding hurt.

Emma nodded, "Yes, for a Human to be buried in this manner is a great honor. It is not given to many Humans. All Elves who pass this grave will know that your friend was unusually special."

"But they didn't know her," Sara wondered aloud.

Sasha's voice soft and gentle interrupted them. "But we know you. Come with me," Sasha said taking Sara's hand.

Iselin took Keither's and Opes took Emma's.

Emma walked in line as Elves came and pressed their palms to the tree. Sara looked confused as they stood next to Sasha and she closed her eyes and touched the tree. Then Sara gave a slight sob. It was Emma's turn. Her mind joined with Opes' as he touched the tree. She felt life run from her own body to the plant, and with it a prayer in her heart wove itself with the energy and love of others before her.

Emma stood off to the side as people walked up to the tree. She felt something bump against her leg and looked down to see Sasha's ruby familiar, Princess. She picked the cat up, scratching its ears. "Hey girl, how are you?" she asked as the cat rubbed its face against her neck.

"We are about to leave," Cynta's voice came from behind her.

Emma turned around, looking up before she remembered that Cynta was in her Elf form. "It's been awhile since I've seen you in that form," Emma apologized.

Cynta's brown eyes warmed as she smiled, "It's fine; when you're as short as I am, you get used to people having to look down on you." She winked.

Emma approached Sara and Keither, who spoke. "Are you leaving?" he asked.

Emma nodded, "Sara, once again, I'm sorry for your loss. Are you going to be in Salez long?"

"We will be for some time, yes," Keither said. "I don't think the Pawdin Empire is going to be pressing as hard on this front until the northwest has fallen," he added.

"I wouldn't know," Emma said honestly.

She looked around her, "This place is so far in the mountains, it reminds me of home."

Keither nodded, "We are close to Salmont; well, close if you're on a Dragon. It would take you a couple of weeks with the terrain around here, but on a Dragon's back, I would guess you're not more than an hour or two away."

"About an hour and a half," Cynta said, "We have cleared most of the air space in this area. Emma, are you ready?"

Emma waved goodbye and joined Cynta. "Are we going directly to Salez?" Emma asked.

Cynta shook her head, "No, there is a battle being fought too close to here; we will head northeast, if you can believe it."

Emma raised her eyebrows.

"To the southwest of here, it looks like the Iumenta had a hidden jump crystal; well, we think they did, but at any rate, they were going to drop in ground units. Pawdin forces headed them off. It's a small fight, but one that we will avoid until we are able to confirm if there is a jump crystal or not," Cynta explained.

Emma met up with Sasha who was waving goodbye to Legon and Iselin's retreating forms. Emma watched them flying off. "Are they going to go join the fight?" Emma asked.

Sasha frowned. "Of course they are. Cynta, are you ready?"

Emma turned to see Cynta in her Dragon form. She climbed on to Cynta's back and felt herself stick in place.

Cynta crouched to the ground, stretching her wings skyward. She leapt, climbing in the air. Emma closed her eyes to the rushing wind. She didn't mind flying anymore, and in a way it was almost relaxing to her now. When she was in the air, nothing could bother her. She opened her eyes, looking back at the co-op they'd been in as it shrunk away.

They angled northeast, moving at a steady pace. She watched Sasha's eyes scan the horizon, her gaze rested in the distance and a frown appeared on her face.

"Cynta, to the north; is that smoke?" Sasha asked.

"Yes, it appears so," Cynta responded.

Sasha's eyes went out of focus, "There are no reports of combat in that area. Let's check it out."

Cynta paused for a moment before saying, "Yes, Un Prose."

As they flew, Emma could see that there was smoke in the distance; columns of it rose in a tightly packed area.

"What do you think it is?" Emma asked.

"I can't see yet, there are too many trees in the way, but that's too much smoke to be a caravan and the only things in this area are small mountain co-ops. They may have a barn on fire or something," Sasha said.

Emma felt uneasy. She didn't like getting closer to the front of the war, but at the same time, she figured Sasha was correct.

"It's a co-op," Cynta said.

As they came overhead, Emma gasped. Below them were the burning remains of a co-op. All of the buildings were on fire and in pieces.

"Where are the people with buckets of water?" Emma shouted.

"They are dead," Sasha said in an icy voice. "Cynta, get us in closer to the ground, I want to know what did this."

They descended. Emma could see bodies. None looked like they had been cut with a sword, and she couldn't see arrows.

"A Dragon did this," Sasha said.

Cynta responded, "Yes; one, maybe two."

"This just happened, Cynta, go high," Sasha ordered.

Emma clung to one of Cynta's spikes as they soared higher and higher. Sasha whispered a spell, helping her eyesight.

"Can you see anything?" Emma asked.

Sasha shared her vision with Emma and she saw smoke all over the horizon. Then there was a flash of red and flame. Emma could make out the shape of an Iumenta Dragon incinerating some town or co-op.

"Un Prose?" Cynta said.

"Take it out!" Sasha ordered, and then looked north to a column of smoke that even Emma could see, "that must be Salkay ... which means-"

"Salmont!" Emma yelled.

Sasha growled. "Cynta, kill the filth and then meet us in Salmont, and call my brother." Emma could feel seething anger in her thoughts. Sasha turned to Emma; her face etched in rage as she grabbed Emma's shoulder, taking her with her as she jumped off Cynta's back.

Emma couldn't help but scream as she fell. Next to her, Princess was a ball of crimson fire that burst into the shape of a Puma. Sasha pushed Emma toward Princess, telling her to hold on. Emma wrapped her arms around the cat's neck, feeling herself stick to its back as they started to slow. When they were almost to the ground, Emma closed her eyes.

She didn't feel Princess touch down but she felt branches brush against her. She opened her eyes to a blur of trees as Princess ran up a hill, Sasha next to them. At the top of the hill, Princess and Sasha jumped, glowing with red magic, sending them to the top of the next hill.

Only occasionally would Princess touch the ground for more than a few strides as Emma felt herself being jostled around. They were moving almost as fast as a Dragon, she realized. She closed her eyes and buried her face in Princess' fire fur, repeating a calming script.

After what seemed like an eternity she heard it, the roars of several Dragons. They came to a stop and Emma opened her eyes. They were on the hilltop overlooking Salmont; the same hill where Edis had convinced her to move in with Laura and him. But the scene below was not that of her memories. Five Iumenta Dragons were over the town breathing torrents of fire on fields as townfolk screamed.

"Emma, get the people to the center of town!" Sasha ordered, and then Princess launched herself in the air.

Time slowed for Emma then. She saw one of the Iumenta, a brown one, look at them. She knew that Dragon; she'd seen her so many years before. Then she looked to Sasha as she drew her fenna.

Scarlet flashed from Sasha's fenna, cracking like thunder against a brown ward.

Emma lost sight of Sasha as she came to an abrupt stop. She let go of Princess, who charged an Iumenta soldier. Emma's eyes widened as she watched a family she'd grown up with running away from an Iumenta. The Iumenta turned just as Princess hit it.

"TO THE CENTER OF TOWN!" Emma yelled at the family.

Shock at her appearance registered on their faces, but she ignored the look and grabbed the mother, pushing her toward the town center.

The sky lit up with magic and Emma clapped her hands to her ears as ruby, orange and yellow streaked across the sky. *How long can Sasha hold them?* Emma continued rounding people up as Princess covered her.

Once in the center of town, Emma tried to huddle everyone together. Iumenta ground units were surrounding them. Princess was doing her best to keep the Iumenta away. Emma saw a flick of red around the townsfolk moments before a yellow ball of magic hit them. The people screamed as the spell was stopped by Sasha's ward.

Emma watched her friend glowing red as she tried to hold back the Iumenta. The brown Dragon swung its tail, hitting her. Sasha's wards lit up as she was sent sailing to the ground and through a building. She skidded to a halt near Emma. Before Emma could help her up Sasha was on her feet, wiping blood from her lip.

Emma had never seen Sasha like this. She knew the rage on her face was that of the White Dragon's, but it frightened her.

The brown Dragon landed and spoke to everyone's mind, "Stupid girl, risking your life for a bunch of apes!"

"It wasn't a risk," Sasha spat, her eyes firing up.

The Dragon laughed, "Powerful you might be, but how arrogant! You can't beat us all, but you can die with these people."

Emma started when Sasha giggled.

"What do you think is so funny?" the brown asked.

"That you think I was planning on fighting you alone. You may want to fly away now," Sasha said.

There was the sound of all the Iumenta laughing. "And why is that?" the brown asked.

Sasha smirked, "Because my brother is here."

As if Sasha's words were a cue, Emma saw flicks of purple, pink and emerald and a deafening roar that she recognized as Legon.

Sasha growled, "This one is mine," and then thrust her fenna forward barking, "IGNOTIS-AURIUM!"

Emma backed away from the flash of heat as a beam of magic launched from Sasha's fenna, crashing into the brown Dragon. The people screamed again as three figures dropped from Legon along with all the Dragons' familiars. Sasha was in the air again and Mage landed next to Emma, his fox familiar the size of a lion. Cynta's green bear was attacking several Iumenta along with Princess, Cat and Bill. Three of Legon's guards were on the ground.

Mage drew his fenna, yelling, "Binnon!" A whip of golden fire lashed out, killing five Iumenta. Another of the guard drove her fenna in the ground, making rocks like spikes shoot from the ground, killing others. The last of his guard swung her blade and caused a blue mist that made the Iumenta thrash on the ground as they died.

Iselin dove next to her husband as he took the lead. Below was a group of five Iumenta Ascended. Sasha was provoking them and they weren't paying the least bit of attention. On Legon's other side was Cynta, and on his back was Mage along with two other of the house guard.

Sasha said something and the Dragons looked up, scrambling. Legon let out an earsplitting roar and said, "There are to be no survivors today!"

"With pleasure," Cynta said, diving.

Iselin sent Cat to assist Mage and the others on the ground and squared off with a yellow class six. It was low to the ground and Iselin sent a spell that thinned the air around it, giving it a hard time climbing. She was faintly aware of Legon engaging two other sixes and then she focused completely on the fight at hand.

She lashed out with her tail and claws, keeping the yellow along the town's rooftops. The Dragon was young and obviously unaccustomed to combat. It was unable to gain any altitude as Iselin delivered one punishing blow after another. For a moment she thought the Iumenta was building her confidence, trying to make her cocky. Its wing caught a building and sent it tumbling. Iselin capitalized on the opportunity by breathing fire, blocking the yellow's view as she moved in close.

Legon looked down at his old hometown. Sasha had done well holding the Iumenta as long as she had; they didn't seem to know what to do with her. Her size made her hard to hit and focused her power. Connected as they were, Legon could feel the rage inside her; truly this wasn't his sister on the ground.

Sasha commented on Legon being there and he ordered that there should be no survivors. Mage and the others, along with Bill, detached and headed to the fight on the ground.

In this form his emotions seemed to be more animalistic; he normally had a violent streak, but in this form ... he wanted to rip and tear. The desire mixed with that of the White Dragon's anger that Sasha felt, giving him a feeling of rightness. Cynta was handling the one class seven, leaving Legon to play with two class sixes.

His eye caught the townsfolk below and he thought, *I need to try not to destroy the town ... I guess I'll make this quick.* There were no other Dragons in the area that he would have to fight; he didn't have to save himself or his energy. Legon felt for the massive well of power in him. He focused on a green Dragon and let the power rip up his body and out his maw as he roared. The simple breaking spell slammed into the green, Legon felt its wards buckle under the weight of his power. The Dragon turned to leave, but too late. Legon's mouth filled with the sweet tangy taste of blood as his jaws closed around the green's neck. Its screams of pain cut off in a gurgle as Legon pushed on its back with his legs pulling its neck, his muscles flaring with power as he assisted them with magic. There was a crack as its back broke and the sound of tearing flesh. Legon turned to face his next victim.

Emma clapped her hands to her ears; never had she been so close to Ascended fighting before. The residents of Salmont screamed as the sky flashed with magic. The concussions of spells on wards shook the ground and sucked her breath away. Legon had defeated one Dragon already and was facing off with another cream-colored one. He charged it as it sent spell after spell at him. The cream was ducking and weaving in the sky, avoiding most of Legon's spells. Legon, however, took every spell sent his way without even so much as a flinch. A lavender ball hit the cream and rent the air; unlike its dead companion, it didn't try to flee but lashed out at Legon, spinning him away.

She turned to see Sasha above her in the sky; her fenna dripping scarlet with power and blood. She shot toward the brown; they were fighting almost entirely with magic. Emma could barely keep up with the fight, so fast was their movement.

Several bright flashes of magic made her look to see Sasha racing toward the brown; Sasha was enveloped in a nimbus of crimson. A flash of light blinded Emma. When her vision cleared, she could see the form of the brown Dragon fall to earth, its chest rent and bleeding.

Sasha flew back to Emma, landing next to her. Legon and the cream hit a building nearby and Emma watched as Legon raked his claws the length of the Dragon's neck, spraying the wrecked building with ruby droplets.

Sasha felt the anger of the White Dragon leave her. Her mind felt fuzzy and she was vaguely aware of Iselin and Cynta dismembering the final Iumenta Ascended high above town. The roars of the familiars were growing faint as they finished clearing the outskirts of Salmont proper. To her side were Mage and Emma, along with the two other guard members. Princess soon joined Mage and the others, coming in close to her. Cynta, the only member of Sasha's personal guard, landed behind her with a gentle thought.

Sasha looked into the awestruck faces of the residents of her former home. It wasn't joy that filled her heart as she beheld them; not a feeling of homecoming. No, years had passed since her time in this town; she'd grown, become powerful and confident. Yet she found all of her old insecurities and fears rushing back to her.

A young woman peered at Emma. Sasha remembered the woman as one of Emma's old friends; she eyed Emma and then turned her gaze to Sasha.

"It can't be," she whispered so softly it pushed Sasha's Elvin ears to their limit. "Sasha?" the girl said and no one else spoke.

Sasha opened her mouth to speak, forgetting her station.

Emma spoke before Sasha could. "Yes, this is Un Prose Sasha of the Great Elvin House Evindass," Emma said formally, introducing Sasha as she had so many times before. She gestured to Legon and Iselin, "Also Un Prosa Legon and Prose Iselin of the Great House Evindass."

"Look at her eyes," someone said, but Sasha couldn't tell who.

She found her knees becoming weak; she could see the fear in the townspeople's eyes as they locked on to the metallic red of her own. "THAT DEMON IS BACK TO KILL US!" Emma's old friend shrieked.

Sasha felt her face fall and then she jumped as Cynta let out a roar, speaking to all. "You have just been saved by the Head of a Great Elvin House, a Head of House who had no reason to risk her own life for yours. You will show proper respect!" she growled.

Cynta added to Sasha alone, in a firm but caring tone, "Remember who and what you are."

Sasha lifted her head and she heard Legon's guard mutter, "Why did we save them?"

Legon spoke to the people who all were averting their gazes in fear. "It is not lost upon us why you think the way you do. You have been influenced by the Iumenta for years, but those times are over. You must now decide for yourselves who is the demon. Is it the girl you all know, the one who has tended to many of your wounds, who has never spoken a harsh word to any? Or is it the filth that sought to kill you and burn your families?"

A man in his early forties stepped forward. Sasha did not know him, but he regarded her with downturned eyes. "I do not know you personally, my lady," he said, addressing her, "I came after your parents left, but I've heard of you. They say you are a demon but never have I been able to hear of an unkind act you performed ..." he looked up to her and then waved a hand behind him. A woman about his age came forward leading a girl probably in her late teens or early twenties. He took their hands, "But today I have proof for myself. If not for you; me and mine would be dead right now, but we were saved by your hand. That doesn't sound like the hand of a demon to me, but that of a kind and protective person." He knelt, his wife and daughter doing the same, and looked up again with resolve, "We owe you our lives. If there is any way we can serve you, just say the word."

Legon's mind joined Sasha's more firmly, and with it came confidence. She spoke. "Thank you. What is your profession?" she asked.

"Healer, highness," he responded.

Sasha resisted the urge to smile, "I dare say that Salmont is well served in my mother's absence." Then she looked to the rest of the town and spoke with a clear voice, "We will heal your wounded, but this area is not safe right now. Salkay has been destroyed by the Iumenta; they meant to do the same here. There are camps near Salez, should you care to leave Salmont until the war is over." She turned and walked away from the gathered group of people, walking toward her old home.

Once out of sight, she felt weak again. Footsteps came up near her.

"Thank you Cynta," she said.

Cynta came up next to her, having resumed her Elf form. Above them, Elf Dragons filled the sky; the rest of Legon's and Sasha's guard, along with Iselin's, had arrived. "Is it wise to have nearly the entirety of the house guard here?" she asked Cynta.

As Dragons flew overhead, several Elves jumped to the ground and took their places around Sasha. As her guard formed, she felt more comfortable.

"The Iumenta will not attack us," Cynta said. "But you do not feel safe here," she pointed out.

"I never really have been safe here without my brother, have I?" Sasha said.

Cynta smirked, "That was before you had us, Un Prose."

Sasha smiled warmly. She stopped, before her was her old home. She thought of approaching it, walking inside one last time and then thought better. *No, it's time Salmont lost its hold on me,* she thought. She turned back to Cynta, "Perhaps we should go back to Salez. I have work that needs to be done and my presence here doesn't seem to be needed anymore."

Chapter Twenty-Four
Arrangements

"Proper planning is the key to any successful venture; you may not always be able to follow your plans, but having them will give you a path and skill that will lead to success."

-The Exiled Captain (Author Unknown)

L egon flew south, honestly not caring about the town of Salmont as it shrunk behind him. To his side were Opes and the rest of his guard, flying in a tight formation. The trip to Salmont had more of an effect on Sasha than it had him, but Legon thought she was going to be fine.

"Opes," Legon said.

"Yes Un Prosa?"

"Why do you think the Iumenta were burning towns?" Legon asked.

Opes considered the question for a moment. "It appears to be some sort of scorch earth policy," he said, and then reading the questioning edge in Legon's mind added, "As you retreat, if you burn everything, leaving nothing for your enemy; in a way it's like a victory."

"I understand that, but why Human towns? You only burn resources ..." then Legon's mind jumped to what should have been painfully obvious, "Humans are just another resource to the Iumenta," he said, feeling deflated.

"I agree that is the only possible conclusion," Opes said grimly.

Legon felt himself speeding up, his guard following suit without question. As soon as he was in range of Salez, he reached out to Sydin's mind.

"Yes, Un Prosa," Sydin asked.

"How is the Ascended reserve in the Pawdin Empire?" Legon asked.

"Mostly young and untrained. We have a backup force along the Pawdin borders and under-trained Ascended in the interior. Why?"

Legon showed Sydin what he'd seen.

"We have been getting reports like that all day; what are you thinking?"

"I would like to look at the possibility of deploying more Ascended before the Iumenta kill everyone," Legon said.

Sydin said that he would meet with Legon once he was back in Salez. This left Legon to his thoughts for the rest of the flight back. The Iumenta had always been tyrants, but outright genocide was new, even for them.

After awhile the twin fortresses of Salez came into view. Legon connected with the Elf base, receiving priority to land. He and his guard circled, turning into the wind, the landscape rushing below them. Legon banked back and forth, slowing himself until he landed. As soon as he touched down, he transformed into his Elf form, and walked off the landing pad to a waiting Sydin.

"I have scheduled a meeting with the commands of the other Great Houses in an hour. Evindass has control over the Ascended as far as the war goes but I would like to consult with them," Sydin explained.

Legon nodded, "That's a good idea, I spoke to Iselin and she will be in attendance as well. We will change and meet you in half an hour."

Sydin nodded walking off.

Legon turned to his wife, smiling. Current situation or not, it was rare to see her in her Elf form lately. She walked up next to him and took his hand. He pulled it to his lips, kissing the back of it. "How is it that you can still give me butterflies?" he asked, making her face flush as she smiled, trying not to roll her eyes.

Iselin followed her husband into a small meeting room. Sydin was already present, along with leadership from six of the other Great Houses. A crystal in the center of the room was lit up; and Iselin knew that leadership from the remaining Houses would be present. The attendants stood as she and Legon entered.

Sydin spoke. "Thank you all for joining us today; I will not be leading this meeting, but rather Un Prosa Legon of House Evindass. We will be discussing possible strategic uses of Ascended currently stationed in the Pawdin interior. Is everyone with us today authorized to make decisions on this level?" he asked.

Everyone said that they were able to. Iselin knew that Sydin was calling this meeting more as a courtesy to the other Houses, but she still sent calming waves to Legon. She didn't want him to appear as if emotion was ruling his decisions.

Legon walked up to the crystal, saying, "My wife and I would like to add our thanks to that of Sydin's. My fellow leaders, I am going to presume that you have been brought up to speed with the happenings here in the north, in regard to the Iumenta aggression toward Humanity."

They said that they had.

Legon continued, "We currently have nearly twenty-five percent of active Ascended stationed inside the Pawdin Empire. Ten percent of our Ascended are assigned to Domes along the Mahj defensive line. These I think, we need not consider moving. But those inside our borders are another story. We think it appropriate to deploy the remaining fifteen percent to securing current Cona lands or to the front lines."

There was no response at first. Iselin knew the other Houses wouldn't be keen on this idea. The Great Houses would be leaving the interior largely unprotected by Ascended.

The representative from House Viridi spoke. "What does House Evindass hope to accomplish?" she asked, sounding uncomfortable.

"The Pawdin Empire is in no threat from the Impa Empire. We need to increase pressure on the Impa to not only stop the inevitable genocide of Humans in the area, but also to bring this war to a swifter end," Legon explained.

"Do you think the Impa will respond by pulling Ascended from their own interior?" the representative from House Amuun asked.

Leena, a brown-haired woman from house Paldin responded, "It may not have that effect. If we increase pressure on all fronts, it could make the Impa Provinces concerned. They could keep their forces at home in case they are needed to defend their homelands."

A severe man with cold eyes spoke, "House Coreen agrees with House Paldin and Evindass. If we want to win the war and minimize losses, we need to pull more Ascended into the fight. We already outnumber the Iumenta in the sky." He turned to Legon, "Un Prosa Legon, may I make a request?"

Legon nodded.

"To the north we are not fairing as well, do you think it would be possible to put a focus on the northern lands?"

Legon glanced to Sydin, his eyes quickly going out of focus and then he looked to the representative from Coreen. "Yes, we can do that," Legon said.

Sydin stood. "We can put an increased effort in the north; this will force the Impa to send more Ascended to that area. Once that is done, we will pull in our reserve, pressing up from the south. If this works right, we will be able to gain some stability in the near future up north, and then when our extra Ascended arrive gain valuable ground in the south."

Members of Houses added other thoughts, but by the end of the meeting every House was behind the new plan. Legon and Iselin would be going north; Legon's presence would not only worry the Iumenta, but give the northern troops a much needed boost in morale.

Legon walked out of the meeting pleased. He and Iselin would be leaving that evening to a Carrier group in the north. He reached out his mind to Sasha to tell her his plans. She wasn't thrilled about him and Iselin leaving, but understood the value of it.

"What are your plans?" he asked her.

"My team jumped in this morning, we are taking the jump crystal in the north fortress. We are getting ready to move in by the end of the day tomorrow or whenever the House guard has cleared the building," she said, sounding irritated.

"What's got you upset?"

"Nothing, we just have to include a security force from the Human military, is all. They are feeling underutilized, but I have my choice of units so that's not too bad," she said.

"Are you going to make Barnin and his men do it?" Legon asked, knowing the answer.

"Of course," she said brightly "They may not like the idea of sitting around, but they have been on the lines too long and there's no reason not to at least have some more good company," she said.

"Have you told Barnin yet?"

She paused, "Well, coward that I am, I made the Human officers do it. I mean, they wanted to be more involved, so they can tell Barnin that he is going to be babysitting a group of Elves that really don't need babysitting." Then changing tack, asked, "Are you going to have time for dinner tonight?"

"Yes, we are going to be jumping and need to rest and get a bite to eat. Ise and I will be eating here, so let's keep it low key."

"Perfect, I'll let Emma and Edling know," she said, and broke the connection.

Barnin stood at attention, trying not to let his eyes glaze over. He was being told that his unit was going to be assigned to assist in security for the Lady Sasha and her team of researchers. Ankle stood next to him, looking equally bored. The man speaking was named Johnson and was new to the area, he was sandy haired with a hook nose.

"Men, this is a key opportunity for us; you should feel honored to be selected for a mission like this," he said, looking down his hooked nose at Barnin. Johnson looked up at Ankle, "Is that a smirk I see, son?"

Son? Barnin thought. *We have to be older than this guy; who is he calling son?*

"Not smirking, Sir," Ankle answered.

Johnson's eyes narrowed. "It is unlikely that you can be trusted on your own with this, so I will be accompanying you in your assignment. You are to speak only when spoken to by representatives of House Evindass, am I clear?" he said firmly.

Barnin refrained from rolling his eyes. He gathered his men and waited for Johnson before heading over to where the Elves were. Johnson insisted on leading them even though he had no idea where he was going. Finally they arrived at an open Dragon hangar. Elves moved, stopping to look up at Barnin's unit, which was marching in formation.

A figure walked from the building in a lavender robe. It was Emma, looking confused. She looked at Barnin and he nodded to Johnson.

"My name is Emma, I'm Un Prose Sasha's assistant; may I help you?" she said, keeping a polite but formal tone to her voice.

Johnson looked at Emma, regarding her passively, "I am Major Johnson, and I am here to speak with Lady Sasha. Please fetch her."

Barnin heard Heath whisper, "Bad call."

Emma puffed up, "Fetch her?" She turned her gaze to Barnin. "Barnin, who is this man?" Emma asked, dropping all hints of politeness.

Johnson spoke before Barnin could. "As I said before, I am Major Johnson. Please do not address my men. From this point on, I will be Lady Sasha's sole contact. Now yes, fetch her for me," he said, closing the subject.

Barnin saw Cynta walking out of the hangar, her purple House guard overcoat catching the breeze. That, coupled with her being followed by a bear cub familiar of bright green, made her rather intimidating. Barnin repressed the urge to smile.

Before Johnson could speak, Cynta said coolly, "I am Cynta, Head of Un Prose Sasha's security, you will be under my command. For further reference, we selected Barnin and his men; not you. You do not *fetch* Heads of House; when their assistants greet you, they are standing in proxy as the Head of House and should be treated as such. And lastly, Un Prose Sasha will address whomever she chooses whenever she chooses, am I clear?"

Johnson shrunk back a bit,"Y-yes um ... Cynta. Forgive me, Emma, what may I do?"

Emma eyed him, "Not talking would be a start."

She walked up to Barnin and hugged him, kissed Heath on the cheek and asked Ankle if he'd grown.

Ankle smirked. "Someone has to make up for how short you are," he said, earning a slap to the arm.

"Come on in, Sasha is inside." She turned to Cynta, "I leave Major Johnson, along with the rest of Barnin's men in your capable hands," Emma said to Cynta, making Johnson blanch.

Ankle walked inside the hangar with Barnin and Heath. Elves were moving about, no longer paying them any attention. Toward the back of the building, they found Sasha next to a table of glass jars. She turned and smiled at them.

"How are you guys today?" she asked warmly. "I hear your new boss is a bit stuffy."

Barnin chuckled. "Stuffy is an understatement. So why did you ask for us, Sash?" he asked.

She shrugged. "Well, we needed to make the Cona government feel involved. I thought of your men because we are friends and I thought you could use some time away from the front and could go for the comfort of Salez," she explained.

Ankle stopped listening; he was fine with the assignment, since he knew that he and his men wouldn't be doing any real work on this mission. It was for PR and the thought of not having people try to kill him seemed wonderful. He and Heath turned their attention to the tables.

He bowed in close, seeing a glass filled with some black liquid in it. He sniffed and wrinkled his nose. "Smells like sewage," he said.

"It's dead algae," Emma explained. "We pulled it from a vat in the fortress."

"Why did you do that?" Ankle asked.

Emma shrugged, "There isn't much we can learn from it but we wanted to make sure."

He must have looked confused as she explained, "It's from the base of a jump crystal ..."

"A power vat?" Heath asked excitedly.

She nodded, "Yes, it appears to be relatively standard, but like I said it's hard to tell."

"What's a power vat?" Ankle asked.

Emma looked at the glass, making a face, "It's a mixture of a couple different kinds of algae and some yeast. The Iumenta use the vat to power crystals."

Ankle thought about asking more but decided that it would be over his head. Instead he asked, "So, do you know where we are going to be staying during this assignment?"

"Yes, you will be with our staff in the north fortress, I believe you will be in some of the barracks there," Emma said.

"Hmm, well it sounds better than a tent to me."

Heath took in the gates of the north tower and urged his horse through. From the outside, it had looked like one big structure, but Heath could see now that it was a collection of buildings. A few were destroyed but for the most part everything was in good shape; he'd heard the south fortress hadn't done as well. He left his mount at the stables and followed a boy in a brown pair of pants and white coat to a building that said, "Housing building twenty-three," in Glosso.

"You are room 305, Sir," the boy said, moving on to tell others where they were to stay.

He entered the building, walking along its smooth stone floors, the sound of his and others' shoes reverberating. He made his way up a graceful staircase and along another hall until he stood in front of a red-wood door. The Number 305 was in brass. He turned the handle and pushed the door, which swung without a sound.

He stepped into a room that was only built to accommodate one. He let out a whistle, taking in the fine rug on the floor. He walked to the bed, sitting on it and feeling himself sinking in, running his hands along the silken sheets. He looked out of the large window, getting a view of Salez. He didn't want to get off the bed; it was so soft. His desire to explore got the better of him and he examined a writing desk with a marble inlay top and oak armoire. Next he found that he had a bathroom to himself and, "A shower!" he said. "You landed in it this time Heath."

There was a knock at the door and he opened it to see Ankle.

"Pretty amazing isn't it?" Ankle said.

"You can say that."

"Hey I was wondering, do you know what these little discs on the wall do?" Ankle asked pointing to a little brass disc in the wall.

Heath touched it, making a light in the ceiling go on and making Ankle jump, "Looks like they control lights."

"So there is still magic here?" Ankle asked, concerned.

"Looks like it. I bet the Iumenta only had time to disable the jump crystals and anything the military would need. That's good for us; it looks like we'll have hot water and the building will stay warm," Heath said, not sharing Ankle's concern.

Barnin wrapped a towel around himself and stepped out of the shower. He knew some of his men were worried about the magic the building used, but for his part; if the place was safe enough for the House guard to let Sasha stay in it, it was safe enough for him. When he got out of the shower and in his room, there was a knock at the door.

"Coming!" he said, putting on pants and a shirt.

He answered the door to a girl in a brown skirt and white shirt. She bowed. "Master Barnin, may I interest you in some dinner?"

"Um sure, but you don't have to call me master," and then, "Do you work here?" he asked, wondering why any of the Human staff was left on.

"Yes master Barnin, I do. I assume you, like the others, are wondering about my trustworthiness." She turned, lifting her hair, exposing a mark on the back of her neck, "I am – well, was -- in the care. Most of the Human staff here was killed by the Iumenta as you know, but I and a few others hid. We showed the Elves how to get around the passageways."

"You don't mind staying here?" he asked.

"Oh no, we are still of use to the Elves and I don't really have anywhere else to go, now do I?" Then she said, "If you follow me, I will take you to the dining area."

Keither cantered along, not paying attention to the countryside as it passed around him. Over the years he had become more confident on Pixie, but still didn't care for horseback. Ahead, there were spirals of smoke from a refugee camp that he was to assist. *I wonder what I will find?* He thought, *perhaps an issue with clean water or maybe a housing problem?* In a way, he should be thankful that he had seen and fixed most issues that arose from the various camps. But as he drew closer, he could see that this camp and its problems were in many ways the same and different from that of former camps. Hordes of people were in the fields around it, clogging the main entrance. The high linked fence that surrounded the camp looked like it could burst with the numbers inside.

People cleared out of the way for him the best that they could, and a group of soldiers on horseback rode out to meet him. One was holding up a thick hand. "Whoa there," he said, sounding both frustrated and concerned. "Where do you think you're going?" he asked.

Keither held out a sheet of parchment that the man unfolded and read. The look on his face didn't harden or perk up as he looked at Keither. "Sorry about that, we have been getting people trying to come in to camp with all manner of livestock, please follow us to the command building."

Keither did as he was asked, still not saying a word. Rather, he tried to take in the hundreds if not thousands of disheveled and dirty people. *Where did they come from?* He wondered.

Inside the camp, he could smell waste and death; the people having no room to move about and for a moment Keither thought that those outside of the camp were better off. As he looked, he could see that the camp was set up properly; even boasting several Elvin structures. *No, this camp is different; it suffers not from poor organization, but from being overrun.* They came to what he presumed was the command building. One of the Human house's banners flew outside, ash staining the fine fabric. Inside, he was met by a portly man named Sith, who lead him to a small room where several others sat around a table. All looked worn out, and Sith didn't bother to introduce the attendees to Keither.

"This is Keither; he is here to consult us," Sith said with a tone of exasperation.

Those in attendance eyed Keither not with distaste, but rather a lack of faith. He took his time before speaking, "I can tell by the looks on your faces that you aren't overly confident in me."

Sith waved a hand, "It's not personal; it's just you are the fifth person sent to try to help us deal with our situation. So far no one has been able to fix our camp. But I suppose we should try; would you like a report?"

"Let's start with that," Keither said.

He listened to people report back what he assumed was going on. The camp had neither the room nor the staff to handle all those around.

Adding insult to injury, the chief of security said, "We are running into issues with security now as well."

"How so?" Keither asked.

The burly man looked down, a tint of shame on his face, "Some of the men are obviously getting frustrated, thieving is rampant, and just with the amount of congestion in the camp, they are getting to their wit's end. I'm not making excuses, but we are finding that some of the guards are getting rather abusive. Sadder still with leadership being overwhelmed, we have found that some of our staff is engaging in still rather worse activities."

"Such as?"

The man turned redder still, "You name it; theft, assault, prostitution, kidnapping, even murder and rape are running rather rampant. We have been trying to keep things under control, but it hasn't been easy."

Keither nodded, he was using the Mahann, helping him to think clearly, and the reports of abuse did not bother him in this state, but were just another bit of information. He paused, closing his eyes for a long while until someone cleared their throat, to which Keither raised a finger. Prior to leaving Salez that morning, he'd read over reports from every camp in the occupied land as he did every day. He could name the commander in each, how many supplies they had, along with every other detail.

His mind reached out, connecting with a set of individuals assigned to relaying messages back and forth with Salez. Soon he was hearing his assistant's voice in his head clear as day. They spoke for a moment before the assistant reached out to the Elvin communication network. A short time later, Keither broke the connection, opening his eyes to the room.

"There is no way to fix this camp; you have been overrun and stretched too thin. This in no way is a failure on anyone's part," Keither said.

"But then what are we to do?" Sith asked, worry etching his face.

"I have been in contact with my office; there are many camps in the area that are under-capacity. Still further southwest, there are some that can handle many, many more people. We will arrange river boats from Salez to go down the Kayloose, transporting refugees elsewhere. In the meantime, I will petition the Pawdin Empire to send Ascended to the area to help calm people. I will also see if I can get some Venefica to the area to help you police your staff and help take care of local tensions," Keither explained.

The people in the room seemed to relax and respond to him with a bit more respect, but before they could speak, Keither went on, "Do you know why you are getting so many more refugees? Our estimations show you should be getting a tenth this many."

Sith shook his head, "It's the Iumenta burning towns as they leave I think, people don't want to be near the front and are fleeing."

Keither shook his head and stood, "Thank you for your time, I do not mean to be rude, but I will be able to better serve you from Salez where I can personally procure transport and resources for you. I will be back in the next few days. In the meantime, please try to find out from which parts of the Empire people are coming from." He spoke with a few of the attendants briefly, but left as soon as he could.

Chapter Twenty-Five
Bellum Omega

"We tell ourselves that hindsight is perfect, that we can see what could and should have been. The reality is that hindsight is just as blind as foresight. We pick apart whatever the outcome of something was, as though if we'd done something different the troubles of today would not exist. This is a falsehood, we may have an idea of the imminent outcome had we acted differently, but past that we know nothing. The only difference between hind and foresight is with foresight we don't yet know at least one of likely many outcomes."
-Rivulets of Time

Legon's nostrils filled with the scent of sea air as his wings opened, catching the breeze. He could feel Iselin's mind join his as she completed her jump. Below them was the roiling northern sea. The battle group moved in perfect formation. Several Carriers, along with many other ships moved along seemingly unfazed by the rough waters. Legon angled to one of the Carriers and made his descent. Wind buffeted him and he remembered back to his first attempt at landing on a Carrier. The thought amused Iselin as she read his thoughts. Legon moved in with confidence now, using just a bit of magic to help stabilize himself with the wind and the ship's movements.

He landed inside the hangar, transforming into his Elf form as his feet touched down. Iselin came in behind him doing the same, followed by Opes who stayed in his Ascended form. Legon and Iselin were met by an attendant who ushered them down the ship's corridors to a meeting room near the bridge. An Elf woman in purple robes stood and introduced herself, waiting for Legon and Iselin to be seated.

"It is an honor to have you aboard Un Prosa and Prose," she said in a warm tone.

"Thank you Captain," Legon replied with equal warmth. "Has the weather been like this long?" he asked, making small talk.

The captain smiled, "Yes I'm afraid so; it hasn't been bad enough to keep Ascended from flying, but it has made for much less contact with the Impa Navy."

"How have things been going with the Impa Navy?"

The Captain gave an unconcerned look, "They have not posed much of a threat in several months now; it was like this in the War of Generations as well, once they have been beaten, they keep their fleets close to land."

"Hmmm, I wonder why that is," Legon wondered aloud. The Impa ships were a force to be reckoned with, though not to the same quality of the Pawdin Navy.

The attendant who brought him and Iselin to the room re-entered, caring a tray of glasses and Poti, along with several cakes and other snacks. Legon took of sip of his drink, making more small talk until the Captain came around to the point of their meeting.

"We have received word from the front; we are taking losses here in the north," she said.

"How bad?" Iselin asked.

The Captain took a sip of Poti, "Not catastrophic, but enough for House Coreen to pull out of some areas. I dare say with the poor weather and being so close to Impa air space, we have been unable to properly control the skies."

Legon nodded, "Yes, we have been told that the Impa have been making a strong presence up here."

The Captain waved her hand at the wall, opening a panel that revealed a crystal that shone with a map of the northern Cona lands. Symbols represented different groups varying from civilians to military units. To the south were mountains, that bottlenecked a stretch of land holding several large cities. These cities needed to fall. Beyond them, the mountains opened back up. Once clear of the mountains, the Pawdin forces could come on the Capital from the north, cutting off its retreat. Bailaya rested against still more mountains, its strategic advantage being that there was only one way for an army to make an efficient run at it. That meant coming from the south, but to do that they would have to deal with a Dragon Dome.

"We have to control the north," Legon said, "if we don't, the Impa will be able to keep the Capital supplied and move troops in."

"What is our plan to retake the north, Un Prosa?" the Captain asked.

"We are sending many Ascended to the area; some like Iselin and I will be Carrier-based, but still more will be land-based. We need to make a hard push inland."

Legon continued to outline the strategy that he and the other houses had agreed on before returning to his hangar with Iselin. In the morning, they would be flying their first sortie in the north. *I wonder if my friend will be here,* he thought, thinking of the green class eight.

Umbra scanned the land as she flew. It was light out, which would normally be a bit of a liability for a Dragon who stayed alive based on her ability to fade into darkness, but today she wasn't looking for Iumenta. She, like the rest of the Pawdin military, knew where the Iumenta were. No, today she was looking for groups of refugees from the eastern lands. The area was thick forest, making it hard to see the ground, and Umbra found herself staying low as she and her squad flew in a zig-zag, scanning with all their senses.

The mission was a consequence of the Iumenta's scorch earth policy. From what the Elves and resistance had been told by survivors, the Iumenta would move into an area, quickly destroying what they could, and then leaving. Still, the majority of townspeople were being wiped out, but those who hid or fled prior to the Iumenta's arrival found that they could survive. Refugee camps had been overwhelmed with people seeking any type of help they could get, but within the last week the hordes of people had stopped almost alltogether.

Festina contacted her. "Are you seeing anybody?" he asked.

"No I'm not," then to the rest of her squad, "Has anybody seen any signs of people?"

"I found a town, but from what I can tell, it's empty; not even burned," Festina said.

Umbra could see the town in his mind, ordering him to drop lower and take a closer look. "If people are leaving, we will see tracks," she said.

She changed course to head toward the town, ordering her squad to do likewise. She flew overhead, looking down at the town. Nothing was out of place, except that there were no people. Umbra felt a shiver run down her spine. Ground forces hadn't cleared the area yet and she was under orders to not go on the ground.

"Boss, we have our orders ..." one of her squad said.

"I know, but we have to get on the ground, we just can't see with all the trees," Umbra said, landing in the town's center.

She walked around town, trying not to run into any of the buildings or break anything with her tail.

"What's it looking like?" Festina asked.

"Well ..." she said, taking in a large set of tracks heading into the woods, "it looks like everyone or nearly everyone left, but it doesn't look like there was a struggle of any kind." She sniffed the air at the edge of the woods, "Something isn't right here ..."

She took her Elf form, cursing that the last thing she wore was a dress. Her squad was none too happy, but stayed close overhead, wards flicking around her. She could smell recent death. *Someone put up a fight.* She walked into the woods, following the tracks, the smell of the trees was too strong ... she walked up to one, seeing a small crystal embedded in its trunk. She went to look at it, hearing a snap behind her. She whirled and drew her faloon, startling a man holding a small boy.

She lowered the weapon. "Where did everyone go?" she asked.

The man shook his head, "Don't know miss, my son and I stayed the night in the woods having some father-son time, you know? We came into town about an hour ago and there's no one home."

"You've been here for an hour, you say?"

He nodded, Umbra turned her attention to her squad, "you heard that they've been here an hour and we didn't sense them."

"Concealment spells. What's with the crystal in the tree?" Tacita asked.

"I don't know yet, but fan out. Go to active seeking spells and breakers; I want to find out what is being hidden. Tacita, call in for backup," Umbra ordered and looked back to the man. "I'm sorry, I'm talking to my squad, are you injured?" she asked.

"No miss, just a little concerned, my wife and daughters aren't around either, and I'm worried."

He looked it too. Umbra asked him to stay close, as she walked on. There was the telltale crack of magic as wards broke, but it wasn't loud. She doubted the man or boy even heard it.

Festina's voice rang in her head, "Broke a pod of crystals about five minutes north of you, they weren't strong, maybe had enough power to last a week."

She looked back at the man, "I am going north of here just a ways, I need you to stay here, please?"

He looked worried, but nodded anyway.

She started to move; as soon as she was out of sight, she pulled a large crystal from a bag on her shoulder, releasing her familiar. It took the form of a wolf, walking just ahead of her. The scent of death grew stronger, much too strong, and Umbra picked up her pace, coming over a small hill and stopping cold. Her gut clenched as she looked down at the bodies. They were stacked almost neatly in a ditch area. She walked up to the small pit, trying to wrap her mind around what she was looking at. The people were naked; their clothes nowhere to be seen. Only a few of the bodies were pierced with arrows or cuts. She could see deep furrows from carts leaving the area. She started to shake.

A new mind joined hers, it was Sydin. "What are you doing on the ground ..." he started and stopped, seeing her thoughts.

"There's still no sign of struggle ... these people trusted their killers ... how ... how can this happen?" she said, walking up and touching a body. The hand in hers was cold to the touch. "They had to use magic ..." she looked at the few bodies with damage, "those must have resisted ..."

"Umbra, stay put," Sydin ordered, but she wasn't listening.

She heard a cry and turned to see the man and the boy running toward the pit, the man grabbing at one of the bodies and mumbling to himself. Umbra shook herself and looked down at the tracks. She could see them going north.

"I have to stay put Tacita, but you don't -- these people have only been dead a few hours; find those carts!" she ordered.

Tacita acknowledged the order, flying north. Umbra was angry; she didn't want to be stuck on the ground, but she'd received a direct order. She tried to calm the man and boy and help them to find their loved ones. It wasn't long before Sydin and a contingent of ground units were in the area. Sydin was in his Elf form to better inspect the site.

"It appears that the Impa weren't looking for a scorched earth policy," he said.

"What do you mean?" Umbra asked.

"You saw the town, nothing was burned or harmed, only the people. I dare say the Iumenta saw how we reacted to them burning towns and decided to be more subtle about their doings." He took in the heap of people, adding, "And it appears they also have become far more efficient. I bet these people thought they were being evacuated from the front," he said, shaking his head. He placed his hand on her shoulder. "You did well today."

She spun, "Did I? How did I, Sir? I went off orders and found that despite upping our presence, people are still being killed by the hundreds." A thought occurred to her and she recoiled. "Did we do this?" she asked, more to herself.

"Umbra, this war was inevitable, you know that ..."

"Not this time ... the last time ... did we do this? What if we'd finished what we'd started?" she asked, looking up at him. "What if at Bellum Omega we'd have pushed on ... none of this would have happened ..." she said, feeling shame, thinking of all of the death in the land, of those in the care and Mors. Rachel's sunken face burned in Umbra's mind. Yes, if only Bellum Omega had been different.

Legon touched down in his hangar. The ship rocked back and forth in the rough waters of the north, but it didn't bother him. There was something he found oddly soothing about the movement of the ship. Magic kept him from motion sickness and with his size, the movement just didn't feel that extreme. He and Iselin's hangars were joined, and he found her curled up sleeping. She didn't stir when he curled up next to her. It was odd sleeping next to his wife in his Dragon form. It was necessary in case of attack; Ascending took energy that could be used in a fight.

She was warm next to him, but her scales were rough and he couldn't hold her. Memories flooded his mind. Times when they could lay in bed together, having his arms wrapped around her sleeping form, fingers running through her long hair or scratching her back. He could still do that, but with claws, he doubted it would have the desired effect.

He let himself get lost in a daydream. Kissing her soft skin, feeling her body mold to his ... her lips ...

Iselin grunted, only half awake. "Stop thinking about that," she muttered in his head.

Legon pushed his nose against her neck, "I would love to be nibbling on your neck and ears right now love, you know that?"

She turned her head, opening one eye, "You're mean. Careful; I'll fight back."

He made a few other comments and true to her word she fought back, sending him memories of some of his favorite times with her.

He chuckled. "Fine, you win," he said.

They had been in the north for the better part of a month. When they'd arrived, the Elves had started losing ground. Since then they'd retaken much of that ground back. With Legon's arrival and reinforcements from the south, morale had boosted and the Elves were making progress. News of the mass graves also encouraged many to fight with more vigor.

"Should it be a shock?" Iselin asked.

"No, not after Mors. In truth, I thought things would be worse than they are," he said honestly.

Iselin nodded in agreement. The images they'd seen from that camp still haunted him. Human and Elf forces had also found the dark warriors; they were becoming a regular part of daily warfare. They were of little consequence for the Elves, skilled they may have been, but on the same level as Elves with centuries of experience they were not. Still, the Dark Warriors did their damage. He didn't see any of the green Iumenta class eight. Opes thought that the Iumenta were using him as a battle standard, a way of boosting morale in the area; Legon was hoping for another shot at him. *Maybe at the Dome,* he thought. With that thought he nodded off to sleep.

Neelya walked down the dimly lit hall, approaching the Queen's study. She knocked twice, softly.

"Who is it?" the Queen's voice came from inside.

"Neelya, Un Prose."

The Queen asked her to come in. Neelya walked through the door, taking in the fine rug of two Dragons on the floor. The room never seemed to change; it was a constant. She found the Queen on a terrace overlooking the city. The moon was dim this evening, making the lights of Bailaya seem all the more bright. The Queen was leaning on a stone railing with her arms crossed, something very uncharacteristic of her.

"Join me at the rail, Neelya," she said with as much warmth as the Queen could possess.

Neelya came next to the Queen, resting against the rail as well. They didn't speak for some time; Neelya would on occasion look over to the Queen, wondering why she was summoned.

"Neelya, do you enjoy serving me?" the Queen asked.

"Yes of course Un Prose, it is a great honor," she said in earnest.

The Queen looked at her with what looked like the hint of a smile, "I was like you once you know, young, trusting and filled with ideas." She looked back out over the city. "We see the fruit of many of those ideas now here, in this city," she said.

Neelya looked out over the city and said, "You have done great things."

The Queen looked at her again, "Do you think so? I'm not so sure anymore."

Neelya looked down; what was she to say to that? The Queen never showed a second thought about anything.

"I don't mean my end goal, but how I've tried to go about doing it. Neelya, learning from mistakes is the mark of a great leader," the Queen said.

"What mistakes could you have possibly made?" Neelya asked, worrying she had gone too far.

"Neelya, I am as much your mentor as you are my assistant, you have nothing to fear this night from me." Then she pointed to one of the mansions surrounding the castle, "Do you see that house?"

Neelya said that she did, adding with a bit of disgust, "That house belongs to the Human, House Ceeder," she said looking at the dimly lit house. It was large, one of the largest buildings in the area.

"Yes that is Ceeder; they were once a Great House you know, maybe even the greatest of them all. Once I turned them, turning the rest of the great Human Houses was simple. Ceeder is now the only House left that has the resources and pull to keep a property so close to the Palace. The day will soon come when they will be forced to sell that property and finally, the noble Houses will have no more pull," the Queen said.

"It will be another victory," Neelya said.

"I'm not so sure anymore. The first thing I did was to destroy the Human nobility, I made the people dependent on me, but it was that same nobility that had put me in power. They were the ones who paid and ran the war efforts and kept the people in order; now they are gone and I have puppet lords in their stead. And now when I need real leaders to take charge of Humanity, the Elves are at our doorstep." The Queen looked to Neelya, reading the look on her face, "You are confused? I'm not saying that destroying the Human leadership wasn't going to be necessary, but now I wonder if I should have waited until the Pawdin Empire had fallen first."

"They will Un Prose, they will," Neelya reassured her.

The Queen took her hand, leading her inside to a writing desk. On it was a map of the area. "I'm not so sure," the Queen said pointing to a spot on the map. "This is the Bailaya Dragon Dome, south of it is the Elves, to the north we are losing ground again. The only thing between us and the southern Elves is that Dome," she said fingering the dot.

"But a Dome has never fallen," Neelya said with confidence.

The Queen gave a weak laugh. "You are correct but this, like the Elves' Dome outside of Manton, is merely a public relations piece; it is half the size of other Domes. It isn't a matter of if it will fall, but how long it will take."

Neelya felt concern for the first time. "If it is so small, might the Elves just go around it?" she asked.

The Queen looked over at her, eyes sharp, "You do not pass a Dome; that is the road to death. Have you not studied the War of Generations?"

Neelya said that she had, but hadn't made it far into the histories yet.

The Queen relaxed, saying, "Toward the end, we had the Elves beaten … we thought. We'd push them back to what they call the Mahj line. We took the last of our offensive strength and hit the line pushing past a Dome, not taking it, just making it around. We thought ourselves geniuses; it was a straight shot to Seeon, but we were naive. The Elves let us pass that Dome. Once our armies were well past it, the Elves jumped hundreds of Ascended to the Dome. In so doing, they cut off retreat and supplies. They came behind our army and overwhelmed it. In that battle, we lost our ability to form an offense again. There were no survivors." Neelya tensed as the Queen went on, "The world saw that you do not pass a Dome. A lesson the Elves remembered at Bellum Omega. Never forget," she said.

The Queen changed tack, asking Neelya to retrieve some paperwork, the night's reflections over. Neelya gladly did as she was asked; thinking about what the Queen had told her.

Emma found herself with nothing to do for a while and was walking around the building. Sasha was hard at work, having made some discoveries she thought could aid the immediate war effort. Sasha had Edling with her, along with the rest of the team; many had been going without sleep, so intense was their focus. As for Emma, she had a fairly good grasp on what they were doing, but research wasn't really her job. She found herself most days acting as a messenger for Sasha with the other Houses. She saw Ankle standing next to a window, looking out it.

She came up behind him, not really trying to sneak up, but he still jumped when she touched him. His hand went to the handle of his sword, the blade sliding part way out of the sheath.

Emma jumped back. "Ankle, it's me!" she cried, scared.

He breathed out; grabbing his chest, "Emma I am so sorry. You caught me off guard ..." he trailed off.

"I'm wearing heels on a marble floor, how off guard could you be?" she asked, concerned and a little miffed.

Then she looked at him more closely. His face was droopy, his eyes had bags underneath. *You should be looking better after a month of being here.* "Ankle, since you aren't doing a really great job of guarding, why don't you walk with me for awhile and keep me company," she said.

He grimaced, "I don't think that's a good idea, Em. If the major finds out ..."

"Finds out that you left your post at my request, he'll what?" she demanded. Emma did have a reasonable amount of power, but she didn't often use it.

"He could punish me and going off mission is punishable by death," Ankle said half-heartedly, he knew he wasn't going to get executed for walking around a heavily guarded building.

Just then, the major in question came bouncing around the corner and gave Ankle a stern look, "Why are you not at attention?!"

Before he could answer, Emma turned coolly to the major, "Because I am talking to him and asked him to relax. Also, he is going to be spending the rest of his shift with me." She turned to Ankle, "Commander, come with me."

Ankle looked like he didn't know what to do and Emma turned back to the Major, whose mouth was open. He shut it with a snap. "You heard her man, get to!" he grunted, bowing to Emma and walking off.

Emma started down the hall, and after a few moments Ankle came trotting up behind. "You like messing with him, don't you?" he asked, once they were out of earshot.

She smiled, "I can't even tell you how much; maybe if he hadn't been so rude the first time I met him, it'd be different."

She kept walking until they were at her office. She entered the room and indicated for Ankle to take a seat at a table by the window. She grabbed two glasses and a bottle of Poti, taking the chair across from him. She poured the dark amber liquid in the glasses, handing him one and raising it in a toast. "To House Evindass," she said.

"To House Evindass," Ankle repeated and then took a sip.

He relaxed in his chair, glancing at a book on the table, picking it up, "Bellumm O-Omega?" he asked.

She sighed, content, "Yes, Bellum Omega, it means 'the end'."

"That sounds happy; what's it about?" he asked, flipping the pages.

She smirked; the book was written in the Elf language Glosso. Ankle picked up on that, and placed the book on the table.

"It's about the last battle in the War of Generations. Would you like to hear about it?" she asked.

He nodded.

"The Iumenta had the Elves against their own border once; they passed by the Domes of the Mahj Line, a mistake that cost them nearly their entire army. You see, at the time the war had been raging for nearly fifty years. Both sides in truth were crippled beyond immediate repair. After that victory, the Elves pushed the Iumenta back to their own border. The Impa army was so weak, the Elves were all but able to run across the land. But the Impa had a Mahj Line of their own; though I don't know its name.

"The battle of Bellum Omega lasted for weeks, the Pawdin troops breaking like waves against a Dragon Dome. Each wave got closer to victory. On the last day, the Pawdin and Impa generals met in the field that separated the two armies. Neither general is alive today, but legend says that the Iumenta and Elf knew that the Dome would fall, but that the losses it would cause would make it impossible for the Elves to take the rest of the Impa lands, nor would they be able to defend themselves. On the flip side, the Impa would also take such losses that they too would not be able to fight the Pawdin Empire. They say that the generals looked out at their tattered armies, both defeated. There was going to be no winner, there couldn't be; both Impa and Pawdin Empires had lost the war. The two generals parted ways, the Elf telling his army to go home, to console their families and to rebuild what they could.

"After that, the Iumenta were spotted only a handful of times for nearly two thousand years." She looked at Ankle. "This is Bellum Omega; today some Elves feel that had they sacrificed their own nation, the tyranny of the Impa wouldn't be here today," Emma said.

Ankle looked thoughtful for a moment. "Is that why they are so sad?" he asked.

"Who, the Elves? Yes, they feel the blood of our race is on their hands."

Ankle shook his head. "I've seen what our race does to each other; tyranny was going to be a part of this world regardless. How can they blame themselves for something that they could not control?" he asked, looking at her.

"Don't you do the same?" she asked.

His face darkened, "What do you mean?"

"Mors," she whispered.

He puffed up a bit and then deflated, "You're right; but I see them whenever I close my eyes, I see her ..."

"Rachel," Emma confirmed. "Do you write her?"

"Yes often, and she writes back. I'm glad she's in Seeon, safe."

Emma could feel her heart breaking for Ankle; this war was all but lost for him too, just as the War of Generations had been a loss for the Elves and Iumenta. But it didn't have to be a total loss, she realized. She stood, taking his hand. "Follow me," she said, flicking out her mind to an assistant. She led him down a hall, past Elf guards and into restricted areas. They entered a room with a high ceiling and a crystal the size of a bathroom mirror on the wall. She walked to it, flicking her mind out.

"Here," she said placing him in front of the crystal. An image appeared, a timid-looking girl came into view, her eyes narrow and then wide with recognition

"Ankle!" she said.

"Rachel ..." Ankle said.

She patted his arm. "Take your time, I'll be waiting for you outside," she said.

As she walked, she could hear the tension in his voice break, could hear the weight of guilt lift as he saw the now-healthy girl. He could see that though he couldn't save them all, he could save at least the one and that's all that mattered.

Chapter Twenty-Six
Decisions

"Figure out what it is you want to accomplish and then get to work."
-The Wondering Way (Author Unknown)

Neelya tried to keep pace with the Queen while not losing the many papers she held in her arms. Next to the Queen was Parkas, his gait was confident if not slightly haggard. They entered the Queen's study, Neelya placing the papers on the desk.

"This was a wise move, Hoelaria," Parkas was saying.

It was a mark of their relationship that he could address the Queen by name.

"I think it is the only option we have at this point," the Queen growled, "if only they had dedicated more at the beginning." She started, then shook her head, "No matter. Thank you Parkas, you may leave."

Parkas left, leaving Neelya and the Queen alone. "Is there anything else I can do for you, Un Prose?" Neelya asked.

The Queen waved her hand dismissively, "Tell me Neelya, what have I accomplished today."

This was a test she needed to answer correctly, "By convincing the Heads of all the other Provinces to stay in Bailaya, you were able to force them into committing more resources to the war effort. Perhaps force is the wrong word."

"No I forced them; make no mistake, but in forcing them, they are now in a live or die situation, at this point none can back out. What are the possible consequences of today?" she asked.

Neelya thought. "We will hold the Capital and drive the Pawdin Empire back," she said, gazing into the fire, looking at the bronze Dragons; the shifting firelight on them helped her focus. "We will likely lose most of the Humans bred at Mors, however Human numbers have been greatly depleting and the Mors units were never intended to hold off an Elvin assault. The Pawdin Empire will be forced now to match our numbers." She looked up at the Queen, "We will win the battle for the next few months, but will have a long road ahead," she said.

The Queen nodded, "A very long one indeed."

Legon stepped into a large conference room. To his right was Iselin; to his left was Sasha. Edling, Emma, Sydin and a few others trailed behind them. Seats filled the room, assistants from all the Great Houses in attendance; also in the wings were the Heads of many of the Houses Minor. In the center of the room, a round table stood with a crystal in it, and next to the table stood the Heads of every Great Elvin House. Legon took his place. As he stopped, a crystal the size of a marble floated to his lips, the same was at the lips of every Head of House; today, all in the room would hear clearly the discussions of the Houses.

The Heads of House introduced themselves. When everyone was done, the Head of House Coreen looked at Legon, "Evindass, you have spearheaded this war. You and your people have lead it with great competence. I'm afraid without your efforts we would still be standing idly by as the Iumenta executed their plans."

Legon bowed, "Thank you. Indeed, every House has put forth a great deal of effort in this war. Our armies stand at the brink of the Bailaya Dome; with its fall we are a few short miles from the Capital itself. Sadly, this may not be the victory we were all hoping for. The Iumenta have committed genocide, having left the Cona lands nearly void of life in their recent wake. We could have never hoped to capture all of the Impa leaders, but were hoping to maybe at least capture Hoelaria, so that she may stand trial. Today I tell you that those hopes have been dashed."

His words were met with concern and confusion and he went on, "We have recently learned that Hoelaria has brought all of her Heads of Province to Bailaya. Words from spies tell us that they have all committed to Summa Commendo." There were a few gasps from the wings.

———— ∽ ————

Emma was confused and nudged Opes' mind. "What is Summa Commendo?" she asked.

He looked at her darkly. "During the War of Generations, each side committed nearly sixty percent of its population to combat, this is Summa Commendo. We will have to do likewise if we are to hold them back, regardless of our superior numbers of Ascended, Hoelaria just re-started the War of Generations." Opes turned his attention back to the meeting and Emma grew quiet again.

Legon was still speaking. "We predict the first formations will reach the Capital within three months. Even if we are to work as fast as we can, we cannot marshal our own society in time to stop this threat. We will take heavy casualties and lose much of the Cona Empire before we can stop the Iumenta," Legon was saying as he leaned against the table. "We cannot let those troops get here; we must end this war soon," he said.

"I assume that you have come up with a strategy to do this?" The Head of House Insa said.

Legon nodded. "Yes we have; it's far from ideal, but a plan. Stacy," he said, motioning to Arkin's widow, who walked forward.

She waved her hand over the table, bringing up a map of Bailaya. "Thank you for honoring me today," she started. "My organization has mapped the entire city. Bailaya, like all Iumenta occupied Human cities, have two and only two jump crystals." She motioned, bringing up the locations of the crystals. "They are in the southern part of the city, well away from the main Palace; they are heavily guarded, but like most city crystals, have limited power," she said, looking back to Legon.

"Thank you Stacy," he said. "We have all but cut off ground retreat to the north. Those Iumenta troops will not be here for at least three months, this gives us time to secure the city."

"But what good will that do? As soon as the Iumenta see that the Capital is about to fall, they will use the jump crystals to leave; we will take heavy losses at the Dome and the city, just to have the Iumenta retreat on us." The head of House Violaceus said.

Legon got a gleam in his eye. "Not if we get the Impa to surrender first," he said, waiting for a moment and then looking back to the map. "When we crack the Dome and we will, I propose that we send all Ascended in the area to attack Bailaya right away. The Iumenta will be using their jump crystals in the Capital to help fortify the Dome; they have to keep us at bay for several months. They have to hold that Dome and will do whatever they must to hold it. If we attack the city right away, targeting the jump crystals and those alone, we can cut off their retreat."

There were nods and even some smiles Emma could see, as Legon went on, "We are going to lose a lot of good people doing this, but it's our only chance; Hoelaria is betting big on this move. If we can win this battle ..."

"We have the Heads of Province trapped; they will either surrender or die long before their armies get here," House Amuun said.

"And if the tension we've seen with the Impa in the past is any indication of what will happen now, it's highly possible that the Impa Empire will slip into Civil War as Provinces fight for control," the Head of House Insa said. "House Insa is behind this plan."

"As is House Coreen"

The other Houses Great and Minor voted their approval and Emma felt a bit of weight lift. From that point on, she watched as the Heads of House networked their minds along with their generals, developing a battle plan. A few hours later, Emma followed Sasha from the room.

Sasha spoke to Sydin, "Sy, I think we have something that may help us with the Dome."

"What is that?" he asked.

"We have found a weakness in the Iumenta crystals, we think we can exploit it, but the crystal will need to be very taxed for it to work," She explained.

Sydin looked down at her with a smile. "Oh trust me, Un Prose, I fully plan on taxing the crystals of that Dome. Feel free to do whatever you like, so long as it does not interfere with the main battle plan," he said.

Sasha took Emma's hand. "Thank you Sy, come Emma we have work to do."

Barnin finished packing up, taking one last sweep around the room. Heath met him in the hall and they left the building that had been the closest thing to a home he'd had in months. Barnin didn't dislike his time in Salez, but he felt ready for the next leg of the war. Heath felt likewise. As for Ankle; after Emma let him talk to Rachel, Ankle was a new man.

Barnin and Heath made their way across a brick courtyard; Emma was walking quickly in the distance. "HEY EM!" Barnin yelled.

Emma turned, coming over to them. She looked flustered and worried. "Hey guys, what can I do for you?" she asked.

Heath frowned, "We could ask you the same, what's got you so worked up?"

Emma looked back the way she'd been going and turned back to them. "I'm going to pick something up on the other side of the complex; walk with me?" she asked.

They agreed as she started back up at a brisk pace.

"So Em, what's going on?" Barnin asked.

She glanced at him, looking apprehensive.

"You know you can trust us," Heath prodded.

She sighed. "I know; it's something your command knows but likely won't tell you. The Iumenta have gone to Summa Commendo. It's bad, very bad," she said.

"That sounds almost like a gambling term Em, what does that mean?" Heath asked.

"It means that the Iumenta have decided to dedicate at least sixty percent of their citizens to the war effort, they will be here in a few months."

Barnin fought the urge to stop walking as Emma went on.

"We have one chance to end this war before it turns back into the War of Generations," she said.

"And if we don't succeed with this chance?" Barnin asked.

She stopped and looked at both of them. "Humanity was in the wings for the last war, ignored by both sides. That will not be the case this time; we cannot hope to survive this. The Elves and Iumenta will cripple each other beyond repair and we, if we still exist, will be nothing more than small tribes of people hiding in caves again."

Barnin felt goose bumps; Emma believed what she was saying and he did too. His thoughts drifted to Samantha in Manton, her face making his fears ebb away. His jaw clenched, "Thanks Em, you got stuff to do and so do we. Come on Heath." He walked off, taking Heath with him. "No one hears about this. Our command is right for not telling us this information, it will only hurt morale."

They rounded a corner where his three units were getting ready. Barnin yelled at the top of his voice, "LOAD UP WE ARE HEADING OUT!" The men instantly sped up their preparations.

Johnson came up to him, "Barnin ..."

Barnin turned to him "Major, it's been an honor serving with you. I wish you luck in your next assignment."

Johnson looked for a moment like he was going to say something about getting cut off, but decided against it. "It has been an honor; I wish I was accompanying you to the battle's front, good luck."

Trust me major, where we're going, you don't want to be. Barnin saluted him and went back to rousing his men.

Keither trotted along on Pixie, Sara riding next to him. Ahead he could see plumes of smoke, the fires of many camps. They were surrounded by mountains, and the cold evening air hung in his chest. Next to him, Sara was nervous. She was going to be heading her own team of medics, but for his part he just had to worry about feeding the troops. Sara jumped at a roar from above. Both looked up seeing hundreds of Elvin Dragons flying in formation.

"I've never seen so many," she said, talking about the Dragons.

"There havent been this many ground troops either," Keither pointed out. "I dare say this battle will decide the outcome of this war."

The sun was just starting to set on the horizon when Sara and Keither came over a hill. Below them was a wide open space. At the back of it, there was a bottleneck in the mountains. Blocking the view of the mounts was a White Dome that flattened on the top. It resembled a bowl turned upside down. The Bailaya Dome loomed massive; it was the same size as the Precipice Dome. Above it, the sky sparkled as Iumenta jumped into the area. In the air hundreds of Iumenta were in flight.

"Do you think it will start soon?" Sara asked.

"Impa Domes cast no shadow ..." Keither said, remembering a text he'd read. The sun was fast setting and the landscape grew darker, but the Dome let go of none of its brilliance.

"What?" Sara asked.

"They say that an Iumenta Dome has no shadow because it glows. How can something that glows cast a shadow?" He said, looking at his wife.

Never had he felt a sense of awe from the Iumenta, but he did now.

She looked at him, fearful tears misting her eyes. He moved to comfort her, but was stopped by a collective roar from the Elves and Iumenta. His head snapped as the sky filled with artillery fire and magic.

Chapter Twenty-Seven
Crimson Horizon

"Battle, the true test of a warrior, in its tempest we throw ourselves to be tried by death and violence. To the victor songs will be sung, to the vanquished only the memory of history awaits."
- The Exiled Captain (Author Unknown)

Thick musty air passed over Legon's scales and armor. The sun was setting, casting the landscape in dark blues, the Dome standing out; its ivory exterior shining bright and defiant. Legon flew in the lead formation, behind him several hundred Ascended followed toward similar formations of Iumenta. The air below burst with light as both sides fired siege weapons. Trails of smoke and fire streaked the sky, but Legon didn't pay the scene much attention. Instead he focused on the Iumenta ahead of him, their formations growing ever closer. Somewhere in their midst was the green class eight; Legon could feel him in the area, knew that like the last time they had fought, the green would wait until Legon was tired from battle. But not today. Legon was going to use only the minimum amount of magic, he wasn't going to make the same mistake twice.

Sydin bellowed a command, and all the Elves shot spells at the Iumenta, all but Legon. He held his power in, weaving out of the path of several oncoming spells. The air rent with the sound of wards. The two groups closed on each other. Legon turned his attention from roving the ranks of Ascended to looking at one right ahead of him. Legon's lack of focus must have been visible to the Dragon as he saw its face move from confidence to concerned. *Don't worry, you have my full attention,* Legon thought.

"Are you focused, Legon?" Opes asked.

Legon responded by roaring and driving himself faster. The Dragon ahead of him tensed, eyeing Opes. Legon had spent the last several weeks using the same attacks again and again in preparation for today. The

Iumenta assumed that Legon was going to feint and Opes instead was going to attack. The Iumenta angled, expecting a feint that didn't come. Too late its eyes widened as it realized it indeed was going to have to engage Legon. Legon folded his wings, snapping them against his body. He passed just above the Iumenta, dragging his claws the length of its back. It turned up in the air and Legon curled his tail, letting it smack into the Iumenta's neck. Blood sprayed from the Dragon's open wounds, and it lost control. Legon could see in Iselin's mind as she watched Legon pass the Dragon. Then right behind him, another formation of Elves converged on the Dragon, killing it. Legon barreled ahead at a new foe.

Iselin pulled her attention away from her husband, turning it to the wake of chaos that he caused. Legon's main job was to disrupt the Iumenta formation, something that he seemed to be doing quite well. He was bellowing at the top of his lungs and she could feel a distinct sense of amusement coming from him. The Elvin formations collapsed in on themselves as the Elves used their higher numbers to their advantage. Iselin and Cynta focused in on a yellow class seven, both attacking the disoriented Iumenta. Each bit onto a wing and pulled. The Iumenta screamed in pain. Iselin felt muscle and joint pop as she and Cynta pulled on the Dragon like they were playing a game of tug of war. There was a ripping sound of flesh and sinew, and the Iumenta dropped from the sky, twisting in agony in the air. Iselin turned, looking for another target. Similar events were playing out all over and the Iumenta regrouped, watching each other.

"There goes the end to our easy kills," Cynta noted.

"We knew that tactic wouldn't work long," Iselin said, rejoining her formation.

The two groups of immortals separated, for the most part allowing large gaps as they used magic to fight. Iselin jerked in the air, avoiding spells from larger Dragons, while still sending spells of her own. A dull blue spell popped softly next to her and she felt the air from the right side of her body thin to almost non existence. She tottered, flapping hard to correct. A breaking and cutting spell smacked into her wards. The air cracked as she felt two minds pushing on the spells. One of her wards faltered under the pressure, and her chest and front legs burned as they were slashed open. Healing wards sealed the wounds as Iselin righted herself, dodging two more spells. She cast a translucent pink wall in front of her. Iselin was an Energent; she pulled on her minor, altering the wall. When the next spells came at her, they passed the wall with ease but faded and slowed. She avoided a breaking spell with ease, letting a freezing spell hit her. She barely felt it on her wards so weakened was it.

Iselin altered her wards, stretching them out to the area just around her as the pink wall came down. Again, pale blue balls popped around her, this time the surrounding air glowed pink. More spells popped around her and she swore. *I hate elementals* she thought. She was being forced into a small area; if she left where her wards protected, she would be subject to the air changing density. *This can't happen in close combat,* she thought. She cast more walls, avoiding what spells she could. Cynta came to hover behind her, staying behind Iselin's wall, using it as cover, allowing her to fire on the Iumenta. Iselin took a moment to shoot looks at the rest of the battle; others were doing the same as she and Cynta.

It was no surprise to hear Sydin's voice. "Perimeter!" he ordered.

Iselin rolled her eyes, making her wall bigger along the line of Ascended; other Energent's like herself moved forward doing likewise. Other Dragons cast stationary wards on both sides. The Elves and Iumenta entered a standstill in the air.

Barnin looked up at the darkening sky, fighting the urge to cover his ears. As the surroundings grew darker, the glowing white Dome and battle in the sky were in sharp contrast with each other. Missiles flew between the two land armies but Barnin couldn't take his eyes off the formations of Dragons. The two groups were separated by what looked like a river of flashing color and sound.

"What is it?" he asked, more to himself.

Heath responded. "It's a perimeter," he said, almost in awe.

Barnin looked at Heath, on his other side Ankle did likewise. Heath looked at the two men like they were terribly out of the loop and then looked back up. "It only happens when there are large enough groups of Ascended fighting. Use your seeing eyeglass," he said.

Barnin held the glass to his eyes, bringing the fight into view.

Heath went on, "You see the space between the two, on either side of that, separation wards are erected along with other spells; that forms the perimeter. Each side is trying to break the other side's wards; above this main line and to the sides other Dragons will try to flank the perimeter. It won't last too long, I don't think."

"Why's that?" Ankle asked.

"From what I understand, it takes a lot of energy to hold a line like that, and once one side breaches it, they gain a lot of ground. From what I understand they are very rare and only happen with extremely large forces that are trying to hold a small amount of air."

Barnin was about to ask more when a horn in the distance sounded. *So much for watching others fight.* Barnin barked orders to his men, and they moved to their assigned place on the line. His was one of the front line units, something Barnin wasn't overly happy about. Looming before them looming was the white Dome. Fiery missiles shot from it along with magic. Its light lit a massive ground force, in the center of which was rank upon rank of Iumenta. *The immortals aren't your concern,* he told himself.

He leaned forward in his saddle, waiting for the command to charge. He could feel the order coming; the night seemed to grow silent, the battlefield looking oddly calm in the white of the Dome and flashing color of the Dragons above. Barnin could almost hear his heart beat and then a horn sounded and with it the clamor of the army.

"CHARGE!" he yelled, spurring Poison forward.

Fear vanished, replaced by adrenaline-induced confidence. The wind rushed past him as he galloped forward, a pike held in front of him. To his sides were his men; next to them were hundreds of other mounted units.

Ankle swung his blade. It clanged against another and he kicked at the man he was fighting, their mounts biting and kicking at each other. Ankle blocked with his shield, feeling his arm vibrate with the force of the blow. He parried another few attacks before lashing out with a few of his own. He rammed his shield into the other man's, all but pushing him off his horse. Ankle used the opportunity to stab the man, killing him. He yelled a handful of orders before engaging another. Over the sounds of fighting, he could hear the shuffle of infantry. *They'd moved fast.* His own side's infantry wasn't anywhere near the line yet. As he used his horse to knock over another soldier's horse, he looked at the oncoming infantry.

A pit formed in his gut. They jogged in perfect formation, black fabric over their faces. The enemy horsemen retreated as the infantry came to a halt. Shields lined up. making a silvery wall, pikes lowered. To their rear, several men on horses wore light black armor. They thrust their hands forward and magic rushed at Ankle and the others.

Heath felt his power take a hit as one of his wards failed and another man died. The enemy Venefica was the best he'd ever fought. They didn't mix with the main fighting group but stayed well back using only magic. He saw some of his comrades fall as the infantry pushed them back, never breaking formation. The scene was the same all around; the units of Dark Warriors moved forward slowly; but moved forward nonetheless.

Heath dodged a few more spells *how can they have this much power...* and then it hit him. The infantry units were moving at the speed of normal men, allbeit very well trained. Unlike Heath, the other Venefica were not using magic to support their units. Heath hated to do it but he stopped strengthening the men, finding that he was able to hold his own against the other Venefica.

Legon climbed above the perimeter trying to out-flank the Iumenta, other Dragons were doing likewise. Legon would get into small engagements, but after a bit he or his enemy would move on, ever striving for position. He leveled out and that's when he saw him, the Iumenta class eight. He was looking at Legon. Legon looked up, the green taking his lead. Both sailed upwards, moving further and further away from the main fight. Up high, there were fewer Dragons and most of them sixes. Upon seeing the two eights, they cleared away, not wanting to be in the center of Legon and the Iumenta's fight.

Legon leveled out and the green charged at him. Legon did likewise, pushing himself forward. Legon veered to the side at the last moment, the green having the same thought, they didn't touch in the air but spun coming back at each other. Legon blocked a tail attack by countering with one of his own. Neither put much into their attacks, instead drifting apart and hovering in circles. *We both want to see what the other is going to do,* Legon thought.

He decided to test the green. Legon flung a breaking spell from his left paw, it moved fast. The green didn't move, letting the spell hit him full on in the chest. Legon let go of the magic *hmm … either you know I'm testing you or you're cocky …* Legon couldn't decide which. *Ok Green, your turn* he thought.

Almost as in reply, Green roared, sending a river of emerald fire at Legon. Legon folded his wings, dropped in the air a few feet and then opened them again. Legon used magic, shooting up at Green, catching him off guard. Legon came from beneath Green, moving around behind him, raking his claws along his tail. Green spun, breathing fire. Legon pushed a ward out, costing energy but sending the blinding flames away. He launched himself forward, connecting with Green's left wing, making the other Dragon totter. Legon's wards flashed as the green froze the water in the air, sending chunks of ice at him. Legon folded his wings in, focusing his wards. Green came in for a close attack, Legon blocking several swipes and tail swings. Green changed styles at a rapid pace and Legon found himself having a hard time keeping up. *He's good at adaptation.*

Green came in ever-aggressive; Legon tried to break apart, but couldn't. He was starting to take minor injuries. Legon could tell that Green was older than he and a more skilled technical fighter, but seemed to lack experience. Years ago, Legon wouldn't have been able to accept that he wasn't as good of a fighter as another; he would have tried to hold his own, but not anymore. *I need to out-think him,* he thought. Green tried to blind Legon again with fire, which seemed to be a favorite of his. This time instead of dropping in the sky, Legon held fast, waiting for the flames to stop. When they did, Green seemed surprised that Legon was still in front of him. Legon sprayed Green with minor stinging spells, most of which hit ineffectually on wards, but Green backed away.

Legon moved sideways, cutting with his tail, catching Green's right paw. Green launched forward again, this time Legon dodged, getting another hit in. *He's only good straight on,* Legon realized with joy. If he could keep moving, he could wear Green out. Sadly, Legon too had always depended on brute strength in fights. It was only in the last few months that he'd started to learn otherwise.

Legon's moment of introspection cost him; Green was back on him and Legon was again taking damage. Green didn't seem to use much in the way of magic, so Legon sent more energy to his muscles and healing wards. As he got faster, he took less damage and was even able to fight back. Legon couldn't decide if Green just was unskilled with magic, or if he was saving his energy while waiting for Legon to weaken. It was likely the latter. There was only one way to test. Legon glanced down at the perimeter far below. He folded his wings, dropping in the sky. Green dove after him but Legon only angled himself downwards towards the middle section of the two groups of Ascended.

Legon fell like a rock, sending spells at Green; he took almost every one, not even trying to dodge. Right above the divide, Legon breathed a blinding jet of fire, opening his wings. He lashed out at Green, sending the other Dragon tumbling out of control. Legon tried to slow his descent, not wanting to go between the two forces. Magic shot between the two like a river. A river that Green was about to fly into. Green tried to slow himself, but right before he entered the crossfire, his whole body glowed and a spell rocketed from him, hitting Legon's right wing. Legon felt his wards buckle and the membrane of his wing rip. He cried out in pain, his right wing unable to slow his descent. Below Green entered the melee of magic still trying to climb. Legon saw him getting hit by spells from both sides, only the spells of the Elves doing any damage. He got hit by dozens of spells.

Legon was still falling, his wing not healing in time; he too was going to fly into that danger zone. He swore, folding his wings to his body and pointing down. He saw the damage that Green took, Legon was amazed it hadn't killed him. *Speed will be my only chance,* he thought.

He wanted to close his eyes but didn't. Pain exploded all over his body as he was hit by spells. He tried to weave but it was no use. He felt his magic drain, but then it was over. His speed carried him through much faster than Green, and therefore he didn't take anywhere near the damage. Legon's wings snapped back open, his right now healed. The wind was knocked out of him as he was hit by a one of the missiles of the Iumenta artillery. Then he was smacked by one from his own side. He was too far below the battle of Dragons, his descent still moving him down. Legon was forced down again, dodging missiles, the battlefield a mess of men below him. He opened his wings, leveling off near the ground. He was over the Iumenta, but he didn't pay them any attention. Green was down here somewhere too, both of them trapped. He found Green in the distance covered in blood.

Legon sprinted forward, meeting the other Dragon in the air. This time Green was hurt badly and was unable to fight back as well. Legon felt himself winning. Legon felt a small prick in his tail and then hundreds of stabs of pain. He looked down, seeing Iumenta anti-Dragon entrapments below firing at him. Another ballista buried itself in Legon, this time in his leg. It blew, sending shrapnel all over. Legon had to break away from

Green; he couldn't take him plus the ground units. He turned angrily in the air, flying back toward the Elves.

Sara finished healing a soldier's cut arm. "How does that feel?" she asked.

The man flexed his arm. "I'm good; thanks Doc," he said, getting off the bench he was seated on.

She dismissed him, beckoning the next man forward. "Heath?" she asked in surprise.

He smiled. "Hey Sara, any chance I can scrounge some bandages from ya?" he asked sheepishly.

She eyed him, "Why can't you get some from your supply depot?"

"Back log" he said.

She nodded, standing up. "This didn't happen," she said.

He smirked, "I have no idea what you're talking about."

Heath walked next to her as she left the healing tent. Ash fell lightly, the surrounding forest and fields burned to cinders. The noise of Ascended fighting was common to her now. It had only been a week since the battle for the Bailaya Dome had begun, and already Sara had seen more destruction than she had in the entire war previous. Heath next to her was example enough, his armor was blackened and stained with blood, be it his or others she didn't know or care to know. She wanted to ask him about the fighting.

"Heath ..." he turned to her. "What's it like?" she asked. He raised an eyebrow and she refined her question, "What's different about this battle? I see so many injured in such a short time."

His face showed understanding. "This is so much more intense than any other battle; we aren't spread out like we were at Salez or other cities. Plus here the Iumenta and Elves are fighting so much harder. And the Dark Warriors ..." he said with a look of amazement.

This got her attention; every other man she'd heard talk about them seemed scared but not Heath, he seemed ... *respectful?*

"How do you mean?" she asked

"What do you know about them?"

"Nothing really," she answered honestly, "other than that they are good at what they do; all I seem to do is fix the damage they cause."

Heath grunted, "Hardly, they don't injure so much as kill." He went on, "They are amazing really, I don't mean in an 'I like them' sort of way but in a 'respect your enemy' sort of way."

"How so?" she prodded again.

"They specialize like nothing I've seen. For example, you can tell by the way they fight that infantry are only trained to be infantry, to the exclusion of all else. They don't seem like what a normal person would be. Given that I've seen where they are bred, I have a better understanding. But whatever a unit does is all they've done their whole life. And they fight as one, making their formations and ranks near impossible to breach. Behind their front line are Venefica, but they never come close to hand-to-hand combat. The Venefica are skilled in the extreme and where the infantry units seem to think only in terms of the team, the Venefica are not that way. They are smart and adaptive. Behind ranks will be horse-mounted Iumenta with two Human Venefica, it is they who command."

Sara felt goosebumps on her arms, "Tell me about the Venefica. I thought you didn't see them at Mors."

He shook his head, "We didn't see them, but that doesn't mean much. Mors had one purpose; Umbra figured that Venefica must be bred in a different camp."

But not raised the same as the Dark Warriors, Sara thought.

They were at the depot. Sara grabbed Heath a bundle of bandages and then paused. "Why do you need these; why aren't you using magic?" she asked.

"Like I said, the Venefica Dark Warriors are good, they also don't support their men. I can't spare magic like I used to, I have to save it for battle or we'd all die. Thanks Sara, I've got to run," Heath said.

She wished him luck and started back toward the healing tent, thinking about what Heath had said. She had truly under estimated Mors and what the Iumenta were trying to do there.

Legon gritted his teeth against pain. He backed off, feeling his tail knit back together were Green had sliced him. Legon flexed wards in the air around him as Green shot spells under his wings. *He wants to be in close*

combat, Legon thought. Legon backed off more and again Green tried to thin the air around him but this time just on his right side. *Fine.* Legon let his wards fail, seeming surprised. Green shot forward, trying to take advantage of Legon's unsteadiness in the air. Legon used magic of his own, making the air dense on his right side, pushing his wing up. Folding his left wing, Legon rolled in the air opening both wings, solidifying the air. Too late, Green was unable to change course. Legon infused his tail blade with a pain spell and swung. The blade crashed against Green's hind side, his wards only stopping magic and not metal. Legon's blade dug into flesh and bone, moving past wards, he flexed the magic and Green shrieked in pain.

Legon jerked the blade out of the other Dragon's bone, breathing lavender fire, pushing on multiple wards of Green's. In his distraction, Green didn't focus, instead losing control and rushing at Legon, who dodged him by again playing with the air. Green's biological wards weakened, in his rage the Iumenta seemed not to notice. Again, Green rushed Legon, this time getting a grip on his shoulder. Legon felt his muscles burn as they were cut, blood running down his chest and belly. He kicked out at Green and snapped at his neck. Green blocked both, seeming to be getting his focus back.

We can't do this all day, Legon thought. *I need to end this.*

This time when Green rushed him, Legon was counting on the fact that Green expected Legon to feint. It worked, Green darted to where Legon should have gone, but he didn't. Legon made no move to dodge. Green exposed his neck. Legon lashed out his blade, slicing Green's neck but not deep. The Dragon reared in the sky, Legon spewed a river of magical fire. Green did likewise, the two torrents of flames mixing in the sky. Legon sent a breaking spell, finishing off Green's biologic wards. Green's fire stopped and Legon didn't take the time to register the look of horror on his enemy's face. Legon reached down, feeling the well of power in him, tapping his minor. His body glowed, the power running down the length of him flung out in an orb of amethyst energy. It collided with Green.

Time slowed as Legon felt his magic wane drastically, his breath leaving in a whoosh. The spell hit only minor wards which crumbled. Legon watched as all of Green's exposed flesh ripped, shredding into thousands of pieces. The spell wasn't a shredding spell but rather one to vaporize blood. There was a dull pop as Green exploded, scarlet droplets turning the horizon crimson.

All that was left of Green was bloody armor and bone, which started its decent to the battle field below.

Barnin gripped Poison's reins tightly. To his side, the bloody, bony remains of a giant Dragon thudded to earth. He didn't pay it any attention; the sky had been raining gore all week.

He turned his head back to his men, "ON ME! ON ME!"

He yelled at Ankle and pointed. Ankle led his men while holding off a group of Cavalry. Barnin spurred Poison, running around a formation of Dark Warriors, outflanking them. *Let's see how you do with this!* He galloped up, catching the formation off-guard; too late, they were unable to bring pike men to the rear. Barnin drew his sword, leaning over. Poison slammed into men, jumping over others. Barnin attacked with his blade as men pushed back, his men following suit. He couldn't see the Dark Warriors' faces behind the cloth, but he guessed they wore surprised looks; Poison glowed yellow, the enemy blades being deflected. Barnin broke into a clearing. Before him were two Venefica on horseback. These two were the objective. He charged and let out a war cry, making his throat hurt. He ducked and wove as spells came from the startled Venefica.

To his side, several men went down, but Poison rushed on. One of the Venefica turned. Barnin's other unit had flanked them from the other side. Barnin rushed forward, Poison slamming into the Venefica's horse. Barnin stabbed at the Venefica, who pulled a blade, blocking with unnatural speed. Heath's magic was gone and Barnin wasn't fast enough to block the Venefica's slash across his chest. Two more came and he barely deflected them. The Venefica grinned, swinging; Barnin raised his sword, knowing he couldn't make it in time.

His eyes went out of focus as he thought of Samantha and that he wouldn't see her again. Then his arm vibrated. Barnin looked shocked, seeing his blade blocking the Venefica who also looked surprised. Barnin felt a mind, "Sara!"

Her voice was strained. "Yes," she growled, "I'm not losing another friend. I don't have much left; finish this!"

Barnin smiled, "With pleasure."

Barnin rammed his shield into the man, destabilizing him. He swung at Barnin but they were now physical equals and Barnin could tell, extensive magical training or not, the Venefica was no swordsman. He attacked with all his might. The Venefica blocked a few blows and then Barnin stabbed, feeling his blade sink deep in the other man's chest. He fell from his horse. Next to him, the other Venefica turned, but Barnin was already on him, removing his head. Sara's presence left Barnin.

Barnin turned to the infantry, the joy of victory filling him. Pain stabbed in his gut. He looked down to see the tip of a spear in his belly, blood coming from the wound. He grabbed the spear with weak fingers; it was pulled from him by the Dark Warrior holding it. Barnin pressed his hand against the hole in his gut, feeling his life flowing from him. He grasped the horn of his saddle, his own blood slicking his grip. He tottered and fell from his saddle.

Chapter Twenty-Eight
City of Ash

"I often felt as though the weight of the world rested on the shoulders of my sister and me, the Perfectos Compatioa. We felt this way because the weight of the world truly did rest on us. A weight we did not have to bear alone, thankfully."
- The Everser Vald

Sasha looked out over the battlefield, the Dome lighting the ground and hills. It was late in the night, she wasn't sure what time it was, but she knew it was well past midnight. She could feel her brother waking up and readying himself for more fighting. He'd defeated the Iumenta class eight that day; it had an immediate effect on both sides. For the Elves, they'd been bolstered; the Iumenta it seemed felt opposite. The Iumenta spent the rest of the day losing air space, resulting in ground casualties as well. The Dome was falling, but how much longer would it take?

The air above flickered with Dragons jumping in and out of the area.

"Why do they jump out of the area?" Sara wondered beside her.

Sasha looked to her friend, covered in other men's blood.

"We hold the northern air space along with the surrounding area. They need to feed Ascended, but more importantly, they cannot place all of their units here lest we attack Impa cities. So they jump in and out," Sasha explained.

"But what if the crystals are destroyed?"

Sasha shook her head, "The Dome has to fall for that to happen. That won't happen for some time still I think. And besides, the Capital is not far, so the Impa could jump Ascended there instead if needed."

But Sara's question got her thinking. Why did it have to take so long for the Dome to fall? She had ideas of how to deal with the Iumenta crystals, didn't she? Had a plan even, a plan she wasn't expecting to use until they were nearly ready for the Dome to fall ... she excused herself, walking off briskly. The fighting died down at night, only the Elves keeping a large force in the area. She poked Legon with her mind and made her way to Sydin's hangar.

The big black Dragon slept in a large hangar. She walked up, nudging his nose. He didn't respond.

"Sydin!" she said loudly, knocking on the top of his head.

He opened an eye.

"Wake up!" she said again.

"Sasha, what is it?" he asked, not sounding happy to see her.

"I want to attack the Dome," she said honestly.

"OK, you go right ahead and do that, dear," he said, still sounding out of it.

"I think I can crack the defensive crystals," she said.

His eyes opened, "What?"

"I can take them out Sydin. I know I can, but I'll need help."

"I'm listening."

Legon walked over to her, and she waved him over, "We need to hit the Dome hard and now, take the air space so they can't jump anyone in."

"We can't hold that space for long, Sash," Legon said.

"You won't have to, if you attack the Dome it will stress the crystals and I can hit them."

She looked into her brother's eyes, sending a mental argument his way. Legon looked at Sydin, who still didn't look convinced. He looked at the Dome.

"Sydin," Legon said. "Even if Sasha can't do anything, we need to start working the Dome over."

Sydin agreed.

Legon looked back to Sasha, "All right, you have your chance." Then to Sydin, "Give the order to scramble, all hands on deck."

Sydin rose, "Yes, Un Prosa. Sasha, the attack will begin in ten minutes."

She bolted from the hangar over to her work area, waking up team-members. She tapped massive store crystals as she went.

Legon took to the air as sirens blared. Ground units didn't know what to make of anything so they just stared up as hundreds of Ascended took to the air.

Sydin's voice boomed to all, "We are taking the airspace above the Dome. Hold and bombard the Dome," was his simple order.

Legon's guard formed up around him, all tapping into his mind. Joining him were the Ascended from Sasha's guard. "Sevens up front, stay tight," he ordered. They complied without comment. The Dome burst with activity, sirens sounding. Anti-Dragon flack filled the air. Legon rose sharply, coming high above the Dome as others engaged Iumenta Ascended. High above, he turned in the air, angling down, "On me!"

He dove, pushing wards out away from his body as he plummeted. The Dome grew in size. His unit wove in the fighting, coming on a heavy layer of Anti-Dragon flack. His vision tinted purple as his wards activated, deflecting flack. They extended far enough to protect the others. The air was a blur of fire and magic, he could make out Iumenta on the Dome.

"Cynta, Opes" he said.

They darted below him, pushing out wards, focusing all their power on them. Legon let his wards fade, reaching deep, pulling power, and sending dozens of breaking spells at the Dome along with the others in the guard. Other units were doing likewise.

Keither stumbled to where Sara stood transfixed. "What's happening?" he asked.

"I don't know," she said, taking his hand sounding scared.

He tried not to look at the Dome, the lights made him feel sick, and the sound ... all around them people, even Elves watched, not knowing what was going on. Keither had never seen anything like it. The battle raging was so fierce.

He heard an Elf yelling in Glosso. "What are they saying?" he asked Sara.

She looked at him, "They are saying the Everser Vald is attacking the Dome..."

A dull roar built as word spread. At first, Keither couldn't make it out but then he could. They were cheering, they were shouting support, some clapping, others yelling, and still others chanting. The Humans started to cheer as well.

From the center of the Elves' camp, a bolt of ruby flew across the field to the Dome. There was a bright flash and a crack. The Dome flickered and Keither heard the Elves yell louder. Sara started to cheer too, and Keither found himself joining.

Legon pushed harder on his spells, feeling the Dome fighting him. The air around him was filled with explosions; several Dragons had already been forced back away from the battle but Legon wasn't going to stop. A flash of scarlet came from the camp, smacking into the side of the Dome. There was a brilliant flash and Legon heard a crack. The wards of the building flickered and he felt a few spells for just a moment hit the white surface.

Sasha! he thought.

He expanded his connection to her, "You did it!"

"I need help!" she said.

Legon spoke to all the Ascended in the area. "Did you hear that? Did you hear one of the defensive crystals break? My sister did that and she needs our help! Attack with everything you've got, go full power!"

He roared, diving at the building, letting power fill the air. The Ascended bellowed in agreement, the sky lighting brighter than noonday with their magic. Again Sasha fired and again there was a crack. Legon got closer to the Dome; the Anti-Dragon flack failing. The third time Sasha fired, there was another crack and Legon saw the opening of the Dome flicker.

He folded his wings, dropping into the opening. He was plunged into chaos. He landed on the stone floor, empty hangars all around. He spewed forth lavender fire, killing all in the area. Opes, Sydin and Cynta joined him in the Dome. Familiars from all of the Elf Ascended flooded in, taking out infantry.

"The crystals!" Sydin said.

Legon looked to the walls, seeing large blocks where they'd be. He fought through pricks of pain from arrows. Three of the blocks were blackened. He went to one that was not, smashing it with his tail and claws. It broke, as did others as the Iumenta fled.

"The Dome is down!" Iselin said from outside, "Its wards have failed."

Legon came to his senses, looking to Sydin, "The Capital." The old Dragon nodded and they flew out of the Dome.

Edling stood, nervous. He knew his part in this mission; had known his part for some time. He just didn't think it was going to happen tonight. Emma stood with him.

"I can't seem to remember why Sasha and I have to go again," Edling said.

Emma smiled comfortingly, "We can't take chances; jump crystals are tough, Legon and the others won't have long, and you have the best knowledge aside from your wife."

He nodded. He knew why he had to go. He tried to tell himself that everything would be ok. If he was being honest, what had him bothered the most was that Sasha was going and he wouldn't even be with her to protect her. Not that he could protect her if he was with her anyway.

"You protect me," her mind interjected in his.

He was about to answer when he felt Legon's mind touch his, "Edling, get ready, I'm going to fly over."

Edling walked away from the tents and looked toward the Dome. Elves were flying in and out of it, ground units climbing the sides, but it still shone alabaster in the night. Legon's form came toward him. Edling glowed lavender and he flew up in the air with a jolt. Legon passed under him. Edling landed on Legon's shoulders, sticking in place. Wind blew through his hair, pulling at his clothes. He'd been on a Dragon's back before, but not a fully armored one who had been fighting for a week.

The metal of Legon's armor was dingy and scratched, blood stained it in spots and Edling could make out scorch marks. *It's amazing what they can live through,* he thought. Legon turned in the sky, heading back toward the Dome. As he did so, Edling felt Legon connect him with the rest of the Ascended. His head hurt with the noise of Dragons yelling orders and reporting in. It was hard to make out what was going on but from what Edling could tell, the Iumenta lines had split and they were scrambling to reorganize themselves.

Despite the fact that the battle was still raging, Legon flew toward it. Edling looked behind to see Cynta carrying Sasha. He looked forward, gripping Legon's neck. They didn't meet any resistance as they passed over the Dome. The Elves were pushing the Iumenta away.

Sydin's voice boomed, "Legon, I need to stay here and command the Ascended in the area."

"Right, I'll take command," Legon said and then spoke to the Ascended assigned to the mission. "This is Legon of House Evindass. I am assuming command of this mission. Squads report in."

As the Dome faded behind them, Edling watched as Ascended formed up behind Legon. The precision in which they flew inspired him.

"Edling, you remember what we are doing?" Legon asked.

"Yes I do. I am to assist you in taking out a jump crystal." He sighed and thought of his wife being across town doing likewise. He wished Legon was with Sasha.

"You worry about her."

"Don't you?" Edling asked.

Legon took a moment, "Yes, I do. I'm going to be honest with you Ed; there is a very real chance that we won't survive this. We have to take those crystals out at all costs ... if it makes you feel any better, the Iumenta will likely target me, as I'm a class eight."

"So we are the ones most likely to get killed?" Edling asked, oddly feeling better.

Legon was close to the hills and Edling could see the horizon start to glow orange. They were close to the city now; it wouldn't be long. Edling thought about what needed to be done, thought about everything they had learned about the Iumenta crystals. Sasha had proven that they knew how to break them effectively. But this time it would be Edling in a building with hostile Iumenta and Ascended flying all around him.

They crested a hill and Bailaya came into view. The city sparkled even at the late hour. Edling heard the sound of air raid sirens. Ascended filled the sky. The Capital had a small contingent of Ascended to guard it, on top of that the sky was flashing as new Iumenta jumped into the city's air space.

"Hold tight!" Legon said.

Umbra and a group under the command of a red Dragon named Lamma took the lead with a few others. Legon bid fairwell to Cynta. Edling closed his connection completely with Sasha; if something happened to one of them, the other couldn't have it affecting their part of the mission. Edling felt weak. Legon's mind joined more fully with his and instantly he felt his confidence bolster. Sasha told him this would happen connected with Legon; he was a natural born fighter and leader.

Edling braced himself as Legon veered toward the north end of town. Lamma and her squad rushed forward, sending magic at the Iumenta coming to meet them. Legon's guard came in tighter. The air rent with the sound of magic on ward. Edling's confidence vanished as Legon swung in the air dodging magic. It didn't seem to affect him. Edling's mind was abuzz with the talking from the other Dragons, "Up up up!", "To your left!", "Fade back ..." he tried to block the voices.

The sticking spell was getting a workout and Edling used magic to steady his gut. He opened his eyes to a collage of color. His vision flashed purple as Legon took hits. The big Dragon wasn't affected. Legon tilted in the air and Edling almost screamed as an Iumenta collided with them. Legon batted the Ascended away, resuming his original course.

Edling could see where they were heading. The building looked nondescript, all in all a very good hiding spot.

"Take the air space," Legon said.

Umbra and Opes moved over the building, effectively making it so the crystal could no longer bring in reinforcements.

"Here we go, Edling!" Legon said, diving at the building.

Legon and the others fired spells at it. The air around it lit with wards that soon broke under the onslaught.

Edling was concerned by the large group of Iumenta on the roof, though this didn't seem to bother Legon in the least bit. As he came to the roof, his familiar detached from behind his horn to be joined by the familiars of all the other Ascended. Legon breathed straight fire on the roof, burning the wooden structure. Under the dilapidated wooden building stood a sturdy stone one and Legon landed on it, his tail blade glowing. He hit the building, opening it up. Edling saw the jump crystal inside, bringing him clarity.

Legon tore his way into the building and on top of the crystal. Edling cleared his head, guiding Legon in how to best use his magic to break the crystal apart. There was a great crack. Edling watch the crystal split. *More, it needs to be broken more!* Legon's claws flashed amethyst as he dug them in. Chunks broke away as Legon poured energy into breaking the crystal. Finally with a snap, it broke in two. Legon jumped from it, hovering. He sent more spells to break it up.

"It's done, it's done!" Edling yelled out loud.

"You're sure? We don't get another chance at this," Legon said.

Edling thought for a moment "Well, I guess it wouldn't hurt to break it up a bit more or maybe burn the place to the ground."

Legon didn't give a sarcastic remark but spewed a river of lavender flames. Edling heard the crystal shattering into a thousand pieces as the building began to burn. Legon launched into the sky. Edling hadn't been paying attention to the sky. Now that he did, he wanted to go back to the jump crystal. Several of the Elves had perished, holding off the Iumenta. Edling knew that Legon had used a lot of power already and he didn't know if he could fight. Edling yelped as he was sent flying from Legon's back to rest on Iselin's.

"Sorry Edling," she said, dodging attacks. "I'm more nimble, you'll stand a better chance with me."

He looked to see Legon crash into a large Iumenta.

Sara sat on the edge of the cot, checking her patient's vitals. His eyes fluttered open and she smiled at him, "Welcome back; it's been a while."

He started to sit up but she pushed him back down. He put his hand on his forehead. "Wh-what happened?" Barnin said in a rough voice.

"You were stabbed in the gut. It's a miracle you lived, honestly," Sara said. "That was five days ago," she added.

His eyes widened, "I've been out for five days?"

"Sorry, we could only use magic to make you stable, we've had a lot of injured people, thank you very much," She said tartly.

"Sara I need to get up, we have to take that Dome out ..."

Barnin eyed Sara. "I'm missing something," he said.

"Well you see ... about the Dome, it's kind of already fallen," she said, "and I think it's safe to say that Bailaya is about a day away from that as well. So you see, there's no reason to rush yourself, the war is very nearly over," she said brightly.

Barnin looked up at the ceiling, a thousand questions in his mind, "What happened?" he asked.

Sara adjusted herself, "Well, Sasha found a way to defeat the Dome. You should have seen it Barnin, I've never seen anything like it. All the Dragons attacked the Dome and then when it fell, Legon took a bunch of Ascended to the Capital to take out the jump crystals."

"But how has the Capital almost fallen?" he asked.

"Isn't it obvious?" Sara said. "The Iumenta had nearly all their ground units at the Dome. When the Dome fell and the Capital lost its jump crystals, all of the Iumenta Ascended rushed back to protect the Capital. Their armies have almost no air support."

Barnin closed his eyes. He could see it in his head. Even the Dark Warriors wouldn't last long with no air support. They'd be forced to run the twelve miles back to the Capital, the whole time being worked over by the Pawdin Ascended. "How many made it back to the city?" he asked.

"I don't know; not many. Most are pinned down in the hills in between the city and the Dome. It's made for slow moving for our ground units, but I don't think it's going to matter. The Elves have been attacking the Capital with Ascended twenty-four hours a day. I guess at first the Iumenta held fast, but ... there are more Elves, aren't there, and the Iumenta can't get reinforcements, so they are dying off."

Barnin chuckled, "I missed the end of the war, fantastic." Then he remembered something, "Hey, thanks for saving me."

Sara patted his arm. "What are friends for? Now wait a bit longer and I'll see if I can finish healing you," she said.

Neelya walked out onto a balcony overlooking one of the Palace's gardens. She felt tense; would she be found out? She didn't know why she'd hidden the group of servants; she should have killed them as ordered but she didn't. Somehow it just seemed so ... wasteful.

The Queen stood against a rail in light armor, her finger absently running along her Fenna. Neelya felt afraid for other reasons. All around her smoke rose, making flakes of ash like snow. The ever-present roll of thunder and flashing light didn't unsettle her so much anymore. But seeing it get closer did.

"My Queen," she said, bowing.

"Hoelaria now, I think," she said.

Before Neelya could say anything, a runner came up, "My Queen, a message from the front."

"What is it?" Hoelaria asked.

The runner looked up, "I regret to inform you that Parkas has just been killed. He was in the hills slowing the Pawdin forces,..." he trailed off.

Hoelaria nodded deftly, "That will be all."

Neelya stepped up next to the Queen, "Hoelaria?"

"All of the Heads of Province are in the city ... only a few have tried to leave on Ascended and of those, none have survived." The Queen turned to her, "Have the servants been taken care of?"

"Yes," Neelya said.

Hoelaria didn't question her. Neelya asked about the fenna, the Queen held, "Are you going to fight? Do you suppose they won't let us surrender?" she asked.

"They want us to, certainly, however I; as have every other Head of Province, swore on our lives to protect the Empire. No; none of us will surrender; we will fight no matter how low our chances are."

Neelya touched her own blade. She was a class five with the possibility to Ascend; she'd die alongside the Queen. "It will be an honor to die with you, my Queen," she said.

In the near distance she could see one of the Great Houses under attack. Neelya wasn't sure if she was ready to die.

Hoelaria looked into Neelya's eyes intensely, "You will not die today, all of our staff will die fighting or be executed for war crimes; but not you."

"I don-"

"Shhh," the Queen said, placing an envelope in her hand, "we don't have time. You are my messenger, you will carry my last communication to the Pawdin Empire, and this will spare your life." She turned Neelya to the city, "Do you see what has happened here, Neelya? My arrogance has brought the end of the Impa Empire, with the deaths of the Heads of Province, Civil War will break out. It will be as it was before the Empire existed." She turned her back toward her, Neelya feeling a very genuine fear now. "Our Province will be destroyed out of spite for what we brought on. Neelya, you will be the only Iumenta to witness for today. I fear the day will come when it will be up to you and your generation to save our people. You cannot die!"

"But if our Province ..." Neelya started.

"Sue for asylum, beg if you must. Agree to tell the Elves whatever they want to know. Someday you will be able to return to our homelands."

"That's treason," Neelya said, backing away. She felt her eyes, *tears?* She didn't cry; she was Iumenta.

Hoelaria grabbed her shoulders, "Not treason; what I have done is treason. I chose you, Neelya to be my servant, because I saw in you myself; you too can do great things someday. Please Neelya, when you do those things, let it be for your people and not for revenge. Promise me!"

Neelya had never seen the Queen show emotion like this; she didn't even know her, "Yes Highness, I will do as you ask."

There was a crack of a ward. Neelya saw the Palace grounds light up. She dropped her fenna and rushed inside with the Queen.

Legon looked down on Bailaya as it burned. The Iumenta set most of the city on fire as they left areas but Legon hoped that at least a few Humans would live. As for the Impa leadership, he had low hopes of them surrendering. Thus far, all had fought and died; Legon was flying on to the Palace personally and hoped that he could persuade Hoelaria against suicide.

Stacy had told him where the Queen was most likely to be on the ground. It would be at her study which looked out over the gardens, and this is where he flew. Legon sent breaking spells at the Palace, feeling them hit wards. Iselin and Opes did the same, the wards giving way.

Legon landed in the gardens. There were two figures in the doorway. There were no guards which Legon hoped meant that the regent was going to play nice.

Hoelaria stormed outside wearing armor. Just behind her was a girl holding an envelope.

"Hoelaria, this is Legon of House ..."

"I know who you are!" Hoelaria spat, "I killed your ape mother and I killed your father. It was my men who found you, made you; I know who you are, Legon of Evindass, because you are mine!" She yelled, "I made you and I will destroy you!"

She bellowed, holding her sword aloft, glowing a pale green. Hoelaria jumped at his neck. Before Legon could comprehend what was happening or the absurdity of what she was doing, his instincts reacted. Not the instinct to flinch away but to attack.

Legon's head snapped forward, his jaws opening, catching Hoelaria in the air. He brought them down hard, feeling his teeth plunge into her body, crushing her pelvis. He heard her scream in pain. He opened his mouth and snapped it closed again, this time her legs breaking. He was angry now, mad at what this woman had done. He let her screaming form slip a bit from his mouth. He closed it again feeling the bottom of her rib cage against his teeth. Legon shook his head back and forth as a dog would do with a toy and then with a snap he flung her body out of his mouth to smack the stone walkway with a thwack.

The girl ran forward, crying for her dead Queen. Legon lifted a paw to kill her, but she stopped, holding up the envelope in her hand. "I'm a messenger! I'm a messenger, she said you wouldn't kill a messenger," she sobbed.

Legon didn't even know that Iumenta were capable of sorrow, or at least he'd never seen it.

He ordered a small group of ground units to take her into custody.

"Opes, let's get this place secure. I think it's safe to say the Iumenta will know that their government has been killed off, but I'd rather not take chances of them fighting back."

Opes took charge of the Elves in the area.

Ankle went to see Barnin and Heath, walking into the tent, "Hey, do you guys know what's up?" he asked.

Heath shrugged, "I know the Queen is dead but that's about it; I don't know what it would have to do with us."

The tent's flap drifted and Ankle poked his head outside to see Umbra. She was clad in full armor, something that almost never happened.

"Hello boys," she said. "I am here to take you on a very important mission."

Ankle could see Elves were on her back, three spots near the front open. He looked up, questioning.

"You three are the only ones with on-the-ground knowledge of where we are going, therefore you are needed."

"Mors," Barnin breathed.

"I believe we all promised to go back someday," Umbra said.

Ankle felt cold and then he felt resolve. He darted back in the tent grabbing his sword, jogging past Barnin and Heath, "What are you waiting for! Come on move it!"

His friends jumped, joining him.

He was helped up by an Elf. Umbra leapt into the air, joining a formation of twenty-four other Ascended, all laden with Elves.

One of the Elves spoke to him, "Sir, you know more about Mors then we do; we will be under your command on the ground. Where should we go?"

Ankle looked at Barnin saying, "Actually, he's in command; not me."

Barnin reached over, clasping Ankle's arm, "No my friend, you were the one who pulled out Rachel, you were the one who wanted to stay and fight. You've earned this and you're in charge!"

Ankle nodded, thankful, and turned to the Elf, "Can I speak to everyone?"

Umbra joined his mind with everyone's, "The camp is in sections, the center is where the Iumenta stay, that's the only place with magic. We will land ground units on the southeast side, that's where they keep the Humans they breed and take in new victims. They are trained from birth, so anyone old enough to hold a sword that is male is an enemy. Umbra, can you take care of commanding the Ascended?"

"Of course Sir," she said, "hold the sky, burn pockets of Dark Warriors and Iumenta, today we take no prisoners."

After a few hours, the landscape turned rocky as they entered the mountains. The peaks rose up jagged and harsh. In the distance, smoke rose in tendrils. The Elves sped up. Ankle only wondered at the massacre going on at Mors, but there was nothing he could do to get there any faster. As they came over some peaks, the valley of Mors came into view. He could see a Dragon jump from the area and another flying away. There was a flash from the center of camp.

"The jump crystal," Heath supplied.

Umbra dove down to the hovels where people were forced to breed. Some of them were on fire, but there was a lot of activity. Men were pulling pregnant woman by the hair, cutting them with knives and swords.

"Get us down!" Ankle yelled.

He glowed black, sliding from Umbra. He hit the ground with a grunt, drawing his sword and charging a man. The man dropped the woman he was dragging and swung at Ankle. Rage overtaking him, Ankle felled the man with ease. Another came at him but burst into blue flames. The Elf from Umbra came to him, "Sir, your orders."

You're in charge Ankle, keep it together, he thought.

"Save the women, put the buildings' fires out, kill every man in the area; they can't be trusted not to be Dark Warriors."

The Elf barked orders to others. Familiars ran about. Ankle followed one to a hovel, its door locked on the outside, covered in oil. Ankle rammed the door with his shoulder, the wood splintering. He kicked it, breaking it in. He entered, not caring about the smell. Women screamed in fright.

"You're free now! Come out, I'm here to help you," he said.

The Elf came in behind Ankle and stopped looking. Ankle knew what was going through his mind. It was the same thing that had gone through his months before. The frail forms in the hovel were barely alive.

"Bring healers," Ankle said softly. The Elf didn't respond. Ankle shook his shoulder, "Bring healers."

"Y-Yes Sir," he said, leaving.

Booms sounded in the distance as the Elves secured the camp. He turned to leave and felt arms around his legs. He looked down, seeing several people reaching toward him. "Please don't leave us," they begged.

Ankle knelt down, taking one of their filthy hands. "I won't," he said in a shaking voice.

With those words, something in him changed. He felt the cold that had been with him since he'd been here before leave. It was replaced with compassion. He looked at the huddled figures; here was his purpose in life. Rachel had shown him that. *I promised I'd come back.*

Epilogue
A Few Years Later

L egon knelt down, scooping up his son. It was odd that he had a child at such a young age but he'd told himself that it was for his parents' sake. If he was being honest, it was because children brought hope into the world, a peaceful close to the years of turmoil. He put Arkin down after a moment so he could run and play with the other children. They were under the ever-watchful eyes of Emma and Stacy. Sasha hadn't bothered to use their parents as an excuse. She'd wanted to be a mother for as long as Legon could remember. And a good one she made at that.

"How's the shop?" Legon asked Barnin.

He shrugged, "Sales are fine, I suppose. I just don't get worked up like I used to, you know?"

"That I do, and Samantha?"

Barnin winced a bit. "She's mad at me, I don't know why," he smiled "But I figure she'll get over it or I'll figure out what I've done wrong this time," he grinned.

Legon laughed at the now slightly portly man.

As soon as the war ended and the Pawdin Empire pushed the Iumenta back into their own lands, his friends went on with their lives.

"Any word on the Impa?" Barnin asked.

Legon shook his head, "No, it's been nine years since the war ended and from what we can tell, Civil War is still raging. I don't think the Impa Empire will ever exist again."

"Good"

"How's Heath doing?" Legon asked.

"Oh he's still in the military, but they have him training now." Barnin laughed, "Don't think he cares for it much. I offered him a position at my shop and I think he might just take me up on it."

Keither sipped at his drink, talking to Ankle, whose arm was around Rachel. He hadn't left her side in years; Rachel was for Ankle like Sara was for Keither, a reason to be something more. And more Ankle had been. Keither was honored to spend years in service with him as they rehabilitated the people of Mors and those who had been in the Queen's care for so long; Ankle's vision being a guiding light behind everything. He wondered what Ankle would do now.

"Any plans for the future?" Keither asked.

"I'm taking over my family's restaurant, if you can believe it," he said, beaming. "Rach and I are looking forward to being just in Manton," he smiled down at her. Rachel was still soft-spoken, but not as timid as before.

"How goes the Department of the Interior?" Ankle asked.

"Fine I suppose, I'm over Manton, we are looking at some new roadways ..." he stopped talking, "and things that you would find terribly dull. It's good you'll be in town; Heath, Barnin and I get together every week for a guys' night."

Ankle bobbed his head, "I'm game for that."

"Is Sara still the administrator of the Manton healing center?" Rachel asked.

"Yes she is, why?"

Rachel looked sheepish. "Do you think she would mind if I volunteer a few days a week?" she asked timidly.

Keither smiled, "I'll ask her for you and I'm sure she'd like that."

Sara watched Emma watching the kids while still trying to keep a polite conversation going with Sara, Iselin and Sasha.

"Em, how do you do this all day?" Sara asked as kids ran by. "Elf children are so fast!"

Not taking her eyes off them she said, "Well Opes helps me a lot if I'm being honest, but it's nice having Stacy here to help today. Arkin! No we do not do that!"

Sara was happy for Emma; her friendship with Opes gave her some normalcy in life. Iselin told her that they were just as mentally connected as a married couple though neither of them felt anything other than friendship for the other.

Emma took off after one of the kids, one of Sasha's she thought. Stacy scooped up Arkin as he ran by her. Sara turned to Iselin, "Will Opes die when she does?" she asked bluntly.

Iselin smiled warmly, "Yes, I dare say he will. I think Emma is OK with that because she understands him. She told me that knowing that he was going to keep living was so hard for Opes to bear; now he gets a wonderful life with Emma and she does too. At the end of that life he'll get to be with his wife again and she will go with her Kovos; it's beautiful when you think about it," Iselin said.

Sasha enjoyed the rest of her day with her friends. She was looking forward to returning to Seeon but she wasn't in a hurry. The Lux was docked in Manton; they'd spent the day in the city with friends and now she was in her cabin with Edling. Looking out her window, the water in the harbor reflected the moon. Edling wrapped his arms around her.

"What are you thinking of, love?"

"So much has happened, yet so much is the same. Love, family, friends, they are such a constant in life. But still, if you had said to me fifteen years ago living in a small mountain town that Legon would defeat the Empire, that I would be an Elf; well, if you'd told me those things, I'd have thought you were mad. Yet here we are. The girl who would never find love is married to the man of her dreams. She who was once hated and bound to be a slave is now ..." she turned to Edling, "is now the Head of a Great House."

Edling kissed her, "Funny how that happens."

"My brother once said that Salmont was the most inconsequential town in all of the land. But it was that trait that made it seem the perfect hiding spot for his birth parents. My life would have been much different had I been born in Salkay."

Edling tensed a bit, understanding what she meant, "But you weren't."

"I wasn't," she smiled.

Sasha followed Edling to bed, sliding under the sheets, dimming the lights with a flick of her mind. She didn't wonder how long this peaceful happy part of life would last; no, tonight she would think of happy things. Sasha smiled to herself, thankful for everything she'd accomplished in life up to this point. With that thought, she closed her eyes.

THE END

Thank you for reading Legon Restoration by Nicholas Taylor. We hope you enjoyed the book. If you are interested in finding out more about the Legon Series, other books by Nicholas Taylor or to contact him please visit his website at www.NicholasTaylor.co, or connect with him on Facebook, Twitter, Goodreads, and Pintrest. You can also sign up for Nicholas's newsletter at www.NicholasTaylor.co. Thank you again for reading Legon Restoration.

About the Author

Nicholas was born and raised in Denver, Colorado. He didn't want to write until October of 2007. While he was driving around with a friend and said "hey, I wonder if I can write a book." So he thought he would try and write outline and see what happens.

For more about Nicholas Taylor

Visit:

www.NicholasTaylor.co

www.ingramcontent.com/pod-product-compliance
Lightning Source LLC
Chambersburg PA
CBHW030937260626

47169CB00002B/514